［ 人文研究叢書之3 ］

# Qian Zhongshu in others' words

Tiziana Lioi

中央大學出版中心 ｜ 遠流

比較文學的最終目的在於幫助我們認識總體文學（littérature générale）乃至人類文化的基本規律，所以中西文學超出實際聯繫範圍的平行研究不僅是可能的，而且是極有價值的。這種比較唯其是在不同文化系統的背景上進行的，所以得出的結論具有普遍意義。

錢鍾書

The ultimate intent of comparative literature is to help us to grasp the littérature générale, going so far as to the basic principles of human culture. In this way not only the parallel study of Chinese and western literatures that oversteps the limits of the real contacts is possible, but is also of great value. This kind of comparison is precisely to be carried on with a background of different cultural systems and the results thus obtained have a universal significance.

Qian Zhongshu

A che scopo riformulare maldestramente ciò che bravi scrittori hanno già detto così bene prima di noi?
Why express clumsily what good writers have already masterly written before us?

Simon Leys

# CONTENTS

**CHAPTER 6**

**Conclusions**      **237**

# Abstract

Chinese comparative literature has a great representative in the contemporary scholar and writer Qian Zhongshu (1910-1998). His comparative method defies every categorisation and his extensive use of quotations in seven languages-the main characteristic of his style-creates a collage of literary motifs and genres that constitutes a fertile field for analysis to grasp the general principles of world literature.

Chinese scholars have established a discipline, the *Qian Xue* (Studies on Qian); since the 1980s, research on Qian Zhongshu's achievements and methodology plays an important role in understanding of the author's approach to writing and literature. Western scholarship and investigation into the work of such a complex and varied literary production is a step that needs to be further developed, since western literature constitutes a great part of Qian's thematic choices. The number of languages involved in the analysis and the huge number of cross references in Qian's work require a set of skills of which this study is a small yet necessary part, analysing the contribution of Italian literature to the comparative method of Qian Zhongshu.

Italian quotations and the influence of Italian literature on the comparative method of Qian Zhongshu are the main concern of this analysis, and are a topic never before dealt with in mainland and overseas Qian Xue studies.

The study outlines the threads that move Qian Zhongshu in the choice of authors and works that constitute, in quotation, the core of his method. As in a case study, a meticulous analysis of all the Italian quotations that appear in Qian's literary essays, the present study answers questions on the necessity of such a consistent use of quotations and on the role that foreign literatures, with a focus on the Italian one, have in the definition of a comparative method that seems to be all-inclusive and difficult to grasp.

A deductive method is used to delineate the comparative method and the general principles that guide the author through the study and analysis of single quotations.

To seize an understanding of the principles that lead global literatures in an enhancement of mutual comprehension between countries and peoples seems a desirable yet unrealistic goal: Qian Zhongshu, through his use of quotations to establish a dialogue between different historical epochs and distant spatial settings, wants to demonstrates that this desire is attainable.

# 摘要

　　當代著名學者和作家錢鍾書（1910～1998年）是中國比較文學界的一位代表人物。他研究比較文學的方式與眾不同，主要特點在於能在作品中大量地利用七種不同外語的引文，從而創建了一種中外文學主題和體裁的「拼貼」方式，開拓了進行比較分析的一個廣闊領域，以此把握世界文學創作的一般性原則。

　　中國學者八十年代已建立了一門叫做「錢學」的學科，該學科的主要目的是研究錢氏的成就和治學方法。中國「錢學」的價值在於能夠使人們更多瞭解作為學者和作家的錢鍾書的創作意義，不過儘管如此，西方學者的研究仍然是一個必要的補充，因為錢鍾書的創作中很多方面涉及到了西方文學，而面對如此一位學識博大精深的作家，西方的研究需要進一步的發展。

　　因為需要分析的內容包括不同語言和大量的交叉引用，研究錢鍾書對世界比較文學的貢獻是一個宏大的課題，本論文的嘗試只是其中一個微小的，但卻是必要的一部分，它主要分析義大利文學對於錢鍾書的比較文學方法的貢獻。

　　本論文通過對錢鍾書論著中義大利文引文部分的分析，研究錢鍾書在其作品中所引用的義大利作家和作品，最終的目的在於探究錢鍾書比較文學研究方法的內質。

　　本論文的研究方法主要以案例研究為主，通過細緻解析錢鍾書散文中所出現的義大利語引文，進而把焦點集中在錢鍾書與義大利文學的關係上，從而試圖回答以下幾個問題：錢鍾書的著作為什麼能旁徵博引，貫通古今，融會中西？他作品裡出現的外國文獻主要作用是什麼？今天的研究者以何種途徑入手才能全面瞭解其包羅萬象，看似難以把握的比較方法？論文以演繹的方式剖析作為學者的錢鍾書論著的比較方法，並進一步挖掘其研究方式的內質。

　　要抓住世界文學創作的一般原則，加強不同國家和不同國家人民之間的相互理解，似乎是一個過於理想化的願望。不過錢鍾書，這位知識淵博的中國學者，通過在他的著作中精確地援引世界文獻，成功地幫助全球文化開展了跨越時空的對話，他希望能夠證明實現這一願望雖然任重道遠，但畢竟是有可能的。

# Acknowledgments

I would like to thank many people who helped make this research possible.

I would like to express gratitude to my tutor for the research, Professor Zhang Hui 張輝 of the Chinese Comparative Literature Research Institute of Peking University. His patience and guidance encouraged my interest in Qian's works and a better understanding of his role in Chinese literature. I value the time spent with Professor Zhang among the shelves of Peking libraries and bookshops, as well as looking for the location of Qian Zhongshu's former lodging close to Peking University campus.

The person to whom I owe the inspiration for starting a PhD program, and whom I thank, is Professor Federico Masini, professor of Chinese, former Dean of the Faculty of Oriental Studies at Rome University. He exemplifies dedication to research and personal and scholarly advancement. Professor Patrizia Dadò, my supervisor, passed on to me her interest in this versatile and learned author and encouraged me to pursue my research notwithstanding the difficulties of his erudite writing.

Among Qian Zhongshu scholars and experts, my gratitude goes to Professor Ronald Egan of the University of Santa Barbara, California. I appreciate his dedicated and painstaking research on Qian's works. He has been a mentor and a guide through all my PhD research with suggestions, books, encouragements, and an inspiring exchange of ideas during the two international meetings on Qian Zhongshu, which I had the great pleasure of sharing with him. I would like to thank Professor Wang Rongzu 汪榮祖 from Taiwan National Central University for allowing me to take part in the first international seminar on Qian Zhongshu, and Professor Christopher Rea from the University of British Columbia inviting me to the second. Had I not taken part in these two important scholarly exchanges I would have missed the confirmation and encouragement fundamental to pursuing my research. Thanks also to Professor Rea for his editing and suggestions on various papers.

Other scholars who have helped with kind and significant suggestions on occasion at home and during overseas exchanges are: Professor Ji Jin 季進 from Suzhou University, Professor Meng Hua 孟華 from Peking University, Professor Wang Ning 王寧 from Qinghua University in Peking, Professor Yu Hong 于宏 from Munich University, Professor Zhang Wenjiang 張文江 from the Shanghai Academy of Social Sciences, Professor Wen Zheng 文錚 and Professor Liu Xiaopeng 呂小蓬 from Beijing Foreign Language University for their support with important documents, Professor Marina Miranda from Rome University "Sapienza" for her constant presence and methodological suggestions, Professor Lionello Lanciotti and independent scholar Anna Bujatti, whom I met at the very beginning of this project, for their patience in receiving me at home and providing suggestions and ideas on the scope of my research. I will never forget Professor Lanciotti's hearty account of his encounters with Qian Zhongshu.

The collaboration and support of my colleagues at the Faculty of Oriental Studies of Rome University "Sapienza" have been for the whole duration of my PhD as important as the ink with which this work is printed: without them the idea of this research would not have been put on paper; thanks to Edoardo Gagliardi, Luisa Paternicò, Chiara Romagnoli, Paolo De Troia, Davor Antonucci, Bai Hua 白樺, Lara Colangelo, Serena Zuccheri, Emanuele Raini, Sun Pingping 孫萍萍, and Zhang Tongbing 張彤冰. Thanks to Federica Casalin in particular for having always been present whenever most needed.

Sincere thank you to Mary Turner and Dr. Nelly McEwen for their unconditional and patient help with the revision of this book. I also thank my friends Maria João Belchior, Antonia Cimini, Tan Xue 譚雪 and Marina Brancaccio for their support. Finally, thanks to my family for their patience in putting up with my long Chinese stay and to my father for his constant encouragement.

# Introduction

Prior to the 1980s, Qian's work received little attention in China. However, since the 1980s the *Qian Xue* 錢學 (academic research on Qian Zhongshu) has been flourishing. Conversely, outside China, the work of Qian Zhongshu had been analysed and acknowledged, attested to by the large number of translations of the novel *Wei Cheng*, 圍城 (Fortress Besieged), 1947.[1] Nevertheless, interest in his work subsided during the last decades of the 20th century. Thus, much still needs to be done beyond China's borders.

## Scope and purpose of the study

Among the many aspects of Qian Zhongshu's work which could be studied, this study focuses on the comparative method used in the majority of his works. The core of the research lies in the analysis of one particular aspect of this method, the use of quotations, that permeates profoundly the same idea of literature and creative activity. A further step into the study of Qian Zhongshu's use of quotations is undertaken when looking at quotations from Italian authors as the leitmotif and core of this work. The analysis aims to reveal the role and importance of Italian literature in the definition of Qian

---

1 Among the main translations are: *Fortress Besieged* trans. in English by Nathan Mao and Jeanne Kelly, 1979, reissued in 1989, 2003, 2006; *Wei Cheng*, trans. in Russian by V. Sorokin, 1980; *La Forteresse Assiégée* trans. in French by Sylvie Servan-Schreiber and Wang Lou, 1987; *Jiehun Kuangshi Qu* (Wei Cheng) trans. in Japanese by Huang Jingjian, 1988; *Die Umzingelte Festung*, trans. in German by Monika Motsch and Jerome Shih, 1988, reissued in 2008; *Wei Cheng*, trans. in Uighur by Sima Yili and Aizi Maiti, 1991; *La Fortaleza Asediada*, trans in Spanish by Taciana Fisac, 1992; *Wei Cheng*, trans. in Corean by Wu Yunshu, 1994. Theodore Huters in his *Qian Zhongshu*, 1982, talks of Qian Zhongshu as "out of harmony with the main intellectual current of the times" due to his "fiction's detailed descriptions of the urban upper crust and his criticism's evident appeal to patrician taste" (p.1).

Zhongshu's scholarly ideas and more generally the author's contribution to world literature and the enhancement of cultural and literary contacts between east and west in the fields of comparative literature and cultural exchanges.

Italian quotations and the influence of Italian literature on the comparative method of Qian Zhongshu are the main concern of this analysis, and are a topic never before dealt with in mainland and overseas Qian Xue studies. Among those who approach Qian Zhongshu's work and analyse his scholarly career, many evaluate his achievements by paying attention to examples and to textual analysis. Illustrating theories and literary motifs through direct textual references makes it possible to avoid empty pronouncements and baseless assumptions.[2] The present study pursues this method. The core analysis rests on quotations and the way in which quotations are used. The comparative method of Qian Zhongshu is exposed and discussed through the same quotations that constitute nearly all of Qian's work.

The works selected for analysis include all the essays contained in the collections *Xie Zai Rensheng Bianshang* 寫在人生邊上 (Writing on the Margins of Human Life), 1941; *Rensheng Bianshang de Bianshang* 人生邊上的邊上 (On the Margins of the Margins of Human Life), 2001; *Qian Zhongshu Xuanji – Sanwen Juan* 錢鍾書選集散文卷 (Collected Works of Qian Zhongshu, Essays), 2001; *Qi Zhui Ji* 七綴集 (Collection of Seven Patches), 1985; *A Collection of Qian Zhongshu's English Essays*, 2005; *Qian Zhongshu Sanwen* 錢鍾書散文 (Essays by Qian Zhongshu), 1997; and the

---

2 See Zheng Zhining, "Qian Zhongshu's Theory and Practice of Metaphor", a dissertation by Zheng Zhining. Zheng Zhining's work exposes, with a close eye set on Qian's works, his theory about metaphor, the use that he makes of this rhetoric device and the uniqueness of Qian's style achievements. Every point is appropriately supported by relevant examples from Qian's works.

two masterpieces, *Guan Zhui Bian* 管錐編 (The Tube and Awl Collection), 1979, and *Tan Yi Lu* 談藝錄 (Discourses on Art), 1948. Only essays in which Italian quotations are present were analysed, the same principle adopted for *Guan Zhui Bian* and *Tan Yi Lu*, where Qian Zhongshu's Italian quotations were dissected and analysed.

The first phase of this study focused of a survey on general studies on the author and his role in comparative literature, both with reference to Chinese and western sources. Primary sources constitute the main target of analysis, and the reading and dissecting of Qian Zhongshu's essays make up the core of this study, during the second phase of the research. Inquiry into primary sources then proceeded from an analysis of his creative works to analysis of his essays. Creative works account for an important source of information on Qian's life and writing style. Analysis of the essays was supported by the large number of critical studies provided by the *Qian Xue*, the academic discipline that leads the "studies on Qian." Reviewing those studies and personal communication with some of the most important scholars and researchers on Qian Zhongshu and on Chinese modern comparative literature, allowed the present study to define the targets and objectives of research that focuses on Italian quotations.

Participation in two international seminars commemorating one hundred years of Qian Zhongshu fundamentally informed the collection of material, definition and scope of this investigation. A detailed account of those seminars is provided later in this work. Of utmost importance was an academic year, spent as an exchange student in the Department of Chinese Language and Culture at Peking University, made possible thanks to a grant from the European Union, as part of the LiSUM[3] exchange project.

---

3 LiSUM is an acronym for: Linking Sino-European Universities through Mobility, a program aimed at fostering

All quotations in the present study have been transcribed exactly as they appear in Qian's essays, and have been double-checked in their original sources. Incidental mistakes in Qian's quotations have been rectified in footnotes. Whenever possible source texts were checked against the same edition indicated by Qian. Digitisation of old and recent editions of books are on such websites as www.openlibrary.org, www.pelagus.org/it/libri, www. archives.catholic.org.hk, www.gute nberg.org, www.letturelibere.net, www. liberliber.it and www. books. google. it. All quotations were then translated into English and, when the source text of the translated version is not indicated, the translation is by the author of the present study. Sometimes the same work (i.e., *The Divine Comedy* by Dante Alighieri) was consulted in different editions (for example the original Italian and the translated English one) and is thus quoted in footnote, according to the edition used and indicated by Qian Zhongshu.

## Organisation of the work

A brief introduction on the relationship between Qian Zhongshu and 20th century Chinese comparative literature is given in appendix 2 to define the field of studies to which Qian's work might be ascribed and to offer the background for Qian's scholarly career. Since biographical studies on Qian Zhongshu are already available in English,[4] only a brief outline of his life and work is presented here in order to understand the development of his career

---

mutual enrichment and better understanding between the European Union and China through the exchange of persons, knowledge and skills at a higher level education.

4 One of the most complete and reasoned biographies of Qian Zhongshu in English is the one by Theodore Huters, *Qian Zhongshu*. As for works in Chinese, particular attention has been devoted to the work by Zhang Wenjiang, *Yingzao Babita de Zhizhe*.

and the reason for many of his thematic and literary choices. A further step is made in tracing the roots of Qian Zhongshu's method in chapter 3 and in illustrating the way in which Qian's works, with their massive use of quotations, set an important advancement in the practice of Chinese comparative literature. Attention, through examples of the usage of quotations, is then given to the various functions that they have in the corpus of essays by the author. In this first analytical section, both Italian and non-Italian quotations serve to explain his method, touching the roots of his stylistic and thematic choices. The focus then turns to Italian authors and their works, in a chapter in which the quotations examined are divided into two main sections according to a chronological principle. The first is "From Dante to Leopardi: Past theories into the present", where quotations from Italian authors up to the end of the 19$^{th}$ century are used to discuss themes that cover a huge span of time up to the contemporary political situation. The second is "From Pascoli to Eco: Present ideas to shed light on the past" where the focus is on the way contemporary Italian authors discuss classical Chinese texts. In every chapter, sections are named after the authors quoted. Italian quotations are the main target of this study that analyses them by explaining their function and offering a translation from Italian when they are not translated in Qian's texts. Analysis identifies their source text, the literary genre, the historical period[5] and, most importantly, the reasons why he chose them and the role each one plays in the panorama of Qian's literary and aesthetic theory. Little attention is given to quotations that are only present in footnotes in Qian's works, and are not directly functional to the advancement of the motifs discussed, nor is their translation offered. A section is then

---

5 While quotations are always accompanied in Qian's works by the indication of their authors, the same does not happen for their translation from Italian into Chinese and for their source texts and composition details.

dedicated to outline the *Qian Xue* and to illustrate the latest outcomes of this branch of studies in Chinese literature up to the activities commemorating one hundred years of Qian Zhongshu in 2010. Among those activities, were two important international seminars, the first at the National Central University in Taiwan in December 2009 and the second at the Canadian University of British Columbia in Vancouver in December 2010. The author of the present research participated in both seminars, which inspired the present work. Chinese scholars encouraged the author that such an analysis was useful for understanding Qian Zhongshu's thematic and stylistic choices.

Since the scope of this research lies in an explanation of the Italian quotations, the closing remarks summarise the preferred quoted authors and the historical literary trends examined and taken into consideration by Qian, thereby giving more clues to the comprehension of the author's scholarly formation and literary erudition.

Two appendixes follow the conclusion of the book and describe comparative literature studies in the west and in China.

## Limitations of the study

The breadth of Qian Zhongshu's literary interests and scholarly career makes it impossible for the present study to offer a comprehensive account of his method and suggests further investigation into matters dealt with in this study. Many aspects deserve additional attention beyond the scope of this book. For example, an analysis of the evolution of Qian's use of quotations and of his reference to Italian authors in his different works, to determine if Qian's quotations in his initial works differ from the ones in the last phase of his writing career, could be undertaken. The link between his reading notes, published in a scanned version in 2001 with the name *Rong'an Guan Zhaji* 容

安館札記 (Notes from the Rong'an Study), and his essays is another aspect for investigation. The richness of Qian Zhongshu's literary and aesthetic panorama and the numerous implications that lie behind and inside his works constitute a spur to further research and to fill the large gaps left uncovered.

# CHAPTER 1
# Qian Zhongshu and comparative literature

Qian Zhongshu did not like to be considered a comparatist and was often very particular about the definition of comparative literature, for him a different discipline from what was usually intended. However, in the essay "Meiguo Xuezhe Duiyu Zhongguo Wenxue De Yanjiu Jiankuang" 美國學者對於中國文學的研究簡況,[6] (Brief Introduction on American Scholars' Research on Chinese Literature) firstly published by the Chinese Academy of Social Sciences, Qian Zhongshu affirms that his major interest was the study of Chinese classics, but his lingering interest was comparative literature. In this essay, he makes important statements about the utility and interest of comparative literature. He affirms that when comparing literature it is important first to understand one's own literature. Every country's literature has its specificities for artistic aspects and particular developments, and through the analysis of differences between various traditions, similarities emerge. Similarities, in turn, make differences come to light. Therefore, a comparative analysis could give to the study of literature and art the universality of scientific disciplines.[7] This is a noteworthy assumption, since it proves the faith that Qian Zhongshu has in comparative literature and in its scientific value. Another benefit that comparative literature studies have, in the opinion of Qian, is the help that the analysis of literary phenomena relevant to one literature brings to the study of a different literature.

---

6  Qian Zhongshu, *Qian Zhongshu Xuanji*, 69-73.

7  Qian Zhongshu, "Meiguo Xuezhe Duiyu Zhongguo Wenxue de Yanjiu Jiankuang", 186.

Qian Zhongshu's ideas on comparative literature, as expressed in the essay, focus on the belief that comparative literature is nothing more than the first requisite for the study of literatures in a global perspective. He affirms that the first step for China in comparative literature studies should be to arrange and reflect on its own literature. Exchanges with other cultures in China, he notes, had started with Buddhism during the Han dynasty and had been reinforced by the arrival of Marco Polo in the 13th century. During the Renaissance, Marco Polo's *Il Milione* was the most influential book in the west on the eastern world. Qian also notes that in the history of literary and cultural exchanges between China and the west, the play *Zhao Shi Guer* 趙氏孤兒 (The Orphan of Zhao) influenced many French and German authors, and had been used by the Italian Pietro Metastasio (1698-1792) who, in the première of the play, also mentioned its source.

The influence of western literature on China started after the Opium Wars, and continued with Lin Shu 林紓 and Yan Fu 嚴復's translations. A full recognition of this process had been reached with the May Fourth Movement[8]. Authors from that period, such as Guo Moruo 郭沫若, Wen Yiduo 聞一多, Ba Jin 巴金, Lu Xun, Mao Dun 茅盾, Yu Dafu 郁達夫, admitted that they had taken nourishment from western literature and had put much effort in translations and studies. This is the reason why it is impossible to analyse modern Chinese literature without being aware of the foreign languages that often lie at its basis.[9]

In the 1945 essay *Tan Zhongguo Shi* 談中國詩[10] (Discussion on Chinese

---

8 The 1919 May Fourth Movement, 五四運動 *Wusi Yundong*, arose in protest to decisions taken at the Versailles Conference that ended the Great War (1914-1918). China did not get what she was expecting and thousands of students demonstrated to advocate for democracy, a more westernlike organisation of society, a rejection of traditional norms and ideas and language that could reach the majority of the population. A social and political movement thus became a cultural imperative for reform and modernisation.

9 See Zhang Longxi "Qian Zhongshu tan bijiaowenxue yu wenxue bijiao".

Poetry) many of those ideas are reflected upon and there is a thorough explanation and definition of comparative literature and why it is important to move among languages and time periods to appreciate global literatures. In a Biblical reference the curse of Babel was the starting point for men not understanding each other, says Qian. The curse had the greatest impact on literature; that is why translators are necessary to appreciate other literatures. However, translators should not substitute for writers; they should be instead like crafty matchmakers who unveil only partially the beauty of a woman in search of a husband, causing in the man, as in the reader, the curiosity to meet the woman, or to read the original text. Nevertheless, it is not easy to study languages only to appreciate literatures, and the Chinese language happens to be the most difficult in the world. Encounters of Chinese and Anglo-American literatures, continues Qian, seem to be doomed. Early ones were the first Chinese poem to appear in the 1589 *The Arte of Poesie* by George Puttenham and the first English poem to be translated in Chinese, *A Psalm of Life* by Longfellow (written in 1839 and translated in Chinese in the mid 1800s). In his essay, Qian argues that to be able to summarise a country's literature it is necessary to have an overall understanding of it and it is impossible to see the whole of something except through a confrontation with something else. The logical deduction is that to talk about the general imprint of Chinese poetry implies a step into the realm of comparative literature.[10]

Chinese poetry has been precocious because it has not gone through the steps of historical poetry and drama. Instead it directly reached the beauty of lyrical poetry, a significance only understood when compared to other poetic traditions. It is beautiful in its brevity and, since this is a distinctive characteristic, it might be appreciated only through the confrontation with

---

10 Qian Zhongshu, "Tan Zhongguo Shi", 162.

other longer poems. Chinese poetry is full of hints and suggestions and implies more than it states, a point particularly appreciated by western readers and critics. It uses the interrogative tone a lot; this emerges through the confrontation with western poetry that largely does not use questions. Likewise, the confrontation with the use of punctuation in western poetry explains why in Chinese classical poetry the use of punctuation marks could damage the beauty of a nuanced and versatile meaning. The tone of Chinese poetry is subtle and light, bearing nothing of the heroism and strength of western poems. This has something to do with the characteristics of each language. French poetry for instance, is not strong and powerful like German poetry which has not the richness in tone of Latin poetry. The conclusion is nevertheless that the "poetic" inside Chinese poetry exceeds its "Chineseness". The common spirit that lies hidden inside the apparent diversity is traceable only through confrontation and the appreciation of one's own literary realm is even more complete and pleasant when we look to something different.[11]

Qian Zhongshu thinks that the comparative analysis of theories of art and literature and the comparative poetic field are important and very promising fields of research. The main task of comparative poetics should be to make the terminology of Chinese traditional theory of literature and the terminology of western literature explain and enlighten each other. The confrontation between terminologies and literary ideas has in fact always been one of the biggest problems.[12] Qian Zhongshu has gone deeper into the analysis of literature to reach the philosophical principles lying at its core and, showing the possibility to compare those principles and the underlying

---

11  Qian Zhongshu, "Tan Zhongguo Shi", 159-168.

12  See Zhao Yiheng, "Guan Zhui Bian Zhong de Bijiao Wenxue Pingxing Yanjiu", 41-47. Professor Zhao brings the example of the literary concepts linked to the idea of Romanticism and Realism that have unconsciously become part of Chinese literary critic.

theories, he has demonstrated the possibility to compare two literary realms. As Hu Heqing 胡河清 poetically remarks, Qian embodies in quite a representative way both the western Mephistophelian spirit of negation and the eastern "white butterfly" of *Zhuangzi* 莊子 origin.[13] Hu defines Qian as one of the main experts on *Zhuangzi*. Translation is also a fundamental part of comparative literature in the opinion of Qian,[14] who considers "change" (*hua* 化) as the highest standard for translation; the sublime is reached when a text does not show traces of a stiff interpretation and still maintains the flavour of the original text.

There are two main trends in comparative literature, namely the American, focusing on a parallel analysis, and the French, giving more attention to the influences among literatures. Since traditional Chinese criticism had always treasured "concrete evidence" (*shijing* 實景), quite often Chinese critics consciously or unconsciously embraced concepts from the French School. Cultural exchanges treasured by the American School are indeed the stepping stones in Qian Zhongshu's ideas on a comparative analysis of literatures, on linguistics, and on the comparison of languages, fields yet to be explored by scholars and researchers on Qian.[15]

Is it possible, despite great differences, to compare Chinese and western literatures? In answer, Qina Zhongshu stated in the writing of *Guan Zhui Bian* that not only the said comparison is possible, but also that through this comparison the two realms can mutually enlighten each other.[16] Even with the most diverse spheres of literature, through the practical work of comparing, it is possible to show the *shixin* 詩心, poetic heart or the *wenxin*

---

13 Hu Heqing, "Qian Zhonghshu lun", 280-290.
14 See the essay "Lin Shu de Fanyi" in Qian Zhongshu, *Qi Zhui Ji*, 77-114.
15 Gong Gang, *Qian Zhongshu: Aizhishe de Xiaoyao*, 93.
16 See Motsch, "A New Method of Chinese- Western Comparative Literature, 35-42.

文心, literary heart, common to world literature, as the basis for the comparative method.[17] This is a clear escape from historical determinism and a demonstration that possible connections between texts and ideas can be something other than historical, in "an empirical but experimental challenge to the assumption of Chinese uniqueness".[18]

Qian took overt opposition to literary critique in China during the period of the "Gang of Four."[19] According to Qian, the only literary critical trend followed a Marxist and materialistic tendency and no other school was even taken into consideration. Comparative literature, Formalism, and the School of Psychology were not considered legitimate. In the western world instead, critics summed up quite a number of critical schools. Grisenbach counted six schools, Cesare Segre in his *Methodi Attuali Della Critica Italiana*[20] (Italian Criticism's Actual Methods) counted seven schools (he is also recalled in another 1979 essay together with Maria Corti),[21] and Fokkema counted four schools. Qian states that following the "Gang of Four" period, there was a similar proliferation of theories and points of view, since in the humanities, more theories can coexist and be like the "one hundred flowers blooming," that is, not one hundred flowers from the same plant, but one hundred different flowers from one hundred different plants.

Finding common trends in world literatures should not be considered

---

17  See Chen Shengsheng. Qian Zhongshu yu Bijiao Wenxue Piping, 78-80.

18  Haun Saussy, "Comparative Literature?", 339.

19  The "Gang of Four" is the name given to four Chinese Communist Party political officials, namely Jiang Qing (Mao Zedong's wife), Zhang Chunqiao, Yao Wenyuan and Wang Hongwen who were especially active during the latest phases of the Chinese Cultural Revolution (1966-1976). In 1981 they were charged with a series of crimes and condemned.

20  The title should be **I Metodi** attuali della critica **in Italia**, the spelling mistake in the title is here reported as in the original text by Qian. See Corti, M. e Segre, C. *I Metodi Attuali Della Critica in Italia*.

21  Qian Zhongshu, "Meiguo Xuezhe Duiyu Zhongguo Wenxue de Yanjiu Jiankuang", 184.

part of the globalisation of literature, remarks Zhao Yiheng 趙毅衡,[22] but rather an attempt to form, through comparison, a common literature, an *yiban wenxue* 一般文學, tracing the anthropological roots of common stories and common trends.

Qian Zhongshu states that it is important not to consider these common trends as uniformity but to aim through confrontation to a *concordia discors* because: "unison, after all, may very well be not only a synonym of, but also a euphemism for, monotony".[23] These words come from a speech by Qian Zhongshu on the occasion of the Sino-American Symposium on Comparative Literature.[24] Qian hoped that this symposium afforded Chinese and American scholars an opportunity for confrontation and comparison both "of literature and of comparatists [...] for a better understanding of cultural diversity and contextual relativism".[23]

---

22  Zhao Yiheng, "Guan Zhui Bian Zhong de Bijiao Wenxue Pingxing Yanjiu", 41-47.

23  Qian Zhongshu, "A speech by Qian Zhongshu" in *Qian Zhongshu Sanwen*, 562-564.

24  The essay was first published in 1983 in the magazine *Wenyi Lilun Yanjiu* 文藝理論研究 (Studies on the Theory of Art and Literature).

# CHAPTER 2
# "It is commonly said that human life is a big book"

## 2.1 1910-1935 From Wuxi to Beijing

Qian Zhongshu's life[25] and work[26] cover most of the 20th century. He was born in Wuxi[27] in 1910 into a cultured and conservative family and died in Beijing in 1998. His father, Qian Jibo, was a professor of Chinese literature, and his mother was the sister of a popular writer at the time. According to the custom of the time, at the age of one Qian Zhongshu underwent the *zhuazhou* 抓周, grab in a circle. Presented a number of different objects, the one-year-old child chose the one that most captured his attention. In the case of Qian, this object, a book, said to foretell his future and became his "given name", *shu* 書. Qian Zhongshu means, in fact, "Qian who loves books". His grandfather decided that his

---

25  Qian Zhongshu's former name (*yuanming* 原名) is recorded as Yangxian 仰先, his courtesy names (*zi* 字) as Zheliang 哲良 and Mocun 默存, his alternative courtesy name, or pseudonym (*hao* 號) as Huaiju 槐聚, and his former pen-name (*biming* 筆名) as Zhong Shujun 中書君.

26  Biographical notes on Qian Zhongshu are mainly based on: Yang Xiaobin, "Qian Zhongshu"; Theodore Huters, *Qian Zhongshu*, and Zhang Wenjiang, *Yingzao Babita de Zhizhe: Qian Zhongshu Zhuan*.

27  Qian Zhongshu's childhood home was a traditional construction of the Jiangnan 江南 (South of the Yangtze river). It was transformed into a museum in 2001 following a decision of the local city government. The number of visitors has increased annually, reaching 5,000 visitors in peak holiday seasons, proof of a renewed interest in the writer. See Gu Yubao, "Zoujin Qian Zhongshu Guju".

uncle, who had no male heir, would be an exigent master who should adopt this child. Qian alternatively attended public and private-home education for health reasons that kept him away from public schools. Under the guidance of his father, he started to read Chinese classics as well as popular traditional novels following his uncle's interests. When Qian Zhongshu was nine years old his uncle, a mild and cheerful tutor, died and he returned to his father, a more strict and serious mentor. At the age of eleven, he encountered Lin Shu's translations of western literature. Soon after, he was able to read English language literature in the original as he attended a middle school affiliated with the American Episcopal Church. At the age of sixteen, during his summer vacation, he began to write prose and poetry under the guidance of his father. Qian's perfect and elegant classical style resulted in occasionally ghost-writing for his father.

Qian entered Qinghua University, one of the most prestigious schools in China, as a student of foreign languages. It is said his perfect performance in the Chinese and English languages allowed him to enrol at Qinghua, despite his inadequate marks on the math entrance exam. The years at Qinghua included fellow students Li Jianwu 李健吾 and Ji Xianlin 季羨林, and professors Ye Gongchao 葉公超, editor of Crescent Moon, I.A. Richards and Wu Mi 吳宓. Qian particularly admired Wu Mi for his synoptic knowledge of European literary history and his advocacy of traditional Chinese literature in the study of comparative literature.[28] Qian Zhongshu, considered at the time an outstanding student of the Department of Foreign Languages at Qinghua, wrote essays and book reviews for magazines such as *Xinyue* 新月, *Dagong Bao* 大公報, and *Qinghua Zhoukan* 清華周刊.

After graduation in 1933, Qian refused to continue his studies as a

---

28 See Qian Zhongshu, "Correspondence", 427.

postgraduate at Qinghua, preferring instead to move as a teacher of English literature to Guanghua University in Shanghai, where his father was chair of the Chinese Department. In the summer of 1935, Qian married the playwright, translator and essayist Yang Jiang 楊絳, who subsequently documented her life with Qian Zhongshu and his personal and artistic experience. Together Yang Jiang and Qian Zhongshu left for England.

## 2.2 1935-1938 Years abroad

In England, Qian studied English literature at Exeter College, University of Oxford. His thesis on the portrayal of China in English literature of the 17$^{th}$ and 18$^{th}$ centuries, earned him a B. Litt. degree, one of the few awarded to a Chinese student at the time.[29] The years at Oxford were important for Qian's scholarly experience. He studied with Yang Jiang in the Bodleian Library where he could consult the large number of resources, reading incessantly and filling his notebooks with the notes that would constitute the core of his mature essays. Moreover, since Oxford University required at least four foreign languages in its curriculum, Qian also had the opportunity to deepen his knowledge of western literature and languages. Qian Zhongshu and Yang Jiang's only daughter Qian Yuan 錢瑗, was born in Oxford in 1937. That same year, refusing the offer of a job as Chinese literature lecturer at Oxford University, Qian Zhongshu moved to Paris where Yang Jiang attended courses at the Sorbonne while he audited classes, enjoying another year of study and exposure to the western cultural world. In 1938, following the breakout of the Sino-Japanese war and a job offer as English literature teacher at Qinghua University, Qian Zhongshu and Yang Jiang returned to

---

29  See Egan, *Limited Views*, 3.

their homeland.

## 2.3 1939-1949 From Shanghai to Beijing

For Qian, the first half of the 20th century was a very fruitful period that prepared him for his mature works after the Cultural Revolution (1966-1976). He read all the books he found in libraries. His notes of passages he considered noteworthy became prominent background for his major works.[30]

In 1939, after a brief experience, first in Hunan and later in Kunming, Qian was employed by the Xinan Lianda Daxue, an institute made up by merging three Beijing universities which included Qinghua University. Qian moved to Baoqing, Hunan Province, to help establish the Department of Foreign Literatures at Lantian Normal College. The atmosphere and human panorama of Baoqing County in Hunan inspired Qian to create most of the characters and setting of the novel *Wei Cheng* 圍城 (Fortress Besieged), 1947.

## 2.4 The essays: *Xie Zai Rensheng Bianshang*

In 1941, Qian returned to Shanghai to live in the foreign concession with his wife Yang Jiang. In Shanghai, Qian published *Xie Zai Rensheng Bianshang*, a collection of ten essays, mostly written during his stay in Kunming, that deal with disparate topics around cultural conventions. Qian's thesis throughout his essays is that no individual person can offer definitive and valid concepts. Since this is what literati and scholars usually want to do, they are susceptible to being mocked. His essays are full of witty satire and

---

30 For Qian's commitment to reading, see the introduction by Jin Hongda in Yang Lianfen ed., *Qian Zhongshu Pingshuo Qishi Nian*, 1-3.

sharp humour, the same satire we find in his collection of short stories.

## 2.5 Long and short stories: *Ren Shou Gui* and *Wei Cheng*

In 1946, Qian Zhongshu became editor of the journal *Philobiblon* at
Nanjing National Central Library. In the same year *Ren Shou Gui* 人・獸・
鬼 (Humans, Beasts, Ghosts), a collection of four short stories, was published.
The collection is interesting both for its style – elegant, refined, and not in the
least trivial – and for its sociological and political concerns. The stories are full
of sharp sarcasm towards the vanity, greed, and hypocrisy of society and
tragicomic family tragedies. The first short story of the collection, *Shangdi de
Meng* 上帝的夢 (God's Dream), is an allegorical and satirical account of the
creation of man and sees God overcome by human emotions such as solitude,
anger, joy, and boredom. In Qian's narration, God created humanity out of
pure vanity, the consequences being contrary to what he expected. *Linggan* 靈
感 (Inspiration) the second short story, sketches an image of a man of letters,
representative of a whole social class, embracing all the paradoxes and vanities
of this category of people. In this story, a writer, who ends up in Hell, is
hunted by his characters who want him to pay for characterising them badly
and making them suffer in his works. The writer is put on trial and
condemned to become a character in the work of another worthless writer. In
the third story, *Mao* 貓 (The Cat), a couple embodies all the faults of cultured
people. Xenophile and boring, the couple becomes the main subject of the
novel *Wei Cheng*. *Jinian* 紀念 (Souvenir), the last story, is probably the only
one in which characters are given some compassion and sympathy to soften
the stinging sarcasm. Precise description of characters, with all their
insecurities, makes their human nature emerge. All four stories are
overwhelmed by a lack of correspondence between characters' intentions and

the outcome of their actions. The author comments on events through metaphors and descriptions that characterise the inner soul of characters, contributing to a general sense of human life.

*Wei Cheng*, 1947, probably Qian's most successful work, led to others' acknowledging him as one of the greatest Chinese writers. Initially serialized for a full year in the magazine *Wenyi Fuxing* 文藝復興 starting in February 1946, it accounted for the journal's success.[31] The language of the novel is full of wit and rhetorical figures that established Qian's reputation as a great stylist. Dennis Hu and Ted Huters, who have studied Qian's rhetorical inventions in depth, note that the entire novel is informed by extremely able rhetorical imagery. The novel is a stinging narration of a young returnee from abroad with a fake diploma, and his disastrous attempts to deal with a society in which both family and academic pressures are too hard to face. Symptomatic of Qian's attitude towards his works is his capacity to control everything in the novel and the characters' incapacity to control anything. Inspired by noble predecessors the title, *Wei Cheng*, comes directly from a French saying:

> Le mariage est une forteresse assiégée, ceux qui sont dehors veulent y entrer, ceux qui sont dedans veulent en sortir.
> (Marriage is like a fortress besieged: those who are outside want to get in, and those who are inside want to get out.)

The novel is full of similes that originate in Homeric imagery[32] and in Diogene Laertius, while the style and satire exposing hypocrisy and stupidity,

---

31 See Huters, *Qian Zhongshu*, 8.

32 At the end of the Sino-Japanese war, Qian taught in Shanghai Jinan Daxue. One of his courses was "Choice of Euro-American reading" and one of the texts chosen was Homer's *Iliad*.

have their roots in the English novelists Henry Fielding and W.S. Maugham.[33] *Wei Cheng* was not the only novel Qian planned to write. While in Shanghai he started a novel called *Bai He Xin* 百合心, Heart of Artichoke, of which two thousand characters had already been written. Unfortunately, the manuscript was lost in 1949 during the move from Shanghai to Beijing and the new political setting did not allow Qian to pursue this project. Qian affirmed in an interview,[34] that had the manuscript not been lost, this novel would likely have been superior to *Wei Cheng*, and even more liable to criticism and censure during the Cultural Revolution.

## 2.6 Discourses on Art: *Tan Yi Lu*

Based on Qian's wealth of notes and literary critical analysis he had amassed during the previous decade, *Tan Yi Lu* was published in 1948 by the Kaiming Shudian Chubanshe. The title explains the structure of the book and indicates that art is the main object of analysis. Throughout the volume, art and history can be explained together with every epoch containing seeds of the others in a contemporaneity that is not necessarily simultaneity. Different times merge and become part of an epoch – people's thoughts, the events together with the theories and concepts to which they give origin, and the different layers of influences of past on present. *Tan Yi Lu* is a magistral and mature piece of work. Qian Zhongshu, using the comparative method that characterises his work, quotes extensively to discuss themes and create a canon of references on art. In this work, Qian gives importance to the historical sense of the present and realises his intent of creating a literature that

---

33  See Zhang Wenjiang, *Yingzao Babita de Zhizhe.*
34  See Yan Huo, "Qian Zhongshu Fangwen Ji", 91-96.

incorporates both the capacity of expression of individuals in the present and the cultural heritage of tradition that weights on them.[35] Huters identifies two main motives and feelings in *Tan Yi Lu*: a critical spirit on Chinese traditional literature and an aesthetic mood that lies behind the ideas expressed. Literature is the point at which everything converges, an idea that comes from a mixture of Chinese and western concepts demonstrating that literature should be independent of political and ideological purposes.[36]

## 2.7 1949-1969 Years in Beijing

In 1949, upon the Communist takeover of Shanghai, Qian moved to Qinghua University in Beijing and in 1950 was appointed head of the translation committee of Mao Zedong's Selected Works in English. This position, while saving him from criticism and anti-rightist campaigns, helped the government control and restrain him. For Qian Zhongshu, translation was a duty more than a choice and the translation of Selected Works of Mao Zedong and Mao Zedong's Poems was a great compromise between political and artistic matters.[37]

Besides Qian's practice of translation, it is interesting to read his ideas in his essays including: *Lin Shu de Fanyi* 林紓的翻譯 (Lin Shu's Translation, 1963), in which he talks about Lin Shu's translation method; *A Note to the Second Chapter of Mr Decadent*, in the September 1948 issue of *Philobiblon* and the translation of *Laocan Youji* 老殘遊記 (1905) by Liu E 劉鶚 by Yang Xianyi 楊憲益. Even if Qian appreciated this last mentioned work, he

---

35  See Huters, "Traditional Innovation: Qian Zhong-shu and Modern Chinese Letters," Ph.D. dissertation, Stanford University, 1977.

36  See Huters, *Qian Zhongshu*, 37-69.

37  Zheng Xiaodan, "A study on Qian Zhongshu's translation: sublimation in translation", 70-83.

criticised it and its title "Mr Decadent" which he translated to "Taking rest and eating the *resles*." However, he was unable to suggest a more suitable title and resigned himself "with a mild demurrer to 'Mr Decadent' and 'Mr Derelict'." "Mr. Derelict" was the title given by another translator of the same story.[38]

A main source of information on Qian's translation theory rests in his thousands of translated bits and pieces quoted from foreign literatures in his masterpieces of comparative literature *Tan Yi Lu* and *Guan Zhui Bian*. His fellowship with Peking University Institute of Literature resulted in membership in the Chinese Academy of Social Sciences. In 1953, he was appointed Vice President of the Academy while moving to Peking University due to a reorganisation of faculties of Qinghua University, which specialised in scientific disciplines, while Peking University became home of the humanities.

## 2.8 The poetic side: *Songshi Xuanzhu*

In 1958, *Songshi Xuanzhu* 宋詩選注, an anthology of Song verse, and a work that demonstrates Qian Zhongshu's profound understanding of Chinese aesthetics, was published. The collection of Song poems is considered one of Qian's masterpieces. He probably chose Song and not Tang poetry, more prominent as a poetic genre, because there were already many anthologies of Tang poetry but few good commentaries on Song poetry. He included 365 poems with particular attention to poems whose main theme was the difficult condition of common people. This choice bears great significance in relation

---

38 C. S. Ch'ien (Qian Zhongshu 錢鍾書 ), "A Note to the Second Chapter of Mr Decadent", in *A collection of Qian Zhongshu's English Essays*, 390.

both to Qian's ideas about poetry and to his link with a particular time and a certain political condition: it is unsurprising, then, that the book was initially banned from circulation. He included authors that other collections excluded. The selected poems seem plain at first blush, yet full of undisclosed meaning that emerges only after a more careful reading. Qian chose more new poems (*jinti* 近體) than old ones and predominately short poems over long ones. There are 307 seven-character poems (*qiyan* 七言) in a total of 365 poems. This is a strange percentage, 84%, given that in the anthology of 300 Tang poems *Tang Shi Sanbai Shou* 唐詩三百首, one of the canonical anthologies of Tang verse, the number of seven-character poems and of five-character poems is nearly the same.

## 2.9 1969-1972 Years "down-under"

Notwithstanding his position as official translator of Mao Zedong's works, Qian and his family underwent severe hardship during the Cultural Revolution. In August 1966, Qian was denounced for having made derogatory comments about the published works of Chairman Mao. Qian and Yang Jiang were labelled reactionary academics and forced to work cleaning floors and public toilets.[39] In 1968, they were denounced as *zichan jieji xueshu quanwei* 資產階級學術權位 (bourgeois academic authorities) and were sent to the School for Cadres in the Hunan countryside for reeducation through labor. Qian left for the Cadres School eight months before Yang Jiang, who arrived in July 1970, when they were finally reunited, even if forced to live in different places. The couple could not go back to

---

39 See Egan, *Limited Views*. The most accurate account of Qian and Yang Jiang's years in the School for Cadres is given in Yang Jiang's *Ganxiao Liuji*.

Beijing until 1972, following a request by Zhou Enlai that allowed the "old, weak, sick, and disabled" to return to their former lives. In the countryside, access to books was nearly impossible and Qian and Yang struggled to keep alive their attachment to literature and to creative and productive research.

## 2.10 1972-1998 Return to Beijing

The relationship between the historical and social setting of a writer and his literary production is always a close one; this is true for every historical phase, but particularly significant when external conditions are more unstable and in rapid transformation. Qian's thoughts and ideas were not influenced by the controversial period in which they were generated, since he remained the same "out of the loop" scholar and writer notwithstanding his different life experiences. He moved to Europe for a couple of years and returned to China; he underwent experiences both in the best "urban" university in Beijing and in the countryside; he was appointed as translator of the works of Mao Zedong and was criticised as a bourgeois *zhishifenzi* 知識分子.[40] His works were deeply influenced by the events of his life rooted in 20th century Chinese society.

Among the many obituary notices in the Chinese and international press in December 1998, only a Taiwan-based newspaper, the *Zhongguo Shibao*, in praising the life and work of Qian Zhongshu like other newspapers, pointed to Qian's activity as a scholar and writer during the Cultural Revolution. It reported that from 1949 to 1979 many Chinese intellectuals preferred to devote themselves to scholarship instead of creative fiction because scholarly

---

40 *Zhishifenzi* (知識分子) is the term to classify all literates during the Chinese Cultural Revolution and which indicated their belonging to a social class that needed thought rectification and re-education.

works were less affected by political interference.[41] Qian Zhongshu's apparent silence and his covert opposition to the current politics have been criticised by scholar Ge Hongbin 葛紅兵, who, in an interview titled *Qian Zhongshu: bei shenhua de 'dashi'* 錢鍾書：被神話的 "大師" (Qian Zhongshu: the mythicised 'master'),[42] contested Qian's use of a method which added nothing to Chinese literary criticism. Ge says Qian's ideas are moved by the "philosophy of the turtle" (*wugui zhexue* 烏龜哲學), and that the author did nothing but read and copy from other writers. Ge says that Qian is a parasite of literature incapable of creating new trends and of taking part in the debate on culture and politics in the second half of 20th century. Ge seems blind to Qian's need to express his ideas in a more veiled way and to look for a compromise to survive, thus giving birth to witty and sarcastic pieces of works. According to Wang Meng 王蒙, "a writer in the People's Republic of Chine should have the right to remain silent if the official policies are repugnant to him".[43]

## 2.11 The masterpiece: *Guan Zhui Bian*

Wang Rongzu[44] analyses the link between Qian Zhongshu's composition of *Guan Zhui Bian* and *Tan Yi Lu* and the atmosphere of distress and sufferance in which they were composed. He sees a strong link between difficult times, suffering, and literary composition. *Tan Yi Lu* was conceived and composed during the war of resistance against Japan, when the pressure and attack on China was an external one. Even more difficult to endure was

---

41 He Hui and Fang Tianxing, ed. *Yi Cun Qian Si*, 12.

42 Full text at http://www.confucius2000.com/poetry/qzsbshdds.htm. Accessed on November 25, 2011.

43 Ou-Fan Lee. "My Interviews with Writers in the People's Republic of China: A Report", 137-140.

44 Wang Rongzu, "Ai Huan yu Buchang: Shi Tan Tan Yi Lu yu Guan Zhui Bian de Xiezuo Xingqing", 281-306.

the pressure of the Cultural Revolution when the irrationality of internal pressure impacted Qian's vision of the world. The masses became stronger than individuals, whose liberties were greatly limited and whose personalities were nearly cancelled out. Qian could not avoid the agitation and restlessness caused by such a setting, notwithstanding living like a hermit: keeping his old habits of reading books and writing *wenyanwen* 文言文 (classical language), never feeling that the new *baihuawen* 白話文 (written vernacular) should take its place, and never thinking that the country's old written language was useless. For many intellectuals of the first half of the 20th century, like Qian Zhongshu and Zhou Zuoren 周作人, using classical prose was a way to state their aloofness from the current political situation and to keep their individuality out of the immediate social context.[45] Qian Zhongshu believed in the power of both languages, the classical and the vernacular, but worried that in such a big country, once the new language had taken root, fewer than sixty people would still able to write in the old language. The contradiction to the current trend in Qian's use of *wenyanwen* is very strong. If the Cultural Revolution sought to break with the old culture and old traditions, then *Guan Zhui Bian*, both in form and content, strove to enhance studies and annotations on the classics on which traditional culture was based. *Guan Zhui Bian* is a work that fills the gap and the void left by the difficult times China had to overcome, putting Chinese traditional and contemporary literature in a global setting and finding relief through art and criticism. It is fundamental to note the contribution of this comprehensive work in a period in which the appreciation of literature and critical appreciation were seriously compromised. *Guan Zhui Bian* gathers literary treasures when their survival was not considered important. This book touches the *shinian dongluan* 十年

---

45 See Gunn, *Rewriting Chinese*.

動亂 era (the ten years of disorder)[46] and arose from the context in which it was created, full of references to social politics, points of view, and contemporary issues.[47]

The language Qian Zhongshu used is a combination of classical and contemporary language. Qian injected classical language with the logic and the fluidity of spoken language, and wrote in a spoken language with the precision and the essence unique to the classical one, avoiding empty words and creating a dense expression.

Even Chinese scholars considered *Guan Zhui Bian* too dense and disorganised. *Guan Zhui Bian*, a five-volume work, starting from ten Chinese classics – the classics *Zhou Yi* 周易, *Mao Shi* 毛詩, *Zhuo Zhuan* 左傳, the historical work *Shi Ji* 史記, the "Zi" works: *Laozi* 老子, *Liezi* 列子, and the collections *Yi Lin* 易林, *Chu Ci* 楚辭, *Taiping Guangji* 太平廣記, *Quan Shanggu Sandai Qin Han San Guo Liu Chao Wen* 全上古三代秦漢三國六朝文[48] – comments on aesthetics, art, poetry, moral and cultural customs, literature, and society, quoting extensively both from Chinese and western literatures. The work is divided into sections whose relationships are joined in a way that what comes before is the origin of what follows, but what follows sometimes is not directly linked to what precedes. The aim is to delve into details rather than to reach a superficial exposition of different ideas. Usually the first item of every commentary is the theme of the section and expresses the writer's opinion, while subsequent items are commentaries constructed mainly through disparate quotations from every possible tradition and in

---

46  See Chen Ziqian, *Lun Qian Zhongshu.*

47  For an example of those references see Hu Fangzhu and Chen Jiaxuan "'Guan Zhui Bian' Suo Yunhan de Shihui Pipan Yishi" in Ding, Weizhi ed. *Qian Zhongshu Xiansheng Bainian Danchen Jinian Wenji*, 61-76.

48  The translated titles of the ten books on which *Guan Zhui Bian* comments are: *The Book of Changes, The Book of Songs, Zuo Tradition, Records of the Historian, Laozi, Liezi, The Forest of Changes by Jiao, Songs of Chu, Records of the Taiping Era,* and *The Complete Pre-Tang Prose.*

different languages on very specific passages of the book. It is hard to derive from *Guan Zhui Bian* a rationally exposed system of thought when the framework of the book is more an encyclopedic investigation of different entries without the claim of being a rationally organized piece of work. The leitmotifs of the work are what could be called the *datong zhongxi, ronghui gujin* 打通中西, 融匯古今 (break through China and the West, meld old and new) and a continuous reflection and analysis of the different meanings that every word and idea can bear. The opening of the book, with the discussion on *yi zhi san ming* 易之三名 "the three names of the Yi, the Change," is emblematic and presents a concept to which the author repeatedly returns – the changing and different meanings embraced in a sole concept or a single word.

The work does not need to be read from beginning to end and each part can be considered the beginning as well as the end. Even if miscellaneous, *Guan Zhui Bian* is not messy, it is *za er bu luan* 雜而不亂, to use an expression by Qian Zhongshu which means "mixed and not chaotic".[49] The book touches a multitude of themes and subjects, but the leitmotif is literature, and the analysed texts have been viewed with a literary eye. *Guan Zhui Bian* is a book on men; it is meant "not to write at the margin of human life" but "to write in the deepness of human life".

## 2.12 Final Years

The return to Beijing from the countryside in 1972 sets the last phase of literary composition for Qian Zhongshu. Following the 1978 publication of *Guan Zhui Bian*, Qian's essays in *Qi Zhui Ji*, 1985, are a collection from two

---

49 Chen Ziqian, *Lun Qian Zhongshu*, 78.

previous works: *Jiu Wen Si Pian* 舊文四篇 1979 and *Ye Shi Ji* 也是集, 1984, which the author assembled, to address the difficulty of finding editions of the original collections. Qian Zhongshu was convinced that this collection would become representative of his specific method of comparative literature and of his concept of literature in the broadest sense. For this reason, particular attention is given to those essays, together with *Guan Zhui Bian* and *Tan Yi Lu*. *Qi Zhui Ji* consists of seven essays written in *baihuawen* whose composition spans from 1940 with the essay *Zhongguo Shi yu Zhongguo Hua* 中國詩與中國畫 (Chinese Poetry and Chinese Painting) to 1983 with the essay *Yi Jie Lishi Zhanggu, Yi Ge Zongjiao Yuyan, Yi Pian Xiaoshuo* 一節歷史掌故, 一個宗教寓言, 一篇小說 (An Historical Anecdote, a Religious Allegory, a Novel) which is an example of Qian's translation theory and practice.[50] Also included is the posthumous collection of English essays *Yingwen Wenji* – A collection of Qian Zhongshu's English essays (2005) and *Rensheng Bianshang de Bianshang* (At the Margins of the Margins of Human's Life), 2001.

In the mid-1990s, Qian entered the hospital with a high fever, where he spent the last years of his life, cared for by his wife Yang Jiang and his daughter Qian Yuan. In March 1997, Qian Yuan died of cancer. Yang Jiang remained his sole support. Qian slowly understood the fate of his beloved daughter despite Yang Jiang's efforts to avoid giving him such disconcerting news. On December 19, 1998, Qian Zhongshu left this world and his lifetime companion. The formalities were handled in the most common and simple way, without any funeral rites, without flowers, and without tears,

---

50 The other essays of the collection are: *Du "Laaokong"* (Reading Laokoon, 1962); *Tonggan* (Synaesthesia, 1962); *Lin Shu de Fanyi* (Lin Shu's Translation, 1964); *Shi Keyi Yuan* (Complain in Poetry, 1981); *Han Ying Di Yi Shou Yingyu Shi "Rensheng Song" Ji Youguan Er San Shi* (The First English Poem in Chinese Translation and Two or Three Relevant Problems, 1982).

according to Qian's wishes of leaving without "too much ado." When asked about an eventual book of memoirs, Qian replied that a man is different from a dog that urinates to mark his territory.[51]

---

51 He Hui and Fang Tianxing, ed. *Yi Cun Qian Si*, 7.

# CHAPTER 3
# Tracing the roots of Qian Zhongshu's method: a long time legacy

Qian Zhongshu's comparative method, although innovative for reasons the present book is going to examine, is still the heir of a tradition rooted in the Chinese literary world. This tradition seems to be the continuation of the quotation method in the School of Han textual studies *Pu Xue* 樸學 during the Qing era (1644-1911). On one hand Qian's method continues the search for a spirit of concrete textual evidence of that school, on the other hand pursues confirmation and authority of what was affirmed through eastern and western authors' quotations.[52]

As for its form, *Guan Zhui Bian* collects the inheritance of a long tradition of *zhaji* 札記, reading notes that, starting from the Northern Song dynasty, became a characteristic form of the Qing era. It's the heir of Gu Yanwu 顧炎武 (1613-1682)'s *Ri Zhi Lu* 日知錄, Qian Daxin 錢大昕 (1728-1804), Wang Niansun 王念孫 (1744-1832), Yu Zhengxie 俞正燮 (1775-1840) and Chen Li 陳澧 (1810-1882).[53] These authors' *zhaji* are the leading representatives of Qing culture. *Guan Zhui Bian* is very similar to them in length and in structure, while the main difference is that it uses quotes from western works; all these authors' works are constituted by small parts that seem disconnected from one another and that offer the author's point of view on many aspects of culture and thought.

The *zhaji or biji* 筆記 forms – from the Song (960-1279) up to the

---

52 Gong Gang, *Qian Zhongshu: Aizhizhe de Xiaoyao*, 115-119.

53 See Egan, "Tuotai Huangu: *Guan Zhui Bian* dui Qingru de chenzhui yu chaoyue", in *Qian Zhongshu Shiwen Congshuo*, ed. Wang Rongzu, 211-226.

Qing, even in their extreme variety and slippery definition, are an informal prose style. They are informal because they were not produced for special events or for a specific public and because they use a free and clear prose style without prosodic rules. *Guan Zhui Bian* is both the heir of the form used during the Song and Qing dynasties, especially of the *shihua* 詩話 (discourses on poetry) and of the "critical *biji*", sub-genres of the *biji*, and a modern advancement of it. There are differences between the Qing antecedents and *Guan Zhui Bian*, as there are differences between their views on literature and Qian's. Qian was dissatisfied with Qing scholars' absolute faith in a literature subservient to history, sustaining the autonomy of literary creation instead. The greatest literates are the ones who are able to portray what is not linked to a particular time or space or a specific social setting, but the ones who are able to touch and describe the inner core of a situation or a category of people, applicable to each time and space. Qian Zhongshu's satirical works touch on the *zhishifenzi*, the intelligentsia of every epoch, those who believed themselves to be the highest and most sagacious part of society.

If we use only political parameters to analyse and judge the value of a literary work, we will not obtain the work's real value. Literature is not the appendix of politics or history; on one hand it is a reflection of society and the situation of culture and knowledge, but it is also an instrument of art. One of the main characteristics of literature is that it exceeds time and space limits. Literature obeys its inner commands and is not subject to society or politics.[54] Moreover, differently from what Qing scholars did, Qian Zhongshu gave much importance to particular and less important texts instead of the canonical ones, dedicating even longer commentaries than the ones dedicated to the great classics to the non-canonical texts; this is something Qing

---

54 Ze Ming, "Xie Zai Rensheng Bianshang de 'Re n Shou Gui'", 224-244.

scholars would have never done. Another important difference with Qing scholars is also that Qian had strong suspicions towards great systems of thought and complex theories; he often spoke about those ironically. With regard to this it is worth recalling the opening of an essay by Qian titled *Shi Wenmang* 釋文盲 (Explaining Illiteracy), where Qian affirms that to find good and meaningful sentences in works that do not have great value is like finding money that had been forgotten in a pocket when tidying up old clothes.[55]

Another point for which Qian criticised Qing scholars is that they used to focalise on the main ideas of other scholars or on their major works, neglecting secondary opinions and minor works. Qian sustained that an author's thought needs to be considered on the whole without dividing it into grades of importance. A big difference between Qian and his antecedents, this time linked to the historical periods concerned, was his knowledge of western languages and the opportunity he had gained by getting in touch with the western world.

Notwithstanding those big discrepancies, the *biji* form chosen by Qian is still the heir of Qing tradition and allows advantages like flexibility regarding content and style without the need of being consistent with definite stylistic choices or adopting thematic coherence.

Li Hongyan 李洪岩[56] expresses a different opinion; he wants to demonstrate that Qian's masterpieces *Guan Zhui Bian* and *Tan Yi Lu* are not at all written in the *biji* form: this form has never been considered high-level literature in Chinese people's opinion and has been disregarded as lacking of consistency. To ascribe Qian's writing method to this literary form is equal to

---

55  Qian Zhongshu, "Shi Wenmang", in *Xie Zai Rensheng Bianshang*, 47.
56  Li Hongyan, "Ruhe Pingjia Qian Zhongshu", in *Qian Zhongshu Pingshuo Qishi Nian*, 157-174.

affirming that his works lack a solid construction, have random content and do not devote any care to rhetoric expression. If Qian's works had been written in Qing's times, Li's analysis probably would have been correctly formulated. Since they were not, we may well link them to this literary form and state our parallelism.

What we just affirmed is not only valid for the masterpiece *Guan Zhui Bian* but is a characteristic of Qian's writing style and is thus also true for the writer's other scholarly works, as is the case of *Tan Yi Lu*, a great part of which is devoted to the comment of Yuan Mei 袁枚's *Sui Yuan Shi Hua* 隨園詩話. Since the *shi hua* form is an antecedent of Qian's *Tan Yi Lu*, as mentioned above, in giving so much attention to such a work Qian is justifying, confirming the authority of the *shi hua* form, and stating his continuation of such a tradition.[57]

If on one hand Qian Zhongshu is consequently considered the heir of the Qing tradition, on the other hand, it is in continuity with the reform of prose in the first half of the 20th century, as it results from an analysis of Qian's prose style by Theodore Huters. Qian's essays have a deep sense of the European "coupé style" or Baroque style, often exposing an idea at the beginning of the essay, giving the impression that the subject does not need any further discussion to continue with the enrichment of that idea with new meanings and facets of the same topic.[58]

A firm point in the illustration of Qian's prose is the link between form and content. The Baroque prose style serves Qian to express paradoxes and ideas in constant contradiction because the need to express doubt and distrust in fixed and absolute statements is strong. The reader is left as if in front of an

---

57 Huters, *Qian Zhongshu*, 61.
58 Huters, *Qian Zhongshu*, 78-79.

open window to discuss and reflect, rather than in front of truth offered for blind acceptance. It is quite emblematic that Huters puts Qian's style in direct contact with the May Fourth movement and frees the author from most of the accusations he has encountered, as a coward shutting himself up in the classical style and remaining detached from the contemporary historical and social situation. Qian Zhongshu is a son of the May Fourth Literary Revolution, just as Hu Shi 胡適 or Chen Duxiu 陳獨秀 are because he actively participates in the then actual debate on the meaning of literature, on the style to be used and on the themes to be touched upon in literary works. He is modern just like all the other literates of his generation are, because like them he ponders on problems and debates of his time. However, in a way the answer he finds is different from that of both supporters of *baihua* and of *wenyan*. His use of *wenyan* is well studied and bears its own reasons, among others the necessity to demolish literary theories that saw the starting point of literary movements in history, geography, etymology and so on, together with the need to state the independence of literature. In *Tan Yi Lu* he has given an answer to the debate about old and new language affirming that, if enriched by new vocabulary, *wenyanwen* would have been capable of expressing new concepts, just like *baihuawen*. Those who opposed this theory confuted instead that, while *baihuawen* had all the necessary capacities of being a "spoken language", *wenyanwen* could have never been adopted as the common spoken language. The significance of Qian's particular choice regarding the language will be discussed further on with examples rooted in the texts analysed.

A distinctive characteristic of Qian's style is concision. His writing touches on different themes following a line of thought that is peculiar for its massive usage of quotations; that is why Qian's works are different from modern literary pieces both for content and form. Due to their thematic variety, it is impossible to analyse the content of Qian's work by dividing it according to the usual classification of works of history, philosophy, classics and literary collections. However, as innovate as he is, Qian remains a tireless defender of tradition, ratified and surpassed at the same time through a great number of quotations and a comparative method that serves to explain traditional Chinese concepts.[59]

The use of quotations is an old rhetoric device. It was common practice and has been used by many literates like Wang Anshi 王安石 (1021-1086) and Su Shi 蘇軾 (1037-1101) since the *Nan Bei Chao* 南北朝 (North and South Dynasties) during the 4th and 5th centuries up to the May Fourth movement, when Hu Shi made the "do not use quotations" one of the eight pronouncements. And yet the New Literature did not mark a real break with the practice of quoting, since literates such as Lu Xun 魯迅 and Qian Zhongshu continued using textual references after 1919. It is impossible both to write only using quotations "*wu yi zi wu lai chu* 無一字無來處" (there's not a word without a source), as Qian Zhongshu quotes from Huang Jianjian 黃庭堅,[60] and to abolish their use, since quoting is a rhetoric device peculiar to literary style and a way of expressing ideas. In the thirties the same Qian Zhongshu had discussed the appropriateness of using quotations in the essay *Lun Bu Ge* 論不隔[61] (On Non Estrangement). In this essay about translation theory the author affirms that if we do not accept quotations as a literary device, then we should throw away many literary works.

---

59  See Zhang Longxi, "Zhongxi jiaoji yu Qian Zhongshu de zhixue fangfa", in *Qian Zhongshu Shiwen Congshuo*, ed. by Wang Rongzu, 187-210.

60  Huang Jianjian (1045-1105), Chinese literate during the Song dynasty, used this expression meaning literally: "there is not a word without a source" quoted in Qian Zhongshu, "'Songshi Xuanzhu' Shiren Dianping" in *Qian Zhongshu Xuan Ji*, 107.

61  Qian Zhongshu, "Lun Bu Ge", 110-113.

# 3.1 The *Rong'an Guan Zhaji*

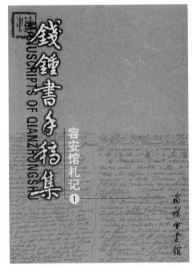

Taking Qian Zhongshu's defence of quotations as a literary device as our starting point, we advance further towards the analysis of how quotations become the same core of literature and the exposition of ideas and concepts for him. We thus try to inquire into his working method. On this regard the collection of scanned writing notes published in 2003 by the Commercial Press, commonly known as the *Rong'an Guan Zhaji* (Notes from the Rongan building), constitutes a source of precious information. It illustrates the process – the choice of books to read which proceeds to the reading and then to the activity of taking notes, up to the reworking of the notes and finally becoming part of Qian's works in the form of quotations. The three volume collection, also named *Qian Zhongshu Shougao Ji* 錢鍾書手稿集 (Collection of Manuscripts by Qian Zhongshu), is the outcome of a meticulous job of collection and reorganization of Qian's notebooks, primarily conducted by Yang Jiang with some support from other helpers like Professor Monika Motsch.

Yang Jiang's introduction to the *Qian Zhongshu Shougao Ji* collection tells us how Qian Zhongshu spent much of his time in the Bodleian Library in Oxford reading and taking notes since books could not be checked out. He read many of the books a second or even a third time, convinced that only then interesting sentences and passages could be perceived. During their years abroad and even after their return to China, Qian and Yang did not have a fixed dwelling. This could be another reason why Qian used to borrow books and keep only the notebooks with all his handwritten notes. Qian Zhongshu's preferential readings were from diverse works of literature: English, French from the 15$^{th}$ to the 19$^{th}$ century, German, and Italian. He also attached considerable importance to periodicals and critical works, building himself a solid construction in many different foreign literatures. Taking notes was his preferential way of reading and he would often read the more significant passages to Yang Jiang, stating nevertheless that they were of no use to anybody but himself. The outcome of this work is one hundred seventy eight notebooks which account for a total number of 34,000 pages in the foreign languages German, Italian, French, English, Latin and Spanish,[62] plus some typewritten pages. Yang Jiang writes that she had some difficulty arranging all the notebooks for posthumous publication because she did not understand German, Italian and Latin and it was thanks to the cooperation of Professor Monika Motsch, who devoted summers in Beijing to the job, that the notebooks have been organized and consequently published as the *Rong'an Guan Zhaji*.

The first volume of the collection, which includes a great amount of Chinese notes and it is not only in foreign languages as Yang Jiang's introduction might lead us to think, would have been used by Qian Zhongshu to write a book in English. This is something Qian will never achieve, presumably[63] because of various subsequent appointments that

---

62 Greek language is quoted as well, but not mentioned in Yang Jiang's preface.

63 Yang Jiang states this quite clearly in the introduction: "Qian Zhongshu both at home and in universities abroad carefully read works in foreign literature; his teaching appointments were also on foreign literatures. After the 'Reorganization of Faculties and Departments' was complete, he ended up belonging to the Literature Research Institute's Research Group on Foreign Literatures. But for many years he had been given other jobs and even transferred for a time to the Classical Literature Research Group, never to return to the Research Group on Foreign Literatures. He

brought him closer to the field of ancient Chinese literature and translation, instead of the English literature he used to teach and research.

The second volume of the collection is made of two different parts merged together: Qian Zhongshu's Chinese literature writing notes and his diary. The reason for this, as explained in the same preface, is that during the first "ideological remoulding" Qian came to know – by the way of a rumour – that the students were authorized to check the diaries of the "old gentlemen", *lao xiansheng* 老先生, and, fearing that his personal matters would become known to the public, he started to cut the diaries into many pieces, pasting them onto the notebooks to disguise them. The amount of these Chinese notes is, more or less, equal to the foreign languages ones.

The third volume is made up of the *rizha* 日札, the daily notes which collect Qian Zhongshu's reading reflections and start from the "ideological remoulding". Qian appears in them with many different pen names and the same notes have different names and titles like: *Rong'an Guan Rizha* 容安館日札 (Notes from the Rong'an building), *Rong'an Shi Rizha* 容安室日札 (Notes from the Rong'an place), *Rong'an Zhai Rizha* 容安齋日札 (Notes from the Rong'an studio). All these names refer to the name of the small one-floor house were Yang Jiang and Qian had been living after the division of departments and schools that had been carried out in 1953 at Qinghua University. Qian refers to the house using a line from a poem by Tao

---

had the composition of a work in English on foreign literatures in mind and he could never satisfy this will. Those notes in foreign languages, according to what he kept affirming, are 'of no use'". The original text is: 錢鍾書在國內外大學攻讀外國文學，在大學教書也教外國文學，「院系調整」後，他也是屬於文學研究所外國文學組的。但他多年被派去做別的工作，以後又借調中國古典文學組，始終未能回外文組工作。他原先打算用英文寫一部論外國文學的著作，也始終未能如願。那些外文筆記，對他來說，該是「沒用了」。in *Qian Zhongshu Shougao Ji – Rongan Guan Zhaji*, vol. I, page 2 of the Introduction. The book Qian intended to write on foreign literatures, and particularly on ten major foreign writers, has been the topic of an exchange of e-mails with Professor Zhang Wenjiang. References to it have also been made in chapter 5 (Italian quotations in Qian Zhongshu's works: a mutual illumination) of the present study.

Yuanming 陶淵明 that says: "*Shen rongxi zhi yi an* 審容膝之易安", in this small place I feel nice and comfortable, which abbreviated becomes *Rong'an*.[64] The third volume is made up of twenty-three notebooks, two thousand pages in total in eight hundred and two entries that carry numbers as titles. This third kind of notebook is manly in Chinese but with a certain amount of foreign languages and it includes material from every period, all countries, and from every literary genre. All this material will help Qian form the core of his major works like *Guan Zhui Bian*, which draws much from these apparently spliced notes. What Yang Jiang points out is that in the *Zhaji* there are many passages remoulded in Qian's other works, but there are also many other passages that do not appear in other books. This means Qian did not have the time and opportunity to use all the material he had collected in his notes. In Professor Zhang Wenjiang's biography of Qian Zhongshu[65] he speaks extensively about a supposed book in English that Qian Zhongshu intended to write, the same one mentioned by Yang Jiang as reported above.

The material contained in the *Rong'an Guan Zhaji* is extremely vast and is representative of Qian Zhongshu's entire life's reading; it spans from his years in Oxford at Exeter College up to the nineties.[66] As mentioned above, the collection of reading notes is in a scanned form and, notwithstanding what has certainly been a painstaking effort for Yang Jiang and Monika Motsch, the notes are still handwritten, they have many layers and the reading is definitely difficult. They appear as a main body that follows the normal structure of the paper to which many other sentences and references have been added. The final aspect is that of notes on notes on notes, which

---

64  See Qian Zhongshu, *Shougao Ji*, vol. I, 1-3.

65  See Zhang Wenjiang, *Yingzao Babita de Zhizhe*, 85-102 and the chapter *Italian quotations in Qian Zhongshu's works: a mutual illumination* of the present study.

66  See Guo Hong, "Shou Gao Shi Yi Zhong Jingshencaifu", 62-63.

sometimes requires the reader to turn the book many times while reading it because they are just inserted in the main text occupying every small blank centimetre of the sheet, going in every possible direction. Thus, reading the manuscript poses incredible difficulties due to the structure of the texts and to the handwriting, which especially in the late notes becomes more frail and uncertain due to the age and bad health of the writer.[66] Furthermore, it is difficult for the reader to guess the Pindaric flights Qian's thoughts were continuously undergoing. There is yet much to discover and extrapolate from the web of literary, social, philosophical, and cultural references Qian "reflected on" while taking notes from his extensive readings and east west comparative literature research would benefit greatly if only the connections Qian had been delineating in his notebooks and the links he had set would have been further analysed and reflected upon.

# CHAPTER 4
# Writing *marginalia* on the book of human life: the use of quotations in the comparative method of Qian Zhongshu[67]

Qian Zhongshu, a scholar who put together works from different contexts in different languages, was able to read and understand Latin, English, German, Spanish, Italian and French. He used to juxtapose passages so that they mutually enlightened each other's meanings in a series of astonishing connections that gave those from the east and west the possibility to see themselves reflected through the eyes of other traditions.

Monika Motsch singles out three phases of Qian's method: dissection, contacts and looking back. The phase of "dissection" is the one in which Qian Zhongshu cuts Chinese literature into many small pieces and quotes extensively from the most disparate works and he does so according to his theory of *liangbing duobian* 兩柄多邊 (two handles, many sides). *Liangbing* stands for the two opposites of positive and negative, *duobian* stands for the many facets these positive and negative can give origin to.[68] In this phase Qian Zhongshu analyses the chosen themes extensively, looking for eventual references in every epoch and the traditions he has the chance to grasp. Usually the quotations he comes up with are *duanzhang* 斷章 (cut chapters) – quotations out of context that are apparently either disconnected from the rest of the discourse or extrapolated from the source text and used in a new composition without any relation to it. In *Guan Zhui Bian*, for example, we

---

67 This chapter was publishe d previously in *Bijiao Wenxue yu Shijie Wenxue*, n. 2, Jan. 2013, Beijing University with the title "In Others' Words – The use of quotations in Qian Zhongshu's comparative method".

68 See Motsch, "A New Method of Chinese- Western Comparative Literature".

find a quotation in a note by Giambattista Basile (1566-1632) which, inserted in a discourse about onomatopoeia, does not consider the meaning it had in the source text. The quotation reads:

> La campane di Manfredonia dice dammi e dòtti[69]
> (The Manfredonia bell says: give me and I'll give you).

Qian Zhongshu uses Basile's quotation as an example of a peculiar onomatopoeia, two verbs used to signify the sound of the bell. He disregards Basile's intent of using an Italian proverb to say that only he who does something good to others might receive good in turn. Qian does not consider the meaning of the quotation in the least and brings our contemplation and attention only to its onomatopoeic implication.

The phase of "contacts" is the one in which Qian tries to show all the points of contacts – synchronic and diachronic – between different traditions and here is where the reader is often shocked by ideas and links he would never have imagined.

Finally, the "looking back" is when past is used to explain present, west is used to explain east and vice versa.

The value Qian ascribes to the fragmentary is fully explained in the introduction of the English translation of selected passages of *Guan Zhui Bian* by Ronald Egan, who states:

> Behind both the expository form Qian Zhongshu has chosen in Limited Views, which has a long history in Chinese letters, and the peculiar way he has reconstructed it, there lies a distinctive mentality or predilection. This mentality

---

69 The quotation bears a mistake since the plural *campane* (bells) has no grammatical accordance with the singular article *la* (the): the correct quotation would have been *la campana*. See Qian Zhongshu, *Guan Zhui Bian*, I, 197.

is marked by an aversion to intellectual systematization as it is usually done in literary or intellectual history, and, contrariwise, a faith in the value of the particular original utterance. [70]

The love for the fragmentary makes Qian treat the works on which he comments in *Guan Zhui Bian* in a very peculiar way, quite often going through passages other critics had neglected or pointing out small and trivial matters. He thus brings to life and to light important fragments of thought, sometimes neglected but fundamental to the creation of a more general idea. *Ronghui* 融匯 (melt together), *canhu* 參互 (mix) and *datong* 打通 (get through) are the Chinese expressions that illustrate Qian Zhongshu's comparative method and that allow us to understand why quotations are so numerous in the work of this author and why they are always reported in their original language.

Qian's method of the *datong*, juxtaposition, like in a stream of consciousness or in a painting of last century's avant-garde movements, wants to juxtapose both to create a more complete and universal understanding and to find relationships where they are not the least expected. To juxtapose means to avoid connective elements and to leave every reflection or summing up to the reader who is confronted with different languages and different codes of interpretation that he needs to exploit and dissect in order to understand the whole and more general meaning. *Datong* is not meant just to see similarities, but also to state differences and the initial affinity from which differentiation could be appreciated: *xiangfan xiangcheng* 相反相成, to be both opposites and complementary at the same time. Reality is multiform and ever changing and needs a complete scheme to be observed. The same

---

70 Egan, *Limited Views*, 10.

*xiangfan xiangcheng* is said to be the main principle enhanced by the Italian Renaissance writer Giordano Bruno (1548-1600), who in *Guan Zhui Bian* is quoted when explaining the "coincidenza dei contrarii" (coincidence of opposites), saying that:

Non è armonia e concordia dove è unità[71]
(There is no harmony nor agreement where there is unity).

*Datong* is applied in Qian's essays in a clear way and Italian literature is a leitmotiv that carries the reader through most of the essays and whose finality is to illuminate Chinese literature with that *mutual illumination* expounded in the essay *Yi Zhong Wenxue De Huxiang Zhaoming: Yi Ge Da Wenti, Ji Ge Xiao Lizi* 意中文學的互相照明：一個大題目，幾個小例子[72] (The Mutual Illumination of Italian and Chinese Literature: a Big Problem, Some Small Examples). In this essay Qian Zhongshu states and proves with many examples that to study the literature of a definite place or time, first of all it is necessary to shift the attention from that literature to one different and far away, and to then go back to the first object of attention to obtain a more clear scheme by analysing different points of view. This belief brings Qian Zhongshu to observe and analyse Chinese literature with the help of logical patterns that come from outside Chinese literature and make quotations the core of his writing practice. In this general scheme Italian literature occupies an important role.

The way in which Qian Zhongshu embodies both the literate and the scholar is proof that this method gives foundation to all the theories set forth.

---

71 Qian Zhongshu, *Guan Zhui Bian* I, 393. See Bruno, *Opere di Giordano Bruno*, 438.

72 Qian Zhongshu, *Qian Zhongshu Xuan Ji*, 65-68.

His scholarly practice and critical theories find the perfect fulfilment in the way in which he creates literary pieces and in his unique style far from the rigor of the scientist and close enough to the fantasy and imaginative power of the artist's expression. He strongly believed that only a good writer could become a good critic and vice-versa, and that no critic is a good one if he is not a writer himself. What Qian Zhongshu wanted to escape with his method of juxtaposing and his flying away from theories that were not embodied in proof of validity was a comparative literature made up only of the study of influences and similarities, which René Wellek (1903-1995) called the "foreign trade of literatures". He wanted to pursue, just as Wellek did "the final objective of comparative literature (that) is to help us to know the basic principles of general literature (literature générale) up to the ones of the culture of human beings; that's why to overstep the boundaries and scopes of a parallel analysis between Chinese and western literatures' practical relations it's not only possible but indeed valuable."[73]

Qian, using J. M. Carré's words, affirmed: "comparative literature is not the comparison of literatures".[73] Qian's new comparative method is not to state similarities and differences but to set up a discussion between motives and writers. Monika Motsch calls this method the *regard regardé* or the *young lady that died of love*: she likens the comparative method to the behaviour of a Chinese coming from abroad that reflects upon China with a new consciousness or to a lady who died of love, whose body lies dead at home while her spirit flies back to look for her lover. Motsch affirms that Qian Zhongshu is a link between China and the West and he has been the sole scholar with such a wide scope of analysis and understanding of both the Chinese and western contexts. She also adds that to read *Guan Zhui Bian* is

---

73 Translated from: Zhang Longxi, "Qian Zhongshu Tan Bijiaowenxue yu Wenxue Bijiao".

an eye-opening experience, which could bring profit not only to the Chinese but also to western readers, offering a readily available field for dialogue and discussion.[74]

*Xiaoshuo Shi Xiao* 小說識小 (1945)[75] is good evidence of Qian Zhongshu's comparative method. It is an essay focusing on what we could call side stories or simply motives of novels and short stories belonging to different epochs both from western and Chinese literatures. There are twenty motives involved and every motif is explained through two or more stories that exemplify it with huge leaps in time and space. There are three references to Italian authors but only one is a direct quotation from the source text.

Quivi due filze son di perle elette, che chiude ed apre un bello e dolce labro[76]
(There are two strings of chosen pearls opened and closed by sweet lips)

is the sentence from *Orlando Furioso* by Ludovico Ariosto (1474-1533) quoted to enhance the theme of teeth like pearls. The motif starts with a quotation from the novel *Der Abenteuerliche Simplicissimus* by Hans Jakob Christoffel von Grimmelshausen where the teeth of a beautiful woman are said to be like "having been chopped from a turnip". A quotation from the *Shi Jing* 詩經 follows with "teeth like melon seeds" and it precedes a reference to E. About and his *Histoire de la Grèce* and J. J. Brousson with *France en Pantoufles*, both with "teeth like piano keys". The theme is further exploited through quotations from Du Mu 杜牧, Boswell, Taine, and the *Journal de Goncourt*, all writing about teeth as "those of an old English lady".

---

74 Motsch, "Qiannülihun fa, Qian Zhongshu Zuo Wei Zhong-Xi Wenhua de Qianxianren", 326-337.

75 Qian Zhongshu, "Xiaoshuo Shi Xiao", 518.

76 Qian Zhongshu, *Xie zai Rensheng Bianshang*, 142. See Ariosto, *Orlando Furioso*, 84.

No conclusion is brought forth and a simple juxtaposition of literary themes and authors serves the scope of demonstrating common processes in the treatment of literary themes.

The other two references to Italian literature that follow the same pattern are from Giovanni Papini (1881-1956) in his critical work *Dante Vivo* (Dante Alive) and Calandrino, a memorable character from Boccaccio's (1313-1375) *Decameron* who, exactly like the Pigsy in *Xi You Ji* 西遊記, thinks he is pregnant and does not understand how to handle giving birth to a child since he is a man.

In the eastern, as well as in the western world, quotations have always had their preferential sphere of usage and have been authoritatively used. In the western rhetorician tradition Aristotle (383-322) and Quintilian (35-100) understood they had a dialectical or logical function, supported by the importance of imitation, the Greek *mimesis*. According to Antoine Compagnon, French scholar and author of a treatise on quotations, quotations have the status of a standard for validity, of a control for statements, of a device for regulation or self-regulation, of the repetition of the already said; a good one qualifies and a bad one disqualifies.[77] Quotations are not details of the book from which they come; they are, on the contrary, a corner stone or a strategic practice to rely on. This assumption endorses and explains the role that quotations have in Qian's works. Compagnon states a simile between the practice of quoting and what he calls the "practice of paper". The author who chooses a few sentences from a text and extrapolates them from it operates like a pair of scissors cutting and shredding a sheet of paper. To cut a strip from a piece of paper makes us master of it, just like

---

77 "La citation a le statut d'un critère de validité, d'un contrôle de l'énonciation, d'un dispositif de régulation, par fois d'autorégulation, de la répétition du dèjà dit: 'bonne', elle qualifie; 'mauvaise', elle disqualifie", Compagnon, *La seconde main*, 12.

copying and pasting from a written text makes us masters of the text. It is also an action that combines reading and writing in one single achievement, since when we quote, we create a new text. To read and extrapolate something from the text worth maintaining helps us to write contents with a solid base. Thus, to read doesn't mean to passively receive content but to extract and re-use it with an awareness that indicates we have eaten and digested what the writer meant to express and are now able to take the energy and the nourishment from our "food" to give it a new life.

Quotations in the West find their paradigm for usage in various theories and literary conceptions that justify and give strength of validity to the usage of this literary device to convey meanings rooted in the reality of things. If we think of Robert Frost (1864-1965) and his theory of "ulteriority": saying one thing and meaning another, or of what T. S. Eliot (1888-1974) was doing with his theory of the objective correlative, they might well remind us of the way in which Qian Zhongshu was using quotations.[78] F. O. Matthiessen reports Eliot writing on the method of Ulysses (1933) in an unpublished lecture:

> In some minds certain memories, both from reading and life, become charged with emotional significance. All these are used so that intensity is gained at the expense of clarity.[79]

It would be difficult to find a more apt definition to describe that density and "intensity," which Qian's works reach through quotations to express the deepest feelings expressed through literary works, lie at the core of

---

78 See Huang Weiliang, "Liu Xie and Qian Zhongshu: Common poetics", 249-280.
79 Matthiessen, "The 'Objective Correlative'", in Harold Bloom, *Bloom's Bio-critiques, T. S. Eliot*, 83.

human experience. The reader is then asked to use his set of references to worldly phenomena to get a summary and all-encompassing conception from that concatenation of events.

The need to study the usage of quotations in literary works is urged by the obligation to analyse the authors' academic ideology, their aesthetic standpoint and their linguistic style, since all of these factors are exemplified and expressed, among other literary devices, also by the way in which quotations are used in literary works. As Wang Peiji 王培基 remarks, the method of the usage of quotations is one of the important problems and factors for analysis both in the linguistic and in the philological fields.[80] As economy studies how to obtain the greatest profit with fewer means, so literature studies how to convey the greatest meaning with more concise language; nothing is more true and representative than Qian's language and style full of quotations with its striking connections and lack of connective elements, the *datong*, which is possible only thanks to the archetypes that lay on the basis of world conceptions and ideas and that allow the play of cross-references and links.[81] Without this common soil it would in fact be impossible to weave the net of allusions that help us grasp a universal meaning from quotations that sweep over time and space. To analyse the method in which Qian quotes is a way to understand both his stylistic and content choices together with the motives he singles out across different traditions.

*Guan Zhui Bian* is Qian Zhongshu's scholarly masterpiece in which he uses approximately two thousand western quotations from nearly one thousand different authors and there are several times as many Chinese ones,

---

80 Wang Peiji, "Yinyong Yishu Xin Tan", 31.
81 Huang Weiliang, in his already mentioned *Liu Xie and Qian Zhongshu* links Qian Zhongshu's *datong* to Northrop Frye's archetypes in *The anatomy of criticism*.

reaching a total number of quotations of nearly one hundred thousand.[82] To understand the link between all the quotations and to trace a panorama of their sources, Zhang Wenjiang[83] has analysed their origin and has come up with a four-sided spectrum whence Qian has quoted: the Four Books of the Chinese literary tradition, The Buddhist texts translated in Chinese, The Taoist material and the western sources.

The reasons for such extensive use of quotations are both theoretical: Qian gives the utmost importance to the study of the texts and considers it futile to talk about what is beyond a poem without a close reading of the poem itself,[84] and methodological: Qian Zhongshu chooses a theme and demonstrates through quotations how different authors in different times have developed and exploited it. Quotations become the way Qian Zhongshu chooses to express his own ideas, giving a hint of tangible proof of validity to the generality of theoretical assumptions based on the words of others. The particularity of this method is that quite often Qian does not explain in his own words what others have said, but prefers to insert the original utterances and expressions of those authors directly into his text, cutting and pasting to develop his thought. In the above-indicated process, Qian rarely makes abstract comparisons; he always starts with a sentence, a tangible idea, a word, and from these explores universal concepts. This method has often been misunderstood and many scholars have not seen the purpose of such a mingling of chopped pieces, thus contesting Qian's lack of consistency for his system of thought.[85] Others convey that nobody should have the right to

---

82  Egan, *Limited Views*, 16.

83  See Zhang Wenjiang, *Yingzao Babita de Zhizhe*, 94-102.

84  Yue Daiyun, *Comparative Literature*, 96.

85  Zhang Longxi in his *Zhongxi Jiaoji yu Qian Zhongshu de Zhixue Fangfa* tries to put a halt to negative critique towards Qian Zhonshu as in the case of Li Zehou 李澤厚 that has affirmed that writers like Qian have culture and knowledge but lack of a system of thought. Professor Zhang affirms that to consider Kang Youwei, Liang Qichao, Chen Duxiu,

criticise the work of the writer without understanding the languages in which he quotes because this would account for a partial analysis. To all those who affirm that Qian Zhongshu does not deserve a place in Chinese literature, or that *Qian Xue* is nothing other than coarse research, or that Qian is not a thinker but a mere scholar because he did not appoint a system of thought, or that he stayed in the sphere of Chinese classical literature and gave no contribution to other fields of research, Li Hongyan[86] gives well documented answers with counter arguments. Professor Li affirms that whoever does not read and understand all the books on which Qian's learning and ideas are based, cannot express a derogatory opinion about the writer because he does not have the means to understand his method. *Qian Xue*, continues Li, cannot be considered as a whole because the contributions to this discipline are numerous and different. As for the creation of a system of thought, this is precisely what Qian opposed and it should be considered that during the 19th and 20th centuries the "magic weapon of systematic doctrines" was being replaced by analytical research. The field of Chinese classical literature then, is of course the point from which Qian sets off, but is nevertheless only a starting point that brings his analysis to cover the range of Chinese contemporary as well as of western literature: nothing different could have happened both because of the May Fourth Movement and because the intellectuals of Qian's generation were exposed to western education and culture.

The reason we cannot consider Qian Zhongshu a comparatist in the

---

Hu Shi and Lu Xun key protagonists of the Chinese literary world and neglect Qian Zhongshu would mean to read history with the eyes of political science then. All those who have criticized Qian Zhongshu, continues Professor Zhang, have done it basing their judgements on misunderstandings and evaluation mistakes like Gong Pengcheng, who completely misunderstood the meaning of Qian's essay *Zhongguo Shi yu Zhongguo Hua*. See *Qian Zhongshu Shiwen Congshuo* edited by Wang Rongzu, 187-210.

86 Li Hongyan, "Ruhe Pingjia Qian Zhongshu", 157-174. Li Hongyan is Professor at Chuanmei University in Beijing.

usual sense of the term is the usage of this particular method. He does not compare themes and works to find similarities and differences; instead, he creates dialogues between authors and works from the past to discover social and psychological reasons behind the motives[87] he analyses. He quite often even involves contemporary developments of the themes or possible links to other disciplines that might have a connection to the same topics.

Another difference between Qian's comparative literature and the "usual one" is that Qian does not compare entire works or poems; instead, he juxtaposes single lines or ideas or a particular literary metaphor or motif. Quotations in Qian's works may fall in the categorisation that Compagnon proposes of all the possible functions quotations might have in literary texts:[88] function of erudition, when we cite other authors and works to show our knowledge and adorn our writings with an halo of importance; invocation of authority, when we quote to demonstrate that our ideas had been asserted previously and then take the strength and the proof of their validity from other authors; function of amplification, when they are meant to expand on a concept; and ornamental function, when they embellish the text with other's appropriate and well written sentences. The first two functions, erudition and authority, are external to texts, or inter-textual, since they move the reader's attention to references outside the texts; the latter, function of amplification and ornamental function, are internal or textual, since they tend to keep the attention on the main ideas expressed and refer to other texts in a marginal way. As for the form of quotations, Tian Jianmin 田建民[89] divides them in encyclopaedic and linguistic quotations. The first form includes all the quotations that come from historical parables or myths; the linguistic ones

---

87 Motsch, "A New Method of Chinese – Western Comparative Literature".

88 Compagnon, *La seconde main*, 99

89 Tian Jianmin, "Yongshi bu shi ren jue – Qian Zhongshu yongdian yanjiu zhi yi", 311-330.

come from expressions or sentences from the Chinese classics. As for the degree of difficulty to understand on the reader's side, quotations can be divided into familiar and rare allusions. As for their usage, there are the clear allusions and veiled ones. Qian often pursued the technique of quoting without letting the reader know it. In the novel *Wei Cheng* there are numerous quotations of this kind, where the quoted words merge completely into the new linguistic setting and become one with it.

Of course the classification just presented is not a fixed one and one type of quotation can merge into the other: for example, the rare allusions in familiar quotations can be transformed from a repeated usage and quotations familiar at a certain time can become rare allusions if the text from which they are taken becomes unpopular. We can add other functions of quotations in Qian's works that have their origin in his previously mentioned re-elaboration of a peculiar Chinese literary style and in his mixing it with theories coming from contemporary western influences to this classification. This work will try to illustrate those usages of quotations particular to Qian's comparative method with the help of a close analysis of a specimen of quotations in his works, and we will see how those usages have Chinese characteristics in a way. The main questions we will try to answer in the following paragraphs are: Which quotations does Qian Zhongshu use in his works? Why is he constantly borrowing others' words to develop and dissect a theme?

Qian Zhongshu's point in using quotations is to build solid foundations for his construction: he does not like empty theories that are not based on real and practical proofs. He thinks that in order to speak about something it is necessary to provide proof of examples of previous assumptions concerning the theme of the discussion. Gong Gang 龔剛 divides Qian's quotations in two different kinds: sentences that need quotations, *yan bi you zheng* 言必有

證, and proofs that need examples, *zheng bi you li* 證必有例.[90] Thus, quotations have the function of erudition and invocation of authority at the same time, but they are also an extremely accurate insertion of other languages into the texture of Chinese sentences, resulting in precious stones in a gold setting, ready to ornate the whole jewel. Sometimes they are also presented in sequence, each one to confirm and add a new turn to the previous one to amplify it.

This study aims at singling out and illustrating, through examples, usages of quotations peculiar to Qian Zhongshu that serve to build his comparative method. Starting from the above-mentioned functions of quotations, Qian, using the *datong* technique, enriches quotations with the following characteristics peculiar to his comparative method:

1) they serve to compare ideas and theories to highlight different opinions or just the many sides and implications of one literary theme;

2) they are the mode to express new ideas like the tesseras of a mosaic work that give life to new figures;

3) they stay for the voice of their authors to overcome time and place in roundtable discussions; 4) they are the way to discover unprecedented links and common concepts;

5) they act as a mirror that helps see one's own image in a clearer way;

6) they are the elements that prove and confirm mistakes discovered by the author in previous works and literary theories and, most surprisingly,

7) they might be a kind of secret code to conceal meaning conveyed from somebody, while unveiling it to others.

---

90 Gong Gang, *Qian Zhongshu: Aizhizhe de Xiaoyao*, 115. Gong Gang is an associate professor of the Department of Chinese at the University of Macao.

## 4.1 Comparing through quotations

Qian Zhongshu did not possess many books; Wu Taichang 吳泰昌, in his *Wo Renshi de Qian Zhongshu* 我認識的錢鍾書 (The Qian Zhongshu I know),[91] describes Qian's house as empty of books and full of writing notes. We may thus assume that Qian Zhongshu, while reading, mostly underlined by heart: he had an extraordinary visual memory that allowed him to read and keep whatever he read in his mind, or at least whatever he would have underlined, to become his mental property. This treasure preserved in Qian Zhongshu's mind gave him the insight that allowed him to make comparisons in order to touch upon many spheres of knowledge. Everything was ready and available in his mental library and striking evidence and parallels could emerge through the analysis of phenomena belonging to the most diverse fields of human experience.

Tian Jianmin finds a strong literary talent and a great aroma of books in Qian's works.[92] The literary talent of course is innate but the acquired knowledge is an ingredient that cannot be neglected and gives Qian's works the strong scent of books that finds its physical expression in the great amount of quotations he employs.

Talking about mystical philosophies in *Guan Zhui Bian*,[93] Qian Zhongshu analyses these philosophical movements through a number of quotations from mystical thinkers and philosophers and eventually explains that the parallels offered are meant to show that Daoism, Buddhism and the mystical philosophies of the West

---

91 Wu Taichang, *Wo Renshi de Qian Zhongshu*, 87.

92 Tian Jianmin, "Yongshi bu shi ren jue – Qian Zhongshu yongdian yanjiu zhi yi", 311-330.

93 Qian Zhongshu, *Guan Zhui Bian* (Beijing: Zhonghua Shuju 1979) 2: 463-465.

Derive from the same human inclination but have acquired different names. [...] Nevertheless, similar as they may be, there is no need to force them together as one.[94]

This sounds more like a reminder from the author that we need to look at different phenomena with a comprehensive mind to strike connections but we also have to pay attention to local and specific conditions that helped differentiate them in the course of history.

Sometimes it is also necessary to be aware of different traditions for the right evaluation of poetic images; it is through a quotation in a footnote in *Guan Zhui Bian* by the poet Torquato Tasso (1544-1595):

La regia moglie, /che bruna è sì ma il bruno il bel non toglie[95]
(The king's wife /that is brunette being beautiful all the same)

and among the other references "modified" by the Chinese saying "*Yuji Xuefu* 玉肌雪膚"[96] (fresh as jade, white as snow) that Qian demonstrates that a woman, to be considered beautiful, should have a dark complexion in some traditions and should be white as snow and jade in others. What Qian Zhongshu sometimes wants to stress are not differences but common trends, as in the entry[97] which illustrates through quotations from the *Extensive Records from the Taiping Era* (Taiping Guangji 太平廣記), from Dong Qichang 董其昌, Bai Juyi 白居易, Pei Xie 裴諧, Friedrich Hebbel, Henri A. Junod, Ernst Cassirer, Plinius, Boccaccio, and many others, that the image

---

94 Egan, *Limited Views*, 306.

95 See Tasso, *Opere*, vol 1, 522.

96 Qian Zhongshu, *Guan Zhui Bian*, I, 182. The Chinese saying actually is *Bingji Xuefu* 冰肌雪膚 and Qian substitutes the word *Bing* 冰, ice, to the word *Yu* 玉, jade.

97 Qian Zhongshu, *Guan Zhui Bian*, II, 1123-1131.

reflected in a mirror or in a painting has always been considered as embodying the spirit of the person there reflected and represents a kind of captivation for which the soul of the person portrayed or reflected is meant to end up being imprisoned in its portrait. This common concept, the same in all quoted authors and works, explains and justifies not only many literary themes that we find in eastern and western literature, but is also a number of sociological and anthropological behaviours such as, for example, the fear that primitive people, like the Bantu tribe in Africa, have for photography.

Another literary cliché is the one of "the other shore" in *Guan Zhui Bian* where both Dante (1265-1321) and Gabriele D'Annunzio (1863-1938) are quoted to support the idea that happiness always lies on the opposite bank of a river, on the opposite shore:

> Ella ridea dall'altra riva dritta
> [...]
> Tre passi ci facea il fiume lontani[98]
> (Erect upon the other bank she smiled
> [...]
> Apart three paces did the river make us)[99]

and

> La gioia è sempre all'altra riva[100]
> (Joy is always on the other shore).

---

98 Qian Zhongshu, *Guan Zhui Bian*, I, 209. See Dante Alighieri, *La Commedia secondo l'antica vulgata* a cura di Petrocchi, 3 volumi, 260.

99 Dante, *Purgatorio* 28, 67-70 from *The Divine Comedy of Dante Alighieri* II translated by Henry Wadsworth Longfellow, 181.

100 Qian Zhongshu, *Guan Zhui Bian*, I, 209. See D'Annunzio, *Alcyone* a cura di Gibellini, 119.

The motif is present in western as well as in eastern literatures; quotations here have the sole function of supporting and proving a similarity. What is worth noting is that while Qian quotes Dante in Italian, his reference in the footnote is from the English translation of Dante's *Divine Comedy*.

The third volume of *Guan Zhui Bian* the entry *Quan San Guo Wen Juan Yi Ling* 全三國文卷一○[101] demonstrates that emotions merge into one another and it was common in Song and Yuan dynasties to designate a spouse or a lover with expressions like "loathsome fellow" or "he (or she) who wrongs me" exactly as in Renaissance literature to find expressions like "sweet foe, o dolce mia guerriera, la mia cara nemica"[102] (sweet foe, oh my sweet enemy, my sweet enemy) and "ma douce guerrière" (my sweet enemy), quotations from Geoffrey Chaucer, Francesco Petrarca (1304-1374) and Pierre de Ronsard.

While comparing, one or more terms of the comparison might be enhanced, while the shortcomings of the other are put in evidence as it strangely happens with a line from Dante's *Paradise* compared to two *Fu* 賦: the *She Zhi Fu* 射雉賦 and the *Zhi Dai Jian* 雉帶箭. The three works are quoted to highlight the way in which animals' movements are described. Even though the works analysed are similar in technique and literary skill, the *Fu*, concludes Qian, is more suitable than western lyrical poetry for this kind of description, giving them more flavour. Dante, always quoted as an example of the utmost imaginative artistry, is quoted here to put Chinese poetic form in a better light. Dante's lines are:

Tal volta un animal coverto broglia,
Sì che l'affetto convien che si paia

---

101 Qian Zhongshu, *Guan Zhui Bian*, III, 1676.
102 See Petrarca, *Rime*, 21, 56.

Per lo seguir che face a lui la 'nvoglia[103]
(Sometimes an animal covered with a cloth moves
As to show
Its feelings through its movements).

This might be taken as a further example of Qian's literary integrity in not considering genres and literary works from the western-centrist perspective by which many Chinese intellectuals from the first half of the 20th century were spoilt.

## 4.2 Quoting as a mode of original elaboration

If we imagine asking Qian Zhongshu his idea about quoting and the function quotations might cover for him, we might find the answer to the question in two passages from *Guan Zhui Bian* that illustrate in practice what the theory is all about. The first passage we are going to observe suggests that quoting is somehow represented in nature by the production of honey made by bees: bees take the substance that becomes honey from different flowers, just as writers take the substance that will become their book – a different product, yet made from already existing content – from different books through quotations. To prove this assumption Qian Zhongshu quotes Zhang Fan 張璠, who in his introduction to *Yi Ji Jie Xu* 易集解序 (Comments on the Book of Changes), writes about bees and their way of obtaining honey and Pei Songzhi 裴松之, in *Shang Sanguo Zhi Zhu Biao* 上三國志注表 (Memorial Presenting the Commentary to Records of the Three Kingdoms), who writes that embroiderers use different colours to obtain a fine embroidery just like bees use different flowers to create a product that tastes even sweeter

---

103  Qian Zhongshu, *Guan Zhui Bian*, III, 1856. See Dante Alighieri, *La Commedia secondo l'antica vulgata*, 391.

than the elements from whence it comes. We find the same simile in western literature: Isocrates (436-338), Lucretius (99-55), Horace (65-8), Seneca (4 B.C.- 64 A.D.), Quintilian, Montaigne (1533-1592), Eckermann (1792-1954) and the Italian Daniello Bartoli[104] (1608-1685) have all written about bees, honey and the work of writers who "gather useful knowledge from every source".[105] We have ten different authors quoted to confirm and prove the truthfulness and validity of the initial statement in just two pages. Quotations are in Chinese, English, Latin, French, Italian and German. In particular Seneca, Montaigne and Eckermann stress that not only bees and writers are similar in their activities, but that the result of both labours is a new original product, completely made up on their own and whose origin from pre-existent components is not to interfere with the originality of the outcome. From Isocrates in the 4th century B.C., the Latin poets from the 1st century before and after Christ up to Zhang Fan and his quoted work from the 3rd century A.D., from Montaigne in the 16th century, Daniello Bartoli, Italian Jesuit from the 17th century to Eckermann of the 18th century, a span of twenty-two centuries is covered, running from the eastern boundaries of the world to the nest of western civilizations. The straightforward and striking sequence of quotations from authors who cover such a huge span in time and space, goes outside the written page and is nearly able to touch our hearing sense, since it is like hearing all those people chatting and expressing their ideas on the theme proposed by the author. It is a virtual journey among all those sages of the past to whom Qian Zhongshu refers in order to create the solid foundation he needs to corroborate his idea.

---

104 Qian Zhongshu, *Guan Zhui Bian*, IV, 1968. Bartoli's quotation reads: "Il lettore deve essere un'ape che colga il miele delle ingegnose maniere di scrivere, dell'imitazione, delle poetiche forme del dire" (The reader who is able to pick up the witty manners of writing, of imitation, of poetic expression). See Daniello Bartoli, *Dell'Huomo di Lettere, Difeso et Emendato*, Parti due, 147.

105 Qian Zhongshu, *Guan Zhui Bian*, IV, 1966.

The second passage in which Qian Zhongshu expresses his ideas on quotations is one that analyses the practice of quoting out of context, that is, of using quotations extrapolated from a text for one's own proper aims, giving the quoted passages a new frame in which to bring new unexpected nuances of meaning. This, specifies Qian, is the technique used in Song parallel prose which had passages made up from "collected lines"[106] with every line coming from a previous composition. Quotations follow to "demonstrate that the practice of 'breaking off a verse' (*duan zhang*) was accorded a place alongside other types of superior writing and conversation, that clever transformations of earlier sayings were not considered inferior to original formulations, and that it was never required that what one said or wrote had to be entirely one's own".[107] Alongside this practice of quoting out of context to build new and original compositions, and keeping the original meaning at a distance from the scope it was first intended to fulfil, there remains the more common practice of quoting to corroborate a specific idea, bringing attention to the first handling of a said utterance without any turn in meaning. What is important, remarks the author to conclude his entry, is that the reader needs to be able to differentiate the two activities and to treat them as two different ways of quoting, understanding if a quotation is meant to bring a new elaboration of an idea, resulting in an original creation, or if it stays simply as an invocation of authority to reinforce and prove a concept. Only being aware of these two functions of quotations, implies Qian Zhongshu, may a reader not be deceived while trying to get the meaning of quoted passages.

A remarkable example of "quotations out of context" is the treatment Qian reserves for a quotation from Dante's *Paradise* and Milton's (1608-1674)

---

106  Egan, *Limited Views*, 222.
107  Egan, *Limited Views*, 222.

*Paradise Lost* in the second volume of *Guan Zhui Bian*.[108] Here the content of the quotations, explained by Qian Zhongshu, comes before the direct quotations. Milton's words are:

> In multitudes,
> The ethereal people ran, to hear and know.

Dante's text reads:

> Come 'n peschiera ch'è tranquilla e pura
> Traggonsi i pesci a ciò che vien di fori
> Per modo che lo stimin lor pastura[109]
> (As in a fishpond which is pure and tranquil
> The fish draw to that which from without
> Comes in such fashion that their food they deem it). [110]

The quotations are quite interesting in that Qian uses them to reverse their original intent. Dante's *Divine Comedy* is a poem deeply rooted in a Christian context: Hell is the place where guilty men encounter their punishment, Purgatory is the expiation field and Paradise is the place where all the joy and beatitude is preserved for the enjoyment of all the purest and lofty men. No reference is ever made in Dante's poem to the boredom that might be experienced in such a perfect place as Paradise, since such an idea might be considered sacrilegious: one cannot define the place where God lives as boring. But with *Guan Zhui Bian*'s placement of these quotations he wants

---

108 Qian Zhongshu, *Guan Zhui Bian*, II, 988-989.

109 Qian Zhongshu, *Guan Zhui Bian*, II, 988. See Dante Alighieri, *La Commedia secondo l'antica vulgata*, 304.

110 Dante, *Paradiso* 5, 100-103 from *The Divine Comedy of Dante Alighieri* III translated by Henry Wadsworth Longfellow, 32.

to prove that people in Heaven are bored and waiting for distractions and amusements like the ones offered by a living man happening to pass by and attracting all those weary people, similar to a handful of food attracting fish in a fish-bowl. Qian defines this unexpected explanation made by the poets Dante and Milton regarding the behaviour of the inhabitants of Paradise, seeking amusement in living beings due to boredom in the place they live, as the "allusion behind the words",[111] which might as well simply be a "quotation out of context" used by the author with a turn in the original meaning, since Dante and Milton would never have implied that to be in the Grace of God could be a boring thing.

An antecedent to this quotation from Dante is another line taken from the seventeenth *canto* of *Paradise* and cited by Qian Zhongshu with the same "out of context" purpose to demonstrate that Paradise was a boring place. We find it in a 1926 essay titled *Lun Jiaoyou* 論交友 (Discussing friendship).[112] The quotation reads:

Che non pur ne' miei occhi è paradiso[113]
(Not in my eyes alone is Paradise)[114]

and it is a sentence with which Beatrice, Dante's beloved, urges him to divert his attention from her and consider what else is happening around him. Qian, following what had already been stated by A. E. Taylor (1869-1945) in his *Faith of a Moralist*, notes that if paradise was such a beautiful and interesting place, Dante (Dante as a character, not Dante as a writer) would

---

111 Egan, *Limited Views*, 336.
112 Qian Zhongshu, *Xiezai Renshang Bian Shang*, 73-81.
113 See Dante Alighieri, *La Commedia secondo l'antica vulgata*, 355.
114 Dante, *Paradiso* 18, 21 from *The Divine Comedy of Dante Alighieri* III translated by Henry Wadsworth Longfellow, 117.

have been more like a countryman going to the city for the first time than like a sad and pensive lover merely in search of the sight of his beloved lady. The assumption about paradise, already derived from A. E. Taylor, is supported in the essay by quotations from the medieval French sung-story from the 13th century *Aucassin et Nicolette* and from Renan's *Feuilles Détachée*.[115] Thus, the divergent meaning that comes from the quotation out of context is supported here by other quotations that sustain it with authority and justification.

## 4.3 Quoting as a debate among sages of the past

Again in *Guan Zhui Bian*,[116] a passage about personal conduct and literary style expresses the idea that it is not possible to know a man from his writings, since a dissolute man might produce upright statements, while immoral compositions might be the product of an ordinary and discreet fellow. Given the starting assumption, Qian goes on with "three subsequent statements [...] to expand among the notion".[117] To *expand* is thus the function of the sequence of quotations that follows; it is an invocation of authority and at the same time an amplification of further proof given to the reader to convince him on the basis of opinions "certified" by the centuries and directly spoken by their authors. There we hear the discussion between Yuan Haowen 元好問 and Huang Dashou 黃大受 from the 13th century, Wang Duo 王鐸 from the 17th century, Zhao Lingzhi 趙令畤 from the 12th century and the Italian critic Benedetto Croce from the 20th century. I will stop to discuss Croce's quotation because it has a characteristic that is

---

115 Renan, *Feuilles Détachées: faisant suite aux souvenirs d'enfance et de jeunesse*.
116 Qian Zhongshu, *Guan Zhui Bian*, IV, 2157-2158.
117 Egan, *Limited Views*, 42.

somehow useful to note in Qian's method: it is made up of two appellatives, two Italian expressions, inserted in the Chinese text without a direct translation in Chinese and preceded only by their Chinese explanation. Egan's English version reports: "Thus, the so-called *persona poetica* should not be lumped together with the *persona pratica*",[118] where *persona poetica*, as Qian explains, is the writer who creates essays, and *persona pratica* indicates the man who 'conducts himself in society'.[119] Quoting with the direct insertion of words and expressions in a language different from the one in which the text is written might be startling enough for the reader but even more effective, resulting like a turn of voice. This technique might be compared to the offstage voice, i.e. the voice of the author, which leaves the scene to the direct interpreters of the *piéce*, resulting in a more enhancing representation. The discussion goes on among those sages and with discordant opinions comes to the point of debating whether or nor a writer needs to have experienced what he writes about. Surprisingly enough, a final quotation by Kant seems to be the peacemaker between the antagonists and seems to summarise the terms of the dispute, carrying on the same idea that belongs to the off-scene author: "knowledge must originate in experience, but it does not derive entirely from experience".[120] This time the German text is supported by the Chinese translation, probably due to a compelling necessity of being understood in the final point of the discussion. The voices of Philip Sidney (1554-1586), Giordano Bruno, Giambattista Vico (1668-1744), C. K. Ogden and I. A. Richards[121] are also supported by the Chinese translations; in the debate between the true and the false in poetic creation they all agree on the need to

---

118  Egan, *Limited Views*, 42.

119  Qian Zhongshu, *Guan Zhui Bian*, IV, 2158.

120  Egan, *Limited Views*, 46.

121  Qian Zhongshu, *Guan Zhui Bian*, I, 167.

distinguish the practical truth, "vero fisico", and the poetic truth, "vero poetico", as in the words of Vico, or what has been called by Bruno the metaphorical sense, "detto per metafora", and the true sense, "detto per vero".[122]

Another interesting debate is recorded in an entry[123] in which Wang Rong 王融, in his *Shangshu Qing Gei Lu Shu* 上疏請給虜書 (*Memorial Requesting to Give Books to the Barbarians*), sustains that it is thanks to the learning that comes from books that even barbarians could become more civilized; their fierceness could be tamed and their military capability could be weakened, leaving Chinese people the way to conquest. In full accordance with him are: Du Ben 杜本, a poet from the Yuan dynasty, a passage from *Zhuangzi*, Yang Xiong 揚雄 from the Han, and Edward Gibbon, English historian from the 18th century, reporting an episode from ancient Greek history when the Goths defeated the Greeks and decided not to destroy their books because it was thanks to the distraction coming from books that the Greeks did not apply themselves to the exercise of arms. It is also because of books, remarks Montaigne, that Rome, in becoming more cultured, saw its warfare successes diminish and that, as the Italian historian Machiavelli[124] (1469-1527) states in his *Historie Fiorentine* (*Histories from Florence*), after a warlike state drops its weapons and passes through to a peaceful period, it sees its power and strength diminish since books soften its valour and bravery. On the other hand a completely different position is maintained by Yu Xiulie 于休烈 in a memorial where he advised that giving books to barbarians means

---

122  Qian Zhongshu, *Guan Zhui Bian*, I, 167. See Vico, *Opere*, 55 and Bruno, *Opere*, 174.

123  Qian Zhongshu, *Guan Zhui Bian*, IV, 2090-2092.

124  Qian Zhongshu, *Guan Zhui Bian* (2001), IV, 2092. Machiavelli's quotation reads: "Perchè, avendo le buone e ordinate armi partorito vittorie, e le vittorie quiete, non si può la fortezza degli armati animi con più onesto ozio che con quello delle lettere, corrompere" (After good and regular arms have caused victories and victories have caused peace, the strength of armed souls is corrupted most of all by literature).

giving them knowledge and understanding even in warfare matters and that the best thing to do would have been to leave them ignorant about the Chinese literary classics and the important principles treasured in them. This time the reader is not given any final key to interpret the argument and the discussion among the sages of the past on the wisdom of giving books and erudition to barbarians is left open to further discussion.

In another passage of *Guan Zhui Bian* the focus is on the word and concept of "barbarian" and a quotation in a footnote by the Italian humanist Benedetto Varchi (1503-1565) analyses the meaning of the word "barbarian":

> Questo nome barbaro è voce equivoca...quando si riferisce all'animo... alla diversità o lontananza delle regioni...al favellare[125]
>
> (This term barbarian is ambiguous...when it refers to the soul...to different and far away regions...to speech).

Further on the debate that arises from Nietzsche's (1844-1900) assumption that happiness sometimes comes from forgetfulness or ignorance of the actual situation is all played amongst Italian poets with brief participation from the Latin poet Horace. The debate is articulated enough with insertions of quotations so as to recount a whole poem by the Italian poet Carlo Innocenzo Frugoni (1692-1768), famous for his prolificacy in blank verse poetry. The poem is called *Poeta e Re* (Poet and King) and here we quote the full text. The lines that Qian translates and gives directly in Chinese have been underlined while the lines in bold are the ones quoted in Italian and translated in Chinese by the author. A translation of the whole poem is offered in a footnote:

---

125  Qian Zhongshu, *Guan Zhui Bian*, II, 821. See Varchi, *Delle Opere di Messer Benedetto Varchi*, 215.

Vi fu un pazzo, non so quando,
Che somiglia un poco a me,
Che **sul trono** esser sognando,
Comandava come un Re.
Nell'inganno suo felice
Conducea contento i dí;
Ma per opra degli amici
Medicato egli guarí.


Guarí, è ver; ma sé veggendo
Pover uomo qual pria tornato,
Disse lor quasi piangendo:
– Voi m'avete assassinato!


Col tornar della ragione
Da me lungi se ne va
Un error, ch'era cagione
Della mia felicità.[126]


Qian chooses to quote the poem partly in Chinese and partly in the original Italian version for stylistic as well as for content reasons. He does not differentiate the quotations from the body of the text because his method is speaking through other authors' words and he does not want to not have credit for those words, and equally does not want to show distance from them by inserting them in quotation marks. On the other hand the Italian in the text is a strong link to the source text; it suggests to the reader that even if the original text comes from afar, it is nevertheless very close to the main theme

---

126 Qian Zhongshu, *Guan Zhui Bian*, II, 762-763. See *Poesie scelte dell'Abate Carlo Innocenzo Frugoni*, tomo IV, 172. A free translation of the poem is: There was a lunatic, and I don't know when, /somewhat similar to me, /he was dreaming of being on a throne, /and gave orders as a king does. /Happy in his deceiving /was happily leading his life; /but thanks to his friends /he was cured and recovered. /He recovered, that is true; but finding out he was back to /his previous normal life, /he told his friends in tears /You have killed me! /I have regained the use of my reason / but I have lost /the belief in a mistake that accounted for /my happiness.

being discussed. Frugoni's poem is preceded by lines with the same subject by Giacomo Leopardi (1798-1837) and Guido Gozzano (1883-1916). Both quotations are not translated. Leopardi's lines are from *Canto Notturno di un Pastore Errante dell'Asia* (Night-Song of a Wandering Shepherd of Asia):

O greggia mia che posi, oh te beata,
che la miseria tua, credo, non sai![127]
(Oh my herd that rests, O flock at peace, O happy creatures,
I think you have no knowledge of your misery!).

Gozzano's lines have the same intent, even if this time the ignorant animals are geese and not a herd of cows:

Penso e ripenso: – che mai pensa l'oca
Gracidante alla riva del canale?
Pare felice! ...
[...]
Ma tu non pensi. La tua sorte è bella![128]
(I think once and again: – what does a goose think
Cackling on the canal's bank?
It seems to be happy!
[...]
But you do not think. Great is your fate!).

In a footnote a few lines later the poet Ariosto answers the poets saying that he who looks for what he does not want to find is a lunatic:

Ben sarebbe folle
Chi quel che non vorria trovar cercasse
(It would be insane

---

127  Qian Zhongshu, *Guan Zhui Bian*, II, 762. Leopardi, *Canti*, 75.
128  Qian Zhongshu, *Guan Zhui Bian*, II, 762. See C. Golino ed., *Contemporary Italian poetry: an anthology*, 2.

A person looking for what he doesn't want to know).[129]

More than a real debate, here we find consent of intent in affirming that oblivion and forgetfulness are sources of happiness because to know the truth is a cause of distress and sad awareness.

Ariosto is one of the characters in another debate that starts from a common theme in literature and social customs: women become old earlier than men and the marrying age should thus be different for the two, being that a gap in age is necessary to allow the couple to have the same vigour and strength throughout their life. The starting assumption comes from Du Qin 杜欽, who writes that men at fifty still like women, while women at forty are already in a declining phase. The answer to Du Qin comes from Chinese as well as western authors among which Euripides (480-406) and Aristotle both affirm that there should be a gap in the age of the marrying couple and Ariosto identifies this ideal gap in ten or twelve years:

De dieci anni o di dodici, se fai
Per mio consiglio, fia di te minore;
[...]
Perchè passando, il megliore
Tempo e i begli anni in lor prima che in noi[130]
(Ten or twelve years, if you
Want to listen to my suggestion, she should be younger than you;
[...]
Because the best
Years of life expire for them earlier than for us).

Balzac (1799-1850) suggests the gap should be of fifteen years and the

---

129 Qian Zhongshu, *Guan Zhui Bian*, II, 763. See Ariosto, *Orlando Furioso*, 710.
130 Qian Zhongshu, *Guan Zhui Bian*, III, 1501-1502. See Ariosto, *Satire*, 36.

English poet Frederick Locker (1821-1895) with a more complicated calculation says that:

A wife should be half the age of her husband with seven years added.[131]

What is the age that sets the turning point for women then? For Hanfei 韓非 (280-233) it is thirty, for Du Qin it is forty, for Italians, adds Qian, it is thirty-five, as Giordano Bruno writes in his comedy *Candelaio*:

Voi siete cosa da cemiterio, perché una femina che passa trentacinque anni, deve andar in pace, ideste in purgatorio ad pregar Dio per i vivi[132]
(You are fit for the cemetery because a woman who is older than thirty-five should go in peace, or to Purgatory to pray to God for people who are still alive).

Western and Chinese seem not to agree on the age at which a woman's beauty declines; an agreement is instead found on the idea that, no matter how old men or women are, they are beautiful and enchanting as long as they are noble or powerful. Stendhal (1783-1842) affirms it and is supported by Lorenzo Magalotti (1637-1712), an Italian baroque poet who writes:

Il viso dal mezzo in giù è assai stretto, onde il ne rimane aguzzo, la bocca è grande e i denti spaventali. La regina è bella perché non s'è mai sentito in questo mondo che una regina sia brutta. Il re d'Inghilterra se fusse un privato cavaliere sarebbe brutto, ma perché gli è e arriva passar per uom ben fatto[133]
(The lower part of her face is narrow and sharp and her mouth is big and her teeth are scary. The queen is beautiful because there has never been an ugly queen. The king of England would be ugly if only he had been a private knight, but since he is the king of England he has a fair appearance).

---

131 Qian Zhongshu, *Guan Zhui Bian*, III, 1502.
132 Qian Zhongshu, *Guan Zhui Bian*, III, 1503. See Bruno, *Opere di Giordano Bruno*, 65.
133 Qian Zhongshu, *Guan Zhui Bian*, III, 1504. See Magalotti, *Relazioni di Viaggio in Inghilterra, Francia e Svezia*, 20.

The counsellor Zou Ji 鄒忌 is of the same opinion; in *Zhanguo Ce – Jice* 戰國策・齊策 (Strategies of the Warring States – Strategies of Qi) he affirms:

My wife praises me as beautiful because she loves me, my concubine praises me as beautiful because she fears me.[134]

And, with the formula Qian likes to use when he finds links and correspondence, he adds "*ke xiang faming* 可相發明" they can mutually expound.

## 4.4 Juxtaposition in quotations: "datong" and striking combinations

In another passage of *Guan Zhui Bian* we might observe still a different way of quoting. This time it is as if Qian Zhongshu wants to give proof that all the literary realms are linked together and the accordance of the quoted opinions becomes more striking due to the difference of languages in which those opinions are expressed. The concept involved here is that the more distant and inaccessible the goal, the more the sense of longing and the desire to reach it is strengthened by the distance itself. Just as all "the various western phrases"[135] prove:

La lontananza; à la nostalgie d'un pays on joint la nostalgie d'un temps; cette nostalgie du pays qu'on ignore; distance lends enchantments; die unendliche

---

134  See Qian Zhongshu, *Guan Zhui Bian*, III, 1504.
135  Egan, *Limited Views*, 79.

ferne, die Entfernung[136]
(Distance; one links the nostalgia for a period of time to the nostalgia for a country; this nostalgia of an unknown country; distance lends enchantments; the infinite distant, the distance).

These sentences from Leopardi, Edmond et Jules de Goncourt (1822-1896), Baudelaire (1821-1967), Lascelles Abercrombie (1881-1938) and Fritz Strich (1882-1963) express basically the same concept of distance and nostalgia and the author puts them together through juxtaposition to prove that "it is as if these statements all came from one mouth".[137] What is important for Qian here is to demonstrate that a common spirit lies among the artistic realms of different times and spaces and that some literary concepts are universal.

Juxtaposition (*datong*) between east and west, between cultural thought of different epochs and between different disciplines are the three major patterns of this technique used by Qian Zhongshu and are a method to obtain maximum meaning through minimum use of language.[138] The striking combinations created by Qian in his quoting from miscellaneous authors and works are the ones that cause in him what he calls the "shock of recognition"[139] which he defines:

In a national literature which apparently never had any truck with the literature of one's own tongue, one often unexpectedly lights upon certain close parallels or similarities to the techniques, themes, dramatic situations and doctrinal formulations found in the literature of one's own country. One has the feeling of seeing a familiar face in a strange land. In an affective tone it is not unlike the

---

136 Qian Zhongshu, *Guan Zhui Bian*, II, 1413.
137 Egan, *Limited Views*, 79.
138 Huang Weiliang, "Liu Xie and Qian Zhongshu: Common poetics", 249.
139 Qian Zhongshu, "The Mutual Illumination of Italian and Chinese Literature" in *A collection of Qian Zhongshu's English essays*, 403; and Qian Zhongshu, "Yizhong Wenxue de Huxiang Zhaoming: yi ge da Timu, ji ge Xiao Lizi", in Qian Zhongshu, *Xie zai Rensheng Bianshang*, 172.

literary experience summed up by De Sanctis in the words 'Ecco una vecchia conoscenza!' in his masterly essays on Hugo's poems.[140]

Here the sentence by the Italian critic De Sanctis means "Here we are old acquaintances!". This quotation by De Sanctis, quoted in Qian's essay, had already been quoted in *Tan Yi Lu* LXXXII[141] where, preceded by Qian's translation, it was used to support a slightly different theory from the one of *The Mutual Illumination*. This time Qian Zhongshu is talking about the genesis of art and the creative process of the artist, who in creating something new needs nevertheless to give the reader the impression of finding an old acquaintance in the piece of art he is confronted with. Only in this way, when arousing such a sensation of familiarity and closeness, can poetry be considered true poetry. Qian Zhongshu explains that this concept can also be extended through the words of Coleridge a few lines further from the reading phase to the creative process, and the writer, in his expression by artistic means, needs to produce something that under new robes contains the seeds of something buried inside himself that comes to life again. The process is expressed through a metaphor in a poem by Luigi Carrer (1801-1850), quoted in Baldacci's (1930-2002) *Poeti Minori dell'Ottocento* (Eighteenth Century Minor Poets) titled "La Sorella" (The sister) and quoted a few lines later by Qian:

> Quel ch'io provassi la prima volta che di vederti m'accadde, ascolta.
> Pareami averti scontrato ancora,
> Maignoti il loco m'erano e l'ora[142]
> (What happened to me the first time I saw you, listen.
> It seemed I had already met you,
> But unknown where the place and the time).

---

140 Qian Zhongshu, "The Mutual Illumination", 404.
141 Qian Zhongshu, *Tan Yi Lu*, 631. The quotation comes from *Saggi Critici* (Critical Essays) by Francesco De Sanctis.
142 Qian Zhongshu, *Tan Yi Lu*, 633. See Carrer, *Opere Scelte*, 3. **Maignoti** should be spelled **ma ignoti**.

In the above-mentioned essay, *The Mutual Illumination*, there are many examples of old acquaintances between Chinese and Italian literatures, which I will briefly mention to illustrate Qian Zhongshu's notion of "striking combinations". Qian Zhongshu talks about Machiavelli, perfect representative of the Italian Renaissance, and about his contrast between *Fortuna* (fortune) and *Virtù* (virtue /ability): this contrast had already been discussed by the Chinese Mozi 墨子 during the 3$^{rd}$ century B.C. and by Liezi 列子 in the 4$^{th}$ century. Machiavelli was not acquainted with either Mozi or Liezi. Still we need not be surprised by their common discussion since, as Qian Zhongshu states, talking about the same arguments is part of the "*condition humaine*" (human condition). What should surprise us instead is that the Machiavellian *virtù* is a topic that, difficult to render in other languages since it is not simply the equivalent of the English "virtue", in the Chinese treatment of the concept by Mozi or Liezi is a perfect translation in the words *li* (力) or *qiang* (強), which both indicate the capacity of man to face the opposing events he has to experience, while "fortune" corresponds precisely to the Chinese concept of *ming* 命. The same example is recalled in the entry about the two words, *li* and *ming*, in the commentary on *Liezi* in *Guan Zhui Bian*.[143]

Another example of striking combinations is the fact that in the 15$^{th}$ century Leonardo da Vinci (1452-1519) used to suggest to his students to observe walls with stains or stones to get inspiration when needed to paint sceneries and the Chinese painter Song Ti 宋迪 gave exactly the same suggestion to his disciples in the 11$^{th}$ century. Other examples are quoted of similar stories narrated by the Italian novelist Boccaccio and the Chinese poet Yuan Mei 袁枚 (1716-1797) of a similar anecdote about the Chinese writer Kung Rong 孔融 of the 3$^{rd}$ century and a Florentine Renaissance boy narrated

---

143 See Qian Zhongshu, *Guan Zhui Bian*, II, 781.

in the *Liber Facetiarum* by the Italian Poggio Bracciolini (1380-1459), which Qian quotes by mistake only with the name Poggio, or in *Il Trecentonovelle* (Three-hundred Short Stories) by Franco Sacchetti (1335-1400). The question left open by Qian Zhongshu in the conclusion of the essay is if those connections and similarities come from willing influences or just from similar responses to similar questions. This will give enough material for dissertation, advises Qian, and will end up in a mutual illumination between the two (in this case the Italian and Chinese) national literatures.[144]

What seems evident is that whenever Qian Zhongshu expresses a concept through unusual combinations and juxtaposes sentences in striking sequences, it is meant to show unexpected similarities more than differences. Another example of this is presented in *Guan Zhui Bian*, where a quotation from the Buddhist classic *Dapan Niepan Jing – Fanxing Pin* 大般涅槃經 · 梵行品 (Sutra of Nirvana – Sanscrit work) affirms that words of rage seem to be engraved on the everlasting stone, while words of praise seem to be inscribed on water and flow away in a short time. Soon after following quotations from Stefano Guazzo (1530-1593), Italian Renaissance writer and author of the *Dialoghi Piacevoli* (Pleasant Dialogues), whence his quotation is taken, who writes:

> Scrivono i beneficii nella polvere e l'ingiurie nel marmo[145]
> (They write good things on dust and offences on marble)

and a quotation in footnote of a proverb from A. Arthaber, contemporary scholar, and his *Dizionario Comparato di Proverbi* (Comparative Dictionary of

---

144  Qian Zhongshu, "The Mutual Illumination", 404.
145  Qian Zhongshu, *Guan Zhui Bian*, I, 315.

Proverbs):

> Chi offende scrive in polvere di paglia,
> Chi è offeso, nei marmi lo sdegno intaglia[146]
> (Who makes offence writes in straw's dust,
> The offended engraves his indignation in marble).

The *datong* is unexpected because of the distance in time and literary genres and serves to point out a common and everlasting truth.

## 4.5 Quotations as a looking glass

The perception we obtain of ourselves through a looking glass is sometimes different from the one based only on self-appreciation: so in order to understand ourselves better, it is useful and fitting to refer to others for a confrontation and an appropriate reconsideration of previous views. This is one of the main usages of quotations that occur in Qian Zhongshu's works, since most of his studies are analyses of Chinese literature, considered and reconsidered, with the help of different perspectives presented by foreign literatures and authors.

Talking about similes and analogies, in the first book of *Guan Zhui Bian*, the author distinguishes between similes in philosophical and poetic writings. There are plenty of similes in *Zhuangzi* as well as in the *Yi Jing* and the treatments they undergo are different and should be considered attentively. Similes in a philosophical work need to remain well separated from the object to which they refer, otherwise the original meaning could be mistaken for the simile itself, as explained by Han Feizi with the similes of the

---

146 Qian Zhongshu, *Guan Zhui Bian*, I, 315.

jewellery case that was more highly praised than the pearl it contained, or of the attendant maid who supplanted her mistress in the mistress' husband eyes.[147] On the other hand, similes in a poetic work need to be linked to the object to which they refer because they are part of the general meaning conveyed by the poetic image. After quoting and referring to Chinese literature, Qian puts it in front of the mirror of western literature with appropriate quotations: Bertrand Russell (1872-1970) once criticized Henry Bergson (1859-1941) for his abuse of metaphors and Bergson defended himself asserting that he used such a great number of metaphors to prevent any of them from becoming a fixed reference to the object referred to. The same concept had been expressed by Freud (1856-1939). Qian Zhongshu concludes: "It is tempting to evaluate the ancient philosopher by this modern rationale: if we attribute to *Zhuangzi* the same intent, we might not be far off".[148]

Another clear example of the usage of quotations as a mirror to reflect and clarify concepts and ideas belonging to Chinese tradition and literature is the explanation of the rhetoric figure of synaesthesia that we find both in the essay *Tonggan* 通感 (Synaesthesia)[149] and in *Guan Zhui Bian*. In ancient Chinese poems synaesthesia is present very often, Qian states, and thanks to the elaboration and explanation of this rhetorical figure created by western criticism, we are now able to see the point in linking a colour – reddish – with a name belonging to the sense of hearing – noise – in Chinese classical poetry as is the case in lines like "*hongxing zhitou chunyi nao* 紅杏枝頭春意鬧" (the noise of spring is on the reddish branches' tips) in Song Qi 宋祁's

---

147  Egan, *Limited Views*, 136.
148  Egan, *Limited Views*, 138.
149  Qian Zhongshu, "Tonggan", in *Qi Zhui Ji*, 62-76.

(998-1061) *Yu Lou Chun* 玉樓春[150] or in the famous poem by the poet Giovanni Pascoli (1855-1912) called *Il Gelsomino Notturno* (Night Jasmine) recalled both in *Tonggan* and in *Guan Zhui Bian*, which we will mention further on in the paragraph dedicated to the poet.[151] Quotations from Buddhist texts, as well as from *Liezi* and *Zhuangzi*, contain claims of the possibility of interchanging the senses of perceptions, the same claims we find in western authors like Shakespeare (1564-1616), Baudelaire and D'Annunzio.

Thus, an eye set on western criticism gives a new perspective to the analysis of ancient Chinese classical texts as when in *Guan Zhui Bian* the "I" of the *Sang Zhong* 桑中 in the *Book of Songs* 毛詩 is explained as "nothing other than a rough copy of this kind of role", that is the role of the libertine, quoted as *l'homme à femme* from G. G. de Bévotte (1867-1938), in *Don Juan* by Mozart. Qian Zhongshu quotes the libretto by Lorenzo da Ponte (1749-1838) from Mozart's *Don Juan* in footnote without a translation in Chinese. The two lines of the quotation tell how the libertine Don Juan had a notebook with a list of all the women he had conquered and the list was so long as to be called a catalogue (*catalogo*).[152] The libertine Don Juan is thus the image reflected in the mirror of the "I" of the *Sang Zhong* 桑中 and is meant to explain and clarify it.

The mirror of western authors and works is also used to cast light upon an intrinsic particularity of Chinese literary criticism as in the 1926 essay *Zhongguo Gu You de Wenxue Piping de Yi Ge Tedian* 中國固有的文學批評的一個特點[153] (An Intrinsic Particularity of Chinese Literary Criticism). The

---

150 Qian Zhongshu, "Tonggan", in *Qi Zhui Ji*, 62.
151 See paragraph 5.2.1 "Pascoli".
152 Qian Zhongshu, *Guan Zhui Bian*, I, 151.
153 Qian Zhongshu, *Xie zai Rensheng Bianshang*, 116.

essay aims to highlight a peculiar aspect of Chinese literary criticism that has always been a distinguishing characteristic and that could be exportable to the western world: it is the humanization of written texts, that is, speaking of literary texts as having flesh, bone and spirit. In dealing with Chinese literary criticism, Qian Zhongshu presents a passage with an extensive amount of western quotations in English, Italian, Latin, Greek, French and German. An impressive *collage* of western terminology and sentences is the mirror in which Chinese literary criticism reflects itself to discover that whenever western critics and writers have described written texts in terms of flesh and bones, it has always been in reference to people (Cicero 106-43: *venustatem muliebrem, dignitatem virile*),[154] to describe a distortion of the style (Longinus 1st or 3rd century B.C.: writings should be like people's body, they shouldn't have swelling)[155] or to write metaphors (Ben Jonson 1572-1637: writings are *likened to a man*, they have *structure and stature, figure and feature, skin and coat* or Wordsworth 1770-1850: people use essays like a *dress* for thought),[156] and never to give the same flesh, blood and spirit that men have to the written text.

According to western critics, spirit is attached to writings but they remain two different things. Chinese literary critical essays and other writings instead, are not just "like having a soul", they just have it. Qian's assumption would not have been so convincing and would not have had such a solid base to prove what he is stating without the help of more than one hundred quotations and expressions from western literature in under twenty pages. The great achievement of Qian Zhongshu's method is that a large part of his

---

154  Qian Zhongshu, *Xie zai Rensheng Bianshang*, 120. The quotation means: grace of women, dignity of men.
155  Qian Zhongshu, *Xie zai Rensheng Bianshang*, 122. The Greek word quoted by Qian Zhongshu to mean "swelling" is "ὄγκοι".
156  Qian Zhongshu, *Xie zai Rensheng Bianshang*, 124.

statements is made up of a careful and well-founded dismantling of eventual counter-arguments to his thesis that confirm and reinforce his argument. While reflecting itself in the mirror of the words of some of the most influential critics and writers in the western literary canon, Chinese literature becomes aware of a distinguishing and substantial feature that has always "intrinsically" (*guyou*) characterized it. The starting point of the essays is that very often what is typically western is considered eastern and vice-versa: the witty example is the Pekinese dog called *yang gou* 洋狗 (foreign dog) in China, and "Pekinese dog" in the west. At the same time what is considered a characteristic peculiar to a place is in fact a motif in common with other places. Take for example the concept of *zhong* 忠, the loyal and superior loyalty without interests and implications: this is not a "typically Chinese concept", affirms Qian, since western criticism as well has discussed concepts, like *zhong* 忠, having a meaning that surpasses the words themselves and that reach a superior level. The example is a quotation from Dante's *Convivio* taken from an English translation of the Italian work.[157] In Qian's text the quotation remains in Italian and refers to the anagogical meaning (senso anagogico) that words may have. This anagogical meaning is one of the four meanings of words discussed in the *Convivio*, the others being the literal, allegorical and tropological ones, and this stands for the utmost level of comprehension of a concept since it indicates the sense above the sense that raises the soul to the divine salvation. Qian Zhongshu states, not an easy concept but exactly the same principle of the *Changzhou Ci Pai* 常州詞派, the Changzhou School of Words.

Again starting from a comment on *Quan Sanguo Wen* 全三國文 in *Guan Zhui Bian*, the mirror of western literature explains and justifies the

---

157 Qian Zhongshu, *Xie zai Rensheng Bianshang*, 117.

phenomenon of attributing a meaning to words according to their sound. The bat is a symbol of good omen in China, while in the west it is used to describe ominous beings like Satan in the *Divine Comedy*:

> Sotto ciascuna uscivan due grandi ali,
> Quanto si convenia a tanto Uccello;
> [...]
> Non avean penne, ma di vivistrello era lor modo[158]
> (Underneath came forth two mighty wings,
> Such as befitting were so great a bird.
> [...]
> No feathers had they, but as of a bat)[159]

or in *Orlando Innamorato* (Orlando in Love) by Matteo Maria Boiardo (1441-1494) "il negromante Balisardo" (Balisardo the necromancer):

> E l'ale grande avea di pipastrello,
> E le mane agriffate come uncine,
> Li piedi d'oca e le gambe de ocello, La coda lunga come un babuino[160]
> (Who had huge bat wings and his hands were sharp like a hook,
> His feet were like a goose's
> And his legs like a bird's, his tail was long like a monkey's).

The fact that in China the bat is a good symbol then is linked only to the sound of the words, as in Chinese *fu* 蝠, bat, sounds like *fu* 福, fortune. This is what happens with the Latin word *lepos*, beauty, similar to *lepus*, hare,

---

158 Qian Zhongshu, *Guan Zhui Bian*, III, 1679. Dante Alighieri, *La Commedia secondo l'antica vulgata*, 142. **vivistrello** should be spelled **vispistrello**.

159 Dante, *Inferno* 34, 46-47-49 from *The Divine Comedy of Dante Alighieri* I translated by Henry Wadsworth Longfellow, 110.

160 Qian Zhongshu, *Guan Zhui Bian*, III, 1679. See Boiardo, *Orlando Innamorato*, 532. **oncine** should be spelled **oncino**.

that made ancient people believe that to eat hare helped beauty! This phenomenon is called "verbal homeopathy"[161] in English and is expressed in *Quan Sanguo Wen* by the sentence "ming sheng jian yi" 名聲見異.

## 4.6 Quotations as proof of truth: unveiling mistakes

Qian Zhongshu's approach in linking east and west is to not accept the two traditions passively: he is not praising one and criticizing the other, or as was customary at the beginning of the 20ᵗʰ century, affirming that China had to use western doctrines for practical scopes to maintain the essence of Chinese culture for abstract concepts. He considers the two different traditions pointing out their achievements and shortcomings as it happens, for example, with the lack of tragic commitment in Chinese tragic works when compared with their parallels in western tradition.[162]

In a particularly long entry in *Guan Zhui Bian*[163] the term of the debate is a discourse on "resonance" in art and literature. Xie He 謝赫 (479-502) had written a treatise called *Gu Hua Pin* 古畫品 in the sixth century. This critical work enumerated six canons for painting at its very beginning. Xie He's "canons" have been renowned throughout centuries by means of a quotation by Zhang Yanyuan 張彥遠 (ninth century), a quotation that completely missed Xie He's initial intent due to a punctuation mistake. In the western translations that Qian Zhongshu had happened to see, he states that Herbert Giles (1945-1935), Raphael Petrucci (1872-1917), A. C. Coomaraswamy (1877-1947), and O. Siren (1879-1946) had all misunderstood Xie He, considering him "as nonsensical – someone talking in

---

161 Qian Zhongshu, *Guan Zhui Bian*, III, 1680.
162 See Qian Zhongshu, "Tragedy in Old Chinese Drama", in *A Collection of Qian Zhongshu's English Essays*, 53-65.
163 Qian Zhongshu, *Guan Zhui Bian*, IV, 2109-2113.

his sleep". The mistake, proven by quotations from the Chinese as well as incorrect western versions, is rectified by Qian Zhongshu's rendering of the canons through correct punctuation marks. More importantly, the meaning that had not been understood is supported here by quotations that come from French, English, Italian, Greek and German literatures that support and build a solid and indestructible foundation for Qian's theory and rectification of the mistake.

In the very beginning of *Guan Zhui Bian*[164] and later in the second volume of the same work *(Guan Zhui Bian* II, 689), Qian makes a fierce and nearly sarcastic critique aimed at the German philosopher Hegel (1770-1831), who in his ignorance of the Chinese language – for which he should not be blamed, states Qian, maintained that German had a semantic richness that even Latin could not reach, let alone a language like the Chinese one, which he considered unsuited for logical reasoning. Since Hegel brought the fact that German had words capable of expressing two opposite meanings as an example of this theory, Qian replies to this assertion with quotations from the *Analects*, *Mozi*, *Laozi* and many other Chinese classics, giving tangible proof that his contradiction of Hegel has a foundation rooted not only in the Chinese language but, as quotations from Heraclitus (535-475), Plotinus (240-270), St Augustine (354-430), Francis Ponge (1899-1988), Shelley (1892-1922), Wordsworth (177-1850) and Coleridge (1772-1834) demonstrate, also in other languages – all capable of embracing different and contradictory meanings in just one single word – like German. What Hegel is culpable of is having seen a difference where there is a similarity, and having based a distance between eastern and western languages comparable to the long distance between horses and oxen on the northern and southern limits

---

164  Qian Zhongshu, *Guan Zhui Bian*, I, 1-2.

of the sea on this supposed difference. This remark by Qian Zhongshu and the counter-argument posed against Hegel's assertion enhance studies on languages and give both east and west a further chance to appreciate differences and understand that they are an approach to mutual enrichment, not a mode to despise and refuse what we rate as inferior only because we do not fully grasp the core of it. By critiquing Hegel and demonstrating that the concept he attributes to the German language is also part of the Chinese language, Qian Zhongshu is also validating that in both the philosophical and linguistic contexts it is possible to have speculative philosophy and that comparison is possible.[165]

In the second volume of *Guan Zhui Bian* the criticism of Hegel is discussed again with further investigation of the meaning that a mere rectification becomes construction of proofs for validation and pretext to build up comparisons and *datong*. The statement in *Laozi* that every opposition ends up in affirmation is the starting point. The word 'opposition,' *fan* 反, has different and opposing meanings; if on one hand this contradicts Hegel, affirming that Chinese words have no semantic richness, on the other hand it confirms and validates his quoted statement that the negation of negation stays for an affirmation and ends up in a circular movement. Then Laozi and Hegel are on the same track and many other quotations from western authors (Blake 1757-1827, Plato 427-347, Plotinus, Proclus 412-485 and Meister Eckart 1260-1328) follow to reinforce Laozi and Hegel's initial statements. Dante is the one who opens the series of quotations with his lines from the XXV canto of the *Divine Comedy*:

> E fassi un'alma sola,

---

165 See Zhang Longxi, "Zhongxi jiaoji yu Qian Zhongshu de zhixue fangfa", 187-210.

Che vive e sente e sè in sè rigira[166]
(And becomes one soul
Which lives, and feels, and on itself revolves)[167]

freely translated by Qian as "the chaos that revolves becomes the soul and the same soul revolves in itself". More appropriately as for its literal meaning we have: "the revolving that goes back to its origin". The quotation is probably lacking the sense of opposition and contrast that Qian was trying to point out in all the other quotations of the entry.

As occurs with the philosopher Hegel, rectification and critic also lie behind the words directed at the English critic Herbert Read (1893-1968) in *Tan Yi Lu*[168] (Discourses on Art), where Qian calls Read's critical analysis superficial. Read had criticized the French priest Henri Brémond (1865-1933) for his supposed attribution to himself in the definition of *poésie pure* (pure poetry) and had made examples of Shelley, Poe (1809-1849) and Pater (1839-1894) to sustain that it was a definition to be attributed to Anglo-Americans. Qian proves with an incredibly high concentration of quotations[169] that not only had the same Brémond never boasted the invention of the definition, but had referred to the Anglo-Americans in talking about *poésie pure* with many more examples than the three made by Read.

In the words of the Italian critic Benedetto Croce, Qian uses an overt rectification (*buque* 補闕) in his theory, considered too simplistic by Lu Ji 陸機, a 3rd century writer and calligrapher, who talks about literary creation in his *Wen Fu* 文賦. It is necessary to rectify his mistake and to state the

---

166 Qian Zhongshu, *Guan Zhui Bian*, II, 691. See Dante Alighieri, *La Commedia secondo l'antica vulgata*, 249.

167 Dante, *Purgatorio* 25, 74-75 from *The Divine Comedy of Dante Alighieri* II, translated by Henry Wadsworth Longfellow, 171.

168 Qian Zhongshu, *Tan Yi Lu (buding ben)*, 268-271.

169 In the entry 88, whose first pages are about Brémond and la *poésie pure*, much more than half of each page is occupied by quotations and their authors' names. See Qian Zhongshu, *Tan Yi Lu*, 268-271.

difference between the immediate or symptomatic expression "espressione immediata o sintomatica": the direct feeling that is not an expression in act, yet it is so only potentially, and the poetic or spiritual expression "espressione poetica o spirituale":[170] a universal and total expression through which poetry connects the particular to the universal – a knowing emotion.[171]

## 4.7 In others' words

Qian Zhongshu does not speak overtly about the existing link between the content of his works and the contemporary historical setting; that is why often this link passes unnoticed. Examining his analysis of past events closer though, his patriotism, humanitarianism and anti-feudal ideas are understood. It is true that in his analysis his main intent is not to display his point of view on contemporary politics, but to correct partial and popular conceptions to get objective and correct ideas and theories. If we look at the treatment of the evaluation of Tang and Song poetry for example, Qian affirms that if there are two kinds of men in the world, there are also two different kinds of poetry and that Tang and Song poetries not only are the product of two different dynasties, but also of two different styles and two different literary genres. Tang poetry is outstanding for emotional sense, Song poetry for concrete and energetic ideas. Moreover, the two different poetries express a style without clear historical demarcation: some Tang poets have written in a style more typical of Song, and vice versa. This point of view is reliable, new and revolutionary in a sense, and is a correction to the mistake of considering

---

170  Qian Zhongshu, *Guan Zhui Bian* (2001), III, 1878.

171  Qian Zhongshu, *Guan Zhui Bian* (2001), III, 1878. The immediate or symptomatic expression is only a potential expression while the poetic or spiritual expression is a knowing emotion through which poetry connects the particular to the universal. See Benedetto Croce, *La Poesia* (Bari: Laterza, 1966), 6-14.

Tang poetry as superior to the Song one.[172] We then see that thanks to quotations from Tang and especially Song poets, Qian attempts to rectify a contemporary wrong literary conception. In the erudite "Foreword to the Prose-poetry of Su Tung Po"[173] first published in 1935, talking about the art of Song with an intriguing deep penetration in the critical spirit of the age, Qian writes:

> The most annoying thing about them is perhaps their erudition and allusiveness which make the enjoyment of them to a large extent the luxury of the initiated even among the Chinese.

The allusiveness here is the same that will characterize most of Qian Zhongshu's prose to the point of becoming a method of writing. We may wonder if Qian imagined that the allusiveness of his work would have become the reason for a certain lack of popularity for his writings and that various critics in China would even have found his style annoying for the excess of quotations and erudite allusions, considering it a boastful method of writing. In all likelihood, he was probably aware of this; additionally, the reason he admired Song prose was also because of the style it adopted, and that among millions of other reasons he probably chose this method both because he wanted to demonstrate that quotations gave a solid structure to theories and assumptions and he wanted his writings to be intelligible only to those people who were capable of extrapolating its deep meaning.

That is why the two main characteristics of *Guan Zhui Bian* surprise the reader at first sight: it has been written in *wenyanwen*, the classical language,

---

172 See Qu Wenjun, "Shilun Qian Zhongshu Datong de Siwei Moshi".
173 Qian Zhongshu, "Foreword to the Prose-poetry of Su Tung Po", in *A collection of Qian Zhongshu's English Essays*, 43-52.

even though the language in use at the time of its composition was the modern language *baihuawen*; it quotes from seven different languages with the obvious difficulties that arise for readers in understanding the words and grasping their meaning. To place the composition of this masterpiece in a historical period might help explain, at least partially, this double particular choice. *Guan Zhui Bian* was composed during the seventies of last century, during the Maoist Cultural Revolution, when writers had a rather difficult time since expressing ideas that were not in full accordance with the on-going political trend was something that could not be done light-heartedly. *Wenyanwen* and quotations in foreign languages were probably the code languages Qian Zhongshu needed to shield himself from critiques and from the watchful eye of political control. They were the "others' words" to express the author's feelings. *Guan Zhui Bian* bears many references to Cultural Revolution but at the same time Qian strongly condemned all those writers who made literature just a satellite of history or politics, believing that literature was just as important as other disciplines and should have had its own independence. In breaking the borders between past and present, Qian Zhongshu, even if in a veiled way, meant to use past in the present without any grade of importance and predominance.

In the first book of *Guan Zhui Bian*[174] the author uses Li Si 李斯's (280-208) words to start his argument of condemnation of those who despise ideas and doctrines simply because they are foreign. Qian says that Li Si had brought forth this concept and this is known to many, but he has never been duly considered as the source of the idea that served in many other historical phases to defend foreign doctrines from the contempt of conservative people. There were two main periods in which Li Si's words served as a defence of

---

174  Qian Zhongshu, *Guan Zhui Bian* (2001), I, 530-536.

foreigners: the time when Buddhist doctrine entered China and was hampered by Confucians and the 19th century when the New Learning was refused by conservatives. Not only are passages by Chinese authors like Mu Rong 牟融 (?-79), Li Shizheng 李師政 (1518-1593), the monk Qi Song 契嵩 (1007-1072), Jiao Hong 焦竑 (1540-1620), Zhao Ming 趙銘, Tan Sitong 譚嗣同 (1865-1898) and others used as appendix and corroborating statements for Li Si's words, but also quotations from the Greek Philostratus (172-247) or the German Goethe (1749-1832) are meant to demonstrate that it would be silly and inconsistent not to use the wise suggestion of Li Si to avoid rejecting theories that come from outside China without any other reasoning than that they are foreign. The power of ideas and books that comes from outside China's borders and that considered capable of mastering people's minds, remarks Qian Zhongshu in a previously mentioned entry in *Guan Zhui Bian*,[175] is something that even ministers of "cultural exchange" in modern times fear.[176]

The words of Montaigne, Dickens (1812-1870), Giordano Bruno and Boiardo in the entry *Ji Ci* 繫辭 in the first volume of *Guan Zhui Bian*[177] also affirm that the time in which the author was living was a difficult one and required a great amount of caution. To step further and go forward, say the quotations from the four authors, it is first necessary to step back and come to a temporary halt. To overcome obstacles sometimes it is necessary to pause and wait for times that are more favourable. The entry from the *Yijing* to whom the quotations are a commentary and the western authors, says Qian

---

175 Qian Zhongshu, *Guan Zhui Bian*, IV, 2090-2092.
176 Egan, *Limited Views*, 383.
177 Qian Zhongshu, *Guan Zhui Bian*, I, 86-87. Bruno's quotation "un fosso da passare, trapassando un fosso" is not directly translated and means "a ditch to cross, crossing a ditch". See Giordano Bruno, *Dialoghi Italiani*, 13; Boiardo's quotation follows and is in footnote: "al fin delle parole un salto piglia: /Vero è che indietro alquanto ebbe a tornare /A prender corso..." and could be rendered as "at the end of his speech he jumped: and he had to step back before taking a run-up"; See Boiardo, *Orlando Innamorato*, 494.

Zhongshu, have a different form but a similar heart: to win with a counter-attack it is first necessary to surrender and yield. The affirmation may easily be seen as an expression of Qian's state of mind.

# CHAPTER 5
# Italian quotations in Qian Zhongshu's works:
# a mutual illumination

In 1946, Qian Zhongshu wrote in *Philobiblon*[178]: "It is a pity that not many Chinese writers read Leopardi".[179] This was quite an unusual statement at a time when not many Italian authors and works were known in China.

Giuliano Bertuccioli, Italian scholar and sinologist, met Qian Zhongshu in 1985 at the Chinese Academy of Social Sciences, and affirmed later that, together with Zhu Guanqian 朱光潛, they were the only two Chinese authors to deal with Italian literature in a serious and competent way. This work investigates the role Qian Zhongshu ascribes to Italian literature. This role is not a marginal one. Given the importance of the Renaissance in particular, among the many other periods covered, Qian Zhongshu's choice of authors and works for quotations, indicates that quotations of Italian authors and works cover nearly one fifth of the total number. This percentage is arrived at through a general analysis of Qian's work, and from information in an unpublished work by Qian that complements and clarifies much of the method used in his other publications, *Guan Zhui Bian* or *Tan Yi Lu*. Information on this unpublished work comes from Zhang Wenjiang,[180] who reports a study by Qian Zhongshu on ten major western authors that would have been filled with more quotations even than *Guan Zhui Bian*. This unpublished work, called *Ganjue-Guannian-Sixiang* 感覺 · 觀念 · 思想

---

178 *Philobiblon* was a review published by the Chinese National Central Library of the Nationalist capital of Nanjing; from 1946 to 1948 Qian Zhongshu acted as main editor commuting from Shanghai.
179 See Bertuccioli "Qian Zhongshu: lo scrittore e lo studioso che si interessa alla nostra letteratura".
180 Zhang Wenjiang, *Yingzao Babita de Zhizhe*, 85-102.

(Feelings, Ideas, Ideologies)[181] was meant to reflect on:

1. two Italian books – *Divine Comedy* by Dante

    *Decameron* by Boccaccio

2. two English – *Collection of Plays* by Shakespeare

    *Paradise Lost* by Milton

3. two French – *Essays* by Montaigne

    another unidentified

4. two German – *Faust* by Goethe

    another unidentified

5. two Spanish – *Don Quijote*

    another unidentified

Zhang Wenjiang remarks that the unavailability of *Ganjue-Guannian-Sixiang* accounts for the fact that all that can be known about Qian's quoted authors and about his preferences can be deduced only from an analysis of the main trends in *Guan Zhui Bian*. Zhang notes that for Italian literature, in his published works Qian Zhongshu quotes mostly from Machiavelli and Leopardi.

## 5.1 From Dante to Leopardi: past theories into the present

Through the explanation and exemplification of Qian Zhongshu's comparative method, it becomes evident that the programmatic intent of his system is to meld and draw ideas from different and distant times and places. This aims at looking for and finding the threads of a global literature and

---

181 The name *Ganjue-Guannian-Sixiang* comes from the "Qian Zhongshu" entry in a dictionary of modern Chinese writers as confirmed in an e-mail from Professor Zhang Wenjiang sent in reply to mine on April 14th 2011.

universal thought. The way in which Qian operates is not a casual and unruly one. A twofold trend can be traced for analysis and further consideration. One of the directions is to use modern authors and their quotations to refer to past ideas; this intent will be discussed in the paragraph "From Pascoli to Eco: Present ideas to shed light on the past".

This section, "From Dante to Leopardi: Past theories into the present," illustrates the way in which quotations from authors of past centuries become the pretext for talking about the present and discussing contemporary issues. From Dante, 13th century, to Leopardi, 19th century, themes that Qian discusses include debates about art and nature, the capacity of words or paintings to express artists' true feelings, the role of literature, the difficult and tricky relations between governors and subjects and the behaviour of governors, the use of torture, the role of metaphor and poetic imagery, the role of women in society as opposed to that of men, the way in which historians leave imperfect testimonies of their times (which has a direct influence on present views of past epochs and events), and the importance of money for people. Quotations from past authors shed light on the present to help readers understand the inner reasons that, for example, make torture today a useless and cruel means used by rulers to extract information or to punish their subjects[182] (or citizens).

### 5.1.1 Dante (1265-1321)

Qian Zhongshu's quotations from Dante seem quite a tribute to the Italian poet whom Qian considered a genius in world literature. The impression is that Dante's quotations serve the function of an invocation of authority for Qian, because he quotes the Italian poet to justify that what he

---

182  See paragraph "The light of reason: Vico, Muratori, Verri, Beccaria".

is assuming has a solid foundation. One of the most evident examples is in *Tan Yi Lu* LXI, where Dante's assumptions follow in sequence without translation into Chinese. Qian affirms that in painting, as in poetry, the expression of the intended meaning is often impossible and it is blocked from the finiteness of expressive means. He says that Dante proclaimed many times that words cannot capture the true meaning of concepts and ideas and the expressive effort does not directly follow the artist's intentions. Follow Dante's words from *The Convivio* and *The Divine Comedy*:

L'altra ineffabilità; cioè che la lingua non è di quello che l'intelletto vede, compiutamente seguace[183]
(The other ineffability; that is to say that language is not a perfect follower of what intellect can see);

Che molte volte al fatto il dir vien meno[184]
(That many times the word comes short of fact);[185]

Chi poria mai pur con parole sciolte ecc.[186]
(Who ever could e'en with untrammelled words etc.);[187]

S'io avessi le rime aspre et chiocce ecc.[188]
(If I had rhymes both rough and stridulous etc.);[189]

Nel ciel che più della sua luce prende ecc.[190]
(Within that heaven which most his light receives);[191]

183  See Dante Alighieri, *Le Opere Minori di Dante*, Convivio, trattato terzo.
184  See Dante Alighieri, *La Commedia secondo l'antica vulgata*, 18.
185  Dante, *Inferno* 4, 147 from *The Divine Comedy of Dante Alighieri* I translated by Henry Wadsworth Longfellow, 181.
186  See Dante Alighieri, *La Commedia secondo l'antica vulgata*, 116.
187  Dante, *Inferno* 28, 1 from *The Divine Comedy of Dante Alighieri* I translated by Henry Wadsworth Longfellow, 89.
188  See Dante Alighieri, *La Commedia secondo l'antica vulgata*, 132.
189  Dante, *Inferno* 32, 1 from *The Divine Comedy of Dante Alighieri* I translated by Henry Wadsworth Longfellow, 103.
190  See Dante Alighieri, *La Commedia secondo l'antica vulgata*, 286.
191  Dante, *Paradiso* 1, 4 from *The Divine Comedy of Dante Alighieri* III translated by Henry Wadsworth Longfellow, 1.

Trasumanar significar per verba non si porìa[192]
(To represent transhumanize in words impossible were);[193]

Vero è che, come forma non s'accorda
Molte fiate all'intenzion dell'arte
Perchè a risponder la materia è sorda[194]
(True is it, that as oftentime the form
Accords not with the intention of the art,
Because in answering is matter deaf);[195]

Da quinci innanzi il mio veder fu maggio ecc.[196]
(From that time forward what I saw was greater etc.);[197]

Omai sarà più corta mia favella ecc.[198]
(Shorter henceforward will my language fall etc.);[199]

Oh quanto è corto il dire e come fioco
Al mio concetto! ecc.[200]
(Oh how all speech is feeble and falls short
Of my conceit! etc.);[201]
All'alta fantasia qui manco possa[202]
(Here vigor failed the lofty fantasy).[203]

---

192  See Dante Alighieri, *La Commedia secondo l'antica vulgata*, 288.

193  Dante, *Paradiso* 1, 70 from *The Divine Comedy of Dante Alighieri* III translated by Henry Wadsworth Longfellow, 4.

194  See Dante Alighieri, *La Commedia secondo l'antica vulgata*, 289.

195  Dante, *Paradiso* 1, 127-129, from *The Divine Comedy of Dante Alighieri* III translated by Henry Wadsworth Longfellow, 6.

196  See Dante Alighieri, *La Commedia secondo l'antica vulgata*, 419.

197  Dante, *Paradiso* 33, 55 from *The Divine Comedy of Dante Alighieri* III translated by Henry Wadsworth Longfellow, 218.

198  See Dante Alighieri, *La Commedia secondo l'antica vulgata*, 420.

199  Dante, *Paradiso* 33, 106 from *The Divine Comedy of Dante Alighieri* III translated by Henry Wadsworth Longfellow, 220.

200  See Dante Alighieri, *La Commedia secondo l'antica vulgata*, 421.

201  Dante, *Paradiso* 33, 121 from *The Divine Comedy of Dante Alighieri* III translated by Henry Wadsworth Longfellow, 222.

202  Qian Zhongshu, *Tan Yi Lu*, 530. See Dante Alighieri, *La Commedia secondo l'antica vulgata*, 421. **manco** should be spelled **mancò**.

203  Dante, *Paradiso* 33, 142 from *The Divine Comedy of Dante Alighieri* III translated by Henry Wadsworth Longfellow, 223.

Quotations are accurate and pertinent to the theme discussed. One of the above quotations is even re-quoted later in an extension of the theme on the limits of language. Qian first talks about mystic poetry and about the process of creation. To produce poetry, poets must distance themselves from reality to see what other people cannot see. They have to reach a state of consciousness that is nearly an encounter with mystical entities. Qian quotes here extensively from western authors who confirm that the mystic experience the poet undergoes in the process of creation is difficult to explain and even recollect. It is a state similar to being in a land of dreams, once awake the vision becomes confused, the remembrance is blurred, and the words are insufficient to express what has just been experienced. Dante had a firm belief that the process of creation in poetry undergoes the just-mentioned stages and the quotation is again from *Paradise* XXXIII and is the full quotation of a shorter passage already quoted in *Tan Yi Lu*:

Da quinci innanzi il mio veder fu maggio
Che il parlar nostro ch'a tal vista cede,
E cede la memoria a tanto oltraggio.
Qual è colui che somniando vede,
Che dopo il sogno la passione impressa
Rimane, e l'altro alla mente non riede,
Cotal son io, ché quasi tutta cessa
Mia visione, ed ancor mi distilla
Nel cor lo dolce che naque da essa[204]
(From that time forward what I saw was greater
Than our discourse, that to such vision yields,
And yields the memory unto such excess.
Even as he is who seeth in a dream,
And after dreaming the imprinted passion
Remains, and to his mind the rest returns not,

---

204 Qian Zhongshu, *Tan Yi Lu*, 705. See Dante Alighieri, *La Commedia secondo l'antica vulgata*, 419.

Even such am I, for almost utterly ceases
My vision, and distilleth yet
Within my heart the sweetness born of it).[205]

A similar amplification has the simile of men who look like worms becoming butterflies quoted from Purgatory:

Non v'accorgete voi che noi siam vermi
Nati a formar l'angelica farfalla[206]
(Do not ye comprehend that we are worms
Born to bring forth the angelic butterfly)[207]

where Dante is quoted among other western writers such as J. Dunlop (1755-1820), Coleridge, I. Disraeli (1804-1881) and Santa Teresa de Jesus (1515-1582). All of them expressed this same simile. Dante's simile, life like a run towards death:

Ai vivi
Del viver ch'è un correre alla morte[208]
(Those who live
That life which is a running unto death)[209]

is accompanied by quotations from Seneca, Jorge Manrique (1440-1479), Henry King (1886-1982), Musset (1810-1857) and F. H. Bradley (1846-1924).

---

205 Dante, *Paradiso*, 33, 55-63 from *The Divine Comedy of Dante Alighieri* III translated by Henry Wadsworth Longfellow, 219.
206 Qian Zhongshu, *Guan Zhui Bian*, IV, 2219. See Dante Alighieri, *La Commedia secondo l'antica vulgata*, 186.
207 Dante, *Purgatorio*, 10, 124-125 from *The Divine Comedy of Dante Alighieri* II translated by Henry Wadsworth Longfellow, 63.
208 Qian Zhongshu, *Guan Zhui Bian*, IV, 2237-2238. See Dante Alighieri, *La Commedia secondo l'antica vulgata*, 282.
209 Dante, *Purgatorio*, 33, 49 from *The Divine Comedy of Dante Alighieri* II translated by Henry Wadsworth Longfellow, 214.

In the second entry commenting on *Laozi* 老子 in *Guan Zhui Bian*,[210] Dante and Croce are quoted to reinforce and comment on a passage which states that sometimes words are not able to express the meaning one would like to convey. The quotation, from Dante's *Il Convivio*, reads:

Il parlare per lo quale dal pensiero è vinto[211]
(Speech that is overpowered by thought)

is not translated by Qian Zhongshu, who only writes about its meaning. Croce is mentioned in a footnote referencing a quotation in German taken from his critical work *La Poesia*.[212] Croce and Dante, together with Metastasio, are quoted in another one of the entries commenting on literary creation, the role of the writer and the best way to convey poetic and literary meanings, and it is one of the longest entries of the third volume of *Guan Zhui Bian*, commenting on *Wen Fu* 文賦 by Lu Ji 陸機.[213] Already familiar with the idea that words can hardly convey an intended meaning, a further advancement of this concept is that after having tried to express an idea, the author enters into the world just created and it is difficult for him to distinguish between creation and reality.

Sogni e favole io fingo; e pure in carte
Mentre favole e sogni orno e disegno,
In lor, folle ch'io son, prendo tal parte
Che del mal che inventai piango e mi sdegno[214]
(Dreams and fables I fashion; and even if on paper

210 Qian Zhongshu, *Guan Zhui Bian*, II, 632-641.
211 Qian Zhongshu, *Guan Zhui Bian*, II, 637. See Dante. *Opere minori, Convivio*, 40.
212 Egan, *Limited Views*, 262.
213 Qian Zhongshu, *Guan Zhui Bian*, III, 1862-1904.
214 Qian Zhongshu, *Guan Zhui Bian*, III, 1877. See Metastasio, *Opere*, 36.

I sketch fables and dreams,
I so much participate in them like a mad man
That I cry and get angry for what I made up).

Metastasio's words attest to the author's immersion in the fictional world he has created.

For a literary author, as for a painter, it is necessary to be able to enter the created world and to act the part of the painted or described thing to give it a feeling of truthfulness.

Poi chi pinge figura,
Se non può esser lei, non la può porre[215]
(Who paints needs to become the thing painted
And if he cannot succeed, he cannot create the image)

affirms Dante a few lines later, commenting on the opinion of Lu Ji who says that just to experience joy and sorrow is enough to write a piece of literature.[216]

It is also true that the result of the poetic creation need not be perfect and lyrical in every moment because only if there is pain is there relief, and only with a lapse of seeming calm can there be an instant of violent emotion.

Senza il piano, non si può avere il rilievo; senza un periodo di apparente calma, non si può avere l'istante della commozione violenta[217]
(Without plain there cannot be relief; without a time of peace there cannot be the moment of violent emotion)

are Croce's words to comment on literary creation. He continues some lines

---

215 Qian Zhongshu, *Guan Zhui Bian*, III, 1878. See Dante Alighieri, *Opere minori, Convivio*, 60.
216 Qian Zhongshu, *Guan Zhui Bian*, III, 1862-1878.
217 Qian Zhongshu, *Guan Zhui Bian*, III, 1894. See Croce, *Conversazioni Critiche*, 66.

later with the image of those plain lines as a wooden bridge to pass from one verdant bank to the other:

> Quei versi sono un ponticello di legno per passare dall'una all'altra sponda verdeggiante.[217]
> (Those lines are a wooden bridge to pass from one greenish bank to the other).

Following the discussion about art and nature in which Ludovico Antonio Muratori had been quoted as representative of the school that believed that art overcomes the beauty of nature, Dante is quoted in *Tan Yi Lu* XV to sustain this same idea with a verse from *Paradise* in which Qian gives the reader an explanation more than a translation. The verse reads:

> Ma la natura la dà sempre scema,
> Similemente operando all'artista
> C'ha l'abito dell'arte e man che trema.[218]
> (But nature gives it evermore deficient
> In the like manner working as the artist,
> Who has the skill of art and hand that trembles).[219]

Dante's meaning is expressed with a metaphor in which nature is compared to an artist who would like to create something in a certain way but has a trembling hand (man che trema) and cannot fully express himself. Nature, explains Qian, needs the help of man to rectify its expression and adjust it to the canons of beauty and art, which, in a quotation at the end of *Guan Zhui Bian* by Giordano Bruno, are considered everlasting and never changing, while nature evolves:

---

218 Qian Zhongshu, *Tan Yi Lu*, 155. Dante Alighieri, *La Commedia secondo l'antica vulgata*, 336.
219 Dante, *Paradiso*, 13, 73-75 from *The Divine Comedy of Dante Alighieri* III translated by Henry Wadsworth Longfellow, 85.

Così, come là la pittura ed il ritratto nostro si contempla sempre medesimo, talmente qua non si vada cangiando e ricangiando la vital nostra complessione[220] (As in a painted portrait we always look the same, our aspect equally does not change again and again).

The quotation devoid of its context is not very clear in Italian, since it lacks the question mark that, in the original text, makes it a question addressed to Venus: do you think," a man asks her, "that as in a portrait we do not change and become older?".

Near the beginning of *Tan Yi Lu*, Qian discusses the senses of hearing and sight, and quotes specific passages from Chinese Song poetry in which it is the sense of hearing that supplies what sight cannot help, or in which it is sight that helps itself. Dante, quoted at the beginning of the annotation as the first poet cited, describes in the X canto of *Purgatory* an engraving on a rock of people chanting, and the sculpture is so vivid that he has the impression of hearing the people's song. Qian translates Dante's passage saying that "one sense said 'no song can be heard' and the other 'yes, there is one'". The Italian text reads:

A due miei sensi
Faceva dir l'uno 'No', l'altro 'si, canta'
(Purg. X. 59-60). [221]

Quotations about the contrast between sound and silence when admiring a painting inadvertently slide into other passages from Chinese

---

220 Qian Zhongshu, *Guan Zhui Bian*, IV, 2370. **Cossì** should be spelled **così**. See Bruno, *Opere di Giordano Bruno*, 128.

221 Qian Zhongshu, *Tan Yi Lu*, 28. See Dante Alighieri, *La Commedia secondo l'antica vulgata*, 134. **miei** should be spelled as **mie**.

poets and from the Greeks, Homer (7<sup>th</sup> or 8<sup>th</sup> c. B.C.) and Philostratus (172-247), who discuss the contrast between colour and non-colour, between black and multicoloured. Qian reflects on the senses of viewing and hearing in paintings; in some paintings, the sense of hearing supplies and completes our visual understanding of a scene and we imagine hearing noises related to the scene. Other paintings, better and more eloquent, are the ones that use only visual imagination to supply meanings not otherwise expressed, such as the face of a dark-skinned person painted in white chalk, the one described by Philostratus.[222] Among the many quotations sustaining one theory or the other, Qian seems to praise the utmost result with the least expenditure of effort, a characteristic of Dante's poetics that Qian particularly admires.

Colours again are the topic in an entry commenting on the *Taiping Guangji* 太平廣記 where many quotations convey the sense that very often poets create images in which similar colours overlap to provide highly poetic imagery. Shakespeare, Jules Renard (1864-1910), Alphonse Allais (1854-1905), Dante, and Marino (1569-1625), play on the image of white on white. Dante's quotation is from the third canto of Paradise:

> Sì che perla in bianca fronte
> Non vien men tosto alle nostre pupille[223]
> (That a pearl on forehead white
> Comes not less speedily unto our eyes).[224]

Similar in intents is Marino's[225] quotation:

---

222 Qian Zhongshu, *Tan Yi Lu*, 30.

223 See Dante Alighieri, *La Commedia secondo l'antica vulgata*, 294.

224 Dante, *Paradiso*, 3, 14 from *The Divine Comedy of Dante Alighieri* III translated by Henry Wadsworth Longfellow, 15.

225 For a detailed description of Marino's quotations see chapter 5.1.6 "Marinisti: Italian baroque poetry".

Ninfa mungitrice [...] ne distinguer sapea
Il bianco umor da le sue mani intatte,
Ch'altro non discernea che latte in latte[226]
(A Nymph that while milking [...] was not able to distinguish
In her hands the white liquid,
Seeing nothing else than milk in milk).

The theme of sound and descriptions, in words rather than in paintings, is recalled in a quotation from Boiardo's *Orlando Innamorato* in *Guan Zhui Bian* where the portrayal of the sorceress Circe accounts for her face being so coloured as to suggest hearing her voice:

Era una giovanetta in ripa al mare,
Sì vivamente in viso colorita,
Che chi la vede, par che oda parlare.[227]
(She was a young woman on the shore
So coloured in her face
That anyone that saw her had the impression of hearing words coming out of her mouth).

Suggestions of sounds from paintings and poems are considered by Qian evidence of a well-conceived piece of art.

In the essay *Du "Laaokong"* 讀《拉奧孔》 (Reading "Laocoon") from the collection *Qi Zhui Ji*, Qian Zhongshu notes that Lessing (1729-1781), author of the *Laocoon*, particularly appreciates the great Italian poet Dante for his capacity to obtain great results with the least effort: "ottiene il maggiore effetto possible coi minori mezzi possibili"[228] (he obtains the greatest effect with the lesser means). The quotation is from Giuseppe Giusti (1809-1850)

---

226  Qian Zhongshu, *Guan Zhui Bian*, II, 1186-1187. Marino, *Poesie Varie*.
227  Qian Zhongshu, *Guan Zhui Bian*, II, 696. See Boiardo, *Orlando Innamorato*, 95.
228  Qian Zhongshu, "Du 'Laaokong'", in *Qi Zhui Ji*, 51.

and his essay *On Two Lines of the Divine Comedy*[229] in which the author analyses two lines from two different canti of the *Divine Comedy*. Qian Zhongshu talks particularly of the line from the V canto of *Hell* which narrates the story of the two lovers Paolo and Francesca:

Quel giorno più non vi leggemmo avante[230]
(That day no further did we read therein).[231]

*Na yi tian women jiu bu duxiaqu le* 那一天我們就不讀下去了, translates Qian. Dante's poetic economy creates the right situation to keep the reader interested and lets him imagine a possible and natural conclusion to the story without telling anything explicitly. This narrative technique is defined as "cliché" (laosheng changtan 老生常談) in *Guan Zhui Bian* where Dante again is quoted to give examples of it from the conclusion of the XXXIII canto of *Purgatory* with a line that says:

Ma perchè piene son tutte le carte
Ordite a questa cantica seconda,
Non mi lascia più ir lo freno dell'arte[232]
(But inasmuch as full are all the leaves
Made ready for this second canticle
The curb of art no farther lets me go).[233]

The second line that Giusti tries to interpret and explain comes from the

229 See Giusti, "Di due versi dell'Inferno", in *Scritti vari in prosa e in verso di Giuseppe Giusti, per la maggior parte inediti*, 235-241, and is not the one Qian Zhongshu read.

230 Qian Zhongshu, "Du 'Laaokong'", in *Qi Zhui Ji*, 51. See Dante Alighieri, *La Commedia secondo l'antica vulgata*, 23.

231 Dante, *Inferno*, 5, 138 from *The Divine Comedy of Dante Alighieri* I translated by Henry Wadsworth Longfellow, 39.

232 Qian Zhongshu, *Guan Zhui Bian*, II, 1136. See Dante Alighieri, *La Commedia secondo l'antica vulgata*, 284.

233 Dante, *Purgatorio*, 33, 140 from *The Divine Comedy of Dante Alighieri* III translated by Henry Wadsworth Longfellow, 219.

XXXIII canto of Dante's *Hell*. In *Guan Zhui Bian*, Qian does not comment on the formal aspect and the rhetorical function of Dante's line, but inserts it as the last quotation in a chapter that discusses the relationship between sorrow and eating. The quotation reads:

Poscia, più che 'l dolor, potè il digiuno[234]
(The hunger did what sorrow could not do)[235]

and wants to support the idea that whenever a person is in a sorrowful state of mind, even though that person may not want to eat, the body requires food. The instinct of eating is always stronger than the will not to eat due to a distressed state of mind.

Another theme discussed and supported by a quotation from Dante, is to mistake somebody else's image for one's own. This sounds the same as mistaking one's image for somebody else's, as demonstrated a few lines earlier by Qian and supported by Dante's quotation:

Tali vid'io più facce a parlar pronte,
Perch'io dentro all'error contrario corsi
A quell ch'accese amor tra l'omo e il fonte.[236]

This quotation presents great difficulties for non-Italian speaking readers for a two reasons: Dante's Italian is not a modern one and requires understanding the classical language and, most of all, Qian does not provide

---

234 Qian Zhongshu, *Guan Zhui Bian*, I, 397. See Dante Alighieri, *La Commedia secondo l'antica vulgata*, 138.

235 Dante, *Inferno*, 33, 75 from *The Divine Comedy of Dante Alighieri* I translated by Henry Wadsworth Longfellow, 107.

236 Qian Zhongshu, *Guan Zhui Bian*, II, 1196-1197. See Dante Alighieri, *La Commedia secondo l'antica vulgata*, 294.

the translation of the quotation, but only summarises its content and the source in a footnote. Thus, the translation offered might be:

Such saw I many faces prompt to speak,
So that I ran in error opposite
To that which kindled love 'twixt man and fountain'.[237]

Again in the second volume of *Guan Zhui Bian*, a reference to Dante and one of the three kingdoms of his Divine Comedy supports two different points of view about ghosts and their second death. There are ghosts who can die and be dead forever (Liu Daoxi in *Taiping Guangji*) and ghosts who would like to die, but are deemed to live forever. This second motif is supported by quotations from Dante's verse from *Hell*:

Che la seconda morte ciascun grida[238]
(Who cry out each one for the second death)[239]

and Ariosto who has the sorcerer Alcina complaining:

E per dar fine a tanto aspro martìre,
Spesso si duol di non poter morire.
Morir non puote alcuna fata mai[240]
(To end such a bitter martyrdom,
Often complaining because it is impossible to die.
No fairy can ever die)

237  Dante, *Paradiso*, 3, 16-18 from *The Divine Comedy of Dante Alighieri* III translated by Henry Wadsworth Longfellow, 15.
238  Qian Zhongshu, *Guan Zhui Bian*, II, 1242. See Dante Alighieri, *La Commedia secondo l'antica vulgata*, 6.
239  Dante, *Inferno*, 1, 118 from *The Divine Comedy of Dante Alighieri* I translated by Henry Wadsworth Longfellow, 5.
240  Qian Zhongshu, *Guan Zhui Bian*, II, 1242. See Ariosto, *Orlando Furioso*, 135.

quoted by Qian Zhongshu in the source language without the Chinese translation. Dante's trip to the supernatural word is often connected to the *Taiping Guangji*: both have ghosts and dead or mysterious souls as their preferential subjects and those characters happen to share, in the two works' imagery, the same characteristics as the one without a shadow or material substance. Dante, in *Purgatory*, is the only living being and the dead souls surrounding him find it out because his body interrupts the rays of the sun, creating a shadow: "il lume che era rotto" (the light that was blocked), quotes Qian in footnote in *Guan Zhui Bian* or "fai di te parete al sol" (you make yourself a shield to the sun).[241]

A study of differences, and not only striking similarities, is the parallel stated between a novel in the *Taiping Guangji*, the *Dongyang Yeguai Lu* 東陽 夜怪錄 (Notes on the Night Ghost) with Dante's *Paradise* and San Francesco's *Il Cantico delle Creature* (Canticle of Creatures). San Francesco (1182-1226) was one of the main figures of Catholic hagiography and his writings, dictated by the saint to his disciples, have gained him a solid place among medieval authors. The reference is to the expressions of family relationships through natural elements – moon, sun, earth, wind and fire. If in the Chinese novel whirling snow represents the role of the father and the bamboo resonating in the wind is linked to a gentleman, there is nothing strange in San Francesco's calling sister the moon, brother the wind, sister the water, and brother the fire:

> Sora luna, frate vento, so'acqua, frate focu.[242]
> (Sister moon, brother wind, brother fire).

---

241 Qian Zhongshu, *Guan Zhui Bian*, II, 1154. See Dante Alighieri, *La Commedia secondo l'antica vulgata*, 162 and 251.
242 Qian Zhongshu, *Guan Zhui Bian*, II, 1367. See San Francesco d'Assisi, *Cantico delle Creature*.

According to Qian, it is strange, curious and bizarre to call the earth both sister and mother: "sora nostra matre terra"[243] (our sister mother hearth) as in the saint's words, and even stranger is what Dante writes in his *Paradise* where Holy Mary is called virgin mother, daughter of her son, both humble and higher than anyone else:

Vergine madre, figlia del tuo figlio,
Umile ed alta più che creatura[244]
(Thou Virgin Mother, daughter of thy son,
Humble and high, beyond all other creature).[245]

Following Qian's reasoning, we find that the French philosopher Edgar Morin (1921) offers another explanation in his *Sociologie*, 1984, p. 131. He states that in the concept of nation, the maternal and the paternal are mixed together, as in the expression "mère-patrie" (motherland-fatherland) and this word might, for Qian Zhongshu, come as well from an old explanation, the ancient Chinese sayings *fumuguo* 父母國 and *fumuzhibang* 父母之邦, precisely "country of mother and father". The oddity of San Francesco and of Dante's novel expressions that mix more than one family relationship in one sole character, are reconciled and explained through ancient Chinese terms.

An ancient Chinese image is "illuminated" through a quotation from the medieval Dante when the view of the earth was small. Commenting on the *Hua Shan Fu* 花山賦 (The Fu of Mount Hua) by Yang Jing 楊敬 in the *Quan Tang Wen* 全唐文, Dante's description in Paradise says:

---

243  Qian Zhongshu, *Guan Zhui Bian*, II, 1367.

244  Qian Zhongshu, *Guan Zhui Bian*, II, 1367. See Dante Alighieri, *La Commedia secondo l'antica vulgata*, 418.

245  Dante, *Paradiso*, 33, 1-2 from *The Divine Comedy of Dante Alighieri* III translated by Henry Wadsworth Longfellow, 217.

Col viso ritornai per tutte quante
Le sette spere, e vidi questo globo
Tal ch'io sorrisi del suo vil sembiante;
L'aiuola che ci fa tanto feroci[246]
(I with my sight returned to one and all
The sevenfold spheres, and I beheld this globe
Such that I smiled at its ignoble semblance; the threshing-floor that maketh us
so proud).[247]

Invocation of authority seems to be the usual function of Dante's quotations. Other western quotations follow the same theme: Milton, Middleton (1580-1627) and Dante Gabriele Rossetti (1828-1882).

## 5.1.2 Petrarca (1304-1374)

After Dante, Francesco Petrarca is one of the most noteworthy Italian poets of the 14$^{th}$ century. His importance is attributable particularly to the development of Italian vernacular poetry and to the development of prosody rules. He is the author of the *Rime* (Rhymes), an important collection of poems and source for Qian when discussing metaphor. As with other poets, figures of speech are precisely what interest Qian Zhongshu the most and what he likes to examine and quote in Petrarca's verse. Petrarca, like Marino, an author discussed further on, is the founder of a poetic school, the Petrarchismo, a sentimental school whose poems' content Qian compares in *Guan Zhui Bian* with the Chinese odes (*pianshi* 篇什). Petrarchismo's poems, remarks Qian, bear some differences compared to the Chinese odes in that when talking about the relationship between love and sleep, the Italians say

---

246 See Dante Alighieri, *La Commedia secondo l'antica vulgata*, 162 and 251

247 Dante, *Paradiso*, 22, 134-136 from *The Divine Comedy of Dante Alighieri* III translated by Henry Wadsworth Longfellow, 148 and *Paradiso*, 22, 151 from *The Divine Comedy of Dante Alighieri* III translated by Henry Wadsworth Longfellow, 217.

that even if poets hate to lose sleep when heartbroken:

Il sonno è'n bando, e del riposo è nulla[248]
(There's no sleep and no relaxing),

is the quotation from Petrarca's *Rime*, they do not hate the fact that in losing sleep, they also lose the opportunity to meet their loved one in their dreams. The two poetic schools are, on the other hand, similar when they say that meeting the loved one in dreams causes a great disappointment upon waking.[249] The number of quotations from Petrarca, is scanty up to the point that in one whole volume of *Guan Zhui Bian*, there is only one quotation from his work, exactly the same as for "minor" poets. This suggests that Qian Zhongshu did not establish any hierarchy among literary authors. Lesser authors and works, provided they were remarkable for stylistic and content characteristics deemed relevant by Qian, were equally as important as literary geniuses such as Dante or Homer. Poets, great ones like Petrarca or minor ones like the Marinisti poets, are quoted particularly when Qian reflects on the figure of metaphor as in the annex to the XXV chapter of *Tan Yi Lu* where two untranslated lines come from two of Petrarca's poems, the 129 and the 219 and are metaphors about the light of the sun, the moon and the stars. Petrarca is here quoted together with both Chinese and western authors. The quotations are:

Come le stelle, che'l sol copre col raggio
(Like the stars that are covered by the rays of the sun)

---

248  See Petrarca, *Rime*, 187.
249  Qian Zhongshu, *Guan Zhui Bian*, III, 1653.

and

Il sole far sparir le stelle e Laura il sole[250]
(The sun makes stars disappear and Laura does the same to the sun).

Qian Zhongshu provides examples to prove that when there are two or more bright bodies, the more luminous one always obscures the fainter one. The same theme is the one exploited in *Guan Zhui Bian* through a quotation from the Italian poet Trilussa (1871-1950), famous for his poems using the dialect of Rome. Here, the glow-worm laments with the cricket that the moon is too bright and obscures its smaller light. The eight-line poem is entirely quoted in Qian's text; while the first four lines are directly reported in the Chinese translation, the last four are quoted in Italian, right after their translation:

Lucciola, forse, nun ha torto
Se chiede ar Grillo: – Che maniera è questa?
Un pò va bè: però stanotte esaggera! –
E smorza el lume in segno di protesta[251]
(The glow-worm maybe is right
If it laments with the cricket: – This is not the way
A little bit might be fine: tonight it is too much though! –
And turns out its light to protest).

A surprising and noteworthy quotation in a contemporary Italian dialect commenting on *Zhuangzi* has a startling and witty effect. As often happens with quotations from minor poets, or simply with poets less quoted in Qian's

---

250  Qian Zhongshu, Tan Yi Lu, 225. See Petrarca, Rime, 189.
251  Qian Zhongshu, Guan Zhui Bian, IV, 1974. See Trilussa, Tutte le Poesie, 30.

works, as is the case with Trilussa's, his quotation comes from a text of literary criticism. Trilussa's quotation is from *Scrittori D'Oggi* (Today's Writers), edited by Pietro Pancrazi (1893-1952).

A farther advancement of the theme is in *Guan Zhui Bian* where Dante explains that the same luminous body may end up obscuring itself:

> E col suo lume sè medesmo cela; Sì come il sol, che si cela egli stessi
> Per troppa luce; che mi raggia dintorno, e mi nascon de
> Quasi animal di sua seta fasciato[252]
> (And who with his own light himself conceals; Even as the sun, that doth conceal himself
> By too much light; Which rayeth round about me, and doth hide me
> Like as a creature swathed in its own silk).[253]

Right before the quotation Qian warns that politicians do exactly as Dante describes in *Purgatory* and *Paradise*, that is, they wrap themselves with too much glory, as the silkworm does with silk threads or the sun with its irradiating light, to disguise their features and real appearance. Qian clarifies in a footnote that the silkworms mentioned by Dante were raised in Italy after Marco Polo introduced them from China, even if their eggs had arrived in Rome in the 6th century. The concept gives way to what may seem a contradiction; a person who wants to be important and covered with glory often ends up being hidden by the same glory. Far from being an incongruity, this process is described by Benedetto Croce in his *Estetica*, and is quoted in a footnote:

---

252 Qian Zhongshu, *Guan Zhui Bian*, II, 904. See Dante Alighieri, *La Commedia secondo l'antica vulgata*, 244; 305; 315. The correct spelling of the last quotation is "che mi raggia d'intorno, e mi nasconde/quasi animal di sua seta fasciato".

253 Dante, *Purgatorio*, 17, 57 from *The Divine Comedy of Dante Alighieri* II translated by Henry Wadsworth Longfellow, 107; *Paradiso*, 5, 133 from *The Divine Comedy of Dante Alighieri* III translated by Henry Wadsworth Longfellow, 33 and *Paradiso*, 8, 53-54 from *The Divine Comedy of Dante Alighieri* III translated by Henry Wadsworth Longfellow, 50.

Lo stesso principio di contradizione non è altro, in fondo, che il principio estetico della coerenza[254]
(The same principle of contradiction is nothing else than the aesthetic principle of coherence).

Nothing strange then, if arrogant and immoderate behaviour leads to a result that is the opposite of the desired outcome. The thread from Petrarca's poems might seem long and tangled, but the striking combination obtained is probably what Qian intended in composing *Guan Zhui Bian.*

Silkworms appear again in a comment on a line from the *Jiuzhang* 九章 (Nine chapters) of the *Chu Ci* 楚辭 (Songs of Chu) that speaks of a heart blocked and tied that does not understand, a thought obstructed that is not released.[255] The same feelings, of a heart tied as a knot and of a thought as a flowing stream that, obstructed, cannot flow freely, is expressed by Dante, Montaigne, Goethe, Tasso, Shakespeare, Webster (1580-1634), and Petrarca. Petrarca wrote in his *Rime*:

Nè per suo mi riten nè scioglie il laccio[256]
(She neither retains me as hers, nor she unties the lace),

Dante's quotations are:

La tua mente ristretta di pensier in pensier dentro ad un nodo[257]
(Thy mind entangled from thought to thought within a knot)[258]

---

254 Qian Zhongshu, *Guan Zhui Bian*, II, 905. **contradizione** should be spelled **contraddizione**.

255 See Qian Zhongshu, *Guan Zhui Bian*, II, 940.

256 See Petrarca, *Rime* di Francesco Petrarca, con l'interpretazione di Giacomo Leopardi e con note inedite di Francesco Ambrosoli, 116.

257 See Dante Alighieri, *La Commedia secondo l'antica vulgata*, 311.

258 Dante, *Paradiso*, 7, 52-53 from *The Divine Comedy of Dante Alighieri* III translated by Henry Wadsworth Longfellow, 43.

and

Della mente il fiume[259]
(The river of the mind).[260]

After the sequence of quotations, Qian concludes that poets have a spirit of observation far greater than that of writers.

## 5.1.3 Italian tales: Sacchetti, Basile, Bandello, Boccaccio
### Franco Sacchetti (1332-1400)

Kong Fangqing 孔芳卿 reports[261] that Qian affirmed in 1980 that during the previous years he had been reading a lot of Italian short stories from the 16th and 17th centuries, finding their style extremely similar to that of Chinese anecdotal short stories. One of the examples he advanced was Franco Sacchetti's *Il Trecentonovelle* (Three-hundred short stories). Qian considered Sacchetti one of the greatest Italian novelists and often quoted him especially when dealing with imagery, figures of speech or literary images. In *Guan Zhui Bian*, Qian quotes Sacchetti's *Il Trecentonovelle* as well as other Chinese and western authors (Petronius 27-66, Thomas Nashe 1567-1601, Cervantes 1547-1616), with the theme of meat dishes made by animals stuffed with other animals. The example from Sacchetti is the one of a goose stuffed with larks and other fat birds:

---

259 See Dante Alighieri, *La Commedia secondo l'antica vulgata*, 197.
260 Dante, *Purgatorio*, 13, 90 from *The Divine Comedy of Dante Alighieri* II translated by Henry Wadsworth Longfellow, 80.
261 See Kong Fangqing, "Qian Zhongshu Jingdu Zuotan Ji", 82-83. Kong Fangqing's is an account of Qian's speech in Japan in 1980 as part of a delegation from the Chinese Academy of Social Sciences.

Una oca piena d'allodole e d'altri uccelletti grassi[262]
(A goose stuffed with larks and other fat birds).


Another metaphor Qian analyses more than once is that of fruit crying like human beings, and a quotation from the Marinisti poets in *Tan Yi Lu* XI is from *Il Trecentonovelle*.[263] The brief quotation is translated and Qian recalls that in Sacchetti's work there is a boy who believes that figs have tears "avevano la lagrime" (had tears) and that before picking a fig to eat it, the boy thus spoke: "Non pianger, no"[264] (don't cry, don't). Qian concludes that this is a true metaphor even if there is a little exaggeration. Many metaphors cited as examples demonstrate Qian's belief of their importance. All the quotations aim at demonstrating that metaphor is an effective rhetorical device, which Qian affirms to be the basis, or a specific characteristic, of literary language.[265] Other quotations in *Guan Zhui Bian* come from *Il Trecentonovelle*. For example, a quotation from Sacchetti reads:


Il tradimento mi piace, ma il traditore no[266]
(I like treachery but not the traitor)


which is in accordance with a sentence from Plutarch's (45-120) *Lives* that says:


He loved treachery but hated traitors.[267]

---

262  Qian Zhongshu, *Guan Zhui Bian*, II, 1158. See Sacchetti, *Il Trecentonovelle*, 225.

263  A very precise reference is given about *Il Trecentonovelle* with edition and page number.

264  Qian Zhongshu, *Tan Yi Lu*, 137. See Sacchetti, *Il Trecentonovelle*, 130.

265  Chen Ziqian, *Lun Qian Zhongshu*, 38.

266  Qian Zhongshu, *Guan Zhui Bian*, I, 547. See Sacchetti, *Il Trecentonovelle*, 9.

267  Plutarch, *Lives*, "Romulus", XVII. 3-4 (Tatius and Tarpeia), 141.

Another quotation is about different perceptions in sleeping and waking where a man dreams of being surrounded by gold and coins:

Era fra oro e moneta
(He was between gold and coins),

but on waking in the morning he discovers that he was covered by a cat's excrement:

E la mattina si coperse di sterco di gatta[268]
(And in the morning he was covered by cat's excrements).

Apart from similes, Qian is attracted to the rich use of common sayings and of proverbs when he draws from Italian novelists. For example, in the comment on the *Yilin* 易林 in *Guan Zhui Bian* the only western quotation in the paragraph is a proverb from *Il Trecentonovelle*:

Egli avessono preso un cane per la coda[269]
(As if they had taken a dog by its tail).

Proverbs and common sayings are, in fact, a characteristic of the style of 15th century short story writers, and constitute an aspect of figurative language that attracts Qian's attention because it is part of that substratum of universal conceptions and knowledge that comes from popular wisdom through which a global literature is possible. Other proverbs are used to

---

268  Qian Zhongshu, *Guan Zhui Bian*, II, 759. See Sacchetti, *Il Trecentonovelle*, 199.
269  Qian Zhongshu, *Guan Zhui Bian*, II, 824. See Franco Sacchetti, *Il Trecentonovelle*, 191.

explain hexagrams from the *Yilin* 易林, as the one from Dante that says:

Tra male gatte era venuto il sorcio[270]
(Among malicious cats came the mouse)[271]

to comment on the hexagram *dun* 遯. The comment on the hexagram *cui* 萃
uses a proverb from *Dizionario dei Proverbi* by A. Arthaber to say that:

Tante volte al pozzo va la secchia,
Ch'ella vi lascia il manico o l'orecchia[272]
(The bucket that goes many times inside the well sooner or later
Loses its handle or other small parts).

## Giambattista Basile (1575-1632)

Quotations from Giambattista Basile are often connected with
metaphors through all of Qian's works. In a *Guan Zhui Bian* commentary on
the *Shi Jing* 史經 (Classic of History), Qian cites many quotations[273] as
examples of living beings functioning as coffins; the whale with the Prophet
Jonah in its belly, as reported in *Leucippe and Clitophon* by Achilles Tatius (3rd
century A.D.); the wolves eating men in *Lauda delle Malattie* (Laud of
Illnesses) by Jacopone da Todi (1233-1306) "Elegome en sepultura /Ventre de
lupo en voratura"[274] (Choose for my burial, The belly of a wolf who shall
devour me);[275] Ariosto's *Orlando Furioso* "nè chi sepolcro dia /se forse in
ventre lor non me lo danno i lupi" (nobody who will bury me, if not for

---

270 Qian Zhongshu, *Guan Zhui Bian*, II, 870. See Dante Alighieri, *La Commedia secondo l'antica vulgata*, 90. **sorcio** should be spelled as **sorco**.
271 Dante, *Inferno*, 22 from *The Divine Comedy of Dante Alighieri* I translated by Henry Wadsworth Longfellow.
272 Qian Zhongshu, *Guan Zhui Bian*, II, 879.
273 Qian Zhongshu, *Guan Zhui Bian*, I, 604-605.
274 Qian Zhongshu, *Guan Zhui Bian*, I, 604.
275 Translated from Italian by Joan M Bruce-Chwatt in *British Medical Journal* Vol. 285, Dec 1982, 1803, 18-25.

wolves who will maybe give me a burial in their belly);[276] people eating people as in C. Lamb (1775-1834) and E. Goudeau (1814-1858); a person who buries himself in Milton's *Samson Agonistes* or a pan and a belly as respectively coffin and burial, as in Basile's *Il Pentamerone* "ti sarà cataletto una padella e sepoltura un ventre"[277] (A pan will be your coffin and a belly your burial).

These images are the counterpart to the initial quotation about You Meng, a famous and clever actor who used to play tricks on the king of the state of Chu during the Spring and Autumn Period (770-454 B.C.). He convinced his king, who cherished his horse more than anything else in life, not to hold a funeral for his horse as he intended but advised him to do the contrary – to hold a funeral fit for a king. Thus operates a reductio ad absurdum or apagoge,[278] a syllogistic method for which the truthfulness of a thesis is proved by demonstrating the falsity of consequences of the contrary thesis.

At the beginning of the annex that follows, there is another untranslated quotation from Basile's *Pentamerone* in the edition translated by Benedetto Croce. It reads:

> Alcuni fichi freschi, chi con la veste di pezzente, il collo d'impiccato e le lacrime di meretrice[279]
> (Fresh figs, dressed in beggar clothes, having hanged men's necks and whores' tears)

and is, in Qian's words, a pertinent remark and another example of figs having tears like whores. A brief quotation in *Guan Zhui Bian* acts as a

---

276  Ariosto, *Orlando Furioso*, 130.
277  Qian Zhongshu, *Guan Zhui Bian*, I, 605.
278  See Qian Zhongshu, *Guan Zhui Bian* (Zhonghua Shuju) I-56, 694-698.
279  Qian Zhongshu, *Tan Yi Lu*, 137.

counterpart to the comment on the *sui* 隨 hexagram of the *Yilin* 易林 is from the introduction to *Il Pentamerone* by Croce. It presents the image of a monkey with clothes that are an undue and inappropriate component indeed:

Si sa che la scimmia, per calzarsi gli stivali, restò presa pel piede[280]
(It is known that the monkey who wanted to wear boots had its foot trapped).

This is the same image Qian provides in *Taiping Guangji* where the orangutan was caught when trying to wear clogs.

The other quotation from *Il Pentamerone* by Basile taken from the eighth tale of the fourth day is not only translated but even explained. No reference to the source text is given as it is unknown, but assumed, that the edition Qian consulted is the same as the previous quotations. "Time" is the topic and its circularity is proclaimed and substantiated with many quotations from western literature (Tieck 1773-1853, Dryden 1631-1700, Shelley, Basile, Marino) that compare the circularity and infinity of time to a snake biting its tail. Basile's quotation reads:

Dove vedrai un serpente che morde la coda, un cervo e un fenice[281]
(Where you will see a snake biting its tail, a deer and a phoenix).

Qian explains that the deer has a quick pace and represents time that flies, the phoenix, once dead, rises again like the continuous alternation between sun and moon, day and night, and the snake biting its tail is the symbol of a non-beginning and non-end, i.e., infinity.

---

280 Qian Zhongshu, *Guan Zhui Bian*, II, 863.
281 Qian Zhongshu, *Tan Yi Lu*, 281. **Un fenice** should be spelled **una fenice** for the feminine concordance between article and noun.

Another image from *Il Pentamerone* is the one of good females who never smile represented by three quotations in a chapter commenting on the *Shi Ji* 史記. The quotations are not translated into Chinese and, as usual, have a very precise bibliographic reference though two of them bear spelling errors:[282]

> Zoza mai non si vedeva ridere; non c'era ricordo che fin allora [Vastolla] aveva mai riso; per lo spazio de sette anni continui [Milla] non si era più vedeta ridere[283]
> (Zoza was never seen laughing; there was no remembrance of Vastolla laughing; for seven continuous years nobody had seen Milla laughing).[284]

The intent of the 27th entry commenting on the *Taiping Guangji* is to point out large-scale similarities and small variations of the same theme and to incite scholars fond of cultural comparative studies to study the differences between European themes and Chinese counterparts.[285] In this entry, Qian points to striking similarities like the one of a Buddhist story that tells of a person who mistakes another person's reflection in a pond for his own, a subject also found in a story by Basile. Qian quotes names in the source language "la schiava nera" (the black slave) and cites an entire sentence:

> Quale vedere, Lucia sfortunata, ti così bella stare, e patruna mandare acqua a pigliare; e mi sta cosa tollerare, o Lucia sfortunata[286]
> (What see, poor Lucia, you so pretty and mistress sends you water fetch. Poor Lucia, me not stand it longer).

---

282 The right quotations are: "Zoza mai non si vedeva ridere; non c'era ricordo che fin allora [Vastolla] avessa mai riso; per lo spazio de sette anni continui [Milla] non si era più veduta ridere".

283 Qian Zhongshu, *Guan Zhui Bian*, I, 420.

284 For a comment on this see: Zhang Wenjiang, *Guan Zhui Bian Dujie*, 101-102.

285 Egan, *Limited Views*, 183.

286 Qian Zhongshu, *Guan Zhui Bian*, II, 1196.

Egan's English translation simulates the poor grammar of the slave.

## Matteo Bandello (1485-1561)

The final essay of Qian Zhongshu's collection of seven patches *Qi Zhui Ji* is *Yi Jie Lishi Zhanggu, Yi Ge Zongjiao Yuyan, Yi Pian Xiaoshuo* and is the one in which Italian literature is most present. An entire short story from the novelist Matteo Bandello is translated by Qian as the short story, the *xiaoshuo* 小說, of the title. Bandello was a 16th century Italian novelist whom Qian Zhongshu points to as the third (after Boccaccio and Sacchetti) greatest Italian novelist of the Boccaccio School. His tale is almost a replication of one of the episodes that the Greek historian Herodotus (484-425) recounts in *Histories*, and represents the *lishi zhanggu* 歷史掌故 of the title. Bandello's tale, a piece of fiction and not an historical account, is much more adorned and full of narrative colours; Qian writes in a footnote that Ser Giovanni Fiorentino, another Italian novelist, in his 14th century *Il Pecorone*, adds even more details to the same historical episode.[287] Herodotus' narration is one in which the author is quite apart from the content and wants to absolve himself of all responsibilities about the truthfulness of what has been said. In both cases, the authors state that what has been written is quite unusual, and the reader is justified in not believing it. Qian finds the same behaviour in Boiardo's *Orlando Innamorato* (1482) and Ariosto's *Orlando Furioso* (1516). The excursus in Italian short-story writing leads Qian Zhongshu to quote Italo Calvino (1923-1985), one of the more translated and renowned authors in China and two of his short stories whose theme, inheritance, is the same as Bandello's tale.

Another example of this same rhetorical device is at the end of the

---

287 Qian Zhongshu, "Yi jie lishi zhanggu, yi ge zongjiao yuyan, yi pian xiaoshuo", in *Qi Zhui Ji*, 182.

second volume of *Guan Zhui Bian* where the Greek Lucian (2<sup>nd</sup> c. A.D.), and Dante, Boccaccio, Lewis Carroll (1832-1898) and Shakespeare are all quoted with expressions through which they wish to inform the reader that something unbelievable and marvellous is about to occur. Dante's lines, from the *Hell*, say:

> Sempre a quel ver c'ha faccia di menzogna
> ...Ma qui tacer uol posso; e vidi cosa, ch'io avrei paura,
> Sanza più prova, di contarla solo[288]
> (Because without its fault it causes shame;
> ...But here I cannot; and saw a thing which I should be afraid,
> Without some further proof, even to recount).[289]

Boccaccio's sentence reads:

> Il che se dagli occhi di molti e dai miei non fosse veduto, appena che io ardissi di crederlo[290]
> (If this had not been seen by many eyes and by myself I would hardly believe it).

Qian concludes in his essay about literary narration that these foreign writers paid attention to historical truth and to the creation of a "not-me", a *fei wo* 非我 literary character on whom authors can unload responsibilities when their tales have doubtful literary or historical value. According to Qian the *Shengjing* 生經, a Buddhist religious parable, *zongjiao yuyan* 宗教寓言 of

---

288 Qian Zhongshu, *Guan Zhui Bian*, II, 1344. See Dante Alighieri, *La Commedia secondo l'antica vulgata*, 68. **uol** should be spelled as **nol**.

289 Dante, *Paradiso*, 7, 52-53 from *The Divine Comedy of Dante Alighieri* III translated by Henry Wadsworth Longfellow, 43 and Dante, *Inferno*, 28, 113-114 from *The Divine Comedy of Dante Alighieri* I translated by Henry Wadsworth Longfellow, 91.

290 Qian Zhongshu, *Guan Zhui Bian*, II, 1344. See Boccaccio, *Decameron*, 26.

the title, and other Buddhist works are boring and often distant from feelings of truthfulness, making them unappealing to the reader. In Qian's opinion, they do not state the right distance between reality and fantasy, mixing the two realms with the result of being unreliable, both as fictional stories or as true accounts of facts.

In *Tan Yi Lu*, in an excursus on authors who have written about war and military practice, Qian quotes Bandello while writing about the Italian Renaissance author Niccolò Machiavelli. Machiavelli had written a treatise on the art of war, *Dell'arte della Guerra* and Bandello's tale[291] makes fun of Machiavelli because, notwithstanding his authorship of the treatise, he is not able to apply its strategies in real situations. The quotation reads:

> Messer Niccolò quel dì ci tenne al sole più di due ore a bada per ordinare tre mila fanti secondo quell'ordine che aveva scritto, e mai non gli venne fatto di potergli ordinare[292]
> (That day Sir Machiavelli made us stand in the sun for more than two hours to draw more than three thousand infantrymen in the order he had arranged on paper, and he never succeeded in doing it).

Giusti calls military generals who can discuss strategies but cannot apply them "strateghi da cafè"[293] (coffee shop strategists).

### Giovanni Boccaccio (1313- 1375)

Bandello and Boccaccio are referenced in *Tan Yi Lu* XXXIX where Qian discusses the ugliness of imitation. The Chinese translation by Qian Zhongshu precedes Boccaccio's quotation from the *Decameron*, while

---

291 From "Il Bandello al molto illustre e valoroso signore il Signor Giovanni de Medici" in *Le novelle*.
292 Qian Zhongshu, *Tan Yi Lu*, 337.
293 Qian Zhongshu, *Tan Yi Lu*, 338.

Bandello's, a corollary to Boccaccio's quotation, is only cited in Italian with all the relevant references to the source text. It reads:

Il suo viso teneva un poco di quelli di Baronzi[294]
(Her face had something similar to the Baronzi's), i.e., she was ugly.

Boccaccio's novel describes the Baronzi family of medieval Florence as one of its most ancient families. Because the Baronzis were of old stock, God, who had not yet learned how to paint well, made them quite ugly, but old and gentle.

In the analysis of imagery and poetic language Qian Zhongshu recalls Boccaccio's *Decameron* and the woman who made fun of her lover. After spending the night out, she asked him if the fire he claimed to have in his heart for her had been enough to keep him warm! This time Qian does not quote directly but narrates the content of Boccaccio's short story, as a few lines before he had done for Giambattista Marino and his *La Ninfa Avara* in the often quoted *Marino e i Marinisti* who affirmed that poets have much wealth in their hands but do not exactly know how to use it to save themselves from hunger and cold.

All the ideas in these passages, concludes Qian, are similar.[295] Quotations here have the simple function of reinforcing and supporting a global and general assumption and a literary cliché. Another quotation from the *Decameron* has this same function. Here Qian is commenting on the *Chu Ci* and on the use of the word "I" that sometimes represents the same subject responding for the person one is talking to:

---

294  Qian Zhongshu, *Tan Yi Lu*, 346. See Bandello, *Novelle*, 336.
295  Egan, *Limited Views*, 169.

E cominciò in forma della donna, udendolo elia, a rispondere a sè medesimo[296]

(And he started to answer himself for the woman who heard him).

Boccaccio's quotations, like those of other short story writers, are nearly always focused on similes and literary clichés. Through them Qian infers the continuous existence from the past to the present of common literary and cultural themes that make writers timely and modern. In *Guan Zhui Bian*,[297] for example, the modernity of Bandello appears through the quotation from one of his short stories in which he wishes that the world went the other way round and that women ruled men instead of the reverse. Another example is Boccaccio's quotation in a footnote, not translated, that highlights the existence, with Ippolito Nievo (1831-1861), Héliodore (3$^{rd}$-4$^{th}$ c. B.C.), Fouqué (1777-1843), Corneille (1696-1684), and other Chinese authors, of the theme of the strong tie, called a blood tie, between members of the same family:

Quasi da occulta virtue mossi, avesser sentito costui loro àvolo essere;
Da occulta virtue mossa, cominciò a piagnere[298]
(As moved by a hidden virtue, 'cause they felt he was their ancestor;
Moved by a hidden virtue he started crying).

Cheating women and the litigious relationship between husband and wife is the theme of the short story by Bandello from *Le Novelle* (Short Stories) quoted in *Guan Zhui Bian*. In this story a married couple's misunderstanding causes a servant to find himself in bed with the wife and when she tries to hold him, believing him to be her husband, he rejects her

---

296 Qian Zhongshu, *Guan Zhui Bian*, II, 915. See Boccaccio, *Decameron*, 363. **elia** should be spelled **ella**.
297 Qian Zhongshu, *Guan Zhui Bian*, I, 44.
298 Qian Zhongshu, *Guan Zhui Bian*, III, 1585. See Boccaccio, *Decameron*, 651.

causing her rage:

> Ma il barbagianni le diede una gran fiancata, di maniera che ella stizzosa e in
> gran còlera montata gli strinse fieramente i sonagli[299]
> (The fool gave her a blow to the side, so that she was greatly upset and hit him).

## 5.1.4 Epic poetry in literary criticism: Ariosto, Tasso, Boiardo

As with other poets from various literary realms, Qian Zhongshu quotes
epic poets especially because of their interest in poetic imagery and rhetoric
figures. Their lines pass very often through the lens of literary criticism and
are functional to the exposition and the analysis of literary techniques and
rhetoric devices.

### Ariosto (1474-1533)

Qian Zhongshu quotes Ludovico Ariosto's *Orlando Furioso* (Mad
Orlando), an epic poem that had great influence on Italian pre-enlightenment
literature, very often. Ariosto lived as an independent thinker even though he
was a Renaissance courtier poet and defined the autonomy of literature with a
subtle and clever polemic with the contemporary world. The first time Ariosto
is mentioned in *Guan Zhui Bian* is to prove that society has always used two
different criteria of judgements about men and women, since a man can be
dissolute and do as he pleases even in choosing a very young spouse at an old
age, while a woman must keep her chastity and is always subject to the will of
man. Sia maledetto chi tal legge pose",[300] says Ariosto through Qian's
quotation, which means: "the one who set this rule be damned" – a very

---

299 Qian Zhongshu, Guan Zhui Bian, IV, 2210. See Bandello, *Le Novelle*, 76.
300 Qian Zhongshu, *Guan Zhui Bian*, I, 44. See Ariosto, *Orlando Furioso*, 52.

modern concept in 16ᵗʰ century Italy and one that can easily be quoted without being considered out-dated in the 20ᵗʰ century.

As often happens with the Italian philosopher Machiavelli, quoted when the subject is war and military administration, the same inevitably happens with Ariosto, whose main epic poem *Orlando Furioso* is quoted when Qian needs to reinforce concepts about soldiers and war. In *Guan Zhui Bian* a short sentence from *Orlando Furioso*: "chi per virtù, chi per paura vale"[301] (some are brave for virtue, some because of fear) reinforces the concept exploited in the whole entry that often soldiers are induced to be brave more because they fear their superiors than because they are valuable combatants.

### Torquato Tasso (1544-1595)

*Tan Yi Lu* is a field for discussion about art and poetic criticism and a great part of the work is devoted to the analysis of metaphor and of its usage. Discussing metaphor, Qian Zhongshu comes to analyse allegory and demonstrates with the usual support of quotations that allegory is best used in didactic poetry and it embellishes contents otherwise boring and "bitter". This is what the Italian poet Torquato Tasso demonstrates with his metaphor of a child drinking a bitter medicine from a vase with rims sprinkled with a sweet liquid. Tasso's words from the poem *Gerusalemme Liberata* (Jerusalem Delivered) as quoted by Qian Zhongshu are:

> Così a l'egro fanciul porgiamo aspersi
> Di soavi licor gli orli del vaso:
> Succhi amari ingannato in tanto ei beve,
> E da l'inganno suo vita riceve[302]

---

301  Qian Zhongshu, *Guan Zhui Bian*, I, 318. See Ariosto, *Orlando Furioso*, 281.
302  Qian Zhongshu, *Tan Yi Lu*, 570. See Tasso, *La Gerusalemme Liberata*, 3.

(This way we offer to the sick child the vase's rims sprinkled
With a sweet liquid:
Deceived, he drinks bitter medicine
And from this deception his life receives).

Qian wants thus to demonstrate that the moral teachings and the didactic function of poetry are often hidden behind more pleasant words and this is something that is not often grasped. In ancient Greece, for example, some philosophers thought that Homeric epic was devoid of true content, while in China historical poetry is misunderstood for a romantic one. Poetry needs to be analysed in-depth in order to grasp contents hidden under the apparent sweet flavour with which poets like to disguise their more didactic intents.

In the first volume of *Guan Zhui Bian* there is another quotation from *Gerusalemme Liberata* and from the same edition published by Riccardo Ricciardi quoted in *Tan Yi Lu*: "rapido si, ma rapido con legge"[303] (quick but in a regulated way) singularly posed as the only western quotation at the end of many Chinese sentences from Hanfeizi 韓非子, Xunzi 荀子 (312-230), Sunzi 孫子 (544-496), to describe the shape and characteristics of armies. Both Tassoand the Chinese philosophers had described soldiers as a flowing stream moving in a compact and regular way. The sentence that follows from Tasso and *Gerusalemme Liberata* in *Guan Zhui Bian* is quoted in an "army" context again and wants to comment and praise a narration mode that Qian Zhongshu considers an expression of high literary talent. In Tasso, like in Dickens, in the *Zuo Zhuan* 左傳, in Homer and in the *Yuan Mi Shi* 元秘史, the narrator is outside the text and writes in a way that makes the events advance even without directly mentioning the movements. We thus know

---

303 Qian Zhongshu, *Guan Zhui Bian*, I, 263. See Tasso, *La Gerusalemme Liberata*, 33.

things happen thanks to the eyes and ears of characters in the narration and we learn what is going on through the reactions of the characters in the situation.

> Conosce Erminia nel celeste campo
> E dice al re[304]
> (...Recognizes Erminia in the heavenly field
> And tells the king)

writes Tasso in *Gerusalemme Liberata*. Qian Zhongshu wants to demonstrate that the narrator's comment tells us that somebody is walking down on the battle field: it is Rinaldo and Erminia steps further and talks about him with the king. Erminia's eyes are thus functional to the advancement of the action. The whole scene is interesting because the movement enhanced is shown to us through Ermina's eyes and not through the author's direct revealing. We should note though that this quotation is extrapolated in an unusual way from the text since it leaves behind the object of the verb that should have been at the beginning of the quotation. *Conosce*, recognizes, is devoid of object and what Erminia recognizes is the bearing and the white beard of one of the warriors. She then presents him to the king. This is an atypical way of quoting since Qian Zhongshu generally ends up with quotations carefully cut and chiselled in the new text without imperfections that make us wonder about his full understanding of the quoted piece.

The *Aminta* – a *pastorale*, one of Torquato Tasso's works, is a lyric poem describing a peaceful and hedonistic golden era. We find the *Aminta* quoted two times in the unfolding of a literary theme through western and Chinese quotations. Epic poems so full of imagery and based on the narration of

---

304 Qian Zhongshu, *Guan Zhui Bian*, I, 345. See Tasso, *La Gerusalemme Liberata*, 38.

conventional events and ever-told stories are often the object of analysis for Qian Zhongshu when looking for common motives in different literary traditions. This time the starting quotation is from the *Taiping Guangji* and analyses the theme of a rhino looking at itself in muddy water, coming out with an unpleasant image.[305] The poetic trend of mirroring in water is a common image in Chinese and western literatures and among the Italians Tasso, Boccaccio and Leopardi find their place in the entry commenting on the theme. Tasso's words are:

> E già non dico
> Allor che fuggirai le fonti ov'ora
> Spesso ti specchi e forse ti vagheggi,
> Allor che fuggirai le fonti, solo per tema di vederti crespa e brutta[306]
> (I'm not saying
> That there will be a time when you'll fly far away from the fountains where you now
> Often mirror and maybe amuse in your image
> The time when you'll fly far away from the fountains, just because you fear seeing yourself ugly and wrinkled).

Thus speaks Dafne to incite her friend Silvia, who doesn't want to accept the shepherd Aminta's offer to become his lover before time puts wrinkles on her face. Boccaccio echoes with sarcasm:

> Figliuola, se così ti dispiaccion gli spiacevoli come tu dì, se tu vuoi viver lieta, non ti specchiare giammai![307]
> (Oh dear girl, if it's true that you don't like unpleasant things, then if you want to live an easy life, never mirror yourself).

---

305 Qian Zhongshu, *Guan Zhui Bian*, II, 1327.
306 Qian Zhongshu, Guan Zhui Bian, II, 1328. See Tasso, Aminta, 265-269, 10.
307 Qian Zhongshu, Guan Zhui Bian, II, 1327. See Boccaccio, Decameron, 395.

This is an uncle's suggestion to his niece, a snobbish girl who dislikes everybody and doesn't consider that she is not such a pleasant sight as she thinks herself to be. Again from *Aminta* comes the quotation that reports a Satyr's words:

Non son io da disprezzar, se ben me stesso vidi
Ne'l liquid del mar[308]
(I am not to despise, if I saw myself clearly
Mirroring in the sea water).

A bird is the one mirroring in Leopardi's quotation, not in water but in a real mirror and Qian quotes the *Zibaldone* where a bird put in front of a mirror is seen "stizzirsi colla propria imagine" (being upset with his own image),[309] while a monkey throws the mirror on the floor and stamps on it: "lo gitta in terra, e lo stritola coi piedi" (throws it on the floor and crushes it with its feet).[310] The creatures' reaction to their image reflected in the mirror is, quotes Qian with sarcasm, the sign of the great love nature has given us towards beings that are similar to us:

Amor grande datoci dalla natura verso i nostri simili[311]
(Great love given to us by nature towards our counterparts).

This is another case of quotations to enforce a concept and to give authority and justification to the author's thread of thoughts.

---

308 Qian Zhongshu, Guan Zhui Bian, II, 1329. See Tasso, Aminta, 758-760, 26.

309 Qian Zhongshu, *Guan Zhui Bian*, II, 1329. See Leopardi, *Zibaldone* in *Pensieri di Varia Filosofia e di Bella Letteratura*, 4280.

310 Qian Zhongshu, *Guan Zhui Bian*, II, 1329. See Leopardi, *Tutte le opere*, XLVIII.

311 Qian Zhongshu, Guan Zhui Bian, II, 1329. See Leopardi, Zibaldone in Pensieri di Varia Filosofia e di Bella Letteratura, 4419.

## Matteo Maria Boiardo (1440-1494)

Following the literary trend that Qian finds in Dante of creating expectation in a piece of writing without fully explaining everything, Qian discovers it as a distinctive characteristic of Renaissance street singers' (*cantastorie*) popular sung poems of ballads and even of dramas. It was common in these kinds of poems, remarks Qian Zhongshu in the essay *Du Laaokong*, to end episodes or stanzas with a sentence that created expectation or suspension and made the reader expect the continuation of the story. Qian quotes the famous Italian epic poems: *Orlando Innamorato* (Orlando in Love) by Boiardo, 1495 and its sequel *Orlando Furioso* by Ariosto, 1516 several times for a reference. In the essay *Du Laaokong*, *Orlando Innamorato* is even strangely quoted without translation in Chinese:

> Però un bel fatto potreti sentire,
> Se l'altro canto tornareti a odire; Nell'altro canto ve averò contato,
> Se sia concesso dal Segnor supremo,
> Gran meraviglia e più strana ventura
> Ch'odisti mai per voce, or per scrittura.[312]
> (But a good story you might hear
> If you keep listening to the following canto; in it I will narrate,
> If the Supreme Lord would agree,
> Marvelous things and the strangest deeds
> You would have ever heard in speech or in writing).

Or

> Ed ecco un altro canto che si interrompe col fiato sospeso!
> (Here you are another canto ending with a suspense)

---

312 Qian Zhongshu, "Du 'Laaokong'", in *Qi Zhui Ji*, 55. See Boiardo, *Orlando Innamorato*, 35.

which Qian translates as: *Zhe you shi bu yikouqi jiang wan de yipian* 這又是
不一口氣講完的一篇.[312]

Again from *Orlando Furioso*:

Poi vi dirò, signor, che ne fu causa,
Ch'avrò fatto al cantar debita pausa;[313]
Ma differisco un'altra volta a dire
Quel che seguì, se mi vorrete udire[314]
(I will tell you later, oh Lord, the cause of it
Right after a pause in speech;
But I will tell you another day
What happened, if you still want to hear)

translated by Qian as *Qing rang wo xianyixia sangzi, ranhou zai jiang laiyou* 請
讓我歇一下嗓子, 然後再講來由.[315]

In the major work *Guan Zhui Bian* Qian does not quote only Boiardo's
version of *Orlando Innamorato*; when talking about the relation between
hand, mind and tools in a creative process, the author quotes a whole *stanza*
from the *Orlando Innamorato* by Berni, a 16th century recasting of Boiardo's
work. The version Qian quotes[316] is from an English translation by John
Hoole. Woman and her deceiving attitude are the subject of the last quotation
by Boiardo in *Guan Zhui Bian* anticipated by Qian's explanation and not
translated in full:

[Origille] era la dama di estrema beltate,
Malicïosa e di losinghe piena;
Le lacrime teneva apparecchiate

---

313 Ariosto, *Orlando Furioso*, 41.
314 Ariosto, *Orlando Furioso*, 158. **differisco** should be spelled **diferisco**.
315 Qian Zhongshu, "Du 'Laaokong'", in *Qi Zhui Ji*, 55.
316 Qian Zhongshu, *Guan Zhui Bian*, II, 780.

Sempre a sua posta, com'acqua di vena[317]
(Origille was a woman of the utmost beauty,
Artful and full of allurement;
She always had tears ready to use
As flowing water).

The quotation finds its place in an annex, commenting on two Chinese passages from the *Wei Shu* 魏書 (Book of Wei) and the *Shi Ji* 史記, in which two scenes of crying are artfully described, exactly as is the case of Boiardo.

## 5.1.5 Renaissance men: Leonardo, Lorenzo De Medici

To be acquainted with Qian Zhongshu's life and works also means being able to perceive his sphere of preferences and his fields of interest. Renaissance represents for Italy, and for European culture as well, a period of great achievements and a time in which brilliant theories and ideas were elaborated; man was the centre of the universe and his experiences the axis of interest. Qian was attracted by Renaissance personalities and when he quotes from authors like Leonardo da Vinci or Lorenzo de Medici (1449-1492), it is often as a request of authority, their voices being the ones of the age of the rejuvenation of art and literature, as the Chinese word for Renaissance indicates.

### Leonardo da Vinci (1452-1519)

For example, Qian quotes Leonardo in *Guan Zhui Bian* to support Aristotle's assumption that direct perception is not wrong but the judgements on it may be incorrect. His quotation is accompanied by the Chinese translation:

---

317 Qian Zhongshu, *Guan Zhui Bian*, IV, 2235-2236. Boiardo, *Orlando Innamorato*, 386.

La sperienza non falla mai, ma sol fallano i vostri giudizi[318]
(Experience never fails, your judgements do).

The two opening essays of the collections *Qi Zhui Ji – Zhongguo Shi yu Zhongguo Hua* and *Du Laaokong* – are two treatises on traditional Chinese critical appreciation and discuss the relation between poetry and figurative arts, denying their equality. This equality had previously been asserted in the course of Chinese history as the poet Su Shi (11th century) had sustained, affirming that poetry and painting move from the same principle, "*Shi Hua Ben Yi Lu* 詩畫本一律",[319] influencing the history of Chinese aesthetic. Qian Zhongshu notes that this idea is present in western tradition too, but it is there that he finds material to support his denial of this assumption. In *Zhongguo Shi yu Zhongguo Hua*, after noting that sometimes critics misinterpret concepts and ideas, making them the same when they are different and distinct, Qian introduces the main theme of the essay: poetry and painting have often been considered sisters, sometimes even twin sisters; instead, they are two different disciplines. Simonides of Ceos (556-468) and are quoted, followed by Leonardo da Vinci's quotation from his *Treatise on Painting* which reads:

La pittura è una poesia muta, la poesia è una pittura cieca
(Painting is mute poetry, poetry is blind painting)

*hua shi zuiba ya de shi, er shi shi yanjing xia de hua* 畫是嘴巴啞的詩，而詩是眼睛瞎的畫.[320]

---

318  Qian Zhongshu, *Guan Zhui Bian*, I, 469. See Leonardo da Vinci, *Aforismi, novelle e profezie*, 4. The correct quotation should be: *La esperienza non falla, ma sol fallano i nostri giudizi*.

319  Qian Zhongshu, "Zhongguo Shi Yu Zhongguo Hua", in *Qi Zhui Ji*, 7.

320  Qian Zhongshu, "Zhongguo Shi Yu Zhongguo Hua", in *Qi Zhui Ji*, 6. See Leonardo da Vinci, *Trattato della Pittura*, 1270.

In Qian's opinion, this reinforces what was said before and puts poetry and painting on the same level. It seems here, as also noted by Wang Linlin 王琳琳,[321] that Qian's understanding is strangely short-sighted, since it does not consider Leonardo's full meaning, which is not of putting the two disciplines on the same level, but of praising painting more than poetry. Poetry lacks sight, and sight is the most important sense in Leonardo's opinion. Painting is meant for sight appreciation while poetry is directed to the hearing sense. Sight is a more noble sense than hearing, so it is particularly from painting that a harmonic proportion comes out. That proportion is what poetry lacks, due to its lack of appeal to the sense of sight. Qian misinterprets Leonardo, stating that he belongs to the category of people who saw painting and poetry on the same level.

The same focus on painting is reported again in *Guan Zhui Bian*, where Benvenuto Cellini (1500-1571), an important Mannerist artist of the Italian High Renaissance, is quoted with a sentence from his autobiography, where he affirms that poetry is nothing more than falsehood and that an excellent painter, just as a liar, wants to disguise falsity under the robes of truth (la pittura non vuol dir altro che bugia; un pittore eccellentissimo, sì come un bugiardo, s'ingegna di somigliare la verità).[322] The passage does not intend to transmit despise for painting; on the contrary, the main message is the power painting has to be the exact representation of truth. The quotation is, among many other western assumptions, on the same concept and follows a sentence by Boccaccio which says that there was a kind of painting that persuaded people to believe painted things to be true:

---

321 Wang Binbin, "Qian Zhongshu Liang Pian Lunwen Zhong de San ge Xiao Wenti".
322 Qian Zhongshu, *Guan Zhui Bian*, II, 1125. See Cellini, *I trattati dell'oreficeria e della scultura*, 230-231; Boccaccio, *Decameron*, 739.

Che il visivo senso degli uomini vi prese errore, quello credendo esser vero che era dipinto[315]

(That men's sight was mistaken believing to be true what was only painted).

## Lorenzo de Medici (1449-1492)

Again in *Tan Yi Lu* in a long series of *buding* 補訂 (notes) and *buzheng* 補正 (corrections) to chapter 2, the discourse is carried through quotations on *carpe diem* and the importance of living the present to the fulest since the future is uncertain and unpredictable. The only quotation, in a foreign language among the many Chinese poems that invites one to make good use of the present because of the uncertainty of tomorrow, is the famous and over-quoted sentence by Lorenzo de Medici from *Trionfo di Bacco e Arianna* (Triumph of Bacco and Arianna):

Chi vuol esser lieto sia:
Di domani non c'è certezza[323]
(Let whomever wants to be happy be so:
There's no certainty about tomorrow)

translated in Chinese by Qian. The series of quotations ends with a sentence by the author that seems to justify and explain the need to put so many different voices close to one another. Qian says *Xin suo tonggan, sui ru yan chu yi kouer* 心所同感, 遂如言出一口耳 (hearts feel the same emotions and it is as if the voices all came from one mouth).[323]

Again at the end of *Guan Zhui Bian*, Marino's *Adone* is quoted on the same theme (We will dedicate the next paragraph to the analysis of quotations from Marino and his poetic school.) but with a sadder tone, since man is

---

323 Qian Zhongshu, *Tan Yi Lu*, 62. See Lorenzo il Magnifico, *Poesie*, 178.

compared with nature and its ever-renewing spring, while his life appears hopeless in that it decreases and can never be born again:

> Pur col nov'anno il fiore e la verdure
> De le bellezze sue fa novo acquisto;
> Ma l'uom, poichè la vita un tratto perde,
> Non rinasce più mai, nè si rinverde[324]
> (With the new year flowers and green
> Reacquire their beauty;
> But man, since he loses life,
> Is not born anew, and does not become green again).

### 5.1.6 Marinisti: Italian Baroque poetry

Here the Marinisti poets are included in one single paragraph, since all the numerous quotations from this group of 16$^{th}$ century Italian poets most likely come from one single text, *Marino e i Marinisti*, edited by G. G. Ferrero. The page reference is always indicated and, supposedly, Qian knew the text well enough to have quotations from the Marinisti poets ready at hand any time the discourse required a quotation to sustain it.

Giambattista Marino (1569-1625) is considered the greatest representative of Italian Baroque poetry, named *marinismo* after him. He takes the merits of clever use of metaphors, musicality of his verses and rich imagery and the demerits of lack of refined taste and an excessive use of poetic devices in the poetic trend he started. He was greatly admired and imitated during his era, not only in Italy but also in France, Spain, Germany and Poland. During the 18$^{th}$ and 19$^{th}$ centuries, Baroque poetry was often despised, while in the 19$^{th}$ century – with careful revaluation made by critics

---

324 Qian Zhongshu, *Guan Zhui Bian*, IV, 2306. See Marino, *Tutte le opere di Giovan Battista Marino*, volume 2, tomo 1, 718.

like Croce – Marino and Baroque poetry have slowly been rehabilitated in the artistic realm of good literature. We may suppose that Qian Zhongshu read Marinisti's poetry thanks to Croce and was able to appreciate it due to the rich use of metaphors that has always been a preferential sphere of analysis and interest for the author. Particular usage of the artifice of metaphor that was meant to create strange and bizarre images, completely out of the schemes and different from the ones that Petrarca and his poetic school had enhanced was characteristic of the Marinisti. No more blonde and ethereal beauties, but ugly yet prosperous red-headed, humpbacked women with squinting eyes with glasses, sometimes with lice or fleas on their bodies, with breasts like rocks; their lice are like gems or ivory beasts wandering around. It is referreing to metaphors and their usages that sometimes differ, sometimes are similar in western and Chinese poetry, that Qian quotes from Italian poetry – that particular kind of poetry, the Marinisti's, so full of imagery and artistic devices.

The Marinisti are also well known for their capacity to elaborate old poetic themes and introduce new ones in Italian poetry and they are quoted in the fourth volume of *Guan Zhui Bian* as the first in 17th century Italian poetry to introduce the subject of glasses: Giacomo Lubrano (1619-1693) and his poem *L'Occhialino* (Spectacles) and Giuseppe Artale (1628-1679) and his *Bella Donna Cogli Occhiali* (Beautiful Lady with Glasses) are quoted together with Bernardo Morando (1540-1600) and his sonnet *Amante Vagheggiator Con Gli Occhiali* (Suitor with Glasses) and Paolo Zazzaroni (17th c.) and his theme of the beautiful lady with glasses (*La Bella Donna che Portava gli Occhiali*).

In the eleventh chapter of *Tan Yi Lu* Qian quotes Cesare Abelli and Federico Mennini (1636-1712) with excerpts from two poems not translated in Chinese. Cesare Abelli's quotation reads:

De li occhi aprendo il lagrimoso varco[325]
(Opening the tearful passage of the eyes)


and nothing, if not the title of the poem, "Vindemia" (Grape Harvest) seems to give a clue that Qian is talking about western poets. Together with Abelli and Mennini, Qian quotes Sant'Agostino (354-430), who talked about liquid coming out of fruit just like tears that come out of eyes. Mennini's quotation from the poem *Gli Alberi E La Sua Donna* (Trees and his Woman) is:


Per dolcezza d'amore il fico piange[326]
(The fig cries for the sweetness of love)


alluding to the white milk coming out of figs. Figs and grapes cry, the liquid coming out of them is like tears, and these tears are similar to the orchid's dew, which, in turn is compared to tears in the words of Li He and to autumn leaves, representing crying, in *Liezi*.

The relationship between a man and a woman is described many times in *Guan Zhui Bian* as the relation between sky and earth, as earth is loved by the sky,


Ama la terra il cielo e il bel sembiante[327]
(The sky loves the earth and its good appearance)


says the quotation from Marino or with Bruno's words,

---

325 Qian Zhongshu, *Tan Yi Lu*, 137.
326 Qian Zhongshu, *Tan Yi Lu*, 137.
327 Qian Zhongshu, *Guan Zhui Bian*, II, 982. See Marino, *Tutte le opere di Giovan Battista Marino*, 227.

Più di sette mesi sono, che non me ci ha piovuto[328]
(It is already been seven months it hasn't rained on me)

where rain represents man and woman is the earth receiving "man's rain"; or again this relation between men and women is perfectly represented in a long poetic tradition, both Chinese, Li Shangyin 李商隱 (813-858) and *Taiping Guanji,* and western, Robert Burton (1577-1640), J. Dunlop, Keats (1795-1821), Hugo (1802-1885) and Marino, through the interweaving branches or roots of trees:

E due piante talor divise stanno,
Ma sotterra però con la radice,
Se non co' rami, a ritrovar si vanno[329]
(And two trees are sometimes separate,
But underground with their roots,
If not with their branches, they find each other)

is the quotation from *Marino e i Marinisti* and the poem *Dipartita* (Departure) by Marino.

Another quotation from the same text edited by G. Ferrero, a passage from *l'Adone* by Giambattista Marino, whose quotation is not translated again:

Sta quivi l'Anno sopra l'ali accorto
Che sempre il fin col suo principio annoda,
E'n forma d'angue inanellato e torto

---

328 Qian Zhongshu, *Guan Zhui Bian*, III, 1402. See Bruno, *Candelaio*, scena IX.
329 Qian Zhongshu, *Guan Zhui Bian*, II, 1288.

Morde l'estremo e la volubil coda[330]
(There rests the Year careful on its wings,
And it always ties its end with its beginning,
And with the shape of an annulated and twisted snake,
Bites its ending and the mobile tail).

The quotation is part of a longer discussion about time and it's never ending cycle, similar to a snake biting its tail, which has pr eviously been analysed in the chapter about Basile and the Italian novelists.

If time is like a snake, eyes are like a mouth in that they can express feelings without talking:

Fanno ufficio di la labra
Le palpebre loquaci, e sguardi e cenni
Son parolette e voci,
E son tacite lingue,
La cui facondia muta io ben intendo; facondia muta e silenzio loquace[331]
(Eloquent eyelids
Act as mouth, while glances and hints
Are words and voices,
They are like silent tongues,
Whose silent eloquence I understand; silent eloquence and eloquent silence).

Marino's quotation here is not translated literally; instead its meaning is given right before the quotation. Two other quotations on the same theme in reference to Marino's are not translated either. They are by Petrarca:

È un atto che parla col silenzio[332]
(It is an act speaking silently)

---

330  Qian Zhongshu, *Tan Yi Lu*, 281. See Marino, *Tutte le opere di Giovan Battista Marino*, 7.

331  Qian Zhongshu, *Guan Zhui Bian*, IV, 1925. **di la labra** should be **di labra**; **eun** should be **ed un**.

332  Qian Zhongshu, *Guan Zhui Bian*, IV, 1925. See Petrarca, "Sonetto CLXXIX" in *Le Rime del Petrarca*, 459.

and by Tasso

E'l silenzio ancor suole
Aver prieghi e parole[333]
(Silence still
Can be prayer or words).

The two quotations, presenting exactly the same figure of silence that is capable of being eloquent, add nothing new to Marino's lines and are thus in footnote with a function of redundancy and amplification.

The quotation Qian uses to prove that artists often make the mistake of looking for inspiration in the work of other authors, while everything they need is already inside them, comes from *L'Adone* by Marino. This quotation is juxtaposed as a parallel to a commented verse from *Laozi* 老子, which affirms that wise men move without going out and know without moving.[334] Marino's passage in Qian's text without translation is:

Quel che cercando va,
Porta in se stesso,
Miser, nè può trovar quel ch'ha da presso[335]
(What he is looking for
He keeps in himself,
And he cannot find what is near).

In Qian's work no other Italian author is quoted in the original without Chinese translations as often as Marino, and in the fourth volume of *Guan Zhui Bian* we find another long quotation by Marino, accompanied by parallel quotations by Torquato Tasso, Sir Philip Sidney, Webster and Keats,

---

333 See Tasso, *Opere*, 29.
334 Qian Zhongshu, *Guan Zhui Bian*, II, 697.
335 Qian Zhongshu, *Guan Zhui Bian*, II, 700. See Marino, *Tutte le opere di Giovan Battista Marino*, 137.

about the image of trees on the shore of streams that seem to establish a relation of mutual protection with the stream joining in a common effort as friends do. This theme was a common one to Marinisti poets, who were keen on seeing love as a force that permeated earth as a whole and that manifested itself in strong ties between every natural element. Western quotations in this short entry of *Guan Zhui Bian* have an effect of redundancy and create the round table around which the authors discuss without any interference from Qian, chairperson of the discussion. Tasso's words are:

> Bagna egli [il canaletto] il bosco e'l bosco il fiume adombra,
> Col bel cambio fra lor d'umore e d'ombra[336]
> (The stream washes the wood and the wood shades the stream,
> In a mutual exchange of moisture and shadow).

Marino echoes saying:

> Quello [l'arbore] con gli spaziosi rami della sua prolezione favoreggiando questo [il ruscello], e questo porgendo a quello con le vive acque della sua feconda vena vita immortale
> (That one [the tree] with its wide branches favours this one [the stream], and this one gives to that one immortal life with its fertile living water).

The other western quotations that, all together, echo and reinforce the Chinese starting quotation from the first emperor Xiao Yi 蕭繹 of the Liang dynasty (502-557) in his *She Shan Qi Xia Si Bei* 攝山栖霞寺碑 (The Stele of the Qixia Temple on the She Mountain) all play around the same idea.

The passage quoted in the expansion n. 3 to the first note in the first paragraph of *Guan Zhui Bian* again comes from the text edited by G. Ferrero.

---

336 Qian Zhongshu, *Guan Zhui Bian*, IV, 2174. See Tasso, *La Gerusalemme Liberata*, 250. **col** should be spelled **con**.

In it Qian talks about the "activity of immobility" attributed to God, and quotes many other examples of this paradox. We read for example about the running fountain which seems iced in Materdona's (1590-1650) poem *La Fontana di Ponte Sisto in Roma* or a fountain that seems still like crystal in M. Barberini's poem *Sopra una Fonte di Bell'Artificio* quoted from J. Rousset (1910-2002) and his *Circè et le Paon*.[337] J. Rousset is a French critic to whom the rediscovery of Baroque poetry in France is attributed; Giovan Francesco Maia Materdona and M. Barberini are two minor Italian Baroque poets. The quotations from such minor poets from this poetic school confirm the interest Qian had for imagery in poetry and his careful reading of Italian Baroque Marinisti poetry.

Lorenzo Casaburi belongs to the southern Marinisti poets and we find a quotation from his poem in the first book of *Guan Zhui Bian* with a witty line, translated in Chinese by Qian Zhongshu, in which a woman tells her husband, who is willing to go to war, that upon his return his head might have been adorned by horns![338] Wit, humour and rhetoric figures are what Qian appreciates from the literary trend of the Marinisti. His appreciation and use of their lines juxtaposed to both Chinese and western authoritative verses could well be the source of a rethinking and reconsideration of that poetry, not necessarily to appreciate it but at least to look at it in a new light and with a new literary background, praising the novelty and wit typical of the school. This is what Qian Zhongshu aimed at in a way by commenting on Chinese literature through other literatures' quotations, to have a mirror in which to reconsider one's own tradition with a glance not spoil by that

---

337  Qian Zhongshu, *Guan Zhui Bian*, I, 12. The reference to the poet Barberini is imprecise since his name is Maffeo, and does not start with N as reported, and the poem's title is *Sopra una Fonte di Bell'Artificio* (On a Fountain of Good Craftsmanship) and not simply *La Fontana* (The fountain). Under the identity of Maffeo, Barberini is disguised as Pope Urbano VIII. It was customary for Marinisti poets to use a penname for their literary career.
338  Qian Zhongshu, *Guan Zhui Bian*, I, 63.

same tradition, in order to be the most objective and have a fresh new vision.

## 5.1.7 Historians and philosophers between Renaissance and Baroque: Machiavelli, Guicciardini, Bruno, Campanella, Castiglione

Philosophy, religion, and history are the disciplines that recur most often after aesthetic and poetic criticism in Qian Zhongshu's works. Even if he prefers the German area for quotations about philosophy, the author draws sentences and ideas to weave his own thread of thoughts more often from Italian, Latin, Greek and British historians and thinkers.

### Niccolò Machiavelli (1469-1527), Francesco Guicciardini (1483-1540)

Niccolò Machiavelli, Italian Renaissance philosopher, humanist and writer, is considered one of the founders of modern political science. Qian reads directly from his works, often from a collection published by Riccardo Ricciardi in Naples, and quotes him as an example of a rational thinker and wise expert of civil and social matters even if he is not always in accordance with his ideas. In discussing religion and faith, in sayings about demons and God, Machiavelli and Tommaso Campanella (1568-1639) are quoted and translated in *Guan Zhui Bian*[339] to prove that when wise men say they believe in religion it is only because they have to pretend to do so, and are instead muttering against it in the enclosure of their lodgings. Further on in the same chapter Machiavelli is quoted again in a witty passage that links past and present in the blink of an eye. The passage starts with the Chinese, Wang Anshi and the Latin, Svetonius (70-130): both of them talk about celestial phenomena like comets that are said to foretell bad omens for the rulers. It

---

339 Qian Zhongshu, *Guan Zhui Bian*, I, 32-33.

happened then, reports Qian Zhongshu with a three line quotation from *Il Principe* (The Prince) by Machiavelli, again in the Ricciardi edition, that while ruling in the province of Romagna in 15<sup>th</sup> century Italy, Cesare Borgia appointed a very cruel man called Messer Remirro de Orco as administrator of the province. This governor was so harsh in carrying on his duties that all the people were unhappy and unsatisfied. Borgia then, to keep his power in the territory and to avoid insurrection, had the poor man killed in public, saying that if any cruelty had followed, it had not been his fault but the minister's, whose nature was still immature (volle monstrare che, se caudeltà alcuna era seguita, non era nata da lui, ma della acerba natura del ministro [messer Remirro de Orco]).[340]

After Machiavelli's account of Cesare Borgia's hypocritical behavior, the same behaviour is attributed to the American President Richard Nixon, in office from 1969 to 1974 and to his theory, the "Nixon formula", quoted and translated by Qian: "I am responsible; the others are to blame".[341] Qian Zhongshu, supported by Wang Anshi, Svetonius, Machiavelli and contemporary American politicians, affirms then, governors are used to find scapegoats for their crimes and this happens in every state and every period. The melody does not change and history explains a present that was under the author's eyes and was deeply marking the course of his life. Governors are not considered examples of moral coherence with principles and trustworthiness, and Machiavelli is the one who gives them advice on how to survive and defeat the possible opponents. One of the suggestions could be to change and adapt to different conditions from time to time and to prove that

---

340 Qian Zhongshu, *Guan Zhui Bian*, I, 36. See Machiavelli, *Il Principe*, 22. It needs to be pointed out that the quotation carries two graphic mistakes and the right spelling would be: "volle monstrare che, se crudeltà alcuna era seguita, non era nata da lui, ma dalla acerba natura del ministro [messer Remirro de Orco]". See Machiavelli, *Opere Complete*, 300.

341 Qian Zhongshu, *Guan Zhui Bian*, I, 36.

Machiavelli had said it various times, Qian quotes the different expressions used by the Italian writer and by Francesco Guicciardini (1483-1540), putting them in a row without Chinese translation: "temporeggiarsi; procedere con le qualità de tempi; accomodarsi alla diversità de' temporali: si concordano col tempo; [...] si discordano e tempi; si discordano dai tempi" (wait for a favorable opportunity; to act according to time; adapt oneself to the diversity of time; they adapt to time; being time at variance; being at variance with time).[342] Again in Guicciardini's words the same theme is presented in *Guan Zhui Bian* in an entry where Bacon (1561-1626) and Montesquieu are quoted on the same motif as well. This quotation seems to have the function of an invocation of authority, since the author, in talking about the advisability of waiting for the right moment for action and the way in which this moment has been called the "ripe moment" in Chinese literature, remarks that Italian political commentator Francesco Guicciardini had given advice on the need to wait for the time to be ripe:

Aspettare la sua maturità, la sua stagione[343]
(Wait for its ripeness, its season).

exactly as the authors of *Shi Ji* 史記, the *Mengzi* 孟子, *Han Shu* 漢書, *Yi Jing* 易經 or *Li Ji* 禮記 had done.

Machiavelli is together with Guicciardini, the other Italian historian at the time, who talks about the difficult and tricky relation between governors and subjects. In *Guan Zhui Bian* Qian reports Guicciardini's words by saying:

---

342  Qian Zhongshu, *Guan Zhui Bian*, I, 430.
343  Qian Zhongshu, *Guan Zhui Bian*, I, 277. See Guicciardini, *Ricordi*, LXXVIII.

Se e principi, quando viene loro bene, tengono poco contode' servidori, per ogni suo pericolo interesse gli disprezzano o mettono da canto, che può sdegnarsi o lamentarsi uno padrone se e ministri, pure che non manchino al debito della fede e dell'onore, gli abandonano o pigliano quelli partiti che sieno più a loro beneficio?[344]

(If princes take little account of their servants and scorn them or push them aside for the slightest reason whenever they please, why should a lord be offended or complain when his ministers – provided they do not fall short of their debts of loyalty and honour – leave him or take up with those parties that better serve their interests?).[345]

If princes want their subjects to be faithful and complant, they should know them, advises Guicciardini, and treat them exactly as they want to be treated. Emperor Taizong suggests in *Song Shu* 宋書 (Book of the Song) that in order to obtain subjects' appreciation and faithfulness and make the country prosper, governors should behave in a way as to not forget the good deeds of subjects, even if they were done long before and the same subjects have carried out bad deeds after the good ones. It is not correct to forget good actions; rather it is necessary not to do so. The same necessity, reports Qian Zhongshu, is interpreted in the opposite way in the work of the Italian Machiavelli, where the word "necessity" is present many times: "E' necessario; uno principe necessitato; obbediscono alle necessità; è bene necessario; non è cosa più necessaria" (It's necessary; a prince needs to; obey necessity; it's aptly necessary; there's not a more necessary thing).[346] What Machiavelli and Qian want to state here is that princes and governors obey the sole principle of

---

344 Qian Zhongshu, *Guan Zhui Bian*, I, 528-529. The quotation carries a few orthographical mistakes and, as in the *Ricordi* edited by Giorgio Masi should be: "Se e prìncipi, quando viene loro bene, tengono poco **conto de'** servidori, per ogni suo **piccolo** interesse gli disprezzano o mettono da canto, che può sdegnarsi o lamentarsi uno padrone se e ministri, pure che non manchino al debito della fede e dell'onore, gli abandonano o pigliano quelli partiti che **siano** più a loro beneficio?".

345 The translation of the passage is from Guicciardini, *Maxims and Reflections of a renaissance Statesman*, 42.

346 Qian Zhongshu, *Guan Zhui Bian*, I, 544. Three small mistakes are present in the spelling of the quotations that should be: "E' necessario; **un** principe necessitato; obbediscono alle necessità; è **ben** necessario; non **esser** cosa più necessaria". See Machiavelli, *Il Principe*, 52, 145, 313.

necessity most of the time, forgetting every moral code of behaviour. As for the subjects, the suggestion given by many authors like Tacitus (56-117), Montaigne, Philippe de Commines (1445-1511) and Machiavelli, is to avoid bestowing princes favours that are too big to receive a reward, because whoever is so good so as to obtain enormous results in favour of a prince is feared and looked at with suspicion by that same prince.

> Una regola generale la quale mai o raro falla: che chi è cagione che uno diventi potenti, ruina[347]
> (A general rule rarely failing: who determines the greatness of somebody else will in turn be ruined)

and it is impossible that gratitude will be bestowed upon those who have contributed to their greatness (è impossibili ch'egli usino gratitudine a quelli che con vittoria hanno fatto sotto le insegne loro grandi acquisti) because suspicion is aroused (nasce da il sospetto).[348]

Necessity is recalled other times as in *Guan Zhui Bian*'s commentary on *Shi Ji* 史記, when again Machiavelli's *Principe* (Prince) and his "necessità, necessario" (necessary, necessity) are quoted together with his core idea of the need to follow the practical truth of things – the way things are, and not the imagination – things as they are supposed to be: "andare dietro alla verità effettuale della cosa che alla immaginazione di essa"[349] (to follow the effective truth of things and not its imagination).

Wit and fraud, this time operated by armies, are again the subject of another of Machiavelli's quotations from *Discorsi Sopra la Prima Deca di Titio Livio* (Discourses on Livy), published by Riccardo Ricciardi, in which

---

347 Qian Zhongshu, *Guan Zhui Bian*, I, 544. See Machiavelli, *Il principe*, 13.
348 Qian Zhongshu, *Guan Zhui Bian*, I, 544. See Machiavelli, *Il principe*, 152. It should be "**dal** sospetto".
349 Qian Zhongshu, *Guan Zhui Bian*, I, 609. See Machiavelli, *Il principe*, XXXII.

Machiavelli states:

> Ancora che lo usare la fraude in ogni azione sia detestabile, nondimano nel
> maneggiar la guerra è cosa laudabile e gloriosa[350]
> (Even if the use of fraud is always deplorable, nevertheless in managing war it is
> laudable and glorious to use it).

Many examples and quotations in previous pages both from western
(Virgil 70-19 B.C., Xenophon 431-355 B.C., Plutarch) and from Chinese
literature (Hanfeizi 韓非子, Sima Qian 司馬遷 145-86) had been in
accordance with this opinion that Qian Zhongshu seems to support.

The philosopher and poet Francesco Guicciardini is quoted after a
quotation about pleasure from the Italian Pietro Verri with a sentence that
says:

> Molto maggior pracere si truova nel tenersi le voglie oneste che nel cavarsele;
> perchè questo è breve e del corpo, quello – raffredo che sia un poco lo appetito –
> è durabile e dell'animo ecoscienza[351]
> (There is much more pleasure in keeping honest desires instead of satisfying
> them; since satisfaction is short and belongs to the body, when desire has cooled
> a little bit, it is long and belongs to the soul and conscience).

The quotation, devoid of a translation like the ones that follow on the
same subject by Pascal (1623-1662), Chassignet (1571-1635) and Flaubert
(1821-1880), means: there is much more pleasure in keeping the honest
desires than in satisfying them, since this pleasure (the one that comes from

---

350 Qian Zhongshu, *Guan Zhui Bian*, I, 311. See Machiavelli, *Il Principe*, 407. **Ancora che** should be spelled **ancorachè**
and the word **nondimanco** is misspelled as **nondimano**.

351 Qian Zhongshu, *Tan Yi Lu*, 75. See Guicciardini, *Ricordi*, XVII. The quotation has two spelling mistakes; the
correct sentence is: "Molto maggior **piacere** si truova nel tenersi le voglie oneste che nel cavarsele; perchè questo è
breve e del corpo, quello – raffredo che sia un poco lo appetito – è durabile e dell'animo **e coscienza**".

the satisfaction of desires) is short and belongs to the body, the other pleasure (that comes from keeping unsatisfied desires), once craving is diminished, is durable and belongs to conscience and soul. The concept at the basis of this assumption is the same expressed in the novel *Wei Cheng*: whoever is in wants to be out and whoever is out wants to be in. When you have not achieved something, you long for it, and when you have got what you were craving and have satisfied your desires, then you are fed up with the object of your craving and want to get rid of it. At the basis of this idea lies Wang Guowei's 王國維 (1877-1927) proper belief, after Shopenhauer (1788-1860), that happiness is born from desire and desire is due to the lack of something. Men desire because they lack something and the search for this something has its meaning in the satisfaction of desire and the filling the previous deficiency. Nevertheless, the happiness thus reached is fleeting and it is soon followed by disillusion and sadness. This is Wang Guowei's opinion, and Qian follows this idea that life, desire and sufferance are on the same level.[352]

The opinion that consenting to pleasures is a source of unhappiness is also discussed in the third volume of *Guan Zhui Bian* through quotations by John Selden (1584-1654), Aristotle, Crébillon le fils (1707-1777), and is seen by Qian as a concept belonging to and supported by Christianity. There is an opposed secular opinion among the westerners supported only by Italian authors; Dante and Tasso are quoted to illustrate that in a good golden age "bella età dell'oro"[353] there was a happy and golden law made by nature itself, that if you like something, then that "something" is legitimate:

Ma legge aurea e felice

---

352  See Chen Ziqian, *Lun Qian Zhongshu*, 3-6. See Dante Alighieri, *La Commedia secondo l'antica vulgata*, 18.
353  Qian Zhongshu, *Guan Zhui Bian*, III, 1463.

Che natura scolpì: S'ei piace, ei lice[354]
(A golden and happy law
That nature made: if you like it then it is allowed).

To say it in Dante's words:

Che [Semiramis] libito fè licito in sua legge[355]
(Who [Semiramis] reasons subjugate to appetite).[356]

Semiramis is a Babylonian queen said to have been led by the law of luxury. The point Qian Zhongshu wants to make is that it doesn't matter if one consents to pleasures or runs away from them; no man who does not consent to pleasures can be considered virtuous if he does not know what pleasures are about.

Qian points to the same literary theme of a neat distinction between body and soul and the different laws that rule the two in quoting in footnote[357] without any translation, as often happens when quotations are in footnote from Boccaccio and Machiavelli. The two authors offer proof of the common notion that mind and body are two different entities and that the only true sin is the one done with the mind. Thus, if the will is pure, it does not matter if the body sins. The three quotations go directly into the argument and are perfectly suited to demonstrate this literary theme.

---

354  See Tasso, *Aminta*, vv 25-26.

355  Qian Zhongshu, *Guan Zhui Bian*, III, 1402. See Dante Alighieri, *La Commedia secondo l'antica vulgata*, 21.

356  Dante, *Inferno*, 5, 39 from *The Divine Comedy of Dante Alighieri* I translated by Henry Wadsworth Longfellow, 19.

357  Qian Zhongshu, *Guan Zhui Bian*, II, 669. Machiavelli's quotation is from the drama *La Mandragola*, 24, and reads: "perché la volontà è quella che pecca, non el corpo" (because the real sinner is will, not the body). Boccaccio is quoted with two passages both from *Il Decamerone*, 414; 1190: "perciò che ella [la santità] dimora nell'anima e quello che io vi domando è peccato del corpo" (sanctity dwells in the soul, what I ask you is only sin of the body); "per questa volta il corpo ma non l'animo gli concedo" (this time I only grant him the body, and not my soul).

## Giordano Bruno (1548-1600)

In *Guan Zhui Bian* Pietro Aretino (1492-1556) and Giordano Bruno[358] are mentioned together with Virgil, Anthony Hamilton (1646-1720), Mérimée (1803-1870) and Dante Gabriele Rossetti, since in their works there is reference to the same *meidao* 媚道 (technique of allurement), which we find in *Records of the Grand Historian* by Sima Qian, quoted at the beginning of the entry. Another quotation from *Degli Eroici Furori* (*On Heroic Frenzies*, 1585) by Giordano Bruno, again, refers to a narrative technique, or a recurrent image in literature "se non è vero, è molto ben trovato"[359] (if it is not true, it is well received), which used to be so popular in Italy it became a common saying. It refers to behaviour of fictitious characters who disguise opposite intent in a perfect way. Qian takes another passage from the same work by Bruno:

Per tema che difetto di sguardo o di parola non lo avvilisca[360]
(For fear that a mistake in his glance or words might debase him)

that fits perfectly in a discussion starting from *Laozi*, saying that the one who knows remains silent, while the one who does not know speaks. Bruno's passage comes from a discussion about blindness and demonstrates that there are people who refuse to see only because they fear seeing in the wrong way, and do not speak because they are afraid of making mistakes while speaking. Bruno adds that this is also the behaviour of those who recognize the

---

358  Qian Zhongshu, *Guan Zhui Bian*, I, 484. Bruno's reference comes from the *Candelaio* in *Opere di Giordano Bruno e di Tommaso Campanella*, 92-93; as recorded in footnote by Qian Zhongshu, the reference for Pietro Aretino is: Pietro Aretino, *I Ragionamenti*, part I. Another quotation from Giordano Bruno is mentioned in the paragraph *In others' words* of the present work.

359  Qian Zhongshu, *Guan Zhui Bian*, I, 507. See Bruno, *Dialoghi Italiani, II, Dialoghi Morali*, 89.

360  Qian Zhongshu, *Guan Zhui Bian*, II, 704. See Bruno, *Dialoghi Italiani, II, Dialoghi Morali*, 104.

superiority of the object in front of them (if this object is God, for example) and avoid interacting with it for fear of doing it in the wrong way, leaving everything unsaid, yet expressed by the same silence.

Another quotation from Giordano Bruno is linked with the speech and silence theme and with the simile of the not-speaking and not-knowing person as a withered tree and a dying ember. Bruno's quotation comments on an obscure passage from *Laozi* which affirms that ignorance can be defined as saintly (santa ignoranza), madness as divine (divina pazzia) and stupidity as superhuman (sopraumana asinità).[361]

History, as with Machiavelli, is also the subject of the discussion when the philosopher and historiographer Francesco Guicciardini is quoted with a sentence that is accompanied by a quotation by the French scholar Jules Michelet (1798-1874) who regrets the silence of historical writing. Guicciardini says:

> Parmi che tutti gli storici abbino, non eccettuando alcuna, errato in questo che hanno lasciato di scrivere molte cose che a tempo loro erano note, presupponendole come note.[362]

The translation, not supplied by the author, might be: it seems to me that all historiographers, without any exception, have made the same mistake of omitting many things that they considered obviously renowned in their times.

Guicciardini, a 16th century historiographer, is juxtaposed with Michelet, a historiographer from the 19th century, and both comment on a sentence

---

361 Qian Zhongshu, *Guan Zhui Bian*, II, 783.
362 Qian Zhongshu, *Guan Zhui Bian*, I, 493. See Guicciardini, *Ricordi*, n. 143.

from *Records of the Grand Historian* by Sima Qian, a Chinese historiographer from the 2$^{nd}$ century B.C.. Sima Qian, considered a great historiographer and one who was perfectly aware of society and events of his time, is nevertheless accused of having forgotten or consciously omitted talking about the background of the events, leaving us opposite a representation where we can see the actors but not the background scene. Writing a historical account without describing in detail all those particulars and usages, which being of that time were considered obvious, causes a great loss for future generations that will not have all the particulars that the historiographer has omitted. Daily and trivial usages and details are deemed as a stock of facts to get lost, since they change rapidly and no trace can remain if nobody takes note of them to communicate them to future generations. Up to twenty centuries after Sima Qian, the mistake recorded by Guicciardini and Michelet is still the same, and the warning against committing it is presented by them together here with Qian Zhongshu.

The quotation from Guicciardini that follows an assumption by the Greek historian Plutarch comes from the work *Ricordi*. All the previous remarks from Chinese literature, as well as Plutarch's quotation, say that enemy and evil can sometimes be a source of happiness and well-being. Guicciardini's quotation reads:

> La buona fortuna degli uomini è spesso el maggiore inimico che abbino...Però è maggiore paragone di uno uomo el resistere a questa che alle diversità[363]
> (Good fortune can often be man's greatest enemy...but it is more difficult to resist than adversities).

Again this is a quotation that seems to be an invocation of authority and

---

[363] Qian Zhongshu, *Guan Zhui Bian*, I, 359. See Guicciardini, *Ricordi*, n. 164.

proof of a universal truth.

## Baldassarre Castiglione (1478-1529)

Baldassarre Castiglione, author of *Il Cortegiano* (The Courtesan), is quoted in *Tan Yi Lu* XI regarding a metaphor. Qian had already talked in a more extensive way about metaphors[364] and about Li He's method. A metaphor, he says, can be elaborated between objects that have something in common but are not precisely the same thing because if they were the same, there would not be any need to compare them through metaphors. Castiglione's quotation is taken from a novel narrated by Qian Zhongshu that tells the story of merchants doing business with clients while standing on different sides of an iced river. The weather was so cold that even words iced before reaching the other bank of the river and they could not be heard. Finally a fire was lit in the middle of the river, up to where the words were supposed to arrive before becoming iced and:

> Le parole che per spazio d'un'ora erano stato ghiacciato, cominciarono a liquefarsi e discender giù mormorando come la neve dai monti il Maggio[365] (Words that for an hour had been frozen started to melt and to flow down, murmuring like snow from mountains in May).

The quotation is from the 1928 edition of the Biblioteca Classica Hoepliana and it carries a mistake in agreement between a feminine noun (*parole*, words) and a participle that should be in the feminine form and instead is in the masculine (*stato ghiacciato* instead of *state ghiacciate*). The quotation is thus probably recollected by heart or copied from not very

---

364 Egan, *Limited Views*, "metaphor has two handles and several sides", 121-129.
365 Qian Zhongshu, *Tan Yi Lu*, 134. See Castiglione, *Il Cortegiano*.

readable notes. The same source has another quotation in *Guan Zhui Bian* where Castiglione, in accordance with other quoted writers (Herodotus, W. Hildesheimer 1916-1991, E. Frenzel) affirms that women are often the source of calamities and disgraces:

> Spesso le bellezze di donne son causa che al mondo intervengon infiniti mali, inimizie, guerre, morti e distruzioni; di che pò far bon testimonio la ruina di Troia[366]
> (Often women's beauty is a source of infinite evils, enmities, wars, death and destruction; proof of this is in Troy's ruin).

Like the previous quotation from *Il Cortegiano*, this one brings two mistakes in agreement as well (verb *intervegon* instead of intervengan) and in spelling (*inimizie* instead of *inimicizie*). Not only women, but also men in general might bring great damage to the world, and here we may as well read a criticism of Qian's contemporaneity.

### Tommaso Campanella (1568-1639)

To this purpose Qian also quotes Tommaso Campanella, a 17th century Italian philosopher, with the French Georges Eugène Sorel (1847-1922) and Guillaume Apollinaire (1880-1918) as the three examples from the western literary world to comment on and reinforce a simile from the Taoist classic *Taiping Jing* 太平經, where men are compared to lice, as small in comparison with earth and sky and as injurious to earth as lice are to men. Campanella's quotation, accompanied by a free translation by Qian, reads:

> Il mondo è un animal grande e perfetto,

---

366  Qian Zhongshu, *Guan Zhui Bian*, I, 354. See Castiglione, *Il Cortegiano*, LXVI.

Statuo di Dio, che Dio laude e simiglia:
Noi siam vermi imperfetti e vil famiglia,
Ch'intra il suo ventre abbiam vita e ricetto.
[...]
Siam poi alla terra, ch'è un grande animale
Dentro al massimo, noi come pidocchi
Al corpo nostro, e però ci fan male[367]
(The world is a big and perfect animal,
Statue of God, similar to him,
We are imperfect worms and base family
Living in his womb
[...]
Compared to earth, that is a big animal,
And we are animals living in it, we are like lice living on
Our body, and very injurious too).

A strong attack, it seems, in an age where men considered themselves absolute rulers of the territory they governed and did not confer nature any right to interfere with their plans.

## 5.1.8 The light of reason: Vico, Muratori, Beccaria, Verri

The love for concrete references and practical assumptions brings Qian to read and appreciate Enlightenment works, quoted for their capacity to throw light on phenomena and events of the world. Vico, Muratori, Beccaria and Verri are the most quoted Enlightenment personalities, together with a reference to the playwright Carlo Goldoni (1707-1793), renowned for his "popular Enlightenment" and his support for a rational and regulated society in which each social class accepts its role and works for the harmony of the whole system.

---

367 Qian Zhongshu, *Guan Zhui Bia*n, III, 1719-1720. The quotation carries two spelling mistakes **statuo** for **statua**, **grande** for **gran**. See Campanella, *Il Nuovo Prometeo*, 46-47.

## Giambattista Vico (1668-1744)

Vico and his *Principi di Scienza Nuova* (New Science) are quoted when referring to the images from *The Book of Changes* that are emblematic, abstract references to signify abstract concepts:

> I caratteri poetici, che sono generi o universali fantastici[368]
> (Poetic characters that are imaginary or universals types).

This idea is based on the same process of conveying intent by borrowing concrete things[369] often used in Chinese poetry. No poetry could do without the help of imagery; all the quotations in the entry of *Guan Zhui Bian*[370] would demonstrate that.

We find a quotation from *Scienza Nuova* again in *Guan Zhui Bian* when Vico's assumption serves only to confirm what was stated in the entry, the common order of ideas should proceed in accordance with the order of things:

> L'ordine dell'idee dee procedere secondo l'ordine delle cose[371]
> (The order of ideas should procees in accordance with the order of things).

Vico, as representative of the light of reason, is the one we find in *Guan Zhui Bian* when, in a series of Chinese and western quotations that comment on the issue of whether one should eat and drink when in grievance, he brings forward an opinion in his *Scienza Nuova* that opposes the majority of the

---

368  Qian Zhongshu, Guan Zhui Bian, I, 19. See Vico, Opere, 56.
369  Egan, *Limited Views*, 134.
370  Qian Zhongshu, *Guan Zhui Bian*, I, 15-24.
371  Qian Zhongshu, *Guan Zhui Bian*, I, 85. See Vico, Opere, 58.

other writers' opinions. In commenting on what Homer wrote about his heroes, Vico considers their eating and drinking attitude despicable when their soul is full of grievance, and considers it unfit to the characterization of whatsoever heroes' behaviour:

sono afflittissimi d'animo, porre tutto il lor conforto in ubbriacarsi[372]
(they are in deep grievance and put all their consolation in getting drunk).

## Ludovico Antonio Muratori (1672-1750)

Qian Zhongshu quotes Muratori from *Genesis of the Romantic Theory in the Eighteenth Century* by J. G. Robertson in a discussion about aesthetic and the relation between art and nature. Muratori states that art has to "make nature distinguished" (far eminente la natura)[373] taking the position of those who, like Plotinus, Bacon, Horace, Baudelaire, Dante, believe that man must force nature. Man, in fact, cannot only imitate and needs instead to add something to create works that embellish and overcome nature.

## Cesare Beccaria (1738-1794)

Cesare Beccaria is very representative of Italian Enlightenment; he became known to the philosophic and intellectual world of his age thanks to a booklet called *Dei Delitti e delle Pene* (On Crimes and Punishments) published when he was only 25. The aim of the booklet was to demonstrate that the current justice system was absurd and could not guarantee the righteousness of state administration. Beccaria contests the death penalty particularly and the way in which both innocents and culprits were tortured

---

372 Qian Zhongshu, Guan Zhui Bian, I, 396. See Vico, Principj di Scienza Nuova, 305.
373 Qian Zhongshu, *Tan Yi Lu*, 155.

to confess crimes. "La tortura", states Beccaria, "è il mezzo sicuro di assolvere i robusti scellerati e di condannare i deboli innocenti"[374] – torture is the assured way to acquit strong wicked men and to condemn weak innocents. Beccaria's words are just one of the portions on the condemnation of torture that with the help of logical reasoning, together with examples from Chinese (*Taiping Guang Ji*) as well as from western literature (Quintilian, Montaigne), seem to convey Qian Zhongshu's ideas about the absurdity of the treatment that governments carry on to establish the guilt or innocence of people. Under torture, says Qian through Quintilian, one who is able to endure sufferance does not confess the truth, and one who cannot endure physical pain confesses falsely just because the body in distress is forced to do so. The temptation to link this criticism with the political and historical situation during the years immediately preceding the publication of *Guan Zhui Bian* is instantaneous if we identify the mild form of physical sufferance that many had to undergo wearing a donkey hat and a poster confessing inconsistent crimes with torture as well.

### Pietro Verri (1728-1797)

The starting point for a discussion about joy and sorrow is the Italian philosopher Verri and one of his important works, *Il Discorso Sull'Indole del Piacere e del Dolore* (Discourse on Pleasure and Sorrow). This work is recalled with the translated quotation that reads:

> Il piacere non è un essere positivo[375]
> (Pleasure is not a positive essence).

---

374 Qian Zhongshu, *Guan Zhui Bian*, I, 536. See Beccaria, *Dei delitti e delle pene*, 83.
375 Qian Zhongshu, Tan Yi Lu, 75. See Verri, Scritti vari, 5.

No further indication is given about Verri's text, apart from the translated title. The sentence comes from an introduction to an edition by Verri of his treatise written in 1781 and the fact that Qian Zhongshu does not give indications about the edition of the book may signify that the sentence is probably taken from Qian's previous notes or from other texts from whence it had been quoted. Verri explains and demonstrates – with the support of other important philosophers and thinkers like Magalotti, Plato, Montaigne and Locke (1632-1704) – that pleasure is born from a temporary suspension and a lack of sufferance.

The Enlightenment playwright Goldoni finds his place in an entry of *Guan Zhui Bian*, commenting on the *Taiping Guangji* about a literary theme Qian finds common in many epochs and places: the swindler who wants to cheat collectors with fake curio and antiques. After many Chinese quotations that spread over the course of two pages, Goldoni's famous drama *La Famiglia dell'Antiquario* (The Antique Dealer's Family) is present with two quotations about the swindler who says an old shoe is Emperor Nero's slipper, the same slipper with which he is said to have kicked Poppea:

> La pantofola de Neron, colla qual l'ha dà quell terribil calzo a Poppea.
> (Nero's slipper, the one used to kick Poppea with much energy).

The swindler also boasts a hair plait to be that of Sesto Tarquini which was taken from Lucrezia Romana's head in a fight:

> La drezza de cavelli de Lucrezia Romana, restada in mano a Sesto Tarquini[376]
> (Lucrezia Romana's tress, that ended up in Sesto Tarquini's hand).

---

376 Qian Zhongshu, *Guan Zhui Bian*, 1188. See Goldoni, *Opere*, 99.

We might find the two episodes of cheating even more ironic if we consider that both Nero kicking Poppea and the fact that Sesto Tarquini pulled a plait from Lucrezia Romana's head are most probably historical falsehoods.

## 5.1.9 Leopardi, Manzoni and 19th century poetry and novels
### Giacomo Leopardi (1798-1837)

*Zibaldone*, by the great Italian poet Leopardi, is a work made of *biji*, notes, and Qian loves to recall it. Leopardi was much appreciated by the author who wrote that it was a pity not many Chinese would read the Italian writers' works. In *Tan Yi Lu* Leopardi is quoted the first time in a discussion about poetry, the lyric and the dramatic one. A quotation by Leopardi says that dramatic poetry is not real poetry, since real poetry is the spontaneous overflow of emotions, and this cannot be reached by a writer who needs to reverse his personality into another fictitious character. Leopardi's quotation is:

> L'estro del drammatico è finto, perchè ei dee fingere... Così delle Orazioni di finta occasione. Or che altro è la drammatica? Meno ridicola perché in versi?[377]
>
> (The inspiration of the dramatist is false, since he has to simulate...It is like odes written for fake occasions. What else is dramatic poetry? Is it less ridiculous just because it is written in verses?)

The quotation is preceded by a Chinese explanation that renders the meaning of Leopardi's words. Notwithstanding Qian's appreciation for Leopardi, we find he is not in accordance with this Italian writer's opinion. If, says Qian, dramatic poetry is not the real type of poetry, how is it that the

---

377  Qian Zhongshu, *Tan Yi Lu*, 96. See Leopardi, *Pensieri di varia filosofia e di bella letteratura*, 2924.

most important literates from the Ming and Qing dynasties took dramatic poetry as an example to study the composition of *bagu* 八股 (eight part essay to be written for the exams in imperial China)? We wait, adds Qian, for scholars willing to do research to answer this question!

Pages later, we find Leopardi again in a discussion about poetry, and he is in the company of many other western poets: Baudelaire, Poe, Whitman (1819-1892), Max Jacob (1876-1944). This time western quotations are not preceded as usual by the Chinese ones, and serve to explain and reinforce a characteristic belonging to Chinese literary tradition. The many voices say that good poems cannot be long and Leopardi affirms:

> La poesia sta essenzialmente in un impeto; i lavori di poesia vogliono per natura esser corti[378]
> (Poetry is essentially an outburst; the essence of poems is brevity).

Pages later a definition given by Leopardi, the one of poetry as "vera e pura poesia in tutta la sua estensione" (true and pure poetry in all its extension)[379] from the *Zibaldone*, is a proof of the existence and canonization of the definition of "pure poetry" to which Qian is devoting the whole CXXXVIII chapter of *Tan Yi Lu*.

One of the main intents in *Guan Zhui Bian* is to prove through juxtaposition that all literary realms are linked together and that there is a common spirit in literatures and cultures belonging to different epochs and places. Qian Zhongshu wants to demonstrate that many concepts and ideas are universal. Proof of this universality of concepts and themes is offered in

---

378 Qian Zhongshu, *Tan Yi Lu*, 511. See Leopardi, *Pensieri di varia filosofia e di bella letteratura*, 2925.
379 Qian Zhongshu, *Tan Yi Lu*, 673. See Leopardi, *Pensieri di varia filosofia e di bella letteratura*, 2796.

*Guan Zhui Bian* commenting on a passage of *Guixi* 詭習 in *Taiping Guangji* and the already quoted *Zibaldone*. In his work Leopardi describes a child born without arms capable of using his feet to perform all the operations he should have done with hands and a girl capable of embroidering with her feet:

> Io ho veduto un fanciullo nato senza braccia, far coi piedi le operazioni tutte delle mani; ho inteso di una donzella benestante che ricamava coi piedi[380]
> (I have seen a child born without arms, and he was doing with his feet all the operations for which hands are usually used; I have heard of a well-off girl who embroidered with her feet).

The same image is the one Qian comments from the *Guixi*.

In the first volume of *Guan Zhui Bian* Qian quotes Leopardi's most famous poem, *L'Infinito* (The Infinity) that would also have suggested ideas of distance that enhance the sense of longing. The quoted beginning of the poem here evokes an image of distance amplified by a near object that shields the view of the far expanding horizon:

> Sempre caro mi fu quest'ermo colle,
> E questa siepe
> Che tanta parte dell'ultimo orizzonte il guardo esclude[381]
> (This hillside has always been dear to me,
> And this hedgerow
> Which shields from sight a huge portion of the horizon).

To an Italian reader this passage would evoke a sense of extreme familiarity and participation, but to others it would surely be obscure and puzzling since the translation of the passage is not provided in Qian's text,

380 Qian Zhongshu, *Guan Zhui Bian*, II, 1122. See Leopardi, *Pensieri di varia filosofia e di bella letteratura*, 1484.
381 Qian Zhongshu, *Guan Zhui Bian*, I, 234. See Leopardi, *Opere*, 50.

and only the explanation of its content is there with the reference to the Italian version of Leopardi's collection of poems *I canti* in footnote.

Leopardi's technique, having a small object (the hedgerow) placed close to the field of vision to make a counterpart to the infinity of space, is considered a skill in poetic practice by Vincenzo Cardarelli (1887-1959), quoted with his *Momenti e Problemi di Storia dell'Estetica* (History of Aesthetics: Moments and Problems) edited by Carlo Marzorati.[382] Today Cardarelli's work is included in the book catalogue of the Bodleian Library, the main source of documents for Qian in 1937-1938, but since the book is dated 1959, it is impossible Qian had read it during his stay at Oxford. It would be a very interesting object of analysis to understand how and where Qian Zhongshu had the possibility to access such rare and not very widespread works like this one during the 60's and 70's of last century.

Leopardi is quoted again when talking about obscurity in poetry; the passages come from *Zibaldone*:

Idée e pensieri vaghi e indefiniti; confonde l'indefinito coll'infinito; una piccolissima idea confusa è sempre maggiore di una grandissima, affatto chiara; il lasciar molto alla fantasia ed al cuore del lettore; descrivendo con pochi colpi e mostrando poche parti dell'oggetto, lasciavano l'immaginazione errare nel vago; sono poetissme e piacevoli, perché destano idee vaste, e indefinite; è piacevole per il vago dell'idea[383]
(vague and indefinite ideas and thoughts; mistakes the indefinite with the infinite; a very small, confused idea is always bigger than a very big, unclear one; leaving much to the fantasy and the heart of the reader; describing with few strokes and disclosing only small parts of the objects, leaving the imagination to wander in vagueness; they are very poetic and pleasant because they arouse big and indefinite ideas; it is pleasant because of the vagueness of the idea).

---

382  Qian Zhongshu, *Guan Zhui Bian*, I, 234.
383  Egan, *Limited Views*, 108. See Leopardi, *Pensieri di varia filosofia e di bella letteratura*, 111; 411; 1046; 90; 134; 1236; 2868. poetissme should be spelled **poeticissime**.

Many different bits and pieces are brought together from Leopardi's works using the technique of juxtaposing many quotations that cross the various fields of artistic creation.

Obscurity in poetry and the sense of indefinite that poets pursue is what Qian finds in *Fronde Sparte* (Scattered Branches) by Giulio Natali, a work quoted in footnote that is a collection of notes and sketches similar to the same *Guan Zhui Bian*, but based only on literary critic.

Nature is a leitmotif that Qian Zhongshu seems to pursue when reading Leopardi, who states in a quotation from the poem *La Ginestra* (The Genista) in *Guan Zhui Bian* that nature is

Madre è di parto e di voler matrigna[384]
(Mother by birth and step mother by will).

In more of a paraphrase than a translation from Italian, Qian explains:

As for its procreation and nurturing, nature is man's loving mother, while as for its aims and desires, nature is man's step mother.[385]

The theme is recalled again further in the third volume of *Guan Zhui Bian* where Leopardi laments nature not being compassionate with men:

La natura [...] pietosa no, ma spettatrice almeno[386]
(Nature [...] not compassionate but at least witness).

---

384 Qian Zhongshu, *Guan Zhui Bian* II, 652. See Leopardi, *Opere*, 106. The right quotation should be: "è madre in parto ed in voler matrigna".
385 Egan, *Limited Views*, 270.
386 Qian Zhongshu, *Guan Zhui Bian* III, 1859. See Leopardi, *Canti*, 31.

The hint Qian seems not to notice in this quotation from Leopardi's poem *Alla Primavera o delle Favole Antiche* (To Spring or on Ancient Fables) is that Leopardi seems to leave a small opening to nature, saying that if it is not compassionate, it could at least be a spectator and participate in a way, even if shallow, to the destiny of men.

*La Ginestra* is quoted again in the fourth volume of *Guan Zhui Bian* with a reference to nature that is well inscribed in the more general panorama of other western quotations on phenomena that happen in nature and that often go unnoticed. Leopardi's words, preceded by Qian's Chinese translation, are:

> Tuoi cespi solitari intorno spargi,
> Odorata ginestra,
> Contenta dei deserti.[387]
> (You scatter around your solitary bushes,
> Fragrant genista,
> Happy with deserts).

Another reference to nature comes from *Dialogo della Natura e di un'Anima* (Dialogue between Nature and a Soul) from Leopardi's *Operette Morali*. Here both a quotation from Leopardi and one from Arturo Graf (1848-1913) are meant to reinforce or offer an opposite view to a concept present in Chinese (Li He, Yuan dynasty, Song dynasty)[388] and western (Babbitt, Schiller, Pascal, Coleridge, Schmack, Keats, La Fontaine) literatures as well.

Literature and the creative process of literary works is a theme that recurs often in all of Qian's works, from the short story *Linggan* 靈感 (Inspiration),

---

387  Qian Zhongshu, *Guan Zhui Bian* IV, 2106-2107. See Leopardi, *Opere*, 103.
388  Qian Zhongshu, *Guan Zhui Bian*, I, 254-257.

where a petty writer goes to hell and is pursued by the characters of his novels because he had handled their lives in a poor way, to *Guan Zhui Bian*, where in many entries Qian comes to discuss literary creation. In the entry *Fa fen zhu shu* 發憤著書 in the third volume Qian uses quotations and examples to support the opinion that happy and satisfied people are less prone to artistic creation, while literates usually are unhappy people. In Jacob Burckhardt's (1818-1897) *Die Kultur der Renaissance in Italien* (The Civilization of the Renaissance in Italy) he quoted the work *De Literatorum Infelicitate* (On the Misfortunes of Literates) by Piero Valeriano (...-1302),[389] an Italian humanist who wrote this book in a dialogical form, and it is recalled by Qian. It is most probable that Qian just heard of the book by Burckhardt, since he would have otherwise quoted from the original instead of reporting the book in footnote whence the reference happens to come.

As for literature, the same is applicable for music and for the appreciation of music in particular, as in the entry *Hao yin yi beiai wei zhu* 好音以悲哀為主[390] where Qian expressly states that he will go through the subject with a few quotations to add clues to the treatment already carried out. Here a passage from Leopardi's *Zibaldone* intends to demonstrate the fact that music, good music, is linked to sadness, while being a truth, it is also something that only advanced and civilized people might grasp. Leopardi's quotation reads:

> In somma, generalmente parlando, oggidl, fra le nazioni civili, l'effetto della musica è il pianto, o tende al pianto...Ora, tutto al contrario di quello che avviene costantemente fra noi, sappiamo che i selvaggi, i barbari, i popoli non avvezzi alla musica...in udirne qualche saggio, prorompono in éclats di giubilo,

---

389 Qian Zhongshu, *Guan Zhui Bian*, III, 1494. In Qian's quotation, both the name of the author and the name of the work are wrong; he reports *De Infelicitate Literatorum* by Pierio Valeriaino.

390 Qian Zhongshu, *Guan Zhui Bian*, III, 1506-1511.

in salti in grida di gioia[391]
(In general terms among civilized nations nowadays music makes people cry, or move towards crying... Now, contrarily to what usually happens among us, we know that barbarians, savages and people not used to listening to music...when they hear it, they are happy and have éclats of joy, they jump and cry for happiness).

Thus, Leopardi's quotation brings forward the point Qian wants to make: it is possible to be happy when hearing good music, but to be happy is not the sign of appreciation that wise people would demonstrate. Those people who express joy while hearing good music are not the right ones to enjoy the best of it.

Other quotations that follow in *Guan Zhui Bian* are again about feelings, this time pertaining to the sky instead of human beings. In nature, creatures that are less conscious of their life, "fornito di minore vitalità e sentimento"[392] (having less vitality and consciousness), reads the quotation from Leopardi, are the ones that live longer and do not grow old because they are not spoiled by feelings, grievances and passions. Li He wrote in a poem that the sky would grow old if it had feelings and Arturo Graf in his poem *L'Azzurro* (Sky-blu) wrote that the sky is the same today, as it was yesterday and as it will be tomorrow:

Tal ieri, tal oggi, tal sarai domani.

The quotation continues:

E tu, privo d'amor, privo di senso

391  Qian Zhongshu, *Guan Zhui Bian*, III, 1508. See Leopardi, *Pensieri di Varia Filosofia e di Bella Letteratura*, 2070. **Oggidì** is here mispelled in **oggidl**.
392  Qian Zhongshu, *Guan Zhui Bian*, I, 220.

(And you, without love and without consciousness),
Tu sol, tu solo incolume, immortale,
Incorrotto, glacial come un coverchio
Smisurato d'avel pesi sul mondo[393]
(You, only you, undamaged, immortal,
Uncorrupted, iced like the huge cover
Of a coffin weighing on the world).

Qian Zhongshu says all these ideas about the sky being unchangeable and immortal, thanks to its lack of feelings, complete one another and make the vision of the sky become a comprehensive one. Moreover, considering both authors' (Li He and Arturo Graf) views and their different spatial and time conditions enriches our point of view. What should be noticed here is that Qian translates the poem by Arturo Graf, which comes from a work edited by Baldocci called *Poeti Minori dell'Ottocento* (Minor Poets of the Nineteenth Century) and his interpretation of a word like "avel," classical form of the world "tomba" (tumb), is precise and well translated in Chinese.

*Du "Laaokong"*, 1962, is an essay that perfectly illustrates Qian Zhongshu's method of justaxposition. The main theme here is the way in which painters can render poetic figures and the link between poetry and painting. Talking about metaphor and rhetoric figures Qian cannot avoid quoting from Italian criticism. A distinctive characteristic of Qian Zhongshu's mastering of quotations appears there: he very often quotes minor literati, sometimes unread even by Italian scholars. Benedetto Menzini (1646-1708) is an Italian poet belonging to the Academy of Arcadia cited in *La Crestomazia Italiana* (Italian Anthology), one of Leopardi's minor works. The quotation does not even come from one of Menzini's major poems but from a critical treatise on the irregular construction of the language of Tuscany, the region of

---

393 Qian Zhongshu, *Guan Zhui Bian*, I, 220. See Graf, *Le Poesie*, 133.

Florence. Menzini affirms in this essay that "Figura è un errore fatto con ragione" (Simile is a consciously made mistake).[394]

*Lin Shu de Fanyi* is a long essay about translation that starts with a quotation from Leopardi and his *Zibaldone* where the poet says that to obtain a good translation the source and the target text should seem not compatible or even contradictory (paiono discordanti e incompatibili e contraddittorie) and the translator should pretend (ora il traduttore necessariamente affetta) to follow the truthfulness and spontaneity of the source text (inaffettato, naturale o spontaneo).[395] Qian is even able to quote a popular Italian saying "traduttore-traditore" (translator-traitor)[396] about the changes a text undergoes when translated into another language. Qian's view on translation, in accordance with Leopardi's point of view, is that "faithfulness requires 'meaning grasped, words forgotten'" *de yi wang yan* 得意忘言, the meaning should be conveyed in such a perfect way that words should be an instrument for it without obstructing it with their strangeness or encumbrance.[397]

The aforementioned is not the only quotation from Leopardi's translation related ideas. In *Guan Zhui Bian*, following a discussion about imitation on one side and artistic or literary creation on the other, Leopardi

---

394  Qian Zhongshu, "Du Laaokong", in *Qi Zhui Ji*, 45. The quotation is from Menzini, *Della costruzione irregolare della lingua Toscana*, quoted in Leopardi, *Crestomazia italiana*, 110.

395  Qian Zhongshu, "Lin Shu de Fanyi", in *Qi Zhui Ji*, 78. See Leopardi, *Pensieri di varia filosofia e di bella letteratura*, 310.

396  Qian Zhongshu, "Lin Shu de Fanyi", in *Qi Zhui Ji*, 78.

397  Zheng Xiaodan, *A study on Qian Zhongshu's translation*, 70-83. Zheng Xiaodan in his article offers an example of Qian's translation practice for a good rendering of meanings and forms in translation with this example: in *Selected Works of Mao Zedong* we find this sentence: "There is a household Chinese saying "*San ge chou pijiang, ding ge Zhu Geliang* 三個臭皮匠，頂個諸葛亮". If we translate it as "even three common cobblers can surpass Zhuge Liang", we can deliver the surface literal meaning, but its true meaning is unmanifested. Besides, few western readers know Zhuge Liang. Even if a reader happens to know who Zhuge Liang is, he might not be able to figure out why Zhuge Liang is connected to cobblers. If we translate with the English proverb, "two heads are better than one" or "collective wisdom is greater than individual wit", the meaning is correct, but the two particular Chinese images of "Zhuge Liang" and "cobblers" are lost. Qian translated it into "three cobblers with their wits combined equal Chukeh Liang, the master mind". This translation avoids the loss of meaning or images in translation. Thus, we can learn from Qian Zhongshu's creative translation ways."

contributes to the conversation saying:

> Questo è imitare...non è copiare nè rifare...Quella è operazione pregevole, anche
> per la difficoltà d'assimilare un oggetto in una materia di tutt'altra natura; questa
> è bassa e triviale, per la molta facilità, che toglie la meraviglia[398]
> (This is to imitate...it is not to copy or to redo...That one is a valuable operation,
> even due to the difficulty of transposing an object in a completely different
> material; this one is a banal and trivial activity because it is too easy and bears no
> wonder).

The kind of imitation that means reworking and that does not simply try to follow a given pattern is thus the most appreciated. This quotation is in line with the preceding one in demonstrating that the translator, as well as the follower of of any kind of artistic trend, needs to recreate to produce an outcome that seems spontaneous and is valuable for it.

In talking about the different expressions caused by joy and sorrow, Qian quotes the Italian poet Leopardi, who in his *Zibaldone* says that joy causes expansion while sorrow causes narrowing (questa tendenza al dilatamento nell'allegrezza, e al restringimento nella tristezza);[399] many expressions in Chinese have the same semantic likeness: *xinhua nùfàng* 心花怒放 (to be elated), *kaixin* 開心 (happy), *kuaihuo de gutou dou qingle* 快活的骨頭都輕了 (the happy bones become light), *xinli da ge jie* 心裡打個結 (a knot in the heart), *xinshang youle kuai shitou* 心上有了塊石頭 (a stone on the heart), *yi kouqi bie zai duzili* 一口氣憋在肚子裡 (separate without a break in the stomach). To demonstrate community of intent in literary themes, Qian quotes Leopardi's *Zibaldone* again with a sentence about the caducity of

---

398  Qian Zhongshu, *Guan Zhui Bian*, I, 424-425. See Leopardi, *Pensieri di varia filosofia e di bella letteratura*, 1806-1807.

399  Qian Zhongshu, "Shi Keyi Yuan", in *Qi Zhui Ji*, 124. See Leopardi, *Pensieri di varia filosofia e di bella letteratura*, 106.

beauty and its link with love:

Il veder morire una persona amata, è molto meno lacerante che il vederla deperire e trasformarsi nel corpo e nell'animo da malattia. Perché nel primo caso le illusioni restano, nel secondo svaniscono[400]
(Seeing a beloved person die is much less painful than seeing this person waste away and be completely devoured by illness. Since in the first case illusions stay, in the other they disappear).

The quotation expresses what other cited authors state in the same paragraph: when beauty disappears, love disappears with it and it is better to die young and beautiful than to wither and become unattractive to the same eyes that have once adored the beauty that now is gone. The author does not express his opinion, and the quotations in succession are just the demonstration of poetic trends common to east and west, past and present.

In *Guan Zhui Bian* another sentence from Leopardi's *Zibaldone* reinforces what was written by other Chinese and western authors and quoted by Qian about a person's eyes being the utmost representation of his soul:

La parte più espressiva del volto e della persona; come la fisionomia sia determinata dagli occhi[401]
(The most expressive part of the face and the person; as eyes determine features).

Expansion on the notion comes from a quotation from Benvenuto Cellini (1500-1571), sole western quotation of the entry, together with a French saying, and it says that an oblique glance is like the one of a pig:

---

400  Qian Zhongshu, *Guan Zhui Bian*, I, 525. See Leopardi, *Pensieri di varia filosofia e di bella letteratura*, 415.
401  Qian Zhongshu, *Guan Zhui Bian*, II, 1127. See Leopardi, *Pensieri di varia filosofia e di bella letteratura*, 1112.

Giunto al papa, guardatomi così coll'occhio del porco, cioè biecamente[402]
(Looking at me with pig's eyes, obliquely).

A person's glance thus gives him precise characterization that is not just a physical one.

The first quotation from Leopardi's *Pensieri* (Thoughts) is in a footnote in the LVII chapter of the first book of *Guan Zhui Bian*:

Colpa non perdonata dal genere umano, il quale non odia mai tanto chi fa male, nè il male stesso, quanto chi lo nomina[403]
(Unforgiven fault of the human race, which never hates who does any evil deed, nor hates evil itself, as much as it hates who speaks of evil).

The quotation finds its place in a discussion about truth and the appearance of truth where other quotations bring the attention to things that are real and true and things that seem to be what they are not.

## 19th Century Poetry

Qian's work does not quote much of 19th century Italian poetry apart from Leopardi. Romantic poetry, also based on imagination and readers' reaction to poetic images, with a minimal grasp on reality and factual things, was not one of the preferential areas for Qian Zhongshu's readings. Exceptions are Leopardi, highly appreciated by Qian, and the young poet and critic Giuseppe Giusti (1809-1850), who often appears in Qian's works with quotations on various themes.

An example of allegory in *Tan Yi Lu* comes from Giuseppe Giusti. With

---

402 Qian Zhongshu, *Guan Zhui Bian*, II, 1141. See Cellini, *La vita di Benvenuto Cellini*, 114.
403 Qian Zhongshu, *Guan Zhui Bian*, I, 608. See Leopardi, *Pensieri di Varia Filosofia e di Bella Letteratura*.

Giusti and his witty poems called *La Chiocciola* (the Snail), many other poets are quoted in the allegory of a snail which always brings its home with itself and that in the words of the metaphysical poet John Donne in his letter to Sir Henry Wotton[404] represents the universe. The same image in *Euphues* by Lyly[405] represents women and in *Fables* by Arnault[406] represents an egoist and self-sufficient person. Qian Zhongshu quotes the second strophe of the seventy-two lines poem by Giusti in full:

Contenta ai comodi
Che Dio la fece
Può dirsi il Diogene
Della sua specie;
Per prender aria
Non passa l'uscio;
Nelle abitudini
Del proprio guscio
Sta persuasa
E non intasa:
Viva la chiocciola
Bestia da casa[407]
(Happy with the premise
That God gave it,
We can call it the Diogenes
Of its species
In order to breathe
It need not leave its door;
In its routine
To live indoors
And it is well contented
And not disturbed
Blessed be the snail,

404  Qian Zhongshu, *Tan Yi Lu*, 572.
405  Qian Zhongshu, *Tan Yi Lu*, 573.
406  Qian Zhongshu, *Tan Yi Lu*, 573.
407  Qian Zhongshu, *Tan Yi Lu*, 573. See *Poesie Italiane di Giuseppe Giusti*, 152.

Housebound creature).

A strong poetic image is also provided in the other poem by Giuseppe Giusti quoted in *Guan Zhui Bian* called *Gingillino*. Gingillino is the name of the main character in the long poem and represents all the people who reach important positions through fraud and evil deeds. Giusti's satire is directed towards them. Gingillino is said to believe in the mint and in her son, called sequin:[408]

> Io credo nella Zecca omnipotente
> E nel figliuolo suo detto zecchino[409]
> (I believe in omnipotent Mint
> And in its son, called sequin).

All the quotations that precede and follow are meant to illustrate how people do everything for money, and that notwithstanding what is commonly believed, to remain honest and avoid cheating for money is more rewarding than fraud and enrichment through every means.

The theme of money is also present in the fourth volume of *Guan Zhui Bian* through a quotation by Cecco Angiolieri (1257-1313), commenting on a *fu* 賦 of the western Jin period titled *Qian Shen Lun* 錢神論 (Saint Discourse on Money), a satire on mammon, the insane and greedy love for money above everything else. Angiolieri is a contemporary of Dante, and an interesting personality contrasting the *dolce stil novo* (sweet new style) in vogue then, the golden and gentle poetry exploring the philosophical, spiritual, psychological and social effects of love in the vernacular of Tuscany.

---

408 Ancient golden coin.
409 Qian Zhongshu, *Guan Zhui Bian*, I, 613. See *Poesie di Giuseppe Giusti*, 247.

Angiolieri's poem, quoted by Qian, similarly to *Qian Shen Lun*, satirizes money calling it the best relative ever:

> I buoni parenti, dica chi dir vuole,
> A chi ne può aver, sono i fiorini:
> Quei son fratei carnai e ver cugini,
> E padre e madre, figlioli e figliole[410]
> (Good relatives,
> Whoever may have them, are fiorins:
> Those are blood brothers and true cousins,
> Fathers and mothers, sons and daughters).

From the western Jin (265-316) to $13^{th}$ century's medieval Italy the theme is the same and Qian Zhongshu seems to speak through the mocking tone of the two authors. It is worth noting that the quotation comes from Enrico Maria Fusco's critical work on Italian lyrical poetry *La Lirica*, again literature visited through the critical filter.

## Alessandro Manzoni (1785-1873)

As with romantic poetry, an even less quoted literary genre is the modern romantic novel. Contemporary novels find their place among Qian's cited works, while scanty references are directed towards big authors of past centuries like Alessandro Manzoni, author of *I Promessi Sposi* (The Betrothed), an absolute masterpiece of Italian literature. The first reference to Manzoni is in *Guan Zhui Bian* and is from the said novel and the second is from a letter, *Lettera a Carlo D'Azeglio* (Letter to Carlo D'Azeglio). The quotation from the novel finds its place in a sequence of quotations that focus on the same concept and are arranged as an invocation of authority but does not constitute

---

410 Qian Zhongshu, *Guan Zhui Bian*, IV, 1939. See Angiolieri, *Rime*, 59.

the focal point of the entry in which it is inserted, being one of a series of similar sentences. It says:

> Fu, da quel punto in poi, una vita delle più tranquille, delle più feici, delle più invidiabili; di maniera che, se ve l'avessi a raccontare, vi seccherebbe a morte[411]
> (From that moment on it was one of the most peaceful, happy and enviable lives; so that if I ever wanted to narrate it you would find it dreadfully boring).

The quotation is preceded by its translation and accompanied by page and edition references. The second quotation, which also functions to reinforce a said opinion like the previous one, reads:

> Il trasgredir le regole è stato un mezzo di far meglio[412]
> (Breaking the rules has been a means to act in a better way).

There are probably various reasons Qian neglects Manzoni: he is a notably religious author and he belongs to a school he did not particularly appreciate, and although he was one of the great masters, Qian did not believe these to be best examples of literature and literary trends – better for him to focalize on less known and important authors; perhaps Qian read Manzoni's works in an advanced phase of his life when it was too late to quote the author in previous works and this not add much to *Guan Zhui Bian*. We cannot neglect considering though that most certainly the Bodleian Library, from where Qian drew out most of his readings, would certainly have had works by such a renowned author as Manzoni in its catalogue.

---

411 Qian Zhongshu, *Guan Zhui Bian*, II, 1036. See Manzoni, *I Promessi Sposi*, 744. **feici** should be spelled as **felici**.
412 Qian Zhongshu, *Guan Zhui Bian*, III, 1882. See Manzoni, "Lettera a Cesare Taparelli D'Azeglio".

## 5.2 From Pascoli to Eco: present ideas to shed light on the past

Even if the amount of quotations from 20$^{th}$ century literature is scanty, due to time constraints and to the difficulty of obtaining reading material in 20$^{th}$ century China, they are the most surprising and fascinating for their striking connections with the past and for the witty combination of references in which they are inserted. This is the case, for example, of the references to the American President, Richard Nixon or to Umberto Eco and Luigi Pirandello's novels. Their presence in Qian's work, as well as the absence of other authors' quotations, on one hand might give us a clue as to which contemporary western authors and works were already present in China before the eighties; on the other hand might it might act as a guide for us to study Qian Zhongshu's influence in introducing western literature and criticism in 20$^{th}$ century China. It is also interesting to note the way in which these western contemporary quotations are functional to the explanation of ancient Chinese classics in a paradigm that might have seemed quite heretical to some of the more traditional Chinese commentators and critics who might have even thought, if not openly declared, that the use of literary critic to study classics was of no use. To use the words of an Italian Romantic poet, Giovanni Berchet (1783-1851), quoted in the essay "Classical Literary Scholarship in Modern China" they might have affirmed:

Al diavolo quelle corbellerie![413]
(To hell those stupid remarks!)

---

413 Qian Zhongshu, "Classical Literary Scholarship in Modern China", in *A collection of Qian Zhongshu's English essays*, 401. See Giovanni Berchet, *Lettera semiseria di Grisostomo al suo figliolo*.

The striking contrast originated by the explanation of Chinese classics through western contemporary authors is exemplified in the already mentioned 1926 essay *Zhongguo Gu You de Wenxue Piping de Yi ge Tedian*[414] where, reflecting itself in the mirror of the words of some of the most influential critics and writers in western literary canon, Chinese literature becomes aware of a distinguishing and substantial feature that has always "intrinsically" (*guyou*) characterized it.

One of the most illuminating examples of Qian's method of using western literature to explain Chinese concepts is exemplified in the mentioned essay *Tonggan* (Synesthesia) in the figure of synaesthesia in eastern and western traditions.

> Le allodole sgranavano nel cielo le perle del loro limpido gorgheggio
> (Skylarks released in the sky the pearls of their clear warble)

translated by Qian as *Yi qun yunquànr mingkuai liuli de xixiguagua, zai tiankong li sakaile yi keke zhuzi* 一群雲雀兒明快流利的咕咕呱呱, 在天空裡撒開了一顆顆珠子,[415] is the quotation from Francesco Perri (1885-1974) extracted from Dino Provenzal's *Dizionario delle Immagini* (Dictionary of Figures of Speech), and in which similar images are presented from the Italians D'Annunzio, Mazzoni (1878-1928) and Paolieri (1878-1928), recalled by Qian in footnote. Qian mentions Rostagni's (1892-1961) comment on Aristotle's *Poetic* in footnote as well and he does so when talking about *sillogismo scientifico* (scientific syllogism) and the *entimema immaginativo e sensitivo* (sensitive and imaginative enthymeme).[416]

---

414  See paragraph 4.6 "Quotations as a looking glass".
415  Qian Zhongshu, "Tonggan", in *Qi Zhui Ji*, 66.
416  Qian Zhongshu, "Tonggan", in *Qi Zhui Ji*, 75.

## 5.2.1 Giovanni Pascoli (1855-1912)

Together with Goethe, Novalis, Wordsworth, Coleridge, Shelley, Dickens, Flaubert and Nietzsche, Pascoli is quoted to sustain the aesthetic principle that it is acceptable and praiseworthy to create something new from the old and to arrange ordinary and common things into an elegant and unusual aspect. Pascoli's quotation is taken from his poem *Il Sabato* (Saturday) and had been quoted in *Momenti e Problemi di Storia dell'Estetica* (The History of Aesthetics: Moments and Problems) by Marzorati. Qian reports it as follows:

> La poesia è nelle cose. Il poeta presenta la visione di cosa posta sotto gli occhi di tutti e che nessuno vedeva[417]
> (Poetry is inside things. Poetry is in things. The poet presents the vision of things under everybody's eyes but nobody sees it).

It is the duty of the artist, poet or painter to express the meaning that goes beyond words or objects because the things that are the most difficult to write or to represent are the ones with boundless meaning, hence more difficult to express in a finite language. During the brief account of the usage of synaesthesia in the history of western literature in the essay *Tonggan*, every century and every literary movement considered is supported by a relevant quotation: 15th and 16th century Baroque loved to use "certi impasti di metafore nello scambio dei cinque sensi" (some mixture of metaphors in the exchange between the five senses) as F. Flora (1891-1962) wrote, quoted from *Marino e i Marinisti* edited by G. G. Ferrero.[418] Stars are very often associated

---

417 Qian Zhongshu, *Tan Yi Lu*, 38. The complete and correct quotation from *Pensieri e discorsi* by Giovanni Pascoli, MDCCCXCV-MCMVI: "La poesia è nelle cose: un certo etere che si trova in questa più, in quella meno, in alcune sì, in altre no. Il poeta solo lo conosce, ma tutti gli uomini, poi che egli significò, lo riconoscono. Egli presenta la visione di cosa posta sotto gli occhi di tutti e che nessuno vedeva".

418 Qian Zhongshu, "Tonggan", in *Qi Zhui Ji*, 72.

with a noise or a buzzing in Italian poetry, as in an already quoted famous poem by Pascoli called *Il gelsomino notturno*:[419]

> La Chioccetta per l'aia azzurra
> Va col suo pigolio di stelle[420]
> (The small hen walks in the azure barnyard
> With his stars peeping).

The same line is quoted in *Guan Zhui Bian*,[421] with the same purpose.

In the critical essay by Natale Busetto (1877-1968) *Giosuè Carducci: l'Uomo, il Poeta, il Critico, il Prosatore* (Giosuè Carducci: Man, Poet, Critic and Prose Writer) it is recorded that for the Italian poet Giosuè Carducci (1835-1907), Romantic poetry is a "secrezione naturale"[422] (natural secretion), in the sense that it is an uncontrolled outcome of sentimentalism. In *Tan Yi Lu* the same essay is quoted[423] when Carducci affirms that in poetry the sound and the rhythm are more important than the words used to express whatever the content may be. It is interesting to note that again Qian Zhongshu has not quoted the poet directly, but has read his works and analysed his outcomes through literary criticism.

## 5.2.2 Literary critics in the essays: Croce, De Sanctis, Provenzal
### Benedetto Croce (1866-1952) and Francesco De Sanctis (1817-1883)

There is much proof in Qian Zhongshu's works of his reading the Italian critic Benedetto Croce. When Qian quotes Croce or other literary critics, often we might refer to these more as references rather than quotations, since

---

419  Pascoli, *Il gelsomino notturno*, 1901.
420  Qian Zhongshu, "Tonggan", in *Qi Zhui Ji*, 72. See Pascoli, *I canti di Castelvecchio*, 56.
421  See Qian Zhongshu, *Guan Zhui Bian*, II, 745.
422  Qian Zhongshu, "Shi Keyi Yuan", in *Qi Zhui Ji*, 119.
423  Qian Zhongshu, *Tan Yi Lu*, 716-717.

the author only writes the name of the critic, the title of his work and the content to which he is referring. In the essays collected in *Rensheng Bianshang de Bianshang* we also find numerous translations of critical passages, like the ones by the Italian critic Francesco De Sanctis. In the 1962 the essay *Fu De Sangketi Qi Wenlun San Ze* 弗・德・桑克梯斯文論三則 (Three Principles in the Essays of Francesco De Sanctis),[424] the idea that the results as the work of a writer often does not correspond to the intentions brought forth by the author and demonstrated through three passages by De Sanctis, two of which are chosen from a collection by Luigi Russo (1892-1961) titled *Gli scrittori d'Italia* (Italian writers), and one from Walter Binni's *I Classici Italiani nella Storia della Critica*[425] (Italian Classics in the History of Criticism). In his introduction to the three translated passages, Qian defines De Sanctis as "the most important critic of the Italian nineteenth century", stating that his influence on the contemporary literary world has been widespread and not only limited to Italy. All outcomes the Anglo-Americans acquired with their concept of the "intentional fallacy" have been nothing more than an expansion of this concept previously expounded by De Sanctis. The three passages translated then are about Dante, Manzoni and Leopardi, undoubtedly three of the foremost Italian writers, and demonstrate that the three writers wrote for a scope and with an idea different from what they ended up obtaining. The point to note here is the accordance of the author with the writers quoted and translated and his knowledge and mastering of their theories and works. The essay on De Sanctis, in addition to its significance in the development and exposition of Qian Zhongshu's ideas on the relation between writers and literary composition, is also important as one

---

424 The essay was published first in the review *Wen Hui Bao*, 15-08-1962. See Qian Zhongshu, *Rensheng Bianshang de Bianshang*, 377-381.

425 Walter Binni, *I classici italiani nella storia della critica*.

of the main achievements for the author in his translation practice.

The same gap between intent and result is quoted in footnote in *Guan Zhui Bian* when De Sanctis' sentence from *Storia della Letteratura Italiana* (History of Italian Literature), who Qian fully read (see Xia Zhiqing, *Zhonghui Qian Zhongshu Jishi*), motivates one to distinguish intentions from reality:

Si ha a distinguere il mondo intenzionale e il mondo effettivo[426]
(We need to distinguish the world of intentions and the world of reality).

A few lines earlier exactly the same concept had been expressed through the previously mentioned passage from Machiavelli:

Andare drieto alla verità effettuale della cosa che alla immaginazione di essa[427]
(It is necessary to follow the practical truth and not the imagined one).

A further expansion on the theory of writers obtaining something different from what they wanted to express is the idea that even disciples of great masters reach an outcome that is a depreciation of their masters' theories. This is what Qian Zhongshu demonstrates in *Tan Yi Lu* with the help of quotations from Renard, Nietzsche, Burckhardt and De Sanctis.

De Sanctis' words, preceded by a translation in Chinese, and from the same above-mentioned *Gli Scrittori d'Italia* edited by Luigi Russo, are:

Ma che cosa è una scuola? Una scuola è la decomposizione del caposcuola. E ne

---

426 Qian Zhongshu, *Guan Zhui Bian*, I, 609 e IV, 1923.
427 Qian Zhongshu, *Guan Zhui Bian*, I, 609. See Machiavelli, *Il Principe*, XXXII.

nasce troppo spesso che tutto quello che nel caposcuola è difetto, ma tenuto a freno dalla forza del genio, per certuni si ritiene bellezza e diventa maniera[428] (What is a School? A School is the decomposition of its leader. It often happens that what in the leader of a School is considered fault and is restrained by his genius is instead considered beauty from others and becomes a trend).

Again, the same idea expressed in a different manner is the one in *Guan Zhui Bian* when Qian quotes De Sanctis in footnote without translation in Chinese and comments on the concept that writers may be influenced by other artists who have preceded them. Thus, their works and mind are not pure and innocent but rely on previous creations. The quotation to support this idea is from the literary critic Francesco De Sanctis again, who, in his *Storia della Letteratura Italiana* wrote:

Lo scrittore non dice quello che pensa o immagina o sente, perchè non è l'immagine che gli sta innanzi, ma la frase di Orazio e di Virgilio[429] (The writer does not say what he thinks or imagines or feels, since what he has in his sight is not an image, but the words of Horace and Virgil).

A quotation from Momigliano (1908- 1987) comes from *La Critica Letteraria Contemporanea* (Contemporary Literary Critic) edited by Luigi Russo,

Noi sentiamo la poesia soltanto quando tutto tace dentro di noi[430] (We feel poetry only when everything else inside us is silent).

This reinforces and supports other quotations from Chinese and western

---

428 Qian Zhongshu, *Tan Yi Lu*, 452-453.
429 Qian Zhongshu, *Guan Zhui Bian*, I, 898.
430 Qian Zhongshu, *Tan Yi Lu*, 671.

authors, affirming that the utmost level of art is reached when there is complete silence around and inside the reader and the artist as well. The same concept had been expressed in the essay *Yi Ge Pianjian* 一個偏見 (A Prejudice), where Qian sustains that only prejudices that are a state of lack of reason for the brain can be aroused from noise and confusion, while good and rational thoughts are originated by silence, where silence is not meant to be the complete lack of sounds, which would spring only from death, but from a transparent state of the sense of hearing.[431] To reinforce the assumption that lack of sound means death, Qian quotes Dante affirming that Hell is the place where even the sun is silent, "dove il sol tace".[432]

Another work by Luigi Russo, *Antologia della Critica Letteraria* (Anthology of Literary Cristicism), is the one that comes from a quotation by Francesco Redi (1626-1697),[433] preceded by the translation in Chinese by Qian Zhongshu. The quotation implies that there is no greater enemy of "good" than the will to change the status of things to pursue "the better"; the quotation is inscribed in a discussion on the need to keep changing and modifying artistic works, poems and paintings as well. The amount of quotations in this LIX chapter of *Tan Yi Lu* suggests that to change too much is not of any help for the sake of good artistic works and seems to point to the author's point of view, "to make perfection more perfect is like adding feet to the drawing of a snake".[434] The same concept had been reinforced a few lines earlier – among other quotations – in a quotation from Vasari's (1511-1574) *Le Vite de' più Eccellenti Pittori, Scultori, e Architettori* (The Lives of the Most

431  See Qian Zhongshu, "Yi Ge Pianjian", in *Xie Zai Rensheng Bianshang*, 44-45.

432  Qian Zhongshu, "Yi Ge Pianjian", in *Xie Zai Rensheng Bianshang*, 45. See Dante Alighieri, *La Commedia secondo l'antica vulgata*, 4.

433  See Qian Zhongshu, *Tan Yi Lu*, 587. Francesco Redi (1626-1697) is an Italian doctor and literate. He carried on important researches on viper's venom and was a member of the Italian *Accademia delle Crusca*, the more acknowledged association for studies on the Italian language.

434  See Qian Zhongshu, *Tan Yi Lu*, 586.

Excellent Painters, Sculptors and Architects) quoted in Pareyson's *Estetica: Teoria della Formatività*[435] (Aesthetic: Theory of Formativity), who all affirmed that sometimes drafts born from an artistic outburst are full of strength and expressivity while the works revised too many times are without any taste. Creative process is also the subject of another quotation from the same *Estetica: Teoria della Formatività* where Pareyson's expressions "l'intenzione formativa" (creative intention) and "la materia d'arte" (material for art)[436] have been quoted to better clarify and explain the meaning of the Chinese words *xin* 心 (heart) and *wu* 物 (object) respectively, words that in Chinese combine many different meanings and acquire clarification from the explanation that the Italian philosopher offers in his work. At the same time his sentence "caricano l'operazione utilitaria di una intenzionalità formativa" (give the utilitarian action creative intent),[437] quoted in the second volume of *Guan Zhui Bian*, explains the divination process of the *Yi Lin* 易林, derived from the classic *Yi Jing*.

In *Guan Zhui Bian* a quotation from Luigi Russo and his *La Critica Italiana Contemporanea* (Italian Contemporary Criticism) proves that to paint according to the words of poetry would make up for a painting by a mad man. Words by Giosuè Carducci are quoted in this regard when he writes:

L'aria è plumbea e l'afa pesante[438]
(the air is like lead and the humidity is heavy).


The weight that concepts have in words – expressing emotional feelings,

435 Qian Zhongshu, *Tan Yi Lu*, 586.
436 Qian Zhongshu, *Guan Zhui Bian*, II, 775.
437 Qian Zhongshu, *Guan Zhui Bian*, II, 816.
438 Qian Zhongshu, *Guan Zhui Bian*, I, 215.

and that ideas have in paintings – expressing sensational feelings, is always different and should be attentively pondered.

In 1979 the Chinese Academy of Social Sciences published a study titled *Waiguo Lilunjia Zuojia Lun Xingxiang Siwei* 外國理論家作家論形象思維 (Foreign Critics Discuss Thought in Terms of Images)[439] in which Qian Zhongshu, Yang Jiang, Liu Mingjiu 柳鳴九 and Liu Ruoduan 劉若端 translated passages from most European and American critics about some crucial concepts in literary critical studies such as fantasy and imagination and their links with literary creation and the work of the mind in understanding the physical and imaginative world. These four authors jointly conducted the choice of whom to translate from among Western Europe's classical authors. Qian Zhongshu and Yang Jiang chose the authors from contemporary Western Europe and America. The content and the translations were revised by Qian Zhongshu and Yang Jiang. Out of a total of thirty-five authors, six are the Italian (Tomitano, Mazzoni, Muratori, Vico, Leopardi, Croce), all classical except one, who was contemporary; and among those, three were translated from English and the others directly from Italian. Among the classical Italian writers we find: Bernardino Tomitano (1517-1576) and his *Della Lingua Thoscana*[440] (On the Language of Tuscany), 1545, translated from B. Hathaway's *The Age of Criticism*; G. Mazzoni with *Della Difesa della Commedia di Dante* (On Defence of Dante's Comedy), 1587, translated from A. H. Gilbert's *Literary Criticism: Plato to Dryden*; and L. A. Muratori and his *Della Perfetta Poesia Italiana* (On Perfect Italian Poetry), 1706, translated from E. F. Carritt's *Philosophy of Beauty*. All of them talk about the difference between fantasy and rational thought and about the

---

439  Qian Zhongshu, *Rensheng bianshang de bianshang*, 382-470.
440  The title is misspelled and should be: *Della lingua Toscana*.

different way in which they interact to create poetic images. We can be quite certain that Qian Zhongshu was in charge of the translations from Italian for Vico, Leopardi and Croce, since the source texts are editions and works from which Qian Zhongshu has quoted quite often. We also suppose that the Qian Zhongshu was also the author of the introduction to the second part of the study about contemporary American and European criticism, since only he and Yang Jiang were in charge of this part and in its introduction we find a precise and adulatory account of the contribution of the Italian critic Benedetto Croce to western aesthetic. The author of the passage writes that Croce was able to clarify the confusion between thought in terms of images (intuitive knowledge) and abstract thought of the Aesthetical School and has also clarified ideas related to thought in terms of images and has enriched the field of western aesthetic.[441] Given the countless quotations of Croce in all of Qian Zhongshu's works, we may take this assumption as his profession of appraisal for the Italian philosopher and literary critic, notwithstanding an initial disapproval of his conceptions. At the end of the translated passage, there is a small summary of Croce's life and main works.[442]

With regard to this, it is necessary to specify that we find a twofold appreciation of Croce from Qian Zhongshu. If the praising account of the Italian critic just mentioned is from a corpus of essays written in 1979 and belongs to the mature phase of Qian's elaboration and reflection on literary themes, opinions on Croce in works from the pre-Cultural Revolution period, like *Tan Yi Lu*, are not equally pleased with the critic's thought. Xia Zhiqing

---

441 See Qian Zhongshu, *Xie zai Rensheng Bianshang*, 440.

442 We find the same opinions on Croce's influence on aesthetic thought and his contribution to the clarification of the difference between intuitive thought and abstract thought in the chapter that Zhu Guanqian dedicates to the Italian critic in his *Xifang Meixue Shi* 西方美學史. Since the expressions used and the opinions involved are nearly the same, we may suppose Zhu Guanqian was a source for Qian Zhongshu.

offers a comment on this in his *Zhonghui Qian Zhongshu Jishi*[443], where the author reports of Qian telling him that he was not so happy about some of the opinions expressed in *Tan Yi Lu* where, for example, sometimes the treatment reserved for the Italian Croce had not been a thorough one and that after reading the whole collection of Croce's works, he had been moved to appreciate the critic's scholarly views. Anyway, even in *Tan Yi Lu* Croce is mentioned for an invocation of authority. For example, reading chapter LXI, the critic – together with Dante, is quoted extensively about the interesting relation between ideas and their representation and the capacity of verbal or pictorial expressions to render in practice what had only been an imagined entity. Croce, whose quotation is not translated here by Qian, says that:

> Ogni vera intuizione o rappresentazione è, insieme, espressione. L'attività intuitiva tanto intuisce quanto esprime
> (Every real intuition or representation together is expression. The activity of intuition senses as much as it expresses).

and

> Intuire è esprimere: e nient'altro (niente di più, ma niente di meno) che esprimere[444]
> (To sense is to express: nothing more (and nothing less) than to express).

A few lines later Croce is quoted again in his reference to *Le Lettere di Michelangelo Buonarroti 1875* (Michelangelo Buonarroti's Correspondence, 1875) by G. Milanesi, where the painter Michelangelo (1475-1564) is said to have written in his letters:

---

443  See Xia Zhiqing, "Zhonghui Qian Zhongshu Jishi", 60-76.
444  Qian Zhongshu, *Tan Yi Lu*, 529.

Lo rispondo che si dipinge col ciervello e non con le mani[445]
(Painting comes from brain, not from hands).

Qian Zhongshu makes this statement to complement a number of quotations from the poet Dante, who sustains that expression does not necessarily follow words because it lacks the power to do so. Qian seems then to use Croce to establish the initial question for the debate: is expression equal to intuition? Dante gives the answer by saying that no, expression is not the exact counterpart of intuition, and Croce again is said to have often quoted artists, painters or poets who affirmed the torment of the inexpressible (questo tormento dell'inesprimibile).[446] One of the artists quoted by Croce happens to be Manzoni, who said:

Ch'io sento come il più divin s'invola,
Nè può il giogo patir della parola[447]
(I sense that the divine flies up
And cannot stand the entrapment of words).

where again words do not have sufficient means to express what is preserved in the minds of the artists. We find further expansion on this concept in *Guan Zhui Bian*'s commentary on *Mao Shi* 毛詩 where Croce is said to sneer at all those who believe the words of poets who praise their lovers, and that if only they had the possibility of meeting the various Lesbia and Cinzia or Beatrice and Laura, they might think that their attentions had been misplaced:

---

445  Qian Zhongshu, *Tan Yi Lu*, 529. The correct quotation would have been: "Io rispondo che si dipinge col cervello e non con le mani".
446  Qian Zhongshu, *Tan Yi Lu*, 530.
447  Qian Zhongshu, *Tan Yi Lu*, 530.

Far la conoscenza personale di Lesbia e di Cinzia, di Beatrice e di Laura[448]
(Personally meet Lesbia and Cinzia or Beatrice and Laura).


This time the subject of the debate is not the lack of a correct respondence between intention and expression but between expression and reality. We find the same inequality exploited in *Guan Zhui Bian* when Tommaso Campanella says wounds and grazes are beautiful, with an obvious contrast of intents; he is quoted by Croce in his *Estetica*: "belle ferite" (beautiful wounds) and "belle scorticature e slogature" (beautiful grazes and dislocations).[449] Both Croce and Qian Zhongshu demonstrate that sometimes ugly and hideous things are beautiful in one's eyes because they find resonance in feelings and interests.

One of the most appealing usages Qian makes of quotations is to arouse questions and discussions through imaginative dialogues between writers whose words he juxtaposes in a striking succession. In *Tan Yi Lu*'s discussion about allegory, the English writer Samuel Johnson (1709-1784) happens to say that:


Allegory is perhaps one of the most pleasing vehicles of instruction.[450]


Francesco De Sanctis echoes this, saying that allegorical poems are


---

448 Qian Zhongshu, Guan Zhui Bian, I, 157. Lesbia is the woman to whom the Latin poet Catullo dedicated much of his love poetry in the 1st century B.C. Cinzia was chanted by the Latin Propertius in the same age; Beatrice is the beloved muse of the poet Dante (1265-1321) and Laura was loved and celebrated in the poetry of Francesco Petrarca (1304-1374).

449 Qian Zhongshu, *Guan Zhui Bian*, I, 357.

450 See Johnson, *The Works of Samuel Johnson*, 212.

Poesia allegorica, poesia noiosa[451]
(Allegorical poetry, boring poetry).

In considering the two points of view, Qian Zhongshu suggests we should contemplate the particular historical and literary circumstances to which the authors belong. Croce, at the same time, wrote a lot about allegory in his *Filosofia, Poesia, Storia* (Philosophy, Poetry, History).[452] The sentence that seems to solve the debate according to Qian is the opinion Milton expresses about Eve in his *Paradise Lost*:

Her loveliness, so absolute she seems
And in herself complete.[453]

Art is complete in itself; it bears its value and its meaning. In Qian's opinion this is what Croce should consider before doubting the utility of allegorical art.

Coming to the evaluation of different artistic currents and artists in the essay *Zhongguo Shi yu Zhongguo Hua*, Qian Zhongshu talks extensively about the painter and poet of the Tang Dynasty, Wang Wei 王維 (701-761) who, even if considered a great poet, compared to Du Fu ended up being a minor poet. In this comparison Qian borrows the expression that the Italian critic Benedetto Croce uses in defining the poet Pascoli:

Da de xiao shiren 大的小詩人[454]

---

451 Qian Zhongshu, *Tan Yi Lu*, 571.
452 Qian Zhongshu, *Tan yi Lu*, 571. Qian writes *Shen zi kao jing* 甚資考鏡：It's worth analysing this material. Croce's work title is mispelled in **Filosofia, Poesta, Storia**.
453 Qian Zhongshu, *Tan Yi Lu*, 571.
454 Qian Zhongshu, "Zhongguo Shi yu Zhongguo Hua", in *Qi Zhui Ji*, 22.

(Un grande-piccolo poeta, o, se piace meglio, un piccolo grande poeta).[455]

a great minor poet, or if you like a minor great poet. With these words the Italian critic wants to debase Pascoli since he does not like his poetry because he considers it too sentimental, too artificial. Qian Zhongshu, on the other hand, borrowing Croce's expression, would like to affirm that even if Wang Wei is a great poet, next to Du Fu he seems to be a minor poet. As with the quotation from Leonardo da Vinci about the relation between poetry and painting,[456] Qian does not catch the full meaning of Croce's expression here but is still able to de-contextualise a quotation and use it for his sole scope. An interesting point to make is that years later in *Guan Zhui Bian* the same opinion about Pascoli by Croce is recalled in a comment on the theme of "playing music to oxes" or giving something valuable to someone who cannot appreciate it; this time, however, grasping Croce's opinion of Pascoli is complete and is obtained through a critical essay on the Italian critic by Fausto Nicolini (1869-1965). Pascoli, explains Qian, wrote an entire poem, *I Due Vicini* (Neighbours), in response to Croce, who despised his poetry. In the poem Pascoli compared the critic to a donkey that appreciates only the cauliflowers born from its excrement (i cavoli nati dal suo fimo)[457] in a vegetable garden and considers the beautiful flowers in the same garden to be of no use. At the same time the donkey, i.e. the literary critic, cannot even be pleased by the song of the nightingale because he says that its song is a waste of time. Instead of wasting that time singing, the donkey – exactly as the literary critic – employs it in a more fruitful way, thinking. Qian quotes:

---

455  Croce, *La Letteratura della Nuova Italia*.
456  See paragraph 5.1.5 "Renaissance men: Leonardo, Lorenzo de Medici".
457  Qian Zhongshu, *Guan Zhui Bian*, IV, 2084. See Nicolini, *Benedetto Croce*, 225.

Oh! Il tempo perso! Canto io forse? Io penso[457]
(Oh! That waste of time! Do I ever sing? I think).

These quotations come after a series of other western examples in which the above mentioned theme of giving valuables to people who cannot appreciate them is discussed in a comment on Hui Tong 慧通 and his *Bogu Daoshi "Yi Xia Lun"* 駁顧道士《夷夏論》.

Among the Italians, Ludovico Ariosto is the one quoted with two works in which he makes the comparison between a dumb person and a donkey. The quotation from *Orlando Furioso* (Mad Orlando) is:

Tanto apprezza costumi, o virtù ammira,
Quanto l'asino fa il suon della lira[458]
(He appreciates morals or virtue
As a donkey does the sound of a lyre)

and the one from *Il Negromante* (The Necromancer) is:

E sa di questa e dell'altre scienzie
Che sa l'asino e'l bue di sonar gli organi[459]
(And he knows about this and other sciences
As a donkey or an ox knows how to play an organ).

Both quotations from Ariosto are preceded by Qian's translation in Chinese but the second one carries an annex added secondarily by Qian in which he says that his translation carries an inaccuracy, since the particularity of Ariosto's simile, that cannot be found in Qian's rendering of his lines, is

---

458 Qian Zhongshu, Guan Zhui Bian, IV, 2083. See Ariosto, Orlando Furioso, 424.

459 See Ariosto, *Il Negromante*, http://www.liberliber.it/mediateca/libri/a/ariosto/il_negromante/ pdf/il_neg_p.pdf. Accessed: 10 december, 2011. **scienzie** should be spelled **scientie**.

that the donkey is not only incapable of understanding but incapable of doing something, that is to play lyre, adding an important nuance of meaning to the theme discussed. Croce again is recalled when talking about usages and ideas so consolidated so as to become tradition. Qian affirms that changes must necessarily occur even in traditional ideas and concepts or in new trends and that these changes need to look for compromises in order to have some influence on a fixed tradition. These compromises are what Croce calls "ipocrisia letteraria" (literary hypocrisy) in his *Estetica*[460], *wenyi li de liangmian pai jia zhengjing* 文藝裡的兩面派假正經[461] in Qian's translation, to show that tradition is not rigid and must be flexible, both stating rigid regulations and providing the possibility for these regulations to be violated by new trends. Qian Zhongshu, reflecting on metaphor and on how it can be rendered in paintings, recalls Charles Philipon's caricature of King Louis Philippe whose face is transformed into a pear (1834) in *Du Laaokon*. He also mentions some modernist paintings like the one in which a bicycle is rendered as an ox head with horns as handles, or the one of a nice girls' face whose lips seem like a sofa and make the whole face similar to a room, as recorded in Mario Praz's (1896-1982) work *Beauty and Oddity* (Bellezza e bizzarria).[462] Praz's example reminds Qian Zhongshu of the portrait of Li Duanduan in Cui Ya's 崔涯 poem *Chao Li Duanduan* 嘲李端端.[463] Both the Italian Praz and the Chinese Cui Ya are examples of how painting tries to give a physical aspect to words. Words, on the other hand, need to be effective enough to give readers a tangible feeling of reality. The critic Mario Praz is recalled again with his essay *La Grandezza dei Traduttori* (Translators'

---

460  Croce, *Estetica come scienza dell'espressione e linguistica generale.*

461  Qian Zhongshu, "Zhongguo Shi Yu Zhongguo Hua", in *Qi Zhui Ji*, 2.

462  Qian Zhongshu, "Du Laaokong", in *Qi Zhui Ji*, 59.

463  Qian Zhongshu, "Du Laaokong", in *Qi Zhui Ji*, 59.

Greatness) where he states that the more of a mess a translation is, the more interesting it is.[464]

## Dino Provenzal (1877-1972)

Provenzal is an Italian critic and literate whose interests are directed towards analysing the particularities and curiosities of the Italian language. He is the author of many children's books and the translator of Grimm's tales from German. *Perchè si dice così* (Why do we say it like this?) is a book in which Provenzal explains common and popular sayings and Qian quotes from it in *Guan Zhui Bian* to reinforce the concept that opposites are complementary. For example the upper and lower jaws are opposites and when we bite, even if they go against one another, neither is harmed by the movement. In modern times, Qian writes that scissors and our jaws in mastication are opposites that have both been compared that do not harm one another. This finds its parallel in the Italian language where the two opposing parts in a quarrel are said to be like the blades of scissors, "le lame delle forbici"[465] as Provenzal wrote, since they receive the attacks of the other part but are not offended and the only harmed person is the defendant between the parts.

Dino Provenzal's *Dizionario delle Immagini* (Dictionary of Figures of Speech) is a reference book quoted often by Qian Zhongshu, who sometimes takes very particular and seemingly trivial references like the quotation from Vitaliano Brancati's (1907-1954) *Don Giovanni in Sicilia* (Don Juan in Sicily):

---

464 Qian Zhongshu, "Lin Shu de Fanyi", in *Qi Zhui Ji*, 82.
465 Qian Zhongshu, *Guan Zhui Bian*, I, 41. See Provenzal, *Perché si dice così*.

Quel pezzo di donna che fa fermare gli orologi[466]
(The type of woman that makes clocks stop)

referring to an astonishingly beautiful woman, so beautiful as to make the hands of a clock stand still. The metaphor is used to reflect on how sometimes the same image is used with opposite aims, since the same metaphor of the clock had also been used to describe a woman so ugly as to make a clock stop working.[467]

In *Tan Yi Lu* XXXIX another image from Provenzal's dictionary is recalled to signify a very ugly woman:

Un pentimento d'uomo, una donna brutta come un rimorso[468]
(A man like a repentance, a woman ugly like a remorse).

The quotation, not translated, finds its place in a discussion about the ugliness of imitations.

Another quotation from Provenzal's *Dizionario delle immagini* is reported in the fourth volume of *Guan Zhui Bian* where other western authors seem to use a consonance of voices in the image of writing as on a (blue) sky. After Iona and Peter Opie's quotation from *The Oxford Dictionary of Nursery Rhymes*, where the sea is seen like ink and the world as paper, Qian quotes Leonardo Giustinian (1388-1446) from a critical study by E. M. Fusco, *La Lirica* (Lyrical Poetry), with his simile of trees that can speak, leaves that are like tongues, ink like seawater, earth like paper and grass like pens. The author comments that even if these similes were to become reality,

---

466 Qian Zhongshu, *Guan Zhui Bian*, I, 66.
467 Egan, *Limited Views*, 124.
468 Qian Zhongshu, *Tan Yi Lu*, 346. See Provenzal, *Dizionario delle Immagini*.

nothing could be adequate to sing the beauty of his lady:

> Se li arbori sapessen favellare,
> E le lor foglie fusseno le lingue,
> L'inchiostro fusse l'acqua dello mare,
> La terra fusse carta e l'erbe penne,
> Le tue bellezze non potria contare[469]
> (If trees could speak
> And their leaves were tongues,
> If seawater were ink,
> Earth were paper and grass were pens,
> Even then I could not tell your beauty).

Then Claudian's (370-404) *De Bello Gildonico* and Curtius (1866-1956), with Robinson Jeffers (1887-1962), find their place ending the series of western quotations. The next to the last one is Vitaliano Brancati again from Provenzal, writing:

> Nel cielo azzurro le rondini scorrono come una veloce scrittura[470]
> (In the blue sky swallows flow like quick calligraphy).

It is emblematic that Italian authors, more so than others, are the majority belonging to the field of literary criticism and that Italian literature is one that quite often is analysed through the critical filter in Qian Zhongshu's works.

## 5.2.3 20th Century Poetry and Novel

Since criticism is often the starting point for Qian Zhongshu's reading

---

469 Qian Zhongshu, *Guan Zhui Bian*, IV, 2303. See D'Ancona, *La poesia popolare italiana*. http://www.archive.org/ stream/lapoesiapopolare00dancuoft/lapoesiapopolare00dancuoft_djvu.txt Accessed December 12, 2011.
470 Qian Zhongshu, *Guan Zhui Bian*, IV, 2303.

choices, and in criticism he finds clues about novelists and poets, it is possible that in reading Croce's appreciation for Carlo Collodi's (1826-1890) novel *Pinocchio* in 1903, the appreciation that ratified the novel's role in Italian contemporary literature, Qian was inspired to read it. A quotation from Collodi finds its place in a sequence of Chinese and western quotations that, commenting on *Yilin* 易林, describes all situations in which two deficiencies supply one another and make for a functioning body:

> La Volpe, che era zoppa, camminava appoggiandosi al Gatto, che era cieco, si lasciava guidare dalla Volpe[471]
> (The Fox, that was lame, leaned on the Cat, that was blind, which was led by the Fox).

"Dialogue between sages of the past" might be the category in which this quotation falls together with the others that precede and follow, because according to the previously given definition, they all express the same concept notwithstanding time and space gaps.

In the footnote to one of Leonardo's quotation in *Zhongguo shi yu Zhongguo hua*, which we have already analysed in paragraph 5.1.5 "Renaissance men: Leonardo, Lorenzo De Medici", Qian Zhongshu quotes Gabriele D'Annunzio's novel *Il Fuoco (The Fire)* with a passage in which the author says that it is well known that da Vinci's favourite sentence is:

> Ci appare evidente la sentenza preferita da quel Vinci cui la Verità balenò un giorno co' suoi mille volti segreti: – La musica non ha da esser chiamata altro che sorella della pittura. – La lor pittura non è soltanto una poesia muta ma anche una musica muta[472]
> (It is clear the favourite sentence of Leonardo Da Vinci whom Truth, with its

---

471 Qian Zhongshu, Guan Zhui Bian, II, 834. See Collodi, Pinocchio, 78.
472 Qian Zhongshu, "Zhongguo Shi yu Zhongguo Hua", in *Qi Zhui Ji*, 30.

thousands of secret faces, manifested one day: Music is nothing other than the painting's sister. Their painting is not only mute poetry but also mute music).

D'Annunzio here intends to praise painting calling it similar to music, and music, notes Qian Zhongshu, was even more important than poetry or painting during romanticism. D'Annunzio is then in full accordance with Leonardo da Vinci, and both, even if unconsciously, may support Qian Zhongshu in not considering poetry and painting on the same level. D'Annunzio's quotations, even if not consistent in number, are somehow worth analyzing since the Italian author, who reached China during the twenties and thirties of last century, was later forgotten and banned as a symbol of a clear link with Fascism during the years of Cultural Revolution and Communist China. Lü Tongliu (1938-2005) was the fist scholar in China to repropose D'Annunzio's work in translation with the publication of one of his short stories, *Chuanfu* 船夫 (The Ferryman) in the journal *Zhongshan* 鐘山 (Mountain Bell) in 1982.[473] His choice was guided by a consideration of the writer's literary and artistic merits that eluded his commitment to the rightist party. Qian Zhongshu quoted D'Annunzio's work, inserting it in the general panorama of the literary debate before Lü Tongliu did, without considering the negative role attributed.

*Guan Zhui Bian*, published in 1978, nevertheless has been revised and republished many times. Not only did Qian continue correcting and adjusting minor mistakes in the text but, following his usual approach of taking notes, he added new references and quotations from his continuous readings to later editions. We find one of the latest additions in *Guan Zhui Bian* where an interesting web of quotations winds into a ball of references

---

473 Leonesi, "La Cina, la Letteratura Italiana e Lü Tongliu. Un Progetto di Traduzione Lungo una Vita", 445-446.

starting from the Buddhist sentence "to go off on the shore leaving the raft", which can be interpreted as a metaphor of ingratitude just like the English saying "to kick down the ladder one rises by".[474]

The German philosopher Wittgenstein in his 1978 *Tractatus Logico-Philosophicus* uses something similar to the meaning conveyed by the above-mentioned quoted metaphors and Umberto Eco (1932-), Italian contemporary literary critic and novelist, in his masterpiece *Il Nome della Rosa* (The Name of the Rose) edited by Bompiani in 1980 (Qian used an edition dated 1986), quotes Wittgenstein just like Qian Zhongshu, pretending it is a quotation from a mystic of the Middle Ages. Eco then, in the note to the text, explains this particular usage of quotations that he de-contextualises and extrapolates from their time attributing them a new and fictitious epoch:

> Mascheravo citazioni di autori posteriori (come Wittgenstein) facendole passare per citazioni dell'epoca[475]
> (I used to disguise quotations of later writers (like Wittgenstein) as quotations of that time).

A double jump across time occurs here: Wittgenstein and Eco inside Qian Zhongshu's work, Wittgenstein and Middle Age inside Eco's novel.

The other quotation from Eco's *Il nome della rosa* is again in an annex with precise indications of the edition used and with the chapter's name and page reference. This time the quotation comments on *Jiu Ge* 九歌 of the *Chu Ci* 楚辭 and recounts of two monks debating about irony and laughter in the novel with one of the monks saying that they make the world appear the contrary of what it shoud be:

---

474  Qian Zhongshu, *Guan Zhui Bian*, I, 447.
475  Qian Zhongshu, *Guan Zhui Bian*, I, 447.

Mostrano il mondo al contrario di ciò che deve essere[476]
(They show the world in a contrary way of how it should be)

and that laughter and this topsy-turvy world should be avoided more than anything else because they even debase God's deeds and will to obtain an upright world. Other quotations from Burton, Curtius and Rousset express the same about a world that is upside-down. Eco's quotation, being an annex, is clearly only a reference to the main theme and amongst other western poems is the only example from a novel.

With an eye towards western criticism, Qian Zhongshu always gives a new perspective to the analysis of ancient Chinese classical texts as in *Guan Zhui Bian* when D'Annunzio and his lines

Sotto il cielo bigio, il giallo grida, il rosso squilla[477]
(Under the grey sky yellow screams, red blares)

are drawn near lines quoted by Yang Wanli 楊萬里 (1127-1206) and Yan Suicheng 嚴遂成 (1694- ?). To quote what sometimes results as trivial bits and pieces of literary works might seem a controversial method of analysis. The explanation for this comes once again from Qian himself who states:

I have bored holes in these many texts to string selected passages together, hoping thereby to call attention to a single literary technique that manifests itself in a thousand different ways.[478]

---

476  Qian Zhongshu, *Guan Zhui Bian*, II, 918.
477  See *Guan Zhui Bian*, 744. D'Annunzio's lines are from the poem "Notturno" quoted and discussed in Eurialo De Michelis *Tutto D'Annunzio*, once more Qian Zhongshu accesses a poet through a critic's essay on the poet.
478  Egan, *Limited Views*, 177

A variation of a theme already presented through Leopardi's words is supported by a quotation from the Italian poet Ungaretti (1880-1970) that reads:

Balaustrata di brezza
Per appoggiare stasera
La mia malinconia[479]
(Gentle breeze balustrade
On which to lean tonight
My melancholy).

It is always about sadness and Ungaretti, among others, expresses in poetry the concept that being on a high brings forth the latent sense of sadness that one might feel. Sadness and weariness also emerge from another quoted poem by Ungaretti, *Si porta* (Brings with himself) where the poet says:

Si porta l'infinita stanchezza
Dello sforzo occulto
Di questo principio
Che ogni anno
Scatena la terra[480]
(It brings eternal weariness
Of the hidden effort
Of this principle
That every year
Arouses the earth).

---

479 Qian Zhongshu, *Guan Zhui Bian*, III, 1412. See Ungaretti, *Stasera*, in *L'Allegria*, 1916.
480 Qian Zhongshu, *Guan Zhui Bian*, IV, 2306. See Ungaretti, *Si porta*, in *Vita d'un Uomo*, 1918.

Qian Zhongshu continues quoting Aldo Vallone (1916-2002) and his *Aspetti Della Poesia Italiana Contemporanea* (Aspects of Contemporary Italian Poetry) in which the author observes that what is expressed by Ungaretti is:

Strikingly similar to the mood and scenes so often evoked in our nation's poetry.[481]

Another theme that Qian finds the same in both Chinese and western literatures, inserted in a comment on a passage from *Laozi* about the contrast and the relation between body (*shen* 身) and fame (*ming* 名), is illustrated by passages from *Zhuangzi, Bai Juyi, Fan Zhongyan* 范仲淹 (989-1052), *Tang Yin* 唐寅 (1470-1523), Edward Gibbon, Eckermann and La Bruyère (1645-1696) among the others, and involves a contemporary Italian writer, Tomasi di Lampedusa (1896-1957) and another of the Marinisti poets, Tommaso Gaudiosi (17th sec.). Life, as long as it might be, is extremely short if we count only the happy moments for true life. Quotations are freely translated into Chinese and their assonance is complete:

Dieci lustri di vita o poco meno
Porto sul dorso; e se ricerco quante
Son l'ore lieta, a numerar l'istante,
Posso a pena formarne un di sereno[482]
(I am nearly fifty years old;
And if I try to count
The happy hours in my life I can barely
Make them add up to one day)

---

481 Egan, *Limited Views*, 78.
482 Qian Zhongshu, *Guan Zhui Bian*, II, 792. See Croce, *Lirici Marinisti*, 505. **lieta** should be spelled as **liete**.

is the quotation from the poem *L'Infelicità Umana* (Human Sadness) by Gaudiosi and

> Ho settantatrè anni, all'ingrosso ne avrò vissuto, veramente vissuto, un totale di due...tre al massimo. E i dolori, la noia, quanto erano stati? Tutto il resto: settant'anni[483]
>
> (I am seventy-three years old and I have probably lived only two or three years at most. Pain, boredom, how much do they amount to? All the rest: seventy years)

is the sentence from *Il Gattopardo* (The Leopard), an internationally recognized novel by Tomasi di Lampedusa. The only way to make life longer, Qian seems to suggest through a quotation by Blake a few lines later, is to pursue one's desires by trying to increase the amount of happy moments:

> He who desires but acts not, breeds pestilence; Sooner murder an infant in cradle than nurse un-acted desires.[484]

As for the meaning of these happy moments and the way to fulfil desires, an incredibly real survey draws from *Harrap's Slang Dictionary*, 1984, quoted in an annex, and mentions that LSD (Lysergic Acid Diethylamide) is considered a way of reaching immediate satisfaction. It then goes on quoting a Portuguese-Italian philosopher, Leone Ebreo (1460-1530), who in his *Dialoghi d'Amore* (Dialogues of Love) suggests that copulation is the way to reach beatitude:

> L'atto copulativo de l'intima e unita cognizione divina; copulazione è la più

---

483 Qian Zhongshu, *Guan Zhui Bian*, II, 792. See Tomasi di Lampedusa, *Il Gattopardo*, 210.

484 Qian Zhongshu, *Guan Zhui Bian*, II, 794. See Blake, *The Marriage of Heaven and Hell*, 13.

propria e precisa parola che signifchi la beatitudine[485]
(The copulative act of the intimate and united divine knowledge; copulation is
the most appropriate and precise word to signify beatitude).

Another passage from Ungaretti in *Tan Yi Lu* LVII that follows the
western quotations from Rambler and Reverdy, reads:

La poesia moderna si propone di metter in contatto ciò che è più distante.
Maggiore è la distanza, superiore è la poesia[486]
(Modern poetry wants to link what is very far away. The farther the distance, the
more superior the outcome of poetry is).

Ungaretti's passage comes from an essay by G. Mariani reported in the
proceedings of the Second International Congress of Italian Studies about
Stylistic Critic and Literary Baroque. All the quotations in this passage serve
to prove what Qian Zhongshu believes to be true: it is very important for the
sake of good poetry to make antithesis and striking connections to link
different realms and make them the same in a way that astonishes the reader
both for its unlikelihood and for its originality and well-founded relationship.
What is true about poetry is also true about method of work, both the
author's and his *datong*.

The reference to Luigi Pirandello's novel *Uno, Nessuno, Centomila* (One,
No One and One Hundred Thousand) is remarkable because it is a reference
to a work that still does not exist in a full text edition in Chinese. Luigi
Pirandello (1867-1936), although an author of the utmost importance for
20th century literature, is not very well-known in China and, if the existing

---

485  Qian Zhongshu, *Guan Zhui Bian*, II, 798.
486  Qian Zhongshu, *Tan Yi Lu*, 478.

translations in mainland China include only two collections of narrative,[487] it is a good sign that a performance of his *Sei Personaggi in Cerca d'Autore* (Six Characters in Search of an Author) has been enthusiastically greeted when performed by the Shanghai Theatre Academy at the Shanghai 2010 expo. Qian quotes from one of Pirandello's most representative works in an entry that takes its move from *Liezi*'s sentence about the need to continually pursue truth.[488] Men need to keep searching for truth and for the *dao* 道 because they themselves always change in a continuous metamorphosis:

Riconoscerete forse anche voi ora, che un minuto fa voi eravate un altro?[489]
(You too will now admit that a minute ago you were another person?).

Pirandello's quotation is followed by many other sentences with similar meaning and all of them confirm and support *Liezi*'s assumption.

In opposition to traditional Chinese filial piety, *xiao* 孝, instead are all the quotations from Chinese and western authors that come from the mouths of both parents and children to exclude every sense of gratitude or respect due to the reciprocal role.

Alberto Moravia (1907-1990), contemporary Italian novelist, is quoted with a sentence from his short stories spaced out from Qian's translation:

Guarda che non dovresti rispondere così a tuo padre, [...] alzava le spalle, [...]. Io non avevo chiesto di venire al mondo. Mi ci avete fatta venire.[490]
(You should not talk back to your father this way, [...] shrugging her shoulders, [...] I did not ask to come into the world. It was you who gave birth to me).

---

487 Pilandelou 皮蘭德婁, *Zisha de gushi: Pilandelei Duanpian Xiaoshuo Xuan* 《自殺的故事：皮蘭德婁短篇小說選》, Liaoning Jiaoyu Chubanshe, 2000 and *Pilandelei Zhongduanpian Xiaoshuo Xuan* 《皮蘭德婁中短篇小說選》, Zhongguo Wenlian Chubanshe, 2009.
488 See Qian Zhongshu, *Guan Zhui Bian*, II, 727-736.
489 Qian Zhongshu, *Guan Zhui Bian*, II, 734-735. See Pirandello, *Uno, Nessuno, Centomila*, 33.
490 Qian Zhongshu, *Guan Zhui Bian*, III, 1630. See Moravia, *Opere complete*, 581.

Qian's words in concluding this entry are critical enough toward the lack of filial piety.

A few lines later, in the following entry, another quotation from the same work by Moravia echoes all the others (among which an expression used by Michelangelo, "la figura serpentina" – serpentine figure) on the image of woman like a snake:

> La donna...era flessuosa come un serpente; camminando dimenava le anche e dondolava di testa[491]
> (The woman...was sinuous like a snake, she wiggled her hips and swayed her head).

If the operation of explaining the present through the past is something critics, historians and observers of society have usually carried out, the same cannot be said of the reverse operation of explaining the past through the present. This can be seen as an original contribution offered from Qian Zhongshu in terms of methodology and is probably the part of his theories that might give new clues to a thorough and in depth examination of Chinese and world literature.

---

491 Qian Zhongshu, Guan Zhui Bian, III, 1634. See Moravia, Opere complete, 177.

# CHAPTER 6
# Conclusions

This study of Italian authors and works in Qian Zhongshu's works contributes to a greater understanding of his use of foreign language quotations, with a focus on the Italian literary world. Included are sections on language, historical period, authors and quotations.

## 6.1 Language

Qian Zhongshu quotes all authors in their original language, nearly always accompanied by a Chinese translation, especially when quotations are in the main body of the text and not in a footnote. This clear indication of Qian's understanding of the Italian language is supported by his link with Italian scholars and literati. Lionello Lanciotti affirmed this in an interview.[492] In a letter to Professor Lü Tongliu, Qian wrote that he received articles from some popular Italian magazines. Wu Taichang reported in *Wo Renshi de Qian Zhongshu* that in 1984, on the occasion of the fourth National Meeting of Representatives of Chinese Writers, Qian completed a form where one of the fields was "foreign languages" and he wrote: English, French, German, Italian.[493]

Being able to read foreign works in their original language helps a true comparatist appreciate the flavour of texts without misunderstandings due to

---

492 Lanciotti, discussion with author, Rome, February 17, 2009.
493 Wu Taichang, *Wo Renshi de Qian Zhongshu*, 116.

translation errors. Qian Zhongshu's obituary in the *Guangming Ribao* of December 22, 1998, includes excerpts of interviews with Qian's colleagues from the Chinese Academy of Social Sciences. In an interview Dong Heng, an expert in American literature, affirms that he often helped Qian to borrow books and discovered that Qian would borrow books in English, French, German, Italian, Latin, Greek, and that this method of reading texts in the original language was of great inspiration to fellow scholars.[494]

The present study demonstrates that reading and quoting texts in their original languages is one of the main characteristics of Qian's method, and one that places him in the field of comparative literature without fear of translation errors, not uncommon in comparative studies. Quotations in Italian – an Italian that sweeps over classical times and contemporary years – are always perfectly integrated into the main body of the text, and delight in their refinement and accuracy.

## 6.2 Historical Periods

Qian Zhongshu was able to read and understand Italian from a variety of historical periods and authors. Table 1 summarises the historical periods, the number of authors in each period and examples of cited authors.

Qian chose ten authors up to and including the Middle Ages going back as far as Saint Augustine in the 5th century A.D. The languages from the Middle Ages and Baroque Italy are the most difficult to understand for non-native speakers who lack specific training or familiarity with those codes. The language of the Middle Ages is the most distant from contemporary Italian usage and the Baroque language is the most affected by imagery and rhetorical

---

494  He Hui and Fang Tianxing, ed. *Yi Cun Qian Si.*

speech. From the 15<sup>th</sup> to the 16<sup>th</sup> century, the age of Humanism and the Renaissance, Qian cited twenty-eight different authors such as Leonardo Da Vinci, Lorenzo de Medici, Benvenuto Cellini.

| Historical Period | Number of Authors | Examples of Authors |
|---|---|---|
| 5<sup>th</sup> century to the Middle Ages | 10 | Saint Augustine, Dante Alighieri, Giovanni Boccaccio. |
| 15<sup>th</sup> and 16<sup>th</sup> centuries Humanism, Renaissance | 28 | Matteo Bandello, Giambattista Basile, Niccolò Machiavelli. |
| 17<sup>th</sup> century Baroque and Marinisti Poets | 12 | Cesare Abelli, Lorenzo Magalotti, Carlo Innocenzo Frugoni. |
| 18<sup>th</sup> century Age of Enlightenment | 8 | Cesare Beccaria, Pietro Verri, Giambattista Vico. |
| 19<sup>th</sup> century Romanticism | 12 | Giacomo Leopardi, Alessandro Manzoni, Giuseppe Giusti. |
| 20<sup>th</sup> century Contemporary period | 32 | Umberto Eco, Alberto Moravia, Gabriele D'Annunzio. |
| Total | 102 | |

In Qian's writings, the 17<sup>th</sup> century, the century of Baroque and Marinisti poets, is represented by twelve authors – such as Giambattista Marino or Giovan Francesco Maia Materdona. The 18<sup>th</sup> century Age of Enlightenment provided Qian with eight authors with its main representatives being philosophers and thinkers such as Cesare Beccaria, Pietro Verri, Giambattista Vico, and writers such as Carlo Goldoni, Carlo Innocenzo Frugoni, Pietro Metastasio, with their elegant and classical oriented language. He quoted from twelve authors of 19<sup>th</sup> century Romanticism including the poet Leopardi and the writer Manzoni. Of the 102 authors selected by Qian, he quoted from thirty-two authors of the 20<sup>th</sup> century including Benedetto Croce, Giuseppe Ungaretti, Giovanni Pascoli.

Table 1 indicates that Qian emphasised two literary periods – the Humanism and Renaissance period from the 15$^{th}$ and 16$^{th}$ centuries and the first half of the 20$^{th}$ century.

The Renaissance began in Italy and spread to the rest of Europe up to the 17$^{th}$ century, leaving indelible and long – lasting changes in the cultural and social spheres of a vast area of the western world. The great genius Leonardo da Vinci represents Renaissance man and is a clear symbol of society's progress based on continuous training in classical education, with a firm belief in the power of art to instil a sense of eternity in a finite world, as Qian notes in a quotation near the end of *Guan Zhui Bian* where Da Vinci affirms that:

> Cosa bella mortal passa e non dura
> (A beautiful mortal thing passes and does not last)

and

> Cosa bella mortal passa e non d'arte[495]
> (A beautiful mortal thing passes away, but not if it belongs to art).

The Italian language was solemn and preciously carved in every one of the literary pieces, slowly evolving in the Baroque to elaborate an artificial love for figures of speech and plays on words.

The first half of the 20$^{th}$ century was the period in which Qian lived and worked. It was an age of extraordinary transformation in the history of the western as well as the eastern world. It was marked by two atrocious world

---

495 Qian Zhongshu, *Guan Zhui Bian*, IV, 2284.

wars, the end of the Chinese empire, and a new global perspective that revolutionised the social and cultural order. In the cultural crisis that affected society, a need for new values emerged and literature played a fundamental role in the process.

Creative writers and literary critics reasserted the centrality of literature as a guide to the perplexities of the age. A sense of doubt developed into a spirit of revolt and experimentation in an attempt to create a new system of reference. New methods were tried as well as a new language to develop rich patterns of meaning to explore modern experiences and consciousness. Modernism was in fact a powerful international movement reaching throughout western cultures, dominating the sensibility and aesthetic choices in literature. Most movements emphasised the loss of a sense of continuity between past and present through a radical break with tradition, whereas some intellectuals held onto tradition, which coexisted with innovation. The past was remoulded in an original way by writers and poets who were influenced by contemporary authors from abroad, giving literature a cosmopolitan flair. This is a period in which literature seemed to search for a new language to express new feelings. Western modernism influenced the language and the expression of ideas while critics tried to understand and explain this evolution of culture.

## 6.3 Authors and quotations

Most of Qian Zhongshu's readings are guided more by a critical than a narrative eye: he quotes the Italian critics Mario Praz, Dino Provenzal, Benedetto Croce, Giuseppe Giusti, and through them accesses Dante, Leopardi, Pascoli, D'Annunzio, Ariosto, Boiardo, or talks about Italian poetry and its characteristics as found in critical treatises such as *Poesia Bernesca e*

*Marinismo* (Berni's poetry and Marinismo) whose author, R. Macchioni Jodi, is quoted with examples taken from the poets Francesco Berni (1497-1535) and Torquato Tasso who describe beautiful women as having ebony teeth and silver eyes or hair.[496]

Qian Zhongshu writes in *Zhongguo Shi yu Zhongguo Hua* that from a critical perspective it is possible to understand the flavour of one author and his work just as from the rippling of water or sand indicates the direction of the wind.[497] This is a concept that occupies an important part in Qian Zhongshu's ideas about literary appreciation and to which he returns in *Guan Zhui Bian* where he states that nothing can really be extrapolated from context. The implications are that to understand the meaning of a sentence it is necessary to understand the origin of characters; to understand the sense of a text, it is necessary to understand the meaning of the sentences making up the text and only then can the concepts and the ideas be deduced. The small clarifies the big; the big and general, give understanding to the small and particular; the final implications, lead to consideration of the starting principles and from the basic principles, details emerge. The prevalent style of writing when a work is composed, or the critical and rhetorical trends in which an author writes, are, in Qian's opinion, fundamental to understanding an author, and only with a full picture in mind can the meaning of particular sentences and even words can be analysed. An interesting aside as noted by Hu Fanzhu 胡范鑄 and Chen Jiaxuan 陳佳璿,[498] is that if the background is important to understanding every act of speech, it is also true that as soon as an act of speech is enunciated, it modifies the background in which it has

---

496  See Qian Zhongshu, *Guan Zhui Bian*, III, 1656.
497  Qian Zhongshu, "Zhongguo Shi yu Zhongguo Hua", in *Qi Zhui Ji*, 2 . "...hao bi cong fei sha, mailang, bowenli fachule feng de zitai" …好比從飛沙、麥浪、波紋裡看出了風的姿態.
498  Hu Fangzhu, Chen Jiaxuan, "'Guan Zhui Bian' suo Yunhan de Shihui Pipan Yishi", in Ding, Weizhi ed., *Qian Zhongshu Xiansheng Bainian Danchen Jinian wenji*, 61-76.

been generated.

Two authors helped Qian Zhongshu prove the validity of his assumptions. Pareyson (1918-1991), an Italian philosopher, supported the introduction of German existentialism[499] into Italy and maintained that the understanding of reality is a matter pertaining essentially to an individual's capacity of interpretation. Giordano Bruno (1548-1600), a philosopher whose ideas were considered heretical and condemned by the Church, assumed that God was a pantheistic diety in which thought and substance merge without distinction. Quotations come from Pareyson's *Estetica: Teoria della Formatività* and Bruno's *Spaccio de la Bestia Trionfante* (The Expelling of the Triumphant Beast) and are not translated, in footnote. Pareyson's quotation, accompanied by an opinion of the German philosopher W. Dilthey (1833- 1911), reads:

> La parte è contenuta dal tutto solo in quanto a sua volta lo contiene,
> E il tutto è formato dalle parti solo in quanto le ha esso stesso reclamate e ordinate[500]
> (The single part is contained in the whole only to the extent to which itself contains the whole; the whole is made up by the parts only to the extent to which itself has demanded and arranged them).

Bruno's assumption, which finds its perfect counterpart in a line from the Huayanjing (The Avatamsaka Sutra Scripture) is:

> La unità è nel numero infinito ed il numero infinito nell'unità; l'unità è uno infinito implicito, e l'infinito è la unità explicita[501]

---

499 For the influence of existentialism on Qian Zhongshu see Wang Ning, "Confronting Western Influence", 916.
500 Qian Zhongshu, *Guan Zhui Bian*, I, 281.
501 Qian Zhongshu, *Guan Zhui Bian*, I, 283. The quotation is from *Opere di Giordano Bruno e di Tommaso Campanella*

(Unity is in the infinite number and the infinite number is in the unit; unity is an implicit infinite and infinite is the explicit unity).

The parts cannot be understood without the whole, nor the whole without the parts – unity and infinity converge. These passages illuminate the understanding that quotations in Qian's work are justified only in light of their context and of the general critical atmosphere which surrounds literary works, and that the author's intent is far from a fragmented reality without cohesion and coherence.

Qian Zhongshu's point of view is an aesthetic and critical one, and his focus is on rhetoric, artistic commitment, and literary criticism more than on content and narrative scopes. His main intent is to delve into the artistic conception of Chinese and western works to look for common principles, common poetic or artistic spirit. For Qian, it is nevertheless true that a good critic is the only one who can understand poetry because he is able to write it; a poet can be a good critic, but a good critic is not necessarily a good poet.[502]

The reason why quotations in his essays are drawn from the 15th and 16th centuries is probably that in the Italian Renaissance Qian Zhongshu finds the expression of the spirit he wanted to disclose in his difficult times. Italian Renaissance authors like Machiavelli, Ariosto, Boiardo, offered Qian Zhongshu the words he could not directly use. During the Renaissance, with its cult of the classical world, the need for revival of the old culture lived within a new and revolutionary spirit.

During the 20th century, on the other hand, an Italian man of letters could oppose the contemporary society. Once more Qian Zhongshu uses the

---

in the edition published by Riccardo Ricciardi from which Qian quotes often.
502 See Qian Zhonghu, *Guan Zhui Bian*, III, 1665-1677.

words of Italian authors to say what he could not have said in his own voice.

It is interesting to note that all the Italian works quoted are functional to the analysis of Chinese traditional literature: Bandello, Boccaccio, Sacchetti and Calvino. The Italian novelists are quoted to make some observations and criticism on the Chinese narrative pieces in religious works, when Qian Zhongshu says that all these Italian novelists created in their works a *feiwo* 非 我 (not me) character, that had the function of creating a distance between the author and the things described, so as to give to the mirabilia[503] a feeling of truthfulness. This feeling, warns Qian Zhongshu, is what Chinese religious literary works, like the *Jiusheng Jing* 舅甥經 of the last essay of the collection *Qi Zhui Ji*, lack, and is a necessary element that should be incorporated into narrative works.

The theory of "literary hypocrisy"[504] from the *Estetica* by Benedetto Croce is used to legitimise changes and revolutions in traditional ideas, while Dante and his method, validated by Ariosto and Boiardo,[505] of creating expectation in a piece of art, be it a painting, a literary work or a sculpture, justifies and explains all the suspense created in Chinese serial novels, and legitimises these works as literary works able to create expectation and pleasure of a noble kind.

Even if the works of Qian Zhongshu, their biji form and the huge span of time they cover, seem to be, and in a certain sense are, all inclusive, it is still possible to find recurrent themes and a choice of authors and literary trends that weave through the fabric of Qian's essays.

By analysing first the function of quotations in Qian's work and secondly by dividing and grouping those quotations according to the quoted authors,

---

503  Marvellous and extraordinary things.
504  Qian Zhongshu, "Zhongguo shi yu Zhongguo hua", in *Qi Zhui Ji*, 2.
505  Qian Zhongshu, "Du 'Laaokong'", in *Qi Zhui Ji*, 51-55.

we may note that nothing is left to pure chance and that it is possible to find order and a cause-effect sequence in his comparative method.

The relationship between men and women is, for example, a theme that recurs many times. Quotations by Boiardo and Ariosto address the injustice of the different treatment the two sexes receive from society. The longest passage on this theme, and particularly on the possibility for women to compose poetry and be scholars, at the end of the second volume of *Guan Zhui Bian* where many quotations, both Chinese and western, demonstrate that this behaviour has been unjustly perpetrated over the course of history as all the quoted authors demonstrate. The Italian poets Giosuè Carducci and Gaspara Stampa (1523-1554) stand on the side of the Chinese, the French, the German, and the British. Carducci's quotation, echoing the others, is:

> Nel mio codice poetico c'è questo articolo: ai preti e alle donne è vietato far versi[506]
> (In my poetic code there is this clause: women and priests are forbidden to be engaged in poetry).

This is a quotation out of context, since the continuation of the sentence, in an excerpt of a letter sent by the poet to a poetess he appreciated, is that he would abrogate this clause for her. The quotation from the *Sonnets* (Sonetti) by Gaspara Stampa is only a reference to herself as a despicable and vile woman:

> Così come sono abietta e vile
> Donna[507]
> (Thus as I am a despicable and vile

---

506 Qian Zhongshu, *Guan Zhui Bian*, II, 1315. See Carducci e Vivanti, *Addio Caro Orco*, 18; Stampa, *Rime*, 7.
507 See Stampa, *Rime*, VIII.

Woman).

The theme was an important one for Qian as he mentioned it so many times; the dryness with which he presents it, without value judgment, is even more a call for the reader's judgment.

More than in other essays, Italian literature is overwhelmingly present in the essay *Tonggan* – Pascoli, Perri, D'Annunzio, Carducci, Paolieri, the Marinisti poets – where Qian Zhongshu explains a rhetorical figure ever present in Chinese literature but never fully understood by previous Chinese commentators. He affirms at the beginning of the essay that in Chinese poetics there is a narrative technique that critics and rhetoricians of the past had limited understanding or did not know.[508] This is a fundamental contribution to a mutual understanding that Qian Zhongshu wishes, and functions in demonstrating that due to this literary and critical exchange, this rhetorical figure has been understood in China.

Figurative language attracts Qian for its evocative power and the capacity to play with words and their meanings, to give life to inanimate objects and to give rationality to irrational things, or simply to relate in metaphor things that are usually distant in attributes and semantic fields. Most of the Italian authors quoted are masters of figurative language, from the Marinisti poets with their rich use of imagery to Dante's absolute excellence in Italian literature for his similes; from the novelists of Boccaccio's school with their fables and metaphors, mostly functional in arousing amusement and a sagacious rethinking of popular themes, to the most subtle figures of Italian medieval and romantic poetry, more intimate and meant to enrich

---

508 Qian Zhongshu, "Tonggan", in *Qi Zhui Ji*, 62. The original text is: *Zhongguo shiwen you yi zhong miaoxie shoufa, gudai pipingjia he xiucixuejia sihu dou meiyou lijie huo renshi* 中國詩文有一種描寫手法, 古代批評家和修辭學家似乎都沒有理解或認識.

descriptions and evocative language.

Since the present study focuses on the contribution of Italian literature to the comparative method of Qian Zhongshu, mere analysis of Qian's use of quotations of metaphors and similes falls outside the scope of this research; it would nevertheless be a promising field of study as a main vehicle to guide the choice of authors and their works. This explains why Marinisti's poetry, often condemned as empty in Italian literary criticism, is so present in the selection of Qian's quoted lines. It is necessary to point out that Qian's theory about metaphor, as demonstrated throughout his works and particularly explained in *Guan Zhui Bian*,[509] is of western derivation. I. A. Richards, a British critic, poet and theorist on western metaphor, spent time at Qinghua University and discussed literature with Qian. Richards pointed to metaphor as juxtaposed images; western opinion about such a rhetorical device might well be expressed in Goodman's words that metaphor is

A matter of teaching an old world new tricks,[510]

a matter of unknown and unprecedented links – the more an author is capable of finding similarities and complementarity between different and distant things, the more able he is considered. According to Michelle Yeh, synthesis based on antithesis, reconciliation on opposition, juxtaposition and the focus on differences and opposition is what constitutes the western idea of metaphor and not the Chinese. In Chinese, metaphor is called bi 比 and the same etymology of the word carries the meaning of complementarity, of phenomenological, not ontological differences.[511] Things appear different, but

---

509 Egan, *Limited Views*, "metaphor has two handles and several sides", 121-129.
510 Yeh, "Metaphor and Bi", 244.
511 Yeh, "Metaphor and Bi", 247.

their essence is the same and in Qian Zhongshu's quotation from Ma Rongzu 馬榮祖 (1686-1761), like form and image they combine without the need of a medium.[512] This quotation is at the end of an entry in the third volume of *Guan Zhui Bian* on metaphor and its origin and function. The entry begins with an excursus on the image of the circle opposed to that of the square and continues with all the implications these two images have given in the course of the history of ideas. Knowing the characteristics attributed to the circle and the square explains why a man can be defined as a "square man" and why fortune can be associated with a circular entity (see *La Ruota della Fortuna* – The wheel of fortune – by Sacchetti and his quotation:

> Tu sè nel colmo della rota e non ti puoi muovere, che tu non scenda e capolevi.
> Per questa cagione io t'ho recato quello aguto, acciò che tu conficchi la rota[513]
> (You are at the top of the wheel and you cannot move for fear of getting down.
> That is why I brought you a stingy thing to drive it into the wheel).

Qian Zhongshu implies that metaphor is a combination of two images that are juxtaposed and reveal unprecedented links but at the core of which lies a common idea elaborated through the history of literature and of thought. It might seem surprising to call fortune a wheel, but it derives from the idea of the circle as something that turns. The two connected objects are not the same nor are they completely different so authors must be skilled enough in the common ground of world literature to understand the justifications in making two different objects as one.

Qian follows the western concept of metaphor, even if slightly merged

---

512  Qian Zhongshu, *Guan Zhui Bian*, III, 1481. "*Ru xing yu ying, he bu dai mei* 如形與影, 合不待妹".

513  Qian Zhongshu, *Guan Zhui Bian*, III, 1477. See Sacchetti, *Il Trecentonovelle*, 239. Other Italian quotations support the image of Fortune as a circular object like Machiavelli, who lets the personified Occasion say that it stands on a wheel "è perch'io tengo un piè sopra una rota" to mean that it goes quickly away and Marino who in his Adone defines Fortune as a "volubil palla", a changeable ball.

with some Chinese theory at its core, and applies to Chinese classical and traditional literature. He looks at Chinese things interpreting them with a western eye and, as with synaesthesia, he makes Chinese literature more accessible to western readers, offering a key for its interpretation while explaining aspects of Chinese literature with a new eye.

Qian's choice of foreign quotations demonstrates his deep link with other cultures. Cultural elements refer to all those words and expressions that may be found in books but are most commonly part of daily conversation; elements indicate the specificity of a culture as, for example, proverbs or words indicating objects or things normally used. In *Guan Zhui Bian* III, 132, it is surprising for an Italian reader to find words such as:

"capelli d'angelo" ...................................................................angel's hair

"fiocchetti" ...................................................................................ribbons

"ravioli" ...........................................................................................ravioli

"tortello" ....................................................................................... tortelli

all falling in the category of "la pasta"[514] (pasta) associated with Chinese dishes made of flour, *mian* 麵, and translated by Qian both literally and semantically with the individuation of Chinese varieties of pasta that correspond to the Italian ones. In order they are presented by Qian as

simian 絲麵, noodles
literally tianxianbi 天仙髮, hair of a heavenly immortal
maoerduo 貓耳朵, cat's ears
yunpian 雲片, slices of clouds
hundun 餛飩, wanton
jiaozi 餃子, dumplings

---

514 Qian Zhongshu, *Guan Zhui Bian*, III, 1850.

It is still more surprising to find these words in a comment on the *Bing Fu* 餅賦 by Shu Xi 束皙 of the Three Kingdoms era in the 3$^{rd}$ century A.D.

As already mentioned in this study, Qian's use of Italian proverbs comes from the *Dizionario comparato di Proverbi* (Comparative Dictionary of Proverbs) by Augusto Arthaber. Sometimes proverbs are simply recalled by the author, as in the opening of his 1980 speech *Shi Keyi Yuan* 詩可以怨 at a Japanese University, when Qian affirmed that to talk about Chinese literature in such a gathering of sinologists was a deed of great courage; the probable consequence might be like the old Italian saying, "Ha inventato l'ombrello"[515] (he has invented the umbrella), a saying used in Italy to laugh at somebody who is convinced he has a new idea, a new invention or a new discovery already well known to everybody but himself. The pertinent use of proverbs and cultural items in Qian's essays is further proof of his acquaintance with the social atmosphere of the literatures from which he quoted, that is, in full cognition of the facts.

Studying the way in which Qian Zhongshu used foreign literatures to analyse Chinese literature for mutual understanding and allowing a more comprehensive grasp of cultural and literary phenomena is certainly a topic that might significantly add to the study of literatures in a global context. It might undoubtedly help illuminate comprehension between foreign concepts that may seem distant and different while they only need to come in contact

---

515 Qian Zhongshu, "Shi Keyi Yuan", in *Qi Zhui Ji*, 115. To support his quotation Qian Zhongshu explains the origin of this saying. A man was walking on a country road when suddenly he was surprised by rain. He then took a stick and placed it on a piece of cloth that he happened to be carrying; this clever stratagem prevented him from being drenched by the rain. He then thought the world should profit from his invention, and went to the Patent Office to register his trick. When the desk clerk saw his invention he started laughing and exclaimed, "He has invented the umbrella!" Qian feels like that useless inventor in making a speech about Chinese literature within a context in which this subject is so well known. It is strange that Qian Zhongshu uses such an unknown saying. Italians like to say "he has invented hot water" when talking about a well known truth that bears no new and unknown content, and it is unknown whether this is a quotation Qian had learnt by direct contact with Italians or from some written reference. (See Lioi, "Yidali Sixiang Duiyu Qian Zhongshu Zhengti Siwei de Gongxian", 2011, 381-400.)

to discover that a different perspective can lead to a better understanding of others and oneself. Huang Weiliang 黃維樑, in *Liu Xie yu Qian Zhongshu* 劉勰與錢鍾書 (Liu Xie and Qian Zhongshu), accurately states that the *datong* Qian applies in his works should have earned him a Nobel Peace Prize![516]

## 6.4 Quotations that stand the test of time

If it is true that big theories and constructs are often not able to stand the test of time, then a meticulous job of building piece by piece permits Qian to create a more solid foundation for his flow of ideas. Quotations in his works, like bricks in a house or trees in a forest, are the solid elements that constitute the whole. Basing the explanation of general theories on so many tangible elements helps to avoid the peril of seeing the forest and not the trees. General theories without substantial concepts to build on, or seeing the trees and not the forest, is akin to having small pieces of ideas without the capacity to link them in a more general context that surpasses time and space boundaries. This last behaviour is the one Qian seems to ascribe particularly to his fellow writers whom he considers incapable of having a view that surpassed time and space.[517]

Nevertheless, to quote only a trifling passage of a source text might seem a controversial and narrow-minded method, but still the justification for this process can be inferred once again from Qian's direct words:

I have bored holes in these many texts to string selected passages together, hoping thereby to call attention to a single literary technique that manifests itself

---

516  See Huang Weiliang, *Liu Xie and Qian Zhongshu*, 2009.
517  See Song Xinli , "Cong 'Du Laaokong' Guankui Qian Zhonghshu de Wenyi Jianshang Guan".

in a thousand different ways.[518]

## 6.5 Becoming a field of study: Qian Xue 錢學

In the short story *Linggan*, Inspiration, published in 1946 in the collection *Ren Shou Gui*, Qian Zhongshu makes fun of a writer so famous that his "name was completely obscured by the reputation"[519] he had acquired. In the year of publication of *Guan Zhui Bian* in 1979, Zheng Chaozong, a friend of Qian Zhongshu, proposed the name of *Qian Xue*, Qian Studies, to indicate the whole field of research on the author.

In 1988 the first issue of the *Qian Zhongshu Yanjiu* review 錢鍾書研究 (Research on Qian Zhongshu) was released and, since the 1980s, the term *Qian Xue* has been widely used to indicate that Qian Zhongshu has a corpus of works worthy of a new discipline.

Qian – a huge personality of great wit and extensive learning – leads naturally for scholars to converge in studies on the author. But the creation of a field of study on him, the *Qian Xue*, did not please the author. Qian always disapproved studies on his life and works. He was always critical of analytical studies and biographies in general and in the course of his life discouraged many critics who wanted to do research on him. Nevertheless, *Guan Zhui Bian* and *Wei Cheng* are such great achievements that, notwithstanding the opposing political situation and the will of the author to stay away from fame and academic honours, nothing could be done to avoid their influence on literature and their incentive to critical analysis.

The years subsequent to the publication of *Guan Zhui Bian* saw the

---

518 Egan, *Limited Views*, 177.
519 Translation by Hu in *Human Beasts and Ghosts*, 153.

growth of Qian Studies with many publications on the subject, including the *Qian Zhongshu Yanjiu* review published by the *Wenhua Yishu Chubanshe* 文化藝術出版社 (Culture and Art Publishing House) and several volumes of research material on Qian edited by Lu Wenhu. The 1980s saw authors analyse Qian Zhongshu's life and works from a variety of fields – translation, comparative literature, philosophy, intercultural studies, linguistic, and history – establishing solid bases for future research. *Qian Xue* is, in fact, a discipline that embraces all the fields related to Qian Zhongshu's works, from the seven different languages Qian quoted to philosophy, religion, history, exegetics, folklore, rhetoric, cultural studies, psychology, and comparative studies.

After the death of Qian, all expressions of appreciation and thoughts of remembrance from the literary world, together with various articles published in the Chinese national and international press, were collected in *Yi Cun Qian Si*[520] 一寸千思 *and in Bu Yiyang de Jiyi*[521] 不一樣的記憶.

As for American and European appreciation, the remarkable and forerunner of ensuing critiques was expressed by Xia Zhiqing in his A History of Modern Chinese Fiction:

The Besieged City" is the most delightful and carefully wrought novel in modern Chinese literature: it is perhaps also its greatest novel.[522]

Outside China Xia Zhiqing's words on *Wei Cheng* were a starting point for research and translations that inspired scholars like Nicolas Chapuis, Christian Bourgois, Ronald Egan, T. D. Huters, and Monika Motsch. In fact,

---

520  He Hui and Fang Tianxing, ed., *Yi Cun Qian Si*.
521  Cheng Bing edit., *Bu Yiyang de Jiyi – Yu Qian Zhongshu Zai Yiqi*.
522  C. T. Hsia, "Ch'ien Chung-shu", in *A History of Modern Chinese Fiction*, 441.

since research on Qian Zhongshu and his works started in China, many western countries started to pursue research on this author and have opened doctoral research classes. At the beginning of the 1980s, reports Chen Ziqian[523], a western scholar defined Qian as "the greatest sage," an epithet previously reserved for the Greek philosopher Socrates. This, remarks the critic, is something of which Chinese people can be proud, even if Qian Zhongshu was not interested in compliments and praise. *Qian Xue* scholars hope that this discipline will spread and become popular, but popularisation means also vulgarisation, because it is rarely linked to deep understanding. Qian Zhongshu always discouraged academic schools of research named after authors; should academics be unwilling to comply with his desire to refrain from scholarly research on his life and works, then it is necessary to conduct this research according to those criteria he indicated: a careful study should precede any pronouncement. A profound understanding of Qian's works should be a requirement before professing to be a scholar belonging to the *Qian Xue*.

Since the publication of the study *Qian Xue Lun* 錢學論 by Chen Ziqian[524], the term *Qian Xue* has been widely used and has started to appear in many articles giving way to jokes on the meaning of the name that plays on the homonym of the surname Qian and the Chinese word for money, qian 錢, thus translating the name *Qian Xue* as "the art of earning money" as in the literary magazine *Hebei Wenlun Bao*.[525]

Nevertheless the development of the discipline started only in the second half of 20$^{th}$ century although most of Qian Zhongshu's masterpieces were written in the 1940s. Qian's literary achievements were not recognised until

---

523  Chen Ziqian, *Lun Qian Zhongshu*, 238-239.
524  Chen Ziqian, *Qian Xue Lun*.
525  Chen Ziqian, *Lun Qian Zhongshu*, 238.

the 1980s and only achieved a complete recognition during the 1990s. Ironically, Qian Zhongshu only learned of Xia Zhiqing's appreciation of *Wei Cheng* in Italy in 1978 when attending a meeting on Sinology in the Italian city of Ortisei,[526] and an Italian scholar told him: "Oh, you're a chapter in a certain Xia's book". Moreover, that was also when Qian became aware of already completed or planned translations of *Wei Cheng* into the French, Russian, Czech, and English languages.[527]

The television series, *Wei Cheng*, directed by Huang Shuqin 黃蜀芹, was broadcast in December 1990. This adaptation of the homonymous novel won Qian Zhongshu's praise as a work better than he expected.[528] The series renewed interest in Qian's writings in mainland China, since up to that period he had been, if not neglected, certainly unappreciated. Zhang Wenjiang, author of a biography of Qian Zhongshu (to which this study has turned for its accuracy and authority), explains the initial lack of interest in Qian's work. With particular reference to the novel *Wei Cheng*, the difficulty of categorising literary accomplishments veered substantially from the main trends set by the Literary Revolution of the first half of the 20th century. More than according to Chinese tradition, *Wei Cheng* had to be analysed in light of world literature. Literary critics were bewildered and confused in having to express an opinion on the novel, and the easiest path was to ignore it. Zhang concludes that for Qian's contemporaries, reading the novel was like encountering an extraterrestrial.[529] According to Ted Huters, Qian Zhongshu was as prolific a writer as Ba Jin and Shen Congwen 沈從文. Qian did not identify himself with either the right or the left, he did not choose a particular

---

526 About the attendance at the Italian meeting see Wu Taichang, *Wo Renshi de Qian Zhongshu*.
527 Xia Zhiqing, "Zhonghui Qian Zhongshu Jishi", 60-76.
528 See Wu Taichang, *Wo Renshi de Qian Zhongshu*, 103.
529 See Zhang Wenjiang, *Yingzao Babita*, 48-49.

language nor a particular literary genre and, more than others, he has always expressed negative comments on his fellow writers, staying aloof from the contemporary literary stage.[530]

Gong Gang divides the *Qian Xue* into two big thematic sections: research on creative works and research on scholarly works, and into four time phases: the Minguo 民國 or Republican period up to 1949, when interest in Qian's work rose; the phase from 1949 to 1979, year of publication of *Guan Zhui Bian*, as the bleakest period; the period from 1979 to 1998, when there was a sudden rise and growth of interest; and the last period from 1998 to the present as the time to cherish Qian's memory and to conduct fruitful and in-depth research.

In the first phase, Qian Zhongshu did not have a leading role among the scholars and literati of his time, and masterpieces like Tan Yi Lu were classified as fragmentary and full of contradictions.[531] The publication of the novel Wei Cheng in 1947 caused contradictory opinions. Positive or negative as they might be, Qian Zhongshu was, with Zhang Ailing, one of the most prominent and popular writers during the Shanghai war of resistance.

From 1949 to 1969 there is nothing remarkable in the history of the Qian Xue but an episode with political connotations; the collection of Song poems, *Song Shi Xuanzhu*, was criticised as leftist by the *Guangming Ribao* 光明日報 of December 14, 1958.

Even if the whole corpus of Qian Xue is repetitive and redundant, it has been important since the first phase of its development to stimulate the interest on the writer and set the pattern for the research on his works.

The majority of publications date from the 1980s to the beginning of

---

530 See Huters, "Traditional Innovation".
531 Gong Gang, Yue Daiyun ed., *Qian Zhongshu: Aizhishe de Xiaoyao*, 25.

the 21st century when a crystallisation of the field of study occurred. New publications continue to appear, but they are mostly reprints of existing collections or collections of essays previously published in magazines or newspapers by well-known names in "commemoration literature." One of the last publications edited by Yang Lianfen and published by the *Wenhua Yishu Chubanshe* in 2009 (with preface and afterword dated 2010) entitled *Qian Zhongshu Pingshuo Qishi Nian* 錢鍾書評說七十年 (Seventy years of comments on Qian Zhongshu) collects extant and published material and the *Qian Zhongshu Xiansheng Bai Nian Danchen Jinian Wenji* 錢鍾書先生百年誕辰紀念文集 (Collected works commemorating the one hundred years of Qian Zhongshu) published at the end of 2010 by the Sanlian Shudian Chubanshe.

## 6.6 One hundred years of Qian Zhongshu

The year 2010, a fundamental date in the development of *Qian Xue*, marks one hundred years since the birth of the writer, and is an anniversary that has been duly commemorated with international conferences in Taipei and in Vancouver and a closed-door meeting in Beijing.

The Taipei "International Conference in Centennial Commemoration of the Late Professor Qian Zhongshu" was held at the College of Liberal Arts of National Central University in Jhong-Li, Taiwan, December 18-19, 2009; it was organised by Professor Wang Rongzu of the same university. This important and official meeting, included contributions from expert scholars on Qian Zhongshu from continental China, Taiwan, Macao, America, and Europe.[532] Yang Jiang, who is often reluctant to authorise meetings on her

---

532 The roster of participant scholars to the Taiwan conference included: Ye Jiaying, Nankai University; Wang Rongzu,

husband and herself, personally approved the list of participants at the meeting. The Taipei conference, with its variety of selected participants and its scholarly attitude, was a unique occasion to reflect on the achievements of Qian Zhongshu and on his influence on the Chinese contemporary literary world.

One year after the Taipei conference, the workshop "Qian Zhongshu and Yang Jiang: A Centennial Perspective"[533] held in Vancouver, Canada, in December 2010, was devoted to the future of studies and research on Qian Zhongshu and Yang Jiang. An occasion to exchange ideas, the workshop was organised by Professor Christopher Rea at the University of British Columbia in Canada to establish a specific focus in *Qian Xue* since its intent (beyond a mere commemoration and rethinking on Qian's works), was to collect scholarly expertise to write a book with the title *China's Literary Cosmopolitans: Qian Zhongshu, Yang Jiang, and the World of Modern Letters*. The book aims to explain to non-China specialists why Qian Zhongshu and Yang Jiang deserve attention. Such a focus is long overdue and strongly recommended for the discipline, *Qian Xue*. Only through opening itself to the outside world could *Qian Xue* advance and promote Qian Zhongshu's practice of literature and literary criticism, that is, to cross disciplines, time and space without being

---

Taiwan National Central University; Zhang Longxi, Hong Kong City University; Huang Weiliang, Foguang University; Monika Motsch, Munich University; Wang Cicheng, Taiwan National Central University; Zhang Jian, Taiwan Chinese Culture University; Jian Jinsong, Taiwan Chinese Culture University; Ronald Egan, University of Santa Barbara, California; Tian Jianmin, Hebei University; Zhang Gaoping, Taiwan Chengong University; Fu Jie, Shanghai Fudan University; Gong Gang, Macao University; Tiziana Lioi, Rome University Sapienza; Yu Guangzhong, Sun Yat-sen University, Shanghai.

533 The roster of participants to the Vancouver workshop included: Judy Amory, Independent scholar; Amy Dooling, Connecticut College; Ronald Egan, University of California, Santa Barbara; Jesse Field, University of Minnesota; Alexander Huang, The Pennsylvania State University; Ted Huters, University of California, Los Angeles; Ji Jin, Suzhou University; Wendy Larson, University of Oregon; Tiziana Lioi, Rome University Sapienza; Christopher Rea, The University of British Columbia; Carlos Rojas, Duke University; Yaohua Shi, Wake Forest University; Wang Yao, Suzhou University; Wang Yugen, University of Oregon; John B. Weinstein, Simon's Rock College at Bard; Zhang Enhua, University of Massachusetts at Amherst.

crystallized into empty rhetoric.

The *Qian Zhongshu Xiansheng Bai Nian Danchen Jinian Hui* 錢鍾書先生百年誕辰紀念會 (Meeting in commemoration of the one-hundred-year birthday of Qian Zhongshu) was a closed-door event at the Chinese Academy of Social Sciences in Beijing, in November 2010, after which the *Qian Zhongshu Xiansheng Bai Nian Danchen Jinian Wenji* 錢鍾書先生百年誕辰紀念文集 (Collected works in commemoration of the one-hundred-year birthday of Qian Zhongshu) was published at the end of 2010 by the *Sanlian Shudian Chubanshe*. In the foreword, the editor of the collection of essays, Ding Weizhi 丁偉志[534], stresses that the fundamental task for all scholars of Qian is to spread knowledge of the author and his works and, quoting Feng Youlan from the Confucian school of idealist philosophy, "we should not speak in accordance with it, but take it over."[535] That should be the wish and the aim of the 21st century *Qian Xue* – to gather Qian's legacy and apply his method to bring new content to Chinese and world comparative literature.

Among the series of activities and publications to commemorate one hundred years of Qian Zhongshu and Yang Jiang, the May 30, 2011 issue of the *Nanfang Renwu Zhoukan* 南方人物週刊[536] edited by the Southern Press Communication Corporation (*Nanfang baoye chuanmei jituan* 南方報業傳媒集團) dedicated its cover to both writers. A twenty-one page article by the journalist Li Naiqing 李乃清 illustrates this literary couple with pictures from their private lives.

---

534  Ding Weizhi is Associate Dean of the Chinese Academy of Social Sciences.
535  Ding Weizhi ed., *Qian Zhongshu Xiansheng Bainian Danchen Jinian wenji*, 3.
536  Li Naiqing, "Duimian Renwu, Cover People, Bainian Jiazu Qian Zhongshu yu Yang Jiang".

# Appendix 1: Brief outline of Western comparative studies

Western comparative literature, which can be traced to the Roman Empire, originated in the 1830s and 1840s as a discipline in France and Germany. The first step in pursuing comparative literature studies is always to settle and arrange a country's own literature and the contact among literatures and authors of other countries. This happened in France which developed a study on "the practical and real contacts" between literatures, or in Germany, whose first forays into comparative literature were to research the history of literatures' comparisons.

Four different phases can be traced to mark the course of comparative literature in the western world. At the beginning of the 19th century the common practice was to compare two or more literary traditions on a regional basis and with a set timeline following the same historiographical method.

In the second half of the century, the start of the second phase of the development of the discipline can be attributed to the French school, where comparing literatures meant to look for influences of one author or of one literary work on another, trying to ascribe a national tradition in a more global scheme. The aim was to make comparative literature a scientific subject with the study of national literatures through quotations, sources, and references to other works. A fundamental contribution to the development of the discipline in the west was an article by the Italian critic, Benedetto Croce, who stated that comparative literature should have a scientific foundation and should study national literatures in a global setting.[537]

The third phase of comparative literature studies is the "American season

---

537 Gnisci and Sinopoli, *Manuale storico*, 77.

of the New Critics", whose leading scholars are Wellek and Étiemble. This is the time when intercultural hints appear and there is an opening towards non-European literatures. Wellek affirms[538] that comparative literature should not have limitations in space, time, and purpose, challenging the limitations imposed by the historic and factual methods. In 1963 Étiemble[539] was the first to insist on the necessity to move towards an intercultural perspective, leaving aside the mere Euro-American borders. Étiemble profiles the characteristics of the "ideal comparatist": a scholar possessing scientific qualities that make him a historian and a sociologist that provide him with common knowledge about general culture. He should be an expert of music and art; he should have encyclopaedic inclinations and should be able to read with intelligence and acumen every text in its original language. The great achievements of the American school made comparative literature less provincial, giving it the status of an intercultural discipline. Wellek's approach to comparative literature sprang from a critique and opposition to the French comparative literature tradition that, in his opinion, confined comparative literature's scope to the study of contacts between literatures. Absorbing the main points of Wellek's critique, Étiemble advanced the discipline, affirming that its main scope was the promotion of mutual understanding between people and that the comparative study of literatures, which had never been in contact, might be significant and capable of enhancing the progress of mankind on a general level. For this reason, comparison in Wellek and Étiemble's method was not the main means of analysis for literatures; instead they maintained that methods such as description, interpretation, narration, explanation, and evaluation be used.[540]

---

538 Gnisci and Sinopoli, *Manuale storico*, 93-108.
539 Gnisci and Sinopoli, *Manuale storico*, 28-29; 109-113.
540 Yue Daiyun, *Comparative Literature*, 84-85.

The fourth and most mature phase of comparative literature as a discipline focuses on cultural studies. Critics belonging to this phase insist on the necessity of freeing comparative literature studies from territorial and temporal limitations and of putting different traditions on the same level taking care to avoid both Euro-American centrism for western critics and Sino centrism for eastern critics, as was the tendency in post-colonial China according to Yue Daiyun.[541] Earl R. Miner, in his article *Etudes compares interculturelles* (Comparative intercultural studies) in 1989,[542] makes an important contribution to the cultural studies phase. He reflects on some specific aspects necessitating attention in cultural studies – lexicon and methodology of research. With literary genres, for instance, Miner warns that it is vital to be aware of fundamental differences in cultures and that it might be illusory to find the same "tragedy" or "novel" in different traditions. This warning is supported by Miner's analysis of basic concepts in world literatures: the western Greek *mimesis*, theorised by Aristotle and the Roman Horace, as imitation of the world by the poet, and the eastern concept of permeation of nature by the artist, based on the same artist's sensations.

Thus, it seems to emerge that Qian Zhongshu's ideas can be traced back to the American school as theorised by Wellek and Étiemble, and that there is full accordance on his side with such an open and intercultural view of the discipline. His ideas nevertheless merge seamlessly in the cultural studies phase, since one of the main points Qian brought to readers' attention has been the specificities of each tradition, and the importance of examining cultural, sociological, and historical motifs as an integral part of literary analysis. The true benefit of his scholarly career is the way he conducted this

---

541 Yue Daiyun is former professor of comparative literature at Peking University.
542 Gnisci and Sinopoli, *Manuale Storico*, 145-181.

analysis and the "comparative method" this study delineates through the specific focus on Italian quotations. This is also the contribution his studies brought to the discipline of global comparative literature.

# Appendix 2: Brief outline of comparative literature studies in China

A brief outline of the main trends of comparative literature studies in China serves as a background for Qian's work to help explain why he is not a comparatist in the usual sense of the term and his original contribution to the discipline.

Yue Daiyun 樂黛雲[543] helps us understand comparative literature studies in China that (as has been the case in the western world) have followed a path towards freedom from provincialism. Analysis of locally and temporally delimited literary phenomena has advanced towards the investigation of encounters outside space and time that surpass the borders of different and apparently far-off disciplines.

As the appendix on comparative literature in the west explains, the credit for this development can be attributed to the American School that influenced Chinese comparative studies; it is from this school that the need to set aside space and time in combining literatures from different cultural worlds originates.

During the 1990s, the works on comparative literature in China of an interdisciplinary character and of multicultural intents have continuously grown and deepened. The 266 works published in 1990 increased to 328 in 1991 and in 1992 there were 271, as reported by Xie Tianzhen 謝天振 in the

---

543  Yue Daiyun is former Professor of Chinese contemporary literature and comparative literature at Beijing University.

article "Le tendenze più recenti della comparatistica letteraria cinese (1990-1992)" (Recent trends in Chinese comparative literature 1990-1992).[544]

Noteworthy studies are: *Xifang Wenyi Sichao Yu Ershi Shiji Zhongguo Wenxue*[545] 西方文藝思潮與二十世紀中國文學 (Western Literary and Artistic Trends and Chinese Literature in the 20th Century) edited by Wang Ning and Yue Daiyun in 1990, and *Lun Ouzhou Zhongxinzhuyi* 論歐洲中心主義 (Discussing Euro-centrism) published in 1990 and 1991 in *Zhongguo Bijiao Wenxue*[546] 中國比較文學 (Chinese Comparative Literature) by Yang Zhouhan 楊周翰, whose main point is the need to cancel western critical and thematic rules, the so-called Euro-centrism, in the practice of comparative literature. In *Lun Ouzhou Zhongxin Zhuyi*, Qian Zhongshu is referred to as the scholar who made a great contribution to the practice of comparative literature[547] with the elaboration of a method capable of conciliating local differences with universally valid principles. Yang Zhouhan affirms that analysing ideas present in one literature with a perspective different from the usual one offers a great advantage in discovering things that would not have been seen otherwise. This is exactly what Qian Zhongshu did, illuminating Chinese and western literatures through comparative literary analysis, making a significant contribution to east-west comparative literature. Other authors (Sun Jingyao 孫景亮 1991, Gan Jianmin 甘建民 1991, Liu Bo 劉波 1992) also advocate setting aside Euro-centrism in Chinese literature and in global comparative literature in general. An essay by Qian Niansun 錢念孫, *Bijiao Wenxue Xiaowang Lun – cong Zhu Guanqian dui Bijiao Wenxue de Kanfa*

---

544 Xie Tianzhen, "Le tendenze più recenti della comparatistica letteraria cinese (1990-1992)", *I Quaderni di Gaia* VI, 9 (1995): 73.

545 Yue Daiyun and Wang Ning, eds., *Xifang Wenyi Sichao yu Ershi Shiji Zhongguo Wenxue*.

546 Yang Zhouhan, "Lun Ouzhou Zhongxinzhuyi", in *Zhongguo Bijiao Wenxue*, 21-46.

547 See also Xia Zhiqing, "Zhonghui Qian Zhongshu Jishi", 69. Xia affirms that Qian has offered to sinological studies a new platform for research on comparative literature.

*Tanqi* 比較文學消亡論——從朱光潛對比較文學的看法談起 (Discussion on the Fading out of Comparative Literature Starting from Zhu Guanqian's Point of View on the Discipline) in *Wenxue Pinglun* 文學評論 (Literature Review) 1990, began the debate on whether or not comparative literature should exist at all, stating that it is a discipline without a specific field and definition and that it cannot be defined as a scientific discipline. Supporting this point of view is that Qian Zhongshu did not define himself as a comparatist. A reply to this 1990 essay given by Du Wei 杜衛 states[548] that we do not have to mix up comparative literature – the study of intercultural mediation and comparative method – the study of one specific literature.

Xie Tianzhen, in the final remarks of the above-mentioned essay, foresees increasing development of comparative studies in many and different fields such as studies on translation and translated literature; studies on popular and folk literature; studies on television, radio and media; and studies on overseas Chinese literature.

The growth of comparative literature studies in China does not necessarily correspond to their quality and value. Meng Hua 孟華[549] notes that it is advisable to distrust the "present generation of Chinese comparatists" who are often unable to read works in the original language and lack the linguistic and literary competence that new generations will be able to gain by travelling abroad to pursue further specialisation. Even today, competence remains the privilege of scholars like Qian Zhongshu who, before the Cultural Revolution, had the possibility to acquire the necessary intercultural skills to pursue comparative literature research.[550]

---

548 Xie Tianzhen, Le tendenze più recenti della comparatistica letteraria cinese (1990-1992), 73-85.

549 Meng Hua is former Professor of comparative literature at Peking University.

550 Meng Hua, discussion with the author, Beijing, 11-08-2009.

Qian Zhongshu wanted the study of literature and literary criticism to have the status of a scientific discipline. In order to do so he was aware that it was necessary to avoid any point of view tainted by the ethnicism that corrupts critical views, the blind adoration of everything that was foreign, and every criticism devoid of significance.

The publication of works like *Tan Yi Lu* and *Guan Zhui Bian*, notes Ning Yunfeng 寧雲峰,[551] gave Chinese comparative literature a place in world literature and impacted the direction followed by the discipline in China. Up to the 1980s, continues Ning, Chinese comparatists had missed the true aim of comparative literature, namely to understand the universal laws that lead the development of art and literature through comparison, together with the peculiarities related to space and time, up to the individuation of a general principle that permeates the development of human civilisation. Due to a deep critical spirit, Qian Zhongshu analysed artistic-literary phenomena without ever leaving aside written texts. He affirmed that he did not talk about comparative literature, he only applied a method.

While Qian Zhongshu and his method are our last step in outlining the development of Chinese comparative literature, tracing the roots of this discipline in China, besides the recent influence of a western point of view, brings us to Wang Guowei 王國維 (1877-1927), one of the pioneers of Chinese comparative literature studies. Wang's article, *Hong Lou Meng Pingxi* 紅樓夢評析 (Criticism on The Dream of the Red Mansion), was serialized in the magazine *Jiaoyu Zazhi* 教育雜誌 (Education Review) in the June-August issues of 1904. Wang Guowei was one of the first to use western theories to analyse Chinese literature. Since then, comparative studies in China have

---

551 Ning Yunfeng, "Shilun Qian Zhongshu de Bijiao Wenxue Guan", 32-37.

flourished through scholars like Lu Xun 魯迅, who examined the functions of literature comparing features of literary traditions in different cultures; Mao Dun, who was the first to compare literatures from England, France and Russia; and Zhou Zuoren 周作人, Zhu Guanqian 朱光潛, Guo Moruo, Wang Yuanhua 王元化 and Qian Zhongshu, each with his own theory and appreciation. In this advancement Zhu Guanqian and Qian Zhongshu particularly have been two scholars with a method that shares similarities such as great erudition and a deep knowledge of western sources. However, their methods also carry some differences;[552] Zhu Guanqian's method can be described as a unidirectional explication coming from the idealism by Benedetto Croce, as it was usually thought, or by Nietzsche, as Zhu himself affirmed.[553] Zhu is considered a proponent of the western aesthetic philosophy. Qian Zhongshu's theory, on the other hand, belongs to Structuralism, a twentieth century western critical theory focused on character and identity of traditional concepts. While Zhu Guanqian's principles are mostly an explanation of others' theories, Qian's theory demonstrates that everything can be directly deduced from texts with the help of aesthetic principles. Both scholars, each in his own way, have contributed to the enhancement of comparative literature studies in China. Zhu Guanqian affirmed that Qian Zhongshu was one of the pioneers in introducing Chinese traditional criticism to western scholarship.[554]

Richards was the first to use the term "comparative literature" in China during his lectures held at Qinghua University in Beijing, in the 1920s and 1930s. Yue Daiyun states that Qinghua University trained a number of outstanding scholars at the start of the 20th century. She includes the

---

552  See Wu Chao, "Zhu Guanqian yu Qian Zhongshu Bijiao Shixue Zhixue Fangfa zhi Qubie", 138-139.
553  See Zhu Guanqian, *Keluoqi*.
554  See Wu Taichang, *Wo renshi de Qian Zhongshu*, 78.

following scholars – Wu Mi, Robert Winter, Chen Yinke 陳寅恪, Ji Xianlin 季羨林, Li Jianwu 李健吾, Yang Yezhi 楊業治, Qian Zhongshu and Zhu Guanqian – trained in Chinese and western literatures as well as comparative literature. Yue Daiyun considers Zhu Guanqian's *The Psychology of Literary Appreciation and Poetics* (1936) and Qian Zhongshu's *Tan Yi Lu* (1948) the most outstanding achievements of comparative literature's studies, praising *Tan Yi Lu* for "its wealth of citations from both Chinese and foreign literatures that were used as evidence to explain and criticize principles and theories."[555]

Yue Daiyun regards Qian Zhongshu's *Guan Zhui Bian*, 1979, a milestone in the revival of Chinese comparative literature; she sees its main achievement as the illustration of the interaction between various subjects of the humanities transcending boundaries between disciplines, time and space. Another aspect Yue Daiyun particularly appreciates in Qian's masterpiece is his theory about translation and his idea of "transformation" as the right vehicle for accurate translation.[556]

The achievements of *Guan Zhui Bian* were decisive in the development of key concepts in Chinese comparative literature; in his work Qian Zhongshu warned scholars to be careful when speaking of origin and influence, since sometimes there are similar theories in contexts that have never been in contact, while big differences arise from ideas sprung from the same origin. He also advocated a reciprocal usage of each other's theories between west and east to interpret literary phenomena.[557] Since its appearance, *Guan Zhui Bian* has had a great influence on Chinese artistic and literary discussion and critical studies. According to Yu Mingfang 俞明芳, all

---

555 Yue Daiyun, *Comparative Literature and China*, 6-7.
556 For Yue Daiyun's appreciation of *Guan Zhui Bian* see her *Comparative literature*, 7.
557 See Yue Daiyun, *Comparative Literature*, 97.

discussions on Chinese literary criticism should consider suggestions by Qian Zhongshu in his masterpiece.[558] Chen Ziqian 陳子謙, author of a study on Qian Zhongshu, expresses his firm belief that *Guan Zhui Bian*, entered in the domain of the international scholarly world, became a point of reference for the Chinese cultural world and the pride of the critics of art, serving as a model for the cultural critique on Chinese culture and civilisation. Chen Ziqian continues: "If a discipline of 'comparative literature' has been started, then we might consider him (Qian Zhongshu) as the founder of said discipline." Because he never conducts an abstract comparison, there is always a practical appraisal to assess people, to understand the real meaning of words, and to know the general mood. Qian himself has compared the need for comparative literature to the need for a discerning attitude when looking at a cat in the dark of night, or the capacity for a cat to distinguish colours during the day. Western critics, lacking the help of comparative literature, tend to view the old multi-coloured Chinese poetry as being grey coloured. When people accustomed to a particular kind of poetic tradition try to consider a different one, they often make no distinction.[559] Differentiation and understanding are possible only with the support of a discipline able to link various literary realms and state points of contacts and appreciation.

An important point Yue Daiyun makes in her essay[560] centres on the legacy of Qian's work. Inspired by the publication of *Guan Zhui Bian*, four professors from Peking University published outstanding works in comparative literature.[561] According to Yue Daiyun, *Guan Zhui Bian*,

---

558  Chen Ziqian, *Lun Qian Zhongshu*, 77.

559  Chen Ziqian, *Lun Qian Zhongshu*, 187.

560  Yue Daiyun, *Comparative Literature*, 98.

561  Yue Daiyun (*Comparative Literature*, 98) reports of four works published in the wake of *Guan Zhui Bian*, these are: *A Stroll in Aesthetics* (1981) by Zong Baihua 宗白華, *Collected Writings on the History of Chinese and Indian Cultures* (1982) by Ji Xianlin, *Collected Writings on Comparative Culture* (1984) by Jin Kemu 金克木 and *Whetstone: Collected Critical Essays* (1984) by Yang Zhouhan.

notwithstanding its difficulty and obscurity, makes a great contribution to Chinese comparative literature, bringing new ideas and influencing other scholars to pursue a new formulation of comparative literature studies. As Xia Zhiqing 夏志清, literary critic and academic, remarks in an essay written in the same year of publication as *Guan Zhui Bian*, Qian's work, even with its limited number of readers in China due to its difficulty, is the most outstanding Chinese achievement in the field of comparative literature studies.[562]

In 1981, the first step for future developments of studies in comparative literature had already been carried out at Peking University by Professor Ji Xianlin, director, and Professor Qian Zhongshu, advisor, of the newly established Peking University Comparative Literature Association.

October 1985 was a milestone for Chinese comparative studies as it was the first conference of the Chinese Comparative Literature Association (CCLA) at Shenzhen University. The congress attracted fourteen distinguished comparatists and a total of 121 papers from around the world. Following the CCLA conference, the development of comparative literature studies took different directions in academic circles in different regions of China, each giving more importance to some aspects. For example, the Beijing School focused on international literary and cultural relations and interdisciplinary studies, and the Shanghai and Hunan Schools on theories of intercultural relations as the theory and history of translation.[563] In her essay, Yue Daiyun carries on a discourse on the need to pursue the idea of "diversity in harmony" that comes from Confucian thought; and she maintains that, based on this concept, comparative literature is a means for understanding

---

562  Xia Zhiqing, "Zhonghui Qian Zhongshu Jishi", 69.
563  For a complete account of Yue Daiyun's description of the different trends in Chinese comparative studies and on the activities of the CCLA see her *Comparative Literature*, 11-13.

diversity and building harmony.[564]

"Notes on comparative literature at the turn of the century"[565] by Yue Daiyun casts a glance at "the last ten years"[566] and the way in which Chinese comparative literature has been approaching maturity, stating that the name comparative literature is no longer sufficient to express the complexity of this discipline that cuts through inter-cultural and inter-disciplinary fields. These are, continues Yue Daiyun, the tasks as well as the challenges of comparative literature at the turn of the century. Both Orientalism, the cultural hegemony of the west on the east, and Isolationism, a mere return to the roots of Chinese culture, should be avoided. Comparatists in the 21st century should consider that every nation, undoubtedly and inevitably, bears its own culture and is affected by it, and that the most important feature of the century should be the interaction among those cultures.

Yue Daiyun foresees that in this century culture will play a fundamental role in the study of comparative literature and that it will be a culture considered in its most real aspects, thanks to a knowledge of its real characteristics and not based on superstitions. In this new perspective, China will play an important role, reaching mutual benefit and understanding of other cultures. A possible canon of the study of comparative literature in China would, as explained in the essay "Teaching Literary History in China and the Canon of Comparative Literature",[567] start from authors such as Mao Dun and Lu Xun who have contributed to modern Chinese literature by absorbing from foreign authors to enrich their national literature.

René Étiemble, at the Congress of the International Comparative

---

564 See Yue Daiyun, *Comparative Literature*, 23-24.
565 Yue Daiyun, *Comparative Literature*, 63-72.
566 Yue Daiyun refers to the period 1994-2004.
567 Yue Daiyun, *Comparative Literature*, 73-80.

Literature Association held in Paris in August 1985, delivered a paper on Chinese comparative literature expressing praise for its rapid growth since the 1980s and faith in its future achievements already noted in its international orientation and in its tendency to link theory and practice. Its role, affirmed Étiemble, was important for the rectification of previous concepts about Oriental literature and for the developments of world literature.[568] On the other hand, Zhang Longxi 張隆溪[569] notes that in China the development of comparative literature as a discipline still needs much work.

Wang Ning[570], reflecting on globalism and the impact on Chinese comparative literature, notes that especially post-modernism, including commercial and popular literature among the field of proper literatures, has caused cultural and comparative studies to be interested in a kind of literature previously underestimated or ignored. Wang Ning also notes that the artificial demarcation between high culture and literature and low culture and literature has thereby been obscured and gradually deconstructed.[571] The strength of Chinese comparative literature is, for Wang Ning, exactly an encouragement for scholars to pay closer attention to popular culture and literature in all of its aspects and perspectives.[572] The challenge that China needs to exploit in a time of both globalism and nationalism is to avoid closure in a mere east-west opposition and to reinforce the dialogue between the two, trying to make the Chinese literary world known to the west in a perspective different from the usual one that studies the east from a western and third-world point of view.[573]

---

568 Yue Daiyun, *Comparative Literature*, 89.
569 See Zhang Longxi, "Qian Zhongshu Tan Bijiaowenxue yu Wenxue Bijiao". Zhang Longxi is Chair Professor of comparative literature and translation at City University of Hong Kong.
570 Wang Ning is Professor of comparative literature at Qinghua University in Beijing.
571 Wang Ning, "Comparative literature and globalism", 591.
572 Wang Ning, "Comparative Aspects of Contemporary Popular Literature in China", 448.
573 Wang Ning, "Comparative Literature and Globalism", 584-602.

As remarked by Monika Motsch,[574] both western and eastern comparative literatures today follow three different patterns: the first one aims at highlighting differences, the second at highlighting similarities, and the third tries to dismantle the two. The first method, derived from the Opium Wars and the unequal treaties, makes east and west distant and without points of contact. Yan Fu 嚴復 has been the first to think that the strength of the west did not come from cannons and the navy but from a vision of the world of Faust and Prometheus. He thought that the fight between east and west was a fight between passive and active, negative and positive, and that while the west represented the correct side, the east was the backward and incorrect side, passive and servile. In the excessiveness of its assumptions, this point of view stimulated discussions; Yan Fu wanted to wake up Chinese people.

The second method, the inclusive one, finds its representative in Lin Yu. He was the first to analyse western novels comparing them to the works of Du Fu 杜甫, Sima Qian 司馬遷 and Li Bai 李白. Even Wang Guowei thought the two realms had something in common. However, Wu Mi was the first to seriously analyse and carry on comparative studies and research. The third pattern, continues Motsch, is the one that sees the presence of three thematic spheres: the Chinese, the western, and the intersection of the two. Muriel Détrie is a strong supporter not only of the possibility of the dialogue between east and west but also of the fruitful encounter between the two. In the article "Où en est le dialogue entre l'occident et l'etrême-orient?" (Where Is The Dialogue Between West And Far-East?), Détrie demonstrates that eastern literatures that encountered the western world in the 20th century were not passive receivers of influences but were able to work out new literary

---

574 Motsch, "Qiannülihun-Qian Zhongshu Zuowei Zhongxi Wenhua de Qianxian Ren". Monica Motsch is former Professor at Bonn University.

patterns from a fusion of new examples with local socio-economic and literary conditions. Détrie shows in her article that the dialogue between east and west is possible and is a fruitful field of analysis between the two worlds in an intercultural context.

# Index of Italian autors

# References

A, Tu 阿塗. *Ting Qian Zhongshu jiang wenxue* 聽錢鍾書講文學. Xian: Shanxi Shifan Daxue Chubanshe, 2008.

ALIGHIERI, Dante. *La Commedia Secondo l'Antica Vulgata*. Milano: Mondadori Editore, 1966-67.

ALIGHIERI, Dante. *Opere minori*, tomo I - parte II *Convivio*, a cura di Cesare Vasoli e Domenico De Robertis. Milano-Napoli: Ricciardi 1988.

ALIGHIERI, Dante. *The Divine Comedy of Dante Alighieri*, translated by Henry Wadsworth Longfellow, Vol I-II-III. Leipzig: Bernhard Tauchnitz, 1867.

ANGIOLIERI, Cecco. *Rime*. Milano: Bur, 1979.

ARIOSTO, Ludovico. *Il Negromante*. http://www.liberliber.it/mediateca/ libri/a/ ariosto/il_negromante /pdf/il_neg_p.pdf. Accessed December 10, 2011.

ARIOSTO, Ludovico. *Orlando furioso*. Milano: Garzanti, 1992.

ARIOSTO, Ludovico. *Satire*. Milano: Rizzoli, 1990.

BANDELLO, Matteo. "Il Bandello al molto illustre e valoroso signore il Signor Giovanni de Medici", in *Le novelle*, edited by Gioachino Brognoligo. Bari: Laterza, 1910.

BANDELLO, Matteo. *Novelle*, parte seconda. Milano: per Giovanni Silvestri, 1813.

BARTOLI, Daniello. *Dell'Huomo di Lettere, Difeso et Emendato, Parti due*. Venezia: Presso Nicolò Pezzana, 1672.

BECCARIA, Cesare. *Dei delitti e delle pene*. Firenze: Tipografia di Luigi Pezzati, 1827.

BERCHET, Giovanni. *Lettera semiseria di Grisostomo al suo figliolo*, a cura di Luigi Reina. Milano: Mursia, 1977.

BERTUCCIOLI, Giuliano. "Qian Zhongshu: lo scrittore e lo studioso che si interessa alla nostra letteratura", *Mondo Cinese* 1 (gennaio 1986 - anno XIV): 23-37.

BINNI, Walter. *I classici italiani nella storia della critica*. Firenze: La Nuova Italia, 1970.

BLAKE, Willliam. *The Marriage of Heaven and Hell*. Boston: John W. Luce and

Company, 1906.

BLOOM, Harold. *Bloom's Bio-critiques, T. S. Eliot*. Broomall: Chelsea House Publishers, 2003.

BOCCACCIO, Giovanni. *Decameron*, a cura di Vittore Branca, correzioni di Natalino Sapegno. Firenze: Le Monnier, 1951.

BOIARDO, Matteo Maria. *Orlando Innamorato*, a cura di Aldo Scaglione. Torino: Classici Italiani UTET, 1984.

BRUNO, Giordano. *Dialoghi italiani, II, Dialoghi morali*. Firenze: Sansoni, 1985.

BRUNO, Giordano. *Opere di Giordano Bruno*. Lipsia: Weidmann, 1830.

BUONARROTI, Michelangelo. *Le Lettere di Michelangelo Buonarroti*, edited by G. Milanesi. Le Monnier, 1875.

CAMPANELLA, Tommaso. *Il Nuovo Prometeo*. Bologna: Edizioni Studio Domenicano, 1993.

CARDUCCI, Giosuè e VIVANTI, Annie. *Addio caro orco*. Milano: Feltrinelli, 2004.

CARRER, Luigi. *Opere Scelte*, vol I. Firenze: Le Monnier, 1859.

CASTIGLIONE, Baldassarre. *Il Cortegiano*. Milano: Hoepli, 1928.

CELLINI, Benvenuto. *I Trattati dell'Oreficeria e della Scultura*. Firenze: Le Monnier, 1857.

CELLINI, Benvenuto. *La vita di Benvenuto Cellini*. Firenze: Le Monnier, 1852.

CH'IEN, C. S. (Qian Zhongshu 錢鍾書). "A Note to the Second Chapter of *Mr Decadent*", *China Heritage Quaterly*, China Heritage Project, The Australian National University, 25 (2011). Accessed November 25, 2011.http://www.chinaheritagequarterly.org/tien-hsia.php?Searchte rm=025_decade nt.inc&issue=025.

CHANG, Shentai. "Reading Qian Zhongshu's 'God's Dream' as a Postmodern Text", *CLEAR* 16 (1994): 93-110.

CHEN, Shengsheng 陳聖生. *Qian Zhongshu yu Bijiao Wenxue Piping* 錢鍾書與比較文學批評. Hunan Shanxueyuan Xuebao (xuang yue kan), vol. 7, n. 4 (2000): 78-80.

CHEN, Ziqian 陳子謙. *Lun Qian Zhongshu* 論錢鍾書. Guilin: Guangxi Shifan Daxue Chubanshe, 2005.

CHEN, Ziqian 陳子謙. *Qian Xue Lun* 錢學論. Sichuan Wen Yi Chubanshe, 1992.

CHENG, Bing 沉冰 edit. *Bu Yiyang de Jiyi – Yu Qian Zhongshu Zai Yiqi* 不一樣的記憶——與錢鍾書在一起. Beijing: Dangdai Shijie Chubanshe, 1999.

COLLODI, Carlo. *Pinocchio*. Milano: Feltrinelli, 1993.

COMPAGNON, Antoine. *La seconde main ou le travail de la citation*. Paris: Aux éditions du Seuil, 1979.

CORTI, M. e SEGRE, C. *I metodi attuali della critica in Italia*. Torino: ERI, 1970.

CROCE, Benedetto. *Conversazioni Critiche*, vol. 1. Bari: Laterza, 1950.

CROCE, Benedetto. *Estetica come scienza dell'espressione e linguistica generale*. Bari: Laterza, 1908.

CROCE, Benedetto. *La letteratura della Nuova Italia: saggi critici*. Bari: Laterza, 1922.

CROCE, Benedetto. *La Poesia*. Bari: Laterza, 1966.

CROCE, Benedetto. *Lirici Marinisti*. Bari: Laterza, 1910.

D'ANNUNZIO, Gabriele. *Alcyone*, a cura di Pietro Gibellini. Torino: Einaudi, 1995.

D'ANCONA, Alessandro. *La poesia popolare italiana*.

DE SANCTIS, Francesco. *Saggi Critici*, edited by Luigi Russo. Bari: Laterza, 1965.

DETRIE, Muriel. "Où est le dialogue entre l'Occident et l'extrême Orient?", *Revue de littérature comparée*, No. 297 (2001/1): 151-166.

DING, Weizhi 丁偉志 edit. *Qian Zhongshu Xiansheng Bainian Danchen Jinian wenji*. 錢鍾書先生百年誕辰紀念文集. Beijing: Shenghuo-Dushu-Xinzhi Sanlian Shudian, 2010.

ECO, Umberto. *Il Nome della Rosa*. Milano: Bompiani in 1980.

EGAN, Ronald. "Qian Zhongshu's Reading of the Chinese Classics: Gauging the Principles of *Guanzhui Bian*", *Program for research of Intellectual-Cultural History*. Beijing: College for Humanities and Social Science National Tsing Hua University, 1998.

EGAN, Ronald. "Tuotai Huangu: Guan Zhui Bian dui Qingru de chengji yu chaoyue" 脫胎換骨——管錐編對清儒的承繼與超越. *Qian Zhongshu Shiwen Congshuo*, edited by Wang Rongzu, 211-226. Taiwan: Airiti Press, 2011.

EGAN, Ronald. *Limited Views: Essays on Ideas and Letters*. Cambridge: Council on East Asian Studies, Harvard University, 1998.

FRANCESCO D'ASSISI, (santo). *Cantico delle Creature*. http://www.liberliber.it/ mediateca /libri/f/francesco_d_assisi/il_canticodifratesole/pdf/ il_can_p.pdf, 3. Accessed December 10, 2011.

FRUGONI, Innocenzo. *Poesie scelte dell'Abate Carlo Innocenzo Frugoni*, tomo IV. Brescia: Daniel Berlendis, 1783.

GE, Hongbin 葛紅兵, LIU Chuane 劉川鄂, DENG Yiguang 鄧一光. *Qian Zhongshu: Bei shenhua de 'Dashi'*. 錢鍾書：被神話的「大師」. http://www. confucius2000.com/po etry/qzsbshdds.htm. Accessed November 25, 2011.

GIUSTI, Giuseppe. *Aggiunta ai Proverbi Toscani di Giuseppe Giusti*. Firenze: Le Monnier, 1855. http://www.Archive.org/stream/aggiuntaaiprove00giusgoog/ aggiuntaaiprove00giusgoog_djvu.txt. Accessed December 10, 2011.

GIUSTI, Giuseppe. *Poesie di Giuseppe Giusti*. http://www.archive.org/stream/ poesiedigiuseppe00 gius/poe siedigiuseppe00gius_djvu.txt. Accessed December 12, 2011.

GIUSTI, Giuseppe. *Scritti Vari in Prosa e in Verso di Giuseppe Giusti per la Maggior Parte Inediti*. Firenze: Successori Le Monnier, 1866.

GNISCI, Armando, SINOPOLI, Franca. *Manuale Storico di Letteratura Comparata*. Roma: Meltemi editore, 1997.

GOLDONI, Carlo. *Opere*. Milano: per Nicolò Bettoni, 1831.

GOLINO, Carlo. ed. *Contemporary Italian poetry: an anthology*. London: University of California Press, 1962.

GONG, Gang 龔剛. *Qian Zhongshu: Aizhizhe de Xiaoyao* 錢鍾書：愛智者的逍遙. edited by Yue Daiyun. Beijing: Wenjin Chubanshe, 2005.

GRAF, Arturo. *Le poesie*. Torino: Loescher, 1922.

GU, Yubao. 顧育豹 "Zoujin Qian Zhongshu Guju" 走進錢鍾書故居. Liaoning Shen Waishi Qiaowu Bangongshi, Liaoning Shen Renmin Zhenfu Qiaowu bangongshi. *Qiaoyuan*, n. 7 (2009): 36-37. Accessed November 23, 2011. http:// http://www.qikan.com.cn/ArticlePart.aspx? titleid=qiyu20090712.

GUICCIARDINI, Francesco. *Maxims and Reflections of a Renaissance Statesman*, translated by Mario Domandi. New York: Harper Torchbooks, 1965.

GUICCIARDINI, Francesco. *Ricordi*, edited by Giorgio Masi. Mursia, Milano, 1994.

GUICCIARDINI, Francesco. *Ricordi*. http://www.filosofico.net/ ricord1iguicciard1nifs.htm. Accessed December 12, 2011.

GUNN, Edward. *Rewriting Chinese: style and innovation in twentieth century Chinese prose*. Stanford: Stanford University Press, 1991.

GUO, Hong. 郭紅. "Shougao Shi Yi Zhong Jingshen Caifu – Ji *Qian Zhongshu Shougao Ji* de Chuban" 手稿是一種精神財富——記《錢鍾書手稿集》的出版. *Beijing Observation data*, n. 7 (2003): 62-63.

HAUN, Saussy. "Comparative Literature?", in *PMLA*, Vol. 118, No. 2 (Mar., 2003): 336-341. Stable URL http:// www.jstor.org/stable/ 1261421. Accessed June 13, 2011.

HE, Hui 何暉 and FANG Tianxing 方天星. ed. *Yi Cun Qian Si: Yi Qian Zhongshu Xiansheng* 一寸千思：憶錢鍾書先生. Shenyang: Liaohai Chubanshe, 1999.

HE, Mingxing 何明星. *Guan Zhui Bian Quanshi Fangfa Yanjiu* 管錐編詮釋方法研究. Wuhan: Huadong Shifan Daxue Chubanshe, 2006.

HSIA, Adrian. ed. *The Vision of China in the English Literature of the Seventeenth and Eighteenth Centuries*. Hong Kong: The Chinese University Press, 1998.

HSIA, C. T. 夏志清. "Ch'ien Chung-shu", in C. T. Hsia, *A History of Modern Chinese Fiction*. 2^nd ed., 432-60. New Haven: Yale University Press, 1971.

http://www.archive.Org stream/lapoesiapopolare 00dancuoft/lapoesiapopolare00 dancuoft_djvu.txt. Accessed December 12, 2011.

HU, Heqing, 胡河清. "Qian Zhonghshu lun" 錢鍾書論. *Qian Zhongshu Pingshuo Qishi Nian* 錢鍾書評說七十年, 280-290. Beijing: Wenhua Yishu Chubanshe, 2009.

HU, Dennis Ting-Pong. "A Linguistic-Literary Approach to Ch'ien Chung-shu's Novel Wei-ch'eng", *The Journal of Asian Studies* 37 (1978): 427-443.

HU, Dennis Ting-Pong. *A linguistic-literary study of Ch'ien Chung-Shu's three creative works*. Phd dissertation. Madison: University of Winsconsin, 1977.

HU, Dennis Ting-Pong. *Humans Beasts and Ghosts – Stories and Essays by Qian Zhongshu*, edited by Christopher G. Rea. New York: Columbia University Press, 2011.

HU, Fanzhu 胡范鑄. *Qian Zhongshu Xueshu Sixiang Yanjiu* 錢鍾書學術思想研究.

Shanghai: Huadong Shifan Daxue Chubanshe, 1993.

HUANG, Weiliang 黃維樑, "Liu Xie yu Qian Zhongshu: Wenxue Tonglun: Jian Tan Qian Zhongshu Lilun de Qian Tixi" 劉勰與錢鍾書：文學通論——兼談錢鍾書理論的潛體系. *Qian Zhongshu Shiwen Congshuo*, edited by Wang Rongzu, 249-280. Taiwan: Airiti Press, 2011.

HUTERS, David Theodore. "Traditional Innovation: Qian Zhong-shu and Modern Chinese Letters", Ph.D. dissertation. Stanford: Stanford University, 1977.

HUTERS, Theodore. *Qian Zhongshu*. Boston: Twayne Publishers, 1982.

JI, Jin. 季進. *Qian Zhongshu Yu Xiandai Xixue* 錢鍾書與現代西學. Shanghai: Shanghai Sanlian, 2002.

JOHNSON, Samuel. *The Works of Samuel Johnson, LL. D. Volume 1*. Jones, 1825.

KONG, Fangqing 孔芳卿, "Qian Zhongshu Jingdu Zuotan Ji" 錢鍾書京都座談記. *Qian Zhongshu Pingshuo Qishi Nian* 錢鍾書評說七十年, edited by Yang Lianfen 楊聯芬, 82-83. Beijing: Wenhua Yishu Chubanshe, 2009.

KONG, Qingmao 孔慶茂. *Qian Zhongshu* 錢鍾書. Zhongguo Huaqiao Chubanshe, 1998.

LANCIOTTI, Lionello. "Qian Zhongshu 1910-1998", *East and West* – IsIAO vol. 48 – No 3-4 (December 1998): 477-478.

LEONARDO DA VINCI, *Aforismi, novelle e profezie*. Milano: Newton Compton, 1993.

LEONARDO DA VINCI, *Trattato della Pittura*. Codice Vaticano Urbinate, 1270.

LEONESI, Barbara. "La Cina, la letteratura italiana e Lü Tongliu. Un progetto di traduzione lungo una vita", in *La Cina e il Mondo* – Atti dell'XI Convegno dell'Associazione Italiana Studi Cinesi. Roma, 22-24 Febbraio 2007, edited by Paolo De Toia. Roma: Sapienza Università di Roma, 2010.

LEOPARDI, Giacomo. *Canti*. Firenze: Le Monnier, 1870.

LEOPARDI, Giacomo. *Crestomazia italiana*. Napoli: Stamperia del Vaglio, 1866.

LEOPARDI, Giacomo. Pensieri di varia filosofia e di bella letteratura. Firenze: Le Monnier, 1921.

LEOPARDI, Giacomo. *Tutte le opere*, vol. I. Firenze: Sansoni Editore, 1969.

LEYS, Simon. *L'Angelo e il Capodoglio*. Roma: Irradiazioni, 2005.

LI, Hongyan 李洪岩. "Ruhe Pingjia Qian Zhongshu" 如何評價錢鍾書. *Qian Zhongshu Pingshuo Qishi Nian* 錢鍾書評說七十年, 157-174. Beijing: Wenhua Yishu Chubanshe, 2009.

LI, Hongyan 李洪岩 and FAN, Xulun 範旭侖. *Wei Qian Zhongshu Shengbian* 為錢鍾書聲辯. Tianjin: Baihua Wenyi Chubanshe, 2000.

LI, Hongyan 李洪岩. *Qian Zhongshu Yu Jindai Xueren* 錢鍾書與近代學人. Tianjin: Baihua Wenyi Chubanshe, 1998.

LI, Mingsheng 李明生 & others. ed. *Wenhua Kunlun – Qian Zhongshu Qiren Qiwen* 文化昆侖——錢鍾書其人其文. Beijing: Renmin Wenxue Chubanshe, 1999.

LI, Naiqing. "Duimian Renwu, Cover People, Bainian Jiazu Qian Zhongshu yu Yang Jiang" 封面人物 Cover People 百年家族錢鍾書與楊絳. *Nanfang Renwu Zhoukan*, n. 17 (30-05-2011): 26-47.

LIOI, Tiziana. "In Others' Words – The use of quotations in Qian Zhongshu's comparative method", in *Bijiao Wenxue yu Shijie Wenxue*, n. 2, genn. Beijing University, 2013. 《比較文學與世界文學》第2期，2013年1月，北京大學期刊.

LIOI, Tiziana. "Yidali Sixiang Duiyu Qian Zhongshu Zhengti Siwei de Gongxian: Qi Zhui Ji Yidali Yinwen zhi Wenhua yu Yuyan Fenxi" 義大利思想對於錢鍾書整體思維的貢獻：七綴集義大利引文之文化與語言分析. *Qian Zhongshu Shiwen Congshuo*, edited by Wang Rongzu, 381-400. Taiwan: Airiti Press, 2011.

LOMBARDI, Rosa. "Polemiche letterarie tra Pechino e Shanghai negli anni trenta", *Mondo Cinese*, n° 93 (sept-dec 1996). Accessed November 24, 2011. http://www.tuttocina.it/mondo_cinese/093/093_ lomb.htm.

LONGFELLOW, Henry Wadsworth. trans. *The Divine Comedy of Dante Alighieri*. A Penn State Electronic Classics Series Publication. Accessed November 23, 2011. http://www2.hn.psu.edu/faculty/jmanis /dante/Dante-Longfellow.pdf.

LORENZO IL MAGNIFICO. *Poesie*. Milano: Bur, 1992.

LU, Wenhu 陸文虎. *Guan Zhui Bian Tan Yi Lu Suoyin* 管錐編談藝錄索引. Beijing: Zhonghua Shuju, 1994.

MA, Guangyu, CHEN, Keyu, TIAN, Huilan. edit. *Qian Zhongshu Yang Jiang Yanjiu Ziliao Ji* 錢鍾書楊絳研究資料集. Wuhan: Huazhong Shifan Daxue Chubanshe,

1990.

MACHIAVELLI, Niccolò. *Il Principe*. Firenze: Le Monnier, 1848.

MACHIAVELLI, Niccolò. *Mandragola*. Torino: Einaudi, 1964.

MACHIAVELLI, Niccolò. *Opere Complete*. Firenze: Passigli, Borghi e Compagni, 1831.

MAGALOTTI, Lorenzo. *Relazioni di Viaggio in Inghilterra, Francia e Svezia*, a cura di Walter Moretti. Bari: Laterza, 1968.

MAIR, Victor H. ed. *The Columbia History of Chinese Literature*. New York: Columbia University Press, 2001.

MARINO, Giambattista. *Poesie Varie*, a cura di Benedetto Croce. Bari: Laterza, 1913. http://www. archive.org/stream/2poesievariecura00mariuoft/2poesievar iecura00 mariuoft_djvu.txt. Accessed December 10, 2011.

MARINO, Giambattista. *Tutte le opere di Giovan Battista Marino*, volume 2, tomo 1, a cura di Giovanni Pozzi. Milano: Mondadori, 1976.

MATTHIESSEN, F. O. "The 'Objective Correlative'", in Harold Bloom, *Bloom's Biocritiques, T. S. Eliot*. New York: Chelsea House Publishers, 2003.

MENZINI, Benedetto. *Della costruzione irregolare della lingua Toscana*, trattato di Benedetto Menzini. Firenze, 1837.

METASTASIO, Pietro. *Opere*, a cura di Mario Fubini. Milano-Napoli: Riccardo Ricciardi Editore, 1968.

MORAVIA, Alberto. *Opere complete*. Milano: Bompiani, 1976.

MOTSCH, Monika. "A New Method of Chinese – Western Comparative Literature: Qian Zhongshu's Guanzhuibian", in *Chinese literature and European context*, edited by M. Gálik. Bratislava: Institute of Asian and African Studies of the Slovak Academy of Sciences, 1994.

MOTSCH, Monika. "Qiannülihun fa, Qian Zhongshu zuo wei Zhongxi wenhua de qianxian ren" 倩女離魂法——錢鍾書作為中西文化的牽線人. *Qian Zhongshu Pingshuo Qishi Nian*, edited by Liang Yanfen, 326-337. Beijing: Wenhua Yishu Chubanshe, 2009.

NICOLINI, Fausto. *Benedetto Croce*. Torino: Unione tipografico-Editrice torinese, 1962.

NING, Yunfeng 寧雲峰, "Shilun Qian Zhongshu de Bijiao Wenxue Guan" 試論錢鍾書的比較文學觀. *Yun Cheng Gao Zhuan Xuebao* 3 (1992): 32-37.

OU-FAN LEE, Leo. "My Interviews with Writers in the People's Republic of China: A Report", in *Chinese Literature: Essays, Articles, Reviews* (CLEAR), Vol. 3, No. 1 (Jan., 1981), 137-140.

PASCOLI, Giovanni. *I canti di Castelvecchio*. Milano: BUR, 1983.

PASCOLI, Giovanni. *Pensieri e discorsi di Giovanni Pascoli*. Bologna: Zanichelli, 1914.

PETRARCA, Francesco. *Rime di Francesco Petrarca*, con l'interpretazione di Giacomo Leopardi e con note inedite di Francesco Ambrosoli. Firenze: Barbera editore, 1886.

PETRARCA, Francesco. *Rime*. Pisa: Tipografia della Società Letteraria, 1805. Petrocchi. Milano: Mondadori Editore, 1966-67.

PHILOBIBLION: a quaterly review of Chinese Publications, The National Central Library, Nanking, (n. 1, June 1946; n. 2 Sept 1946; n. 3, Dec 46; n. 4, March 47; voll. II n. 1 (whole n. 5), Sept 47; voll. II n. 2 (whole n. 6), March 48; voll. II n. 3 (whole n. 7), Sept 48.

PIRANDELLO, Luigi. *Uno, nessuno, centomila*. Firenze: Giunti editore, 1994.

PIROMALLI, Antonio. *Storia della letteratura italiana*. http://www. storiadellaletteratura.it. Accessed November, 23, 2011.

PLUTARCH. "Romulus", *Lives*, XVII, 3-4 (Tatius and Tarpeia), Loeb, I. Cambridge, Massachusetts: Harvard University Press, 1913.

PROVENZAL, Dino. *Perché si dice così*. Milano: Hoepli, 1958.

QIAN, Zhongshu 錢鍾書, "Lun Bu Ge" 論不隔. *Xie zai Rensheng Bianshang* 寫在人生邊上, *Rensheng Bianshang de Bianshang* 人生邊上的邊上, *Shiyu* 石語, 110-115. Beijing: Sanlian Shudian, 2002.

QIAN, Zhongshu 錢鍾書, "Meiguo Xuezhe Duiyu Zhongguo Wenxue de Yanjiu Jiankuang" 美國學者對於中國文學的研究簡況. *Xie zai Rensheng Bianshang* 寫在人生邊上, *Rensheng Bianshang de Bianshang* 人生邊上的邊上, *Shiyu* 石語, 183-189. Beijing: Sanlian Shudian, 2002.

QIAN, Zhongshu 錢鍾書, "Tan Zhongguo Shi" 談中國詩. *Xie zai Rensheng Bianshang* 寫在人生邊上, *Rensheng* Bianshang de Bianshang 人生邊上的邊上, *Shiyu* 石語, 159-168. Beijing: Sanlian Shudian, 2002.

QIAN, Zhongshu 錢鍾書. "Correspondence", *Tian Xia Monthly*, IV. 4 (April 1937): 425-427.

QIAN, Zhongshu 錢鍾書. *Guan Zhui Bian* 管錐編. Beijing: Sanlian Shudian, 2001.

QIAN, Zhongshu 錢鍾書. *Qi Zhui Ji* 七綴集. Beijing: Sanlian Shudian, 2002.

QIAN, Zhongshu 錢鍾書. *Qian Zhongshu Xuan Ji – Sanwen Juan* 錢鍾書選集, 散文卷. Haikou: Nanhai Chuban Gongsi, 2001.

QIAN, Zhongshu 錢鍾書. *Ren Shou Gui* 人・獸・鬼 (firstly published as: Jen Shou kuei men, beasts and ghosts, short stories. Shanghai: Shanghai Kaiming Book Company; Sieh tsai jen-sheng pien-shang on the margin of life, essays. Shanghai: Shanghai Kaiming Book Company, 1946, Philoblioblon n. 2). Beijing: Sanlian Shudian, 2001.

QIAN, Zhongshu 錢鍾書. *Tan Yi Lu* 談藝錄. Beijing: Sanlian Shudian, 2007.

QIAN, Zhongshu 錢鍾書. *Wei Cheng* 圍城. Beijing: Sanlian Shudian, 2001.

QIAN, Zhongshu. *Fortress Besieged*, translated by Jeanne Kelly and Nathan Mao. Beijing: Foreign Language Teaching and Research Press, 2003.

QIAN, Zhongshu 錢鍾書. "Xiaoshuo Shi Xiao" 小說識小. *Qian Zhongshu Sanwen* 錢鍾書散文. Hangzhou: Zhejiang Wenyi Chubanshe, 2006.

QIAN, Zhongshu 錢鍾書. *Guan Zhui Bian* 管錐編. Beijing: Zhonghua Shuju, 1979.

QIAN, Zhongshu 錢鍾書. *Qian Zhongshu Sanwen* 錢鍾書散文. Hangzhou: Zhejiang Wenyi Chubanshe, 2006.

QIAN, Zhongshu 錢鍾書. *Qian Zhongshu Shougao Ji – Rongan Guan Zhaji* 錢鍾書手稿集——容安館札記. Beijing: Shangwu Yinshuguan, 2003.

QIAN, Zhongshu 錢鍾書. *Xie zai Rensheng Bianshang* 寫在人生邊上 (firstly published as: Sieh tsai jen-sheng pien-shang. On the margin of life, essays. Shanghai, Kaiming Book Company, 1941. Philobliblon n. 2), *Rensheng Bianshang de Bianshang* 人生邊上的邊上, *Shiyu* 石語. Beijing: Sanlian Shudian, 2002.

QIAN, Zhongshu 錢鍾書. *Yingwen Wenji* 英文文集 – A collection of Qian Zhongshu's English essays. Beijing: Waiyu Jiaoxue Yu Yanjiu Chubanshe, 2005.

QU, Wenjun 曲文軍. "Shilun Qian Zhongshu Datong de Siwei Moshi" 試論錢鍾書「打通」的思維模式. *Lilun Xuekan* 2 (1999). http://www. cnki.com.cn/Article/CJFDTotal-LLSJ902.034.htm.

RENAN, Ernest. *Feuilles Détachées: faisant suite aux souvenirs d'enfance et de jeunesse.* Paris: Calmann Lévy éditeur, 1892.

SACCHETTI, Franco. *Il Trecentonovelle.* Roma: Einaudi editore, 1970.

SONG, Xinli 宋新麗. "Cong Du Laaokong Guankui Qian Zhongshu de Wenyi Jianshang Guan" 從《讀〈拉奧孔〉》管窺錢鍾書的文藝鑒賞觀. *Zhongguo Xibu Keji, Science and Technology of West China*, vol. 7, n. 15 (2008): 70-71.

STAMPA, Gaspara. *Rime.* Milano: Bur, 1978.

TANG, Yan 湯晏. *Yi Dai Caizi Qian Zhongshu* 一代才子錢鍾書. Shanghai: Shanghai Renmin Chubanshe, 2005.

TANG, Yize 湯溢澤. *Toushi Qian Zhongshu* 透視錢鍾書. Changsha: Hunan Renmin Chubanshe, 2006.

TASSO, Torquato. *Aminta*, edited by Bruno Maier. Milano: Rizzoli, 1963.

TASSO, Torquato. *La Gerusalemme Liberata.* Milano: Feltrinelli, 1961.

TASSO, Torquato. *Opere*, vol. 1. Venezia: Unione Tipografico Editrice, 1722.

TASSO, Torquato. *Opere.* Roma: Newton Compton, 1995.

TIAN, Jianmin. "Yongshi bu shi ren jue – Qian Zhongshu yongdian yanjiu zhi yi" 用事不使人覺 / 錢鍾書用典研究之一. *Qian Zhongshu Shiwen Congshuo,* edited by Wang Rongzu, 311-330. Taiwan: Airiti Press, 2011.

TIAN, Jianmin 田建民. *Zhan Zai Zhongxi Wenhua Pengzhuang de Pingtai Shang Yu Xifangren Duihua* 站在中西文化碰撞的平臺上與西方人對話. Wenxue Pinglun 2 (2004). http:// www.literature.org.cn/ article.aspx?id=6964. Accessed November 24, 2011

TOMASI di Lampedusa. *Il Gattopardo.* Milano: Feltrinelli, 2005.

TRILUSSA. *Tutte le Poesie.* Milano: Mondadori, 1963.

UNGARETTI, Giuseppe. *Vita d'un uomo. Tutte le poesie*, a cura di Leone Piccioni. Milano: Mondadori, 1945.

VARCHI, Benedetto. *Delle Opere di Messer Benedetto Varchi*, vol. 6. Milano: Società Tipografica de' Classici Italiani, 1804.

VERRI, Pietro. *Scritti vari.* Firenze: Le Monnier, 1854.

VICO, Giambattista. *Opere.* Firenze: Tipografia Italiana, 1847.

VICO, Giambattista. *Principj di Scienza Nuova.* Milano: Editore Fortunato Perelli,

1862.

WANG, Binbin 王彬彬. "Qian Zhongshu Liang Pian Lunwen Zhong de San ge Xiao Wenti" 錢鍾書兩篇論文中的三個小問題. *Wen Yi Yanjiu*, vol. 3, 2008.

WANG, Ning. "Comparative Aspects of Contemporary Popular Literature in China", in *Comparative Literature Now Theories and Practice* – Selected papers ed. by Tötösy de Zepetnek and Milan V. Dimic with Irene Sywenky. Paris: Honoré Champion Éditeur (1999): 439-448.

WANG, Ning. *Comparative Literature and Globalism: A Chinese Cultural and Literary Strategy*. Comparative Literature Studies – Volume 41, Number 4 (2004): 584-602.

WANG, Ning. *Confronting Western Influence: rethinking Chinese Literature of the New Period Author(s)*. New Literary History, Vol. 24, No. 4 (Autumn, 1993): 905-926.

WANG, Peiji 王培基. "Yinyong Yishu Xin Tan" 引用藝術新探. *Hanzi Wenhua*, 2 (2006): 30-31.

WANG, Rongzu 汪榮祖. "You Huan yu Buchang: Shi Tan Tan Yi Lu yu Guan Zhui Bian de Xiezuo Xingqing" 憂患與補償：試探《談藝錄》與《管錐編》的寫作背景與心情. *Qian Zhongshu Shiwen Congshuo*, edited by Wang Rongzu, 281-310. Taiwan: Airiti Press, 2011.

WU, Chao 吳超. "Zhu Guanqian yu Qian Zhongshu bijiao shixue zhixue fangfa zhi qubie" 朱光潛與錢鍾書比較詩學治學方法之區別. *Wexue Jiaoyu*, 03 (2008): 138-139.

WU, Taichang 吳泰昌. *Wo Renshi de Qian Zhongshu* 我認識的錢鍾書. Shanghai: Shanghai Wenyi Chubanshe, 2005.

XIA, Zhiqing 夏志清. "Zhonghui Qian Zhongshu Jishi" 重會錢鍾書記實. *Qian Zhongshu Pingshuo Qishi Nian*. edited by Jin Hongda, 60-76. Beijing: Wenhua Yishu Chubanshe, 2009.

XIE, Tianzhen. "Le tendenze più recenti della comparatistica letteraria cinese (1990-1992)", *Quaderni di Gaia*, VI, 9 (1995): 73-85.

YAN, Huo 彥火, "Qian Zhongshu Fangwen Ji" 錢鍾書訪問記. *Qian Zhongshu Ping Shuo Qishi Nian* 錢鍾書評說七十年, 91-96. Beijing: Wenhua Yishu Chubanshe, 2009.

YANG, Jiang 楊絳. *Ganxiao Liuji* 幹校六記. Beijing: Sanlian Shudian, 1981.

YANG, Jiang 楊絳. *Women Sa.* 我們仨. Beijing: Sanlian Shudian, 2003.

YANG, Jiang 楊絳. *Zou dao Rensheng Bianshang de Bianshang* 走到人生邊上的邊上. Beijing: Shangwu Yinshuguan, 2007.

YANG, Jiang. *Il tè dell'oblio*. Torino: Einaudi, 1994.

YANG, Lianfen 楊聯芬. ed. *Qian Zhongshu Pingshuo Qishi Nian* 錢鍾書評說七十年. Beijing: Wenhua Yishu Chubanshe, 2009.

YANG, Xiaobin. "Qian Zhongshu", in *Dictionary of Literary Biography – Chinese Fiction Writers, 1900-1949*. edited by Thomas Moran, 183-191. New York: Thomson Gale ed., 2007.

YANG, Zhouhan 楊周翰. "Lun Ouzhou Zhongxinzhuyi" 論歐洲中心主義. *Zhongguo Bijiao Wenxue* 中國比較文學. Shanghai: Shanghai Waiyu Jiaoyu Chubanshe, n. 1 (1991) 21-46.

YEH, Michelle. "Metaphor and Bi: Western and Chinese Poetics", *Comparative Literature*, Vol. 39, No. 3 (Summer, 1987): 237-254.

YU, Hong. "Qian Zhongshu's Essays", in *The Modern Chinese Literary Essay: Defining the Chinese Self in the 20th Century*, edited by Martin Woesler, 147-69. Bochum: Bochum UP, 2000.

YUE, Daiyun 樂黛雲. *Comparative Literature and China – Overseas Lectures by Yue Daiyun*. Beijing: Beijing University Press, 2004.

YUE, Daiyun 樂黛雲 and Wang Ning 王寧. eds. *Xifang wenyi sichao yu ershi shiji Zhongguo wenxue* 西方文藝思潮與二十世紀中國文學. Beijing: Zhongguo shehui kexue chubanshe, 1990.

ZE, Ming 迮茗. "Xie Zai Rensheng Bianshang de 'Ren Shou Gui'" 寫在人生邊上的「人‧獸‧鬼」. *Qian Zhongshu Yanjiu Caiji*, vol. 2 錢鍾書研究采輯（二）, edited by Lu Wenhu 陸文虎, 224-244. Beijing: Shenghuo, Du Shu, Xinzhi, Sanlian Shudian, 1996.

ZHANG, Longxi 張隆溪. "Qian Zhongshu Tan Bijiao Wenxue yu 'Wenxue Bijiao'" 錢鍾書談比較文學與「文學比較」. http://www.aisixiang.com/data/28340.html. Accessed November 25, 2011.

ZHANG, Longxi. "What Is Wen and Why Is It Made so Terribly Strange?" *College Literature*, Vol. 23, No. 1, Comparative Poetics: Non-Western Traditions of Literary

Theory (Feb., 1996), pp. 15-35. Stable URL: http://www.jstor.org/stable/25112226.

ZHANG, Longxi 張隆溪. "Zhongxi jiaoji yu Qian Zhongshu de zhixue fangfa" 中西交際與錢鍾書的治學方法. *Qian Zhongshu Shiwen Congshuo*, edited by Wang Rongzu, 187-210. Taiwan: Airiti Press, 2011.

ZHANG, Wenjiang 張文江. *Guan Zhui Bian dujie, zengdingben* 管錐編讀解增訂本. Shanghai: Shanghai Guji Chubanshe, 2005.

ZHANG, Wenjiang 張文江. *Yingzao Babita de Zhizhe: Qian Zhongshu zhuan* 營造巴比塔的智者：錢鍾書傳. Shanghai: Fudan Daxue Chubanshe, 2011 (first published 1993).

ZHAO, Yiheng 趙毅衡. "Guan Zhui Bian Zhong de Bijiao Wenxue Pingxing Yanjiu" 管錐編中的比較文學平行研究. *Du Shu* 讀書, no. 2 (1981): 41-47.

ZHENG, Xiaodan. "A study on Qian Zhongshu's translation: sublimation in translation", in *Studies in Literature and Language*, vol. 1, No. 2 (2010): 70-83.

ZHENG, Zhining. "Qian Zhongshu's theory and practice of metaphor", a dissertation for a master of art degree at the University of British Columbia, Department of Asian Studies, Vancouver, April 1994.

ZHU, Guanqian 朱光潛. "Keluoqi" 科洛旗. *Xifang Meixue Shi*, 630-654. Beijing: Renmin Wenxue Chubanshe, 1984.

# Qian Zhongshu in others' words

著者：Tiziana Lioi
執行編輯：許家泰
編輯協力：簡玉欣

出版單位：國立中央大學出版中心
　　　　　桃園縣中壢市中大路 300 號 國鼎圖書資料館 3 樓
　　　　　遠流出版事業股份有限公司
　　　　　台北市南昌路二段 81 號 6 樓

發行單位／展售處：遠流出版事業股份有限公司
地址：台北市南昌路二段 81 號 6 樓
電話：(02) 23926899　傳真：(02) 23926658
劃撥帳號：0189456-1

著作權顧問：蕭雄淋律師
法律顧問：董安丹律師

2014 年 8 月　初版一刷
行政院新聞局局版台業字第 1295 號
售價：新台幣 400 元

**ylib** 遠流博識網　http://www.ylib.com E-mail: ylib@ylib.com